His Rightful Queen

BOOK 3 - THE PAIN SERIES

LYNDA THROSBY

ISBN: 978-1-9196079-0-0
Lynda Throsby Publishing
Email ljtpublishing@gmail.com

Warning

This book is not intended for anyone under the age of 18.

This is for adult reading only and contains counts of violence and sexual content.

His Rightful Queen

Much love
Linda
xx

PART VIII

Svetlana

One

Svetlana
Present

LYING ON MY BED CRYING MY EYES OUT IS NOTHING NEW LATELY. When Sergei came to me and told me Igor was injured, that he may already be dead, it broke me. I thought I was going to die; I had palpitations. I was sweating and I had to sit down. I didn't know the details. Sergei was sent to help. He didn't know all the details either, or so he said. I just told him to make sure he stayed close and loyal to Igor. You never know when he may need a new number two by his side. Waiting for him to get back to me, to tell me what had happened, was the longest time ever. It felt like weeks, but it was only days. Those days dragged, and I cried so much, hidden in my room, that my face was a mess, all puffy and swollen. I had all the 'what-ifs' running around in my head.

What if he was dead?

What if he was hurt so badly that he does not come back to me?

What if she did it?

What if she planned it?

What if he goes to one of his other houses and never comes back here?

What if I never see him again?

If he is dead, will she get rid of me, or will I have to go back to Russia? I couldn't do that. As much as I missed my family, there was no way I was ever going back. I waited and waited on Sergei for news. I didn't know where they were when he left. He never told me where it was he was actually going. I think it was a secret. I know it was difficult for Sergei to contact me because we know all the phones are monitored. He is the one who does most of the monitoring down in the basement.

I'm lying here yet again because I just saw *my love* for the first time in a long time, but it was not the Igor I knew. It was only by chance I saw him. I just happened to be on my way out, walking to the revolving doors to exit the building. I was looking through my purse when I looked up, I froze on the spot. I watched as she entered through the side door, pushing a wheelchair with Sergei and Steve by their side. I was shocked. I gasped and put my hands up to cover my face. *My love.* He looked broken as she wheeled him through the reception area. I hated her so fucking much. She was strutting along with her head held high, pushing my broken king. He didn't look up at anyone, not even me, as she pushed him past me to the elevators. He kept his head down low. He had a Starter cap on and I could see he had on dark sunglasses. He also had a blanket wrapped up around his neck, covering his whole body. Not many people would know it was my Igor, my king, my powerful godfather, *my love*, but I would know him anywhere. My poor broken love. It broke my heart.

Two

Svetlana
Present

IT'S BEEN A FEW DAYS NOW AND I'VE MAINLY STAYED HIDDEN IN MY room. I've been a mess. Seeing him broken like that shattered me. Not being able to run to him and love him like I should be able to had me wanting to kill her, so it could be me looking after him. It should be me. I'm his true love. I should be his rightful queen, not that American bitch. How could my strong, powerful love be so broken like that? I've been pacing in my room, trying to think of a way to get to see him. I need to get access to him, somehow, but I don't know how. If I go to the penthouse, she will not let me see him. I haven't even seen Sergei since the one time we met, so I cannot get any more information from him about *my love*. I have only left the building once to meet him in our secret place and all he told me was that Andrey and Ivan were both dead and that Igor was badly hurt and had to have surgery, but he would not tell me what happened. Andrey and Ivan dead, thank fuck for that. It means my Sergei is now in the number three position with Steve being number two. I was so happy Andrey and Ivan were dead, they deserved it, I hated them and it was the best news.

I used to have Andrey and Ivan in my pocket. They gave me all the information I needed about *my love*. I made them keep me updated on Igor's latest fucks, some of them I never even saw, but now they are dead, which I am elated about. I won't get any of that personal information from Sergei, he doesn't know I love Igor, if he did, he would not fuck me anymore, for the time being, I still need him for whatever snippets of information I can get out of him.

The only thing that got me through all the times I knew Igor was fucking whores was thinking about him fucking me, thinking about the first time I saw him back home in Zhigulyovsk and remembering me flirting, albeit terribly, with him.

———

Age Fifteen

I hated being the eldest of six girls, it was always left to me to look after the others and they were pains in the ass most of the time. Mama and Papa go out to work each day. We live in a poor area of Zhigulyovsk, which is a small town anyway. Where we live is a very poor community with mostly derelict houses and they are tiny. Our house is big considering its two up and two down. There is me at fifteen and Vidana who is almost thirteen, we share what used to be the living room, which is now our bedroom. Then there are my four other sisters who share one of the bedrooms upstairs. There is Dominika who is ten, Klara who is eight, Iskra who is five, and then little Zoya who is two. The kitchen, which is now the hub of the house, the family room, it's just about big enough for a table with six chairs and two stools. This is also where everyone has to wash and in the winter we have to use the pitcher to go to the bathroom, but in the summer we can use the outhouse. It is very difficult living conditions for so many. Whenever Mama and I argue, which is a lot, because it is me looking after my sisters all the time, I always tell her she should have stopped having babies after Vidana came along. I always end up outside being whipped by my papa whenever I say this for being so rude to my elders.

I don't go to school anymore because Mama has to go out and clean for the more well-off people in our town. Papa, well, he does what he can, which isn't a lot, apart from drinking vodka. He got fired from his steady job in the mill about three years ago now. He caused an accident where two people died and he was badly injured himself. Since then he has not been the same person. My papa was always a loving, caring person before the accident but now he is a tyrant and is always whipping me for some reason or other. I am beginning to hate my papa. He does try, I suppose, when he isn't drinking, but that is why Mama had to find work, because Papa wasn't bringing in much money. Sometimes me and Vidana can go a couple of days before we get any food. We let our sisters eat until there is enough for us.

Now that I have to stay home, I homeschool my sisters as best I can. I read a lot of books; I love fiction books on crime and romance. I dream of meeting my prince one day, of him whisking me off somewhere powerful and we will be rich and I will have a bathroom to bathe in. Mama brings a lot of books home from her customers she cleans for. Some are educational which I read as well, but I love fiction. It's the only thing that I can get lost in and pretend I am in another world somewhere. I love my sisters and my mama, but I dream of escaping. I get my little sisters to take a nap in the afternoon. This is my free time to read. I lay on my bed and read, getting lost in my books. Sometimes, I get so carried away that I forget about my sisters until Mama comes home or Vidana from school, whichever one gets home first, and I have to dive up the stairs and pretend to be teaching them school work.

Mama has sent me on an errand to the store in our village to get some bits for our supper and to see if I can find Papa, who hasn't come home as usual. No doubt he will be in the little bar in the village. As I pass, I look inside and sure enough, he is in there. I enter and walk up to him. I stand with my hand on my hip in front of him, waiting for him to notice me.

"Papa, Mama sent me to fetch you. She wants you to come home for supper. I am to fetch some cheese and flour and bring you back with me."

He scowls at me. "Fuck off, Lana, I'll be home when I'm ready."

They all call me Lana at home, but I like my full name. Just as I turn to leave him, I notice a man looking at me. He catches my eye straight away because he is the most beautiful man I have ever seen. I stand staring at him and he stares back.

"Fuck off, Lana, I said," my papa shouts at me.

I turn my head to snarl at him, he's embarrassing me in front of this man. I turn back to look at the beautiful man. He is just sipping his drink, but still staring at me. I kind of sway a little, then I pout my lips and bat my eyes. I saw Anya do that at school when she was flirting with Eriks. It worked because he took her behind one of the outhouses to make out. She told me he played with her vagina under her skirt, that he then stuck his fingers inside her and then he sucked her tits. She said it was the best feeling ever, even if it did hurt at first. I was shocked when she told me but only because I felt jealous. I had read about a lot of things like that in some of the romance books Mama brought me. It's a good thing she didn't read them or she would take them away from me.

This man staring at me looks a lot older than I am. But he is the cutest thing ever. He is in a suit and I can see he has a big watch on his wrist and a gold ring on his pinkie finger. He looks like he has money. He has blond hair that is curly and bright blue eyes. Nothing unusual there being where we are, but for some reason he is different. He seems to exude wealth and power. I stay swaying, gripping my little wicker basket, just staring at him.

"Lana, if I have to tell you to fuck off one more time, I will put you over my knee here and now and whip your bare ass. Now leave," he shouts at me.

I look away from the man and I hang my head and walk out slowly. Just as I get to the door, I turn one more time and give the beautiful man a small smile. I then head to the little store to get the grocery items my mama needed. I should be getting back anyway. I'll tell her I couldn't find my papa like I usually do. We go through this countless times. She knows exactly where he is.

As I leave the store, I come to a complete stop and drop my basket. He's standing there leaning against the doorframe. I gasp, not expecting him to be there. He startled me.

"Hello, Lana, is it? I noticed you in the bar."

I feel my cheeks getting hot even though it's cold out. My heart is beating in my chest so fast, I don't know if it's because he spoke to me or because he scared me. He bends down and picks the basket up, along with the cheese that rolled out, and passes it back to me. As I take it from him, he strokes his thumb over my fingers. I feel little electric shocks pulsating around my body and I have funny feelings in my tummy. I look at him wide eyed and he smiles at me. Here's my chance to flirt, if I can do it without making a fool of myself.

"Well thank you, kind sir. I'm sorry, you just startled me," I say, taking the basket back and fluttering my eyelashes at him.

He laughs slightly and puts his thumb to the corner of his mouth. That annoys me. Is he laughing at me? I don't show I'm annoyed. I don't want him to think I'm immature. He is a lot older than I am, I would say about ten years or more. I can't stop staring into his eyes. I find myself leaning forward slightly to get a better look. It's getting dark out now. My mama is gonna be mad if I'm much later. She needs to make supper for the little ones.

"I heard the way that man spoke to you, Lana. I have to say it made me angry. Is he your papa?"

I nod and look down. He puts a finger under my chin and lifts it up so I can look into his face again. I am tall and skinny as my mama tells me but he is a lot taller than I am. He is beautiful and my cheeks must be bright red. I feel myself getting hot all over.

"It's Svetlana, my name," I say shyly to him. "My family calls me Lana, but I prefer Svetlana. He's just annoyed because my mama wants him to come home for supper, when all he wants to do is drink."

I see the quizzical look on his face.

"How old are you, Svetlana? Does he whip you a lot?"

Oh, he heard that too. I feel ashamed and I just nod again.

"I'm, ermm… I'm eighteen," I lie and he laughs.

"Why did you lie? Don't lie to me, Svetlana, I don't do well with people that lie to me. Just be warned, you will never lie to me again, now tell me how he whips you."

I'm embarrassed, but what does he mean by that. It's not like I will see him again. He lifts my chin up again for me to look at him. He raises his eyebrows, he's waiting for the truth.

"I am sixteen, soon to be seventeen," I say quickly, even though it's two months away until my actual *sixteenth* birthday, so I am technically fifteen right now. I lied. I dare not tell him the truth though. "My papa takes me out the back of my house and puts me over his knee, he then lifts my skirt and he whips my bare ass."

I can see the fury start to spread across his face. He's angry. Is it my age? Did I make him angry? He is hot when he's angry. He suddenly grabs my hand and walks me back to the bar. He marches in, slamming the door and dragging me behind him. He stands in front of my papa. He doesn't speak, he glares at him. My papa slowly looks up and sees this man has me by the hand.

"What is the meaning of this? Lana, I told you to leave. You need to get back home now," he slurs at me.

The man holding me tightens his grip, but I think it is because he is getting very angry with my papa.

"Tell me what it is you do to your daughter? I want the truth. Like I just told Svetlana, I do not do well with lies. You do not want to cross me, old man. I can be your worst nightmare or I can be your best friend. You choose."

He's starting to scare me now. As much as I think he is hot, I am getting scared. He is threatening my papa now. My papa looks him straight in the eye but speaks to me.

"Lana, leave now. Go back to your mama. I will be home shortly."

He is getting protective of me. It's the first time he has ever been like this, but then again, he's never been in this situation. The man doesn't let go of my hand as I try to get free of him. My papa glares at him. He stands up and starts to come around the table to our side. I'm scared for my papa and for me. I don't know this man but I think he could be dangerous.

"Let go of my daughter," he demands.

The man doesn't and he just glares at my papa. I look around, but there aren't many people in the bar to help us. I look to the bartender, but he puts his head down and carries on cleaning the glass in his hand. I see a slight shake of his head as he does this. I think he's warning us. I've never seen this man before and it's one of those small villages that everyone knows everyone. It seems the bartender must know him.

"Please, will you let me go, sir, I need to get back to my mama and sisters. We don't want any trouble with you. I didn't lie to you, so please let me go."

He looks at me but the look isn't anger, it's sorrow. He must think I'm scared of my papa. He doesn't realize it's him that is scaring me. I shake my hand, telling him to let go and he does. I turn and walk out of the door, almost running. I don't want to stay and see what happens. I walk very quickly home. I keep my head down. Just as I round the corner to where my house is, a hand grabs my wrist again and pulls me back. I scream, not knowing who it is. I drop the basket again and I'm suddenly being held tightly. I look up and it's the man from the bar. He must have run after me.

"Shhh, it's okay. I will not harm you. I just want to make sure you are safe. I wanted to make sure you got home safely. Your papa is okay, he is having another drink in the bar. I wanted to walk you home and meet your mama. Is that okay, my angel?"

Holy mother, he called me his angel. What is he doing, he's older and gorgeous and he could snap his fingers and have anyone? Why is he protecting me? I don't even know him. He leans his head down and kisses the top of my head while pulling me into his chest. It's like he wants to wrap me up and protect me. I don't move, I just take in his scent, it's so nice and woodsy. I'm not scared of him. I actually feel safe in his arms. I don't think he is going to hurt me, I think he does just want to protect me. We stay standing like this for a few minutes until he pulls back and bows to look me in the eye.

"My angel, I will not hurt you, and I will make sure you never get hurt again by your papa. I want you to take me to your house where I can speak to your mama alone. I would like to find out more about you and your family. Is that okay with you?"

I just nod. He is so gentle with me. I think I'm in love with him. I want him to whisk me away from here and to take care of me. I know I'm a silly teenager, but I feel all these strange feelings in me. He wants me, I'm sure of it, and I sure as hell want him, I would gladly let him take me and fuck me, just like Anya let Eriks do to her not long after he put his fingers in her vagina, she told me when he got his penis out she had to suck it first to make it wet so he could then put it into her vagina. She said it hurt but it was the best feeling ever to be fucked, I was even more jealous of my friend, I'm thinking about what Anya said and I nod at him.

He bends down to retrieve my basket once again, but this time he carries it for me and takes my hand to hold. We walk along silently. I feel all shy, I don't know what to say or what I should be saying to this man. He looks to me. He must have felt me looking at him and he smiles. He then pulls me into his side and kisses the top of my head again. I hear him whisper in my hair. It's very faint but I know he said 'my beautiful angel'. I smile to myself. I feel so hot pressed against his side. We reach my house and I look up to him to see his reaction. There isn't one. He doesn't judge. I smile to him then pull away and head in through the door, the door that opens straight into mine and Vidana's bedroom.

"Mama, I have someone who would like to talk to you," I shout, turning to make sure the man has followed me.

He is right behind me, I smile up at him again.

"Who is it, Lana? Is it your papa?"

I turn just as she appears in the room from the kitchen, wiping her hands on her apron, I see the look on her face when she notices this gorgeous man standing in my bedroom and who has put his hands on my shoulders and pulled me to his chest. I sigh out and must have the goofiest grin on my face. I instinctively reach up to one of his hands with my own and hold it. I see my mama watching my every move. Her expression goes from a woman in shock at seeing this stunning man standing in her house to a protective mama with a scowl on her face that says it all.

"Lana, who is this man?" She doesn't sound happy, but I don't care.

"This is…" I don't even know his name. It doesn't matter because he answers for me straight away.

"I am Igor. Igor Ustrashkins, it's a pleasure to meet you, hmm…"

Now it's my turn to jump in and save him.

"This is Larisa Baranov, my mama," I introduce her.

He steps out from behind me, and I have to let his hand go. He holds out his hand to take my mama's. She tentatively holds out hers and he takes it, bowing to kiss the back.

"It's a pleasure to meet you, Mrs. Baranov. I just met your husband, Vlad, and Svetlana here in the bar. I have to say what a beautiful, charming daughter you have. May I have a few minutes of your time, alone please, Mrs. Baranov?" he asks.

I see the startled look on her face as it turns to worry and then fear. I am not sure why the fear, he is a gentleman. She nods very slightly then moves her head, motioning me to leave them and go to the kitchen. I do, sulking like a little girl. I want to know what they are going to talk about. I have to see to my sisters while Mama is talking to Igor. I like his name, it's a strong-sounding name, but then if it was Mickey Mouse, I would still say I liked it and it was a strong name. Yeah, I think I'm a love-struck teenager. I sit at the table leaving my sisters to play on their own, Vidana is playing with them, and I just daydream about Igor and him whisking me off somewhere exotic, maybe somewhere that is hot with beaches, that would be real cool.

Mama is gone a long time, or it seems to be a long time. I decide to start supper for Mama. I need a distraction and I know how to cook since I have to cook dinner every day for my sisters. I make bread and put it in the log burner. We make bread every night for the following day or for supper, then I make some dumplings in a potato stew which will be sprinkled with cheese. There will be enough left over for tomorrow's dinner.

The supper is almost ready when Mama finally walks into the kitchen, she doesn't look happy and I see Igor following behind her. He looks okay, apart from being gorgeous but he doesn't seem to look angry. In fact, he looks kind of pleased with himself. My mama looks at me and nods very slightly in his direction, he notices.

"My angel, would you walk me to the door, please?" He's looking at me as he says this. I feel myself burning again and I hear Vidana giggle. I turn and scowl at her as I walk toward him.

"Would you like to stay for supper, Igor?" I ask him just as I reach him and notice my mama scowl and shake her head. He sees this also and laughs slightly.

"No thank you. Will you walk me out?" he asks me again and turns his back to walk out.

I turn to Mama and she nods to follow him. He's at the door with it open and turns to me. He takes my hand and pulls me outside with him.

"I had a good talk with your mama. I assure you that you will be safe if you agree to what she will talk to you about. Please do not be alarmed, I will not hurt you. I give you my oath, and my oath is everything. I will come back to see you tomorrow and see what your mama and you have decided. Just bear in mind this is a once-in-a-lifetime offer for you, my angel." He leans down toward my face.

I think he's going to kiss me, I screw my eyes shut but he kisses my cheek. Oh fuck. He lingers on my cheek for several seconds and I feel him smile. My eyes are still screwed shut, I'm embarrassed, I don't know what to do.

"You can open your eyes, my angel. Go. Go speak to your mama and I will see you tomorrow evening when your mama is home from work. Good night, Svetlana." With that, he turns and walks down the road.

I couldn't speak, not even to say good night. What is he talking about? I am so confused right now, but Mama did not look happy. I will probably have to wait until my sisters are all in bed until she talks to me. I want to know what they talked about and I want to know now. It's going to kill me to have to wait.

We all eat supper, and there is still no sign of Papa. I am starting to worry if he is alright, that Igor did not do anything to him after I left. Mama is not happy, she is snapping at all of us. I'm not sure if it's because Papa isn't home or if it's something to do with Igor. She looks angry and she won't speak to me or look at me. I help wash my sisters and put them to bed. Mama tells Vidana to get to bed and she shuts the door between the kitchen and my bedroom.

"Sit, Lana, we need to talk."

I'm washing the dishes. She is angry with me but I haven't done anything wrong.

"Lana, sit down." I move to the table and I sit opposite my mama. Papa still isn't home.

"Do you think Papa is okay, Mama? He is usually home by now."

She frowns at me.

"Did Mr. Ustrashkins not tell you about Papa?"

I look confused and shake my head. Mama looks upset and looks to her hands.

"Papa will not be home today. Mr. Ustrashkins has paid for him to stay away tonight in a room above the bar. He is okay, apparently, but he had a lot to drink and Mr. Ustrashkins didn't want him to come home in that state. What do you know about him, Lana? How did you meet him?"

"He was in the bar when I told Papa to come home. Then when I went to the store, he was waiting for me outside, Mama. He scared me. Then we went back to the bar where Papa stood up to him, telling him to leave me alone. I have never met him before and I didn't know his name until he introduced himself to you."

She scowls at me.

"I do not believe you, Lana. You are lying to me. You two were very cozy. He was touching you and you were holding his hand on your shoulder. How can you be touching if you only just met? You were acting like lovers."

I blush and look to my hands on my lap.

"Lana, tell me the truth. I know you have little fantasies you like to play out and you often tell lies, but I need the truth."

I scowl at her and place my hands on the table, playing with my nails.

"I am telling the truth, Mama. What did he mean about talking to you and a once-in-a-lifetime offer? I like him, Mama, really like him."

"You are young and foolish, Lana, he is old, too old for you."

I go to speak but she holds her hand up to stop me.

"But, he has made me an offer for you."

What the hell, what does she mean, I'm so confused. She carries on.

"He thinks your papa mistreats you, somehow he has it in his head that your papa does very bad things to you and he wants to rescue you and take you away to safety."

I go to speak again but she scowls at me and puts her hand up stopping me once more.

"I don't know where he has got the information from, but he has offered to pay me a lot of money if he can take you away to live with him."

"But Mama…"

"No, Lana, let me speak. As soon as he told me his name, I knew who he was. His family is from this area and are very well known but not in a good way. They practically run this town and many others like it. Mr. Ustrashkins is not a good man, Lana, he is a very dangerous man. I know the offer he has given me will mean your sisters will all be taken care of for a very long time, but I don't know if I can let you go with him. You are young and sometimes foolish." She looks sad now.

My heart is beating fast, though, from the thought that he wants to take me away with him. I smile and reach for my mama's hand.

"What did he think Papa does to me, Mama? Why does he want to take me away?" I see tears in her eyes.

"It is hard to say, Lana, he has this idea that your papa sexually abuses you. Apparently your papa shouted out he would take you over his knee and whip your bare ass in the bar. Mr. Ustrashkins took this to mean he sexually abuses you. I didn't deny or confirm it to him which solidified the idea in his head."

I am so confused right now.

"But Mama, why did you not tell him that Papa doesn't do anything like that? Papa only whips me, yes he whips my bare ass, but that is all he does, and only because you told him he had to do it."

She looks hurt at my words.

"He offered me so much money for you, Lana, that is why. If, in his mind, he thinks that is what your papa does, then let it be. If neither of us denies or confirms it, then we can't be blamed for his thoughts. I told him I would talk with you tonight and we will decide what to do. If you are happy to go with him, he has promised me he would never intentionally harm you. He said his oath was final. It was the way of his family. Like I said, his family is very well known in all of Russia, they are very dangerous, Lana, that is my only worry if you decide you want to go with him. You are nearly sixteen and you are old enough to make up your own mind."

I scowl, she notices and scowls back at me.

"What is it? I was married at your age. It is the way here, as you know. His offer was more money than I could ever dream of, Lana, I would not have to work again and we could move to a nice area in a nice big house, big enough for each of your sisters to have a room of their own, with bathrooms and a proper kitchen. Oh Lana, this is what dreams are made of, but it is up to you, my sweet girl. I would be lost without you, you know that, and I will not force you to go. Will you think about it? Sleep on it tonight, then we can discuss it tomorrow. If you agree he wants to take you with him tomorrow night as he has a plane leaving, he lives in Los Angeles in the USA, Lana, can you imagine you living in America?"

She's giddy telling me this, and it's making me giddy. I want to go and pack my things now and tell him to take me now. Am I ready to leave? It's what I want to do, to try and make something of myself. There is no way that will ever happen here, not if I stay in this town. There is nothing here for me, I've always known that.

"Mama, I told him I was sixteen, soon to be seventeen. If he knows I am only fifteen, I don't think he would want me."

She looks at me. "If you decide to go, we don't tell him your true age. He must never know. Stick to what you have told him. Okay, Lana, can you do that?"

I nod. "I will sleep on it but my gut is telling me to go with him, I have only just met him but I feel I love him already, Mama. How can that be? I am sure I will have a better future with him, especially in America, Mama.

Can you believe that? America, I've dreamed so long of visiting America." I'm crying, I'm so overwhelmed.

She gets up and comes to me, pulling me to her and hugging me tight.

"I would do this for you, Mama, anyway, for you and my sisters to have a better life, to have the things we all dream of. If he pays you enough, maybe you can all come and visit me in America. How exciting would that be, Mama?" My face drops and she notices. "What will Papa say? Will he let me go?"

She pulls me to her again.

"Don't you worry about your papa, I will take care of that and Mr. Ustrashkins said he would also take care of him."

I look up and see her frowning. She looks back to me and smiles, kissing my forehead. I head to bed, trying not to disturb Vidana. She's not asleep.

"What is going on, Lana? Who is that man? Why is Mama being all secretive and even more angry than usual? She's acting strange, she was being nice for once."

I get into bed and ignore her, I'm too excited, I can't sleep. I think of his beautiful eyes and that gorgeous smile of his, and I fall asleep thinking of my future with him.

Three

Svetlana

Present

I T'S BEEN A FEW WEEKS AND I STILL HAVEN'T SEEN MY LOVE. POPPY
has been to see me a few times. She keeps coming to me and wanting
to talk. She thinks we are like best friends or sisters or some shit
like that. She came asking for my help, asking if I would teach her to
speak Russian. I was surprised she asked me and not Igor. She can speak
broken Russian but she wants to be fluent. We have spent a lot of time
together, so I suppose she thinks we are like bosom buddies now. I just
pretend to like her. I say keep your friends close but your enemies closer.
Is that what she's doing to me, is she just pretending?

She never mentions Igor to me. I wonder why? It doesn't matter, I've
been getting the info I need from Sergei, well some of it. I was mad they
did not make Sergei their number two, but number three will do. It's a
step up and I will still be able to get information from him. I will have to
play it cool though with Sergei. If he suspects I only want info on *my love*,
he will surely stop fucking me and giving me what I need. I've decided
I need another source, and if I do try to become the best friend Poppy
seems to need then I will be that. As much as I hate her and want to kill
her, maybe she will start to open up to me. Maybe if I go see her, she will
let me see Igor. I can try. Then if Sergei suspects my love is for Igor and
not him, it won't matter, I can find anyone to fuck, there's never a short
supply. In all honesty, Sergei is a lousy fuck, especially to what I've been
used to when visiting The Hex Club and from what I was used to from
Andrey and Ivan. They really knew how to fuck.

Sergei and I have been sneaking away for a few months now. I used him so that if I ended up back in the basement for whatever reason, I knew I would be safe. No one would be able to touch me. Well, apart from Igor that is, and Sergei would make sure I was protected. I reeled him in the first time I was put down there, I was there for four days and he was the one to bring me food and water. It wasn't hard. I could tell the first time he laid eyes on me. He was besotted. The second time I was put down there was when Igor thought I had betrayed him with the new arms dealer, Farhad. I played the innocent with Sergei, batting my eyes at him and slowly seducing him. Once I left the basement that second time, I used to wait for him outside of the building. He would stop and talk to me and it went from there. He dated me, no one knew about us, we used to leave at separate times and meet up at our place which was not far from the park. He was a gentleman at first. He wanted to wine and dine me. It was me that ended up making the first move on him. Since then we've been fucking in that dirty motel Andrey and Ivan used to take me to.

I should have told Igor what Andrey and Ivan did to me when he discarded me. I'm not sure they realized Igor was going to keep me around permanently. They did to me what I then found out they did to all his castoffs. They raped, beat, and killed them, okay, so they didn't kill me. They said it was on Igor's orders but I never believed that. Igor would never condone a man raping a woman, he would kill any man he found doing that, which is why I should have told Igor they both raped me, multiple times, together, just waiting for the word from him to make me disappear. I believe Igor did give the word to make the whores disappear but only to make sure they never came back, not to kill them and certainly not anything other than that, like raping them. Andrey and Ivan just wanted his castoffs. I think it empowered them. I think they used their link with Igor to make the whore more submissive, probably telling them they could get them back with Igor, who knows.

The one thing with Andrey and Ivan was, I could still get a fuck from them if I wanted. I only had to threaten them with telling Igor that they raped the girls or what they did to me and they knew he would have had them both killed. Although I hated them both, they were good for a fuck. Having both of them at the same time used to get my juices flowing like never before. That motel I used with Sergei is the one they used to fuck me in. It was one of those pay-by-the-hour places, the ones prostitutes used. Although they had nothing on *my love*, they had amazing bodies, full of muscles, and what they could do with their tongues and cocks was unreal and makes me shudder just thinking about it.

When I came back to Igor after the time I left, he discarded me, Igor got rid of me, and they did actually rape me, I only wanted *my love* and I thought he would be coming back for me, but as time went on and those two kept taking me to the motel, I secretly loved it. I used to put up a fight. I used to hit and kick and spit at them but it was all part of the game for me. Once I had them both that first time, I couldn't get enough and it was better than nothing. I still craved *my love* but if he was getting fucked then why shouldn't I?

That's how I got them in my pocket. The threats to tell Igor everything. We would spend hours in that motel some days. They would take it in turns to fuck me, then both together. It was me in control. I used to demand what they did to me. Some days they would fuck me until I couldn't stand. They used every hole I had over and over. I would be sucking one cock while the other was ramming his cock in my ass, then I would be lying on my back with one sitting over my face with his cock in my mouth but leaning down my body and sucking my clit while the other one was ramming it in my pussy. It was when I was sandwiched between them, usually Andrey on the bottom as he was the biggest in every sense, he would be ramming it into my ass and Ivan would be shoving it in my pussy while biting my tits, that was my favorite position. To feel them both down there thrusting into me, but also the friction they could feel rubbing each other's cocks inside me. It made us all scream as we all ejaculated together, me included. I was a squirter. Igor loved that about me, he could never get enough of the taste of me, or so he told me. I would squirt all over him.

Thinking about those two and what we used to do got me thinking about *my love* again, and when he brought me to America.

Age Fifteen

I woke up in the morning with barely any sleep, I was too excited. I ran into the kitchen when I heard Mama puttering around in there.

"Mama, I'm going. I'm going to leave with Igor and you will all be able to live nice lives. You don't have to work anymore, Mama." I threw myself into her arms.

"Lana, you must never admit your papa didn't do anything bad to you or about your true age. If you do, Mr. Ustrashkins will make us all suffer, if he thinks we deceived him. Do you understand me Lana? If he asks you anything, either tell him you don't want to talk about it or just pretend your papa used to stick his fingers inside you when he whipped you."

I blanch at her words, they sicken me. To have to say my papa did that to me when he's only ever loved me and my sisters. I don't think I can do it. I shake my head at Mama.

"I can't say that, Mama. How can I lie about my papa like that? What if it got out, everyone would hate him."

She looks at me sternly. Grabbing both my forearms hard, she looks me in the face. "You will have to, Lana, for all our sakes. If he takes you and realizes you are a virgin, he will know it was a lie. He will know that the first time. It will hurt you, Lana. When he breaks your hymen, the first time he takes you it will hurt, and you may bleed. He will know then that your papa didn't sexually abuse you unless you tell him it was with his hands only. Do you understand me, Lana? If you don't he will probably kill us all for deceiving him."

I gasp, but nod, she's shaking me and squeezing my arms harder. I do understand because I am still a virgin. I've never even been kissed by a boy or man until Igor kissed me on the cheek yesterday. But she said he will kill us all, is he that dangerous? Somehow the thought of him being so dangerous makes me want to go with him more.

"Okay Mama, I will do that. I want you all to have nice things and have a good life and not to be killed. You, Papa, and my sisters. I will miss you all dearly, but knowing you will all be taken care of will make it so much easier. I love you all, Mama."

She lets go of me.

"Will Papa be home before I leave so I can say goodbye to him? I will be upset if I don't see him."

"I hope so, Lana, I do, but you know what your papa's like. If he gets set in the bar again today, especially staying there last night, who knows what state he will be in."

I know what she means. My papa likes his vodka.

The rest of the day goes by so slowly. I get myself all washed and cleaned and actually wash my hair and put on my best shirt and skirt, ready for Igor to come for me. Mama doesn't go to work, she doesn't have to. I spend time with her and my sisters, and Vidana stays home from school. I told her I was leaving and going to America, she was upset but pleased for me. We never told them they would be moving just yet. Mama wanted to make sure she got the money from Igor first.

It was the longest day of my life. I stood outside on the street watching both ways for any sign of Igor or my papa. Papa never came home today. I will be upset at not saying goodbye, but I know they will all have a good life now.

Finally, after what feels like forever, a car pulls up outside my house, it's a big car. I look in, I don't recognize the driver and the back has blacked-out windows, so I don't know if anyone is inside. It has to be him. I move to the window and put my hands up, shielding my face to see if anyone is inside. I can't see anyone. It's a few minutes before the door eventually opens, I startle back, nearly falling to my ass. I watch as *my love* emerges from the open door. I smile the biggest smile I have, and I fly into his arms. He's laughing at me and he picks me up and twirls me around. I kiss his lips, just a peck. He looks a little taken aback by that.

"You came back for me?"

"Well of course I did, my angel. Someone is eager to see me. I take it you have decided to come with me?"

I smile, nodding my head, and he smiles back at me, putting his forehead against mine and kissing the tip of my nose. I sigh. I am so happy right now. My heart is beating out of my chest and my tummy is doing funny things inside.

"Are you all packed and ready for your new life in LA?"

I nod enthusiastically at him. I'm just like a giddy schoolgirl, which in reality I am. He slowly puts me down, sliding me down his body. I stand back slightly and look behind me. My mama and sisters are all standing there watching me. I see my two bags on the street.

"Is this all you have to take?"

I nod, looking sad. "I don't have many belongings."

"Well, we shall change that," he says, lifting my chin to look at him. "Are you ready to leave? We have to catch my plane soon."

I look around and I have tears in my eyes. Igor walks past me and goes to my mama. He hands her a big bag, I hadn't even noticed he picked a bag up. I walk toward them. I need to say bye to my sisters one by one, I'm sad because my papa is not here. I kneel down to hug each of my sisters, telling them all to be good. I stand to hug Vidana, she's watching Igor hand the bag to Mama.

"You are selling your soul to the devil, Lana. Mama is selling you like a whore," she whispers to me just as I hear Igor telling Mama that is what he promised, and there will also be a monthly allowance sent to her.

Wow, he really wants me. I smile on the inside at the thought. I pretend I don't hear Vidana and I turn to hug Mama to me for what feels like ages.

"I will miss you, Mama, all of you, tell Papa I love him when you see him and that I'm sorry I didn't get to say goodbye." I'm crying as Igor takes my hand and leads me to the back of the car.

He pulls me to his side once we start to drive away. I cry into his chest and he soothes me by stroking my head. I look up to him.

"Why me, Igor? Why did you pay for me? What do you intend to do with me once we are far away from here? Are your intentions good, Igor?" I have so many questions. He unbuckles my seat belt and pulls me onto his lap, turning my face to look at him.

"Because you are such a sweet angel. My intentions are to only help you get a new life, to take you away from a papa that abuses you like that. No one should ever have to suffer the way you have. Tell me, did he do that to your sisters or just you?"

Oh no, I was dreading this conversation and we haven't even left the town yet.

"Just me," I tell him quietly, hanging my head. He lifts my chin up to face him.

"That's good to know. It is why I feel you need a new life, a better chance at life. It is what your mama said. Well, no more. He will not hurt anyone any longer. Now I thought we could maybe see about getting you into modeling or something along those lines once we get you settled in LA, or maybe college. To answer your question, yes, my intentions are good. You are very young, Svetlana. You are certainly underage for anything in LA. Like I told your mama, you will be my ward, like my little sister or niece. I want to look after you and make sure you will be happy and safe."

Oh, his little sister, he doesn't want me? He doesn't want to fuck me? My tummy goes all funny and I feel sick. I think I want to go back home. I thought he loved me like I love him, I thought he wanted me like I wanted him. Not to be my big brother, I don't need a big brother, I need a lover, a husband. Oh no. I put my face into my hands and I cry. I climb from his lap and sit as far away from him as I can. I look out of the window. He really does only want to protect me, nothing more. I cry hard. I miss my family already.

He doesn't speak to me until we arrive at his plane. He then gets out and comes to open my door to help me out. He has someone come and take our bags onto the plane. I don't know how he can take me out of the country, I do not have any documents.

"Hey, look at me." He pulls me round to face him and lifts my chin up. "What's wrong, my angel? You have not spoken to me for a while? Did I upset you? You are still crying. Are you sure you want to do this? You can go back to your mama if you want to. I will not take the money back but there will be no monthly allowance. It is your choice, Svetlana. I only want to protect you." He pulls me into his chest and I just cry, wrapping my arms around him.

This reminds me of being younger and my papa holding me when I hurt myself or when Mama would slap me. That makes me cry harder. I do want to take the chance and go with him, especially as he's giving me the option of going back home before it's too late. He pulls back to look at me. "What do you want to do, my angel?"

"Come with you, Igor. Thank you."

He kisses the top of my head again, in a sisterly manner. It's not what I want, but maybe I can make him fall in love with me, maybe he does love me but doesn't want to admit it because I'm too young, maybe when I turn fake seventeen he will want me. I will work on making him want me. I can do this.

"Igor, how will you get me into America if I do not have any documentation?"

He smiles at me.

"No need to worry your pretty little head about that, my angel. We will clear customs in LA, but the guards are well known to me so they will let us through. Then once you are settled, I will get your documentation to say you can live in America. I like you are inquisitive."

He walks us to the plane, it's huge. Once inside I am speechless, it's smaller inside with only about ten seats but I have never seen luxury like it. Wow, I run along the aisle like the little girl I am, I turn to Igor and he is standing watching me with his thumb at the side of his mouth.

He smiles at me. "I take it you like it?"

"Igor, the plane looks so big outside. I have never seen anything like it, is it safe? I'm scared." I walk back toward him and he just opens his arms for me to walk into. He is my comfort. I feel safe in his arms.

"You will be safe, my angel, do not worry."

Just then someone tells us we need to take our seats so we don't lose our window, whatever that means. I look at all the little windows, wondering what they are talking about. Igor takes my hand and puts me in a seat, fastening my seat belt for me. He takes the seat next to me and he holds my hand the whole time. Someone brings him a glass of what I suspect is vodka, it's what most Russians drink, including my papa, and they hand me a glass and a can of Coke. I have only ever had a can of Coke once before and that was for my birthday. I asked my mama if I could have one as my present, she thought I was silly but I read about it in my books as something all the teenagers drink in America. For someone to just put one in front of me like this, I feel like it's my birthday again. I smile. Igor takes the can and opens it for me. I don't need the glass, so I just take it back from him and drink it.

"Oh my goodness, this is delicious, Igor. I have only ever had it one time for a birthday present from Mama. I love it. It's my favorite thing ever, Igor. Thank you."

He laughs at me just as I feel movement. I stop with the can midway to my mouth. I look to him to see if he's okay, if this is normal.

"It's okay, the plane is moving. It has to get into position on the runway so it can have a run up to taking off. You are safe, my angel, do not worry." He smiles at me then takes my Coke from my free hand and kisses the back of it.

I'm so confused by him. I feel like he likes me, like he wants me, he's always kissing me and holding my hand but he says he's my ward like my big brother.

Suddenly the engines get louder, we start moving again but this time we start to go faster and faster. I watch out the little window and although it's dark, I can see lights whizzing past us. I turn to Igor, I must look scared, he leans over to me and wipes at my cheek, it's a tear. I didn't know I was crying. Just then I'm tilted backward as the front of the plane starts to go upward. I startle and look out the window, seeing the lights getting smaller and smaller as we climb up. I turn to Igor again, crying. I'm gripping his hand so tight and I've squashed the Coke can in my other hand, gripping it tightly.

"Look at me, Svetlana. You are safe. Keep looking at me. The plane will level out very soon, it's just climbing to altitude. Once it levels out, we can leave our seats and walk around. It's a long flight to LA. We have to stop off to refuel in Paris, I thought since it was your first time away from Russia we would stay there for a couple of nights so you can see Paris. Would you like that?"

I look at him, startled.

"You mean Paris in France? Oh Igor, yes, that would be amazing. Can we do that if we don't have documents for me? Will they let me in?"

He nods and laughs, stroking down my cheek.

"Yes, we will not have any trouble. Tomorrow, I have a couple of meetings to attend. I want you to stay in my house, and then I will take you out to see the sights and take you shopping. Would you like that?"

I'm nodding like my head's about to fall off. He laughs at me. Before I know it, he unbuckles his seat belt then leans over to do mine and he pulls me onto his lap.

"This is a shorter flight, it's just over four hours, but the flight from Paris to LA is a lot longer. You see that door over there to the left?" He points to the back of the plane and there are two doors, there are also two scary looking big men sitting there that I didn't notice before. I nod. "That is a bedroom, and the one next to it is a bathroom. If you are tired, you can go and have a little sleep now, but we will fly back at night to LA, so you can use that room to sleep. We shall have something to eat and then you can either go for a sleep or stay here with me, but I have some work to be doing."

I just nod at him and lean into his chest and close my eyes. The next thing I know, I'm being woken up by Igor. He is sitting next to me, on his laptop, but we are on a bed. I sit up.

"How did I get here?"

He laughs at me. He seems to do that a lot.

"You fell asleep on me, so I carried you in here. You missed the food but I have a sandwich here for you with a can of Coke. We will be landing soon. We need to get back into our seats. You will be fine landing. This time the plane nose goes down and then the wheels come out for us to hit the runway. There is absolutely nothing to worry about. Okay?"

I smile as I take the Coke and drink a big mouthful. We land and he was right, it was scary but not too bad. I think I prefer the taking off to landing. We are in a car heading to his house. He has a house in Paris. Wow. It's only a short drive. We pull up to some tall gates and I lean forward and watch as they slowly open for us to drive through. It's a long sweeping drive and when I see the house, I drop my can. Luckily it's empty. I turn to Igor.

"Is this just yours or is it a hotel?"

"It is just mine. I stay often when I am traveling around, which I do a lot. There will be a lot of times I am not at home in LA but you will be safe. I have men to protect you and me."

I just stare openmouthed at him. This seems to be the norm for me right now. I'm really acting my age. Just wait until I get inside this place. I have never seen anything like it, ever. He takes my hand and leads me inside. I don't have time to look at anything because he's taking me up the enormous staircase. He takes me to a bedroom, and another man brings in my bags.

"You will stay in here tonight. I will be in my room on the next floor, up there." He points up to the ceiling.

This room is beautiful with the biggest bed I have ever seen. I'm used to sleeping on a couch, not a bed.

"You have a bathroom right through there all to yourself. You need to take a shower, my angel, you do smell a little."

I look at him. I'm angry.

"I had a fucking wash this morning," I shout at him. I have never been so insulted.

He reaches out, taking my face in one hand and squeezing my cheeks together.

"Ouch, that hurts," I try to say through my puckered-up lips.

He bows right into my face, but drops his hands straight away.

"You will never, ever speak to me like that again. Do you understand? You are sixteen. Words like that should never come out of an angel. EVER," he grits out to me and I recoil slightly, he scares me.

I don't speak and I walk to the bathroom. I leave the door open. I'm used to not having any privacy and I strip out of my clothes. I just stand there not knowing what to do. I have never seen a shower before and I've never had a bath, only in the little sink in the kitchen.

"What the hell are you doing? Why are you standing naked? Here." He throws something around my shoulders.

It's nice and soft. He comes around the front of me and I watch his face as he notices my naked form standing in front of him. I have big tits for a nearly fifteen-year-old. I see him stare at them and he licks his lips just as he pulls the robe around me and ties it at the front to cover me up.

"I was going to take a shower, but I don't know how to use it. I have never been in one before."

He storms over, pulling my hand, and he shows me by getting inside. He presses a button, which makes water come out above us, and then another button makes water come out the side. He gets soaked standing there in his suit.

"Press these to turn it off and on and press this button up or down to turn the temperature hotter or colder. Simple. Now take a shower. I will have some food brought up to you and you need to sleep. Tomorrow stay in the house. There is a pool outside you can use, but make sure you put a bathing suit on first. You will find one in a drawer out there." He points into the bedroom. "You will wait until I return home. Okay?"

I nod and with that, he is gone.

I wake up and stretch out in this huge, soft bed. I had the best sleep ever, well, that I can remember in my life. I don't want to move. It took me a few minutes when I woke to remember exactly where I was. I curl back up into a ball and lay thinking about Igor. I saw the way he looked at my body and especially my tits last night. I know when I am fake seventeen in a couple of months, I'm going to make it my mission to seduce him. I know he has an attraction to me, I saw it.

I don't even know what time it is. I get up and find a bathing suit in one of the drawers; I pull back the curtains and see it's a beautiful sunny day, I hope it's warm. I put on a skirt and tee over my swimsuit and I go in search of food. I find the kitchen downstairs, it took me a little to find it. This place is like a palace, it's huge. I startle in the kitchen when I see a lady there.

"Hello," I say.

She just smiles at me. She opens what I now see is a fridge. We didn't have a fridge at home, it was mostly so cold Mama just kept what food we had outside in a small box. She pulls out orange juice and motions to me. I think she's asking if I want some. Maybe she speaks French and not Russian. I nod and smile. She motions for me to sit on a stool at an island. I do.

She makes me all kinds of things to eat. I don't even know what some of them are. I'm now realizing what a simple life I had back home. The only thing we ate was porridge every morning. Never anything else, except on a birthday, then Mama made us some jam and we had that on bread. This is going from one extreme to another. From being very poor and basic to being very rich with so many choices. The lady puts a little of each down on the side and passes me a plate.

"You eat what you like, she says to me in broken Russian." She points to the different dishes. "Waffles, pancakes, toast, croissants, jam, butter, syrup, bacon, eggs, sausage links, hash brown…" I hold up my hand to stop her. There are just too many things.

"Thank you. I will just taste a little of everything. There is so much. I will not remember them all."

She nods at me.

I do just that, I try bits of everything. I love it all, but I am so full. I ask for a can of Coke. She opens the other side of the fridge and it's full of all kinds of cans. She tells me to just help myself. I take a can and walk around the house, exploring it.

There are so many rooms, all of them are the size of my full house back home where eight of us lived. I can't believe Igor needs this much space. I wander up the stairs back to where my room is and open all the doors to see what is inside. There are lots of different size bedrooms and a big bathroom. I go up the other stairs, which is where Igor said his room was. This is amazing up here. There is only the one room but it spans most of the house. His bedroom has a huge bed also. I move over to it and lay on top, and dream of him taking me in it. I can smell his woodsy smell on the pillows. There are doors and when I open them they lead to the roof of the house. I go out and walk around. Wow, it's so hot out here, I don't think it ever gets this hot back home in the summer, I can see for miles up here, and in the distance I can see the big tower that Paris has. I've seen pictures of it but can't remember the name of it. I walk around the rooftop and spot the pool out the back of the house which I will be heading to very soon, even though I don't know how to swim and have never been in a pool in my life. The garden seems to go on for miles. I can just make out some other houses in the distance. It's very private here. I head back down and through the kitchen, out to the back of the house. I see a little house next to the pool, so I go and see what it is. There are towels and more showers in here. I grab a towel which is big and fluffy and take it with me.

"Enjoying the pool there, my angel?"

He startled me. I didn't hear or see him come out to the pool. I can't swim, so I have stayed in the end where I can stand up and sit on the steps, but I've been on my back floating in this small area above the steps for ages. I didn't realize it was that long. I see the smile on his face and I return it, nodding.

"Oh Igor, I have never been in a pool before, never mind a bath or a shower. This is all so new to me. I can't swim, so I just stay here where I can stand up and hold on to the rail to these steps. I walked around your house, it's beautiful. But Igor, why do you need something so big just for you? Why do you need all this space? I don't understand. All your rooms are bigger than my whole house back home. It is surely too much for one man?"

He laughs at me.

"You are correct, it is too big for one man. You never know what the future holds and who I will share this house with." He looks away as he says this, I can feel my cheeks going red again. I want that to be me, I want it to be me, and we can have a family, lots of children. I look away,

"How many houses do you have?" I look back to him, he looks quizzical, he's sitting on a lounger thinking.

He starts to count on his hand, then uses his other hand. Wow, he doesn't even know how many he has. I move away from him, still in the area where I can stand up.

"Igor, if it's that many you don't even know, then it's far too many in my opinion." I laugh at him.

"Thirteen, I think," he finally says.

He thinks. Wow, he must be so rich. No wonder he could give my mama so much money. It makes me sad to think about them. I feel tears flowing down my cheek and I turn away from Igor so he doesn't see them. I think about my mama and if she told Papa that I loved him? I think of Vidana, we were close and I miss her. I'm wondering if Dominika is now sharing with her and wondering if Mama has gone looking for any houses yet, but then it's not even been a day. I have no way to contact them, so I wouldn't even know when they do move. Suddenly I'm being pulled into Igor's chest gently. He wraps his arms around me and places his chin on my shoulder.

"Hey, what's wrong? Are you thinking about your family?"

I nod and turn in his arms. He's stripped out of his suit. I don't dare look to see if he's naked down below, that scares me.

"Yes, I was just wondering what they were doing, but also I have no way of contacting them. How could I have left not thinking about that? It never crossed my mind that I would want to speak to them, all of them. I do miss them. It makes me sad I didn't speak to my papa before I left. I wanted to say goodbye." I look up as I speak to him.

He suddenly goes rigid in my arms at mentioning my papa. Maybe it's because he's thinking how could I miss someone who treated me like that. But it's not true, and I can't tell Igor that. I rest my head back on his chest. He moves us over to the stone steps and sits down with me on his lap. I think I can feel he has on some shorts or maybe some briefs, I don't dare look. We sit in silence for a few minutes with him stroking down my back.

I know he cares for me, I just get so confused, but like he says, I'm only sixteen, really fifteen, too young for him, even though Mama was married to Papa at my age.

"Okay, are you ready to go sightseeing and shopping? We have this afternoon and then tomorrow for me to show you around. You will need to tell me what types of things you like though so you don't get bored."

I look up to him and smile, and he lowers his head. Oh my god I think he's going to kiss me. I close my eyes, I'm scared, but he laughs and just kisses the tip of my nose.

"No, my angel, I know you want me to kiss you, but I will not. You are far too young for me. I care for you, and I will look after you and protect you, but that is all. There will never be anything romantic between us. Okay? I just want you to know that now so you don't get the wrong idea."

I know my face is red with embarrassment. I get up off his lap and head toward the little house next to the pool, grabbing my towel as I do. I hear him splashing in the water. I turn to look at him and just as I do, he emerges out of the water, dripping wet, and oh my fucking god. He is naked. He didn't have anything on and I was sitting on his lap. I am so embarrassed. I have never seen a penis before, ever. I turn away and head into the little house quickly. He hasn't seen me gaping at him yet, I just caught him grabbing a towel and I can't help it, I stand at the door to the house and turn to look around again. He's drying his hair, but he's just standing there naked, not a care in the world. I'm watching his penis, it's a funny thing, it's just hanging there, it looks like a thick sausage, I don't think I could eat a sausage again without thinking of Igor's penis. I'm still gazing at it.

"Ahem, I thought you had gone to get changed?" He smiles at me, wrapping the towel around his waist and covering up.

I shut the door quickly, mortified he saw me staring like that. I get into the shower and wash off, stripping my bathing suit in there. I don't think I can face him again after that. He was just laughing at me. I put on my skirt and tee that were covering me earlier and creep into the house hoping not to see him. I don't hear him, so I run up the stairs to my bedroom. I find some shorts in the dresser the bathing suit was in and some other tees, I don't know whose clothes these are but I don't think they would mind me borrowing them. I sit on my bed and I pull out one of my books I brought with me that Mama got for me. This one is a love story, it's one of my favorites, I've read it a few times. It's for young adults like me, even though I've read adult books, but this one is so sweet, and I'm sure, or I hope there are others to follow it. Maybe I could ask Igor to find out for me. The book is called *Twilight*, and it's about a human girl and a vampire. I sit reading my favorite part when Igor comes marching into my room.

Shouldn't he knock? He just barges about, not bothering about my privacy. If he is supposed to be like my big brother, then he needs to stop just walking into my space.

"What's that look for?" he says.

I'm scowling at him.

"Shouldn't you knock when you want to come into my room? If you're like a big brother, then I should have privacy. You don't know what I might be doing. Like when you walked into my bathroom last night and I was naked." I burn up again with embarrassment.

He puts his thumb to the corner of his mouth. I know he's thinking when he does this.

"You're right, I'm sorry. It is rude of me, but I am only used to having women I fu—women I fool around with in my company and it's just natural to walk in and out of a room without knocking because well…" He trails off. I know he was going to say they would both be naked with fucking, anyway.

"Well, I'm not one of them you are fuc—"

He holds his hand up.

"Do not finish that sentence unless you want to be put over my knee."

I recoil at that, throwing him a dirty look. Isn't that exactly what he reprimanded my papa for?

"Isn't that the reason you wanted to take me away from my papa? I did not come with you going from one man who whipped me to another one. Doesn't that make you like him?"

He runs over to me and is on the floor in front of me, on his knees and taking my hand. He removes the book from my other hand and lays it on the bed, then takes that hand. He kisses them both.

"Please forgive me, you are right. I would never do that. I don't even know why I said it. It kinda just came out. Yes, it would make me like your papa, but I am nothing like him. I respect females and would only ever do anything that they wanted me to do. I would never hurt a woman intention-ally." He's kissing my hands still. I take one out of his grip and I stroke his hair, it's still damp from the shower he just had but I run my fingers through his curls. "I'm sorry, my angel, I would not do that to you ever."

I know he wouldn't, but it also gives me an idea for the future, a way to make him do things to me. I file it away in the back of my head.

We are up the Eiffel Tower, the big tower I could see from the roof, we've been all over and he's even taken me shopping. He bought me so many new clothes. I think they were expensive clothes. I think one item cost what my entire life's clothes cost Mama for me. He said Paris is the best place to get designer clothes, not that I knew what he was talking about. I love him more and more each minute I spend with him. I know I shouldn't but I loved him the moment I set eyes on him. To have him whisk me away like this is truly a dream. One I will need to keep pinching myself to see if it is real. But without a doubt, I know I love him, and he will be mine. I will make him love me back.

Four

Svetlana
Present

I'VE JUST SEEN *MY LOVE*, I CANNOT BELIEVE IT, BUT IT WAS AN accident, one I know he didn't want to happen. I was just leaving Poppy's office. I have been in there with her for the afternoon going over some ideas she had for the new refuge center. I was at the elevator just talking to Mavra waiting for the cart to arrive when I realized I left my cell in her office. I walked back, but just as I got around the corner, Igor came wheeling himself out of the kitchen area. He didn't see me at first, his head was down. I stood frozen, not wanting to move in case he chastised me for being there. I didn't want to make him angry at me. He looked up just before he was about to run into my legs. It only took a few seconds to notice his appearance. He looked gaunt, his eyes were dull, when they have always been such a vibrant sparkly electric blue. His hair is getting long and he hasn't had a shave for a while. He looked scruffy and looked much older than he is. He just needs someone to love him properly, someone like me. I could take care of him, I could make him happy. I could do a much better job than she is doing. It should be me looking after him. I stood in shock, gawking at his appearance.

"What the fuck, Svetlana, why are you here in my apartment? Who the fuck let you in? Get out of here." He screamed at me with so much venom, really raising his voice, he's quite scary and that's saying something.

I've seen him lose it so many times over the years and he's scared me so many times, but this is not like him. He does look terrible. Not the proud man I've always known him to be. I crouch down in front of him and take his hand. He tries to pull it free from me, but I grip tighter and stroke it down my cheek to my mouth where I kiss his palm. He tries to resist and pulls harder but he's weak, or he's not putting much effort into it and wants me to do this. I have tears spilling out of my eyes following the trail of his hand. I see his face soften. He knows I love him and I always will. I smile tentatively at him.

"How are you, *my love?* I've been so worried about you and not being able to see you has nearly killed me. What happened to you? How long will you be in the chair for? I want to help you, *my love*. You know I will always be there for you, even when she's gone. I love you so much, Igor. Please let me take care of you, she's not looking after you. Look at you. You are not the strong Igor, you are weak and your appearance is shocking. Can I take care of you *my love?*"

His face starts to harden at my words.

"Get the fuck out of my apartment. I don't want you here. I told you that you would never step foot in here again. What the fuck are you doing here? GET OUT." he screams in my face pulling his hand free from mine.

I see him look past me. I know she's there. I hang my head, the tears now streaming down my face as I raise up and turn slowly to leave, keeping my head bowed so I don't look at her. She would have heard everything. I just walk past to the elevators. She holds out my cell as I pass. I take it and then walk straight into the elevator cart waiting for me. Mavra obviously heard too. Fuck, why did that have to happen now. Don't get me wrong, I've waited weeks to see him, since that day he arrived home.

Getting to work more and more with Poppy, I've hoped to see him, hoping she would invite me to the apartment. Yes, she visited me most of the time and I was real friendly with her, putting my plan into action, becoming her best friend. One day we got to talking about drugs. She knew I was using, she wanted to help me get clean and help others. She asked if she could help and I agreed. I only started using when Igor discarded me, he broke me. I needed an out and when Andrey and Ivan started to fuck me they started to bring me heroin, only because I demanded it from them or I would tell Igor what they were doing. Since then I have been using, Igor doesn't know, and I think he would have me killed if he ever found out.

When she actually invited me to the apartment today for a brainstorming meeting I couldn't believe it. She wants to set up a refuge for abused women, those that are in a volatile relationship and need an out so we have been working a lot on that. We usually meet in one of the conference rooms on the seventh floor to discuss the refuge center, but she asked me up there instead, I don't know why, and I didn't care, I was elated when she did, hoping to see *my love*. All through our meeting, I was distracted, I kept listening to see if I could hear him in the apartment. A couple of times she asked if I was okay, I was miles away. I couldn't concentrate. I just wanted to see him. I was even planning on nipping out to the bathroom to see if I could see him, but I feared he would shout at me and I wasn't wrong.

This elevator seems to be taking forever. I'm still questioning why she had me go up there? It's killed me seeing him like that. I still don't know what happened to him, and Sergei will not tell me. He just says he doesn't know. I don't believe him. I've been meeting him a lot in secret lately, over at our fuck-by-the-hour motel. It's more for me than him but to be honest I think I'm getting sick of him now. He isn't telling me anything. I think his job and his loyalty to them is more important. I need to get a release. Not just a quick fuck from Sergei. That's all it is with him, wham bam, and it's over, for him anyway. I very rarely orgasm, I fake it more than I actually have one. I need more. I have needs.

I decide I'm going to the club, The Hex Club, it's an adult-only club. I need a proper release, especially after seeing *my love*. I will just imagine it is him. I do that with almost everyone anyway.

I rush to my room and get changed. What I mean by that is I put on my PVC stuff, ready for the club. I have on long PVC trousers that stick to every part of me. The good thing about these is they are crotchless and they have no ass, which means they do not have to be removed giving anyone easy access. I have on a PVC corset that pulls my waist in making it tiny, but my tits spill out over the top, they are big anyway but the corset pulls them up to under my chin and squeezes them together, on my nipples are tit pasties, just to hide the nipples for now. I like to dance around the club dressed like this, it drives men crazy, especially when they tear them off with their teeth. I get excited just getting dressed for the club. I cover up with sweatpants and an oversized off-the-shoulder top. I have a backpack with my stilettos in it, Louboutin, red leather ones Igor bought me. I wear them every time I go to The Hex, it's so I have a piece of him with me. I think he would die if he saw me like this. I think about him now and how angry he was to see me. I love him so much. I'm his rightful queen. I will make her fall one way or another.

I enter the club, it's a top exclusive club. Actually Andrey knows, or knew, people in high places with being Igor's second and he was the one that got me on the permanent guest list. This club is where all the A-listers come for an escape. No one is allowed cell phones or any kind of recording equipment. If you need to change, then you do that in a room just off the reception area, then you hand over your purse or backpack and your cell. You are not allowed to take any items in with you. On entering the first room you are scanned for any devices. If you beep, you are stripped searched, it's one of the stipulations on signing up. Andrey got me a lifetime membership. I'm not sure if he had to pay, if he did, then I dread to think how much it was. I didn't ask any questions, but a club like this has to run into the thousands for an annual pass. You gain entry from a fingerprint scan and a retina scan. The one thing I love is all the security. I feel so safe here. Andrey brought me the first couple of times. He used to get off watching me work the room, then he would get off in me, sometimes solo, sometimes there were a few. It was another thing I was grateful to him for. I still hated his fucking guts.

There is one guy who is here a lot. As soon as he sees me he follows me around the room, like a little puppy. I've had him take me a few times and he's one of the best fucks I've had in here, so I love it when he's here. He never fails to find me. I've started to look for him each time, he has a cock and a body to die for. I'm not sure if he is anyone important, I have never seen his face, he always wears a mask, different ones. Sometimes he has on full masks and it's only his body I recognize. He has blond hair and blue eyes like *my love*, but he is taller than Igor and he is ripped as fuck. He has muscles on muscles, even his cock has muscles on muscles and it's ridged. It's the best cock I have had in any hole.

I walk the room and spot him right away. I see the moment he notices me and he leaves the woman who has his cock in her mouth and follows me around. I saunter around, swaying my hips. I move gently to the music. I look around, watching what's going on. I head to my favorite room, the room where anyone and everyone can join in. It's like one big fucking orgy. The only thing people keep on, usually, is their masks, or like me today, I don't need to take off my pants. Thank fuck. Peeling them off when it's so hot is a nightmare. I'm exposed, no need for removal. I, too, always were a mask, it's a black lacy mask, full of beads and some feathers, I like to keep my identity hidden for obvious reasons. One being I work for Igor and now Poppy, it would not do me well if I were recognized by any of their clients. Who knows, I may have had a few of them in here already. I twirl around, dancing, making a show of it, just to make sure the big guy is following me. I don't make eye contact, letting him know I know he's there, but I'm in need of his cock in me soon.

I'm almost at my favorite room when I'm being pulled by the wrist. I'm yanked into one of the smaller private use rooms. I don't normally end up in these rooms. I like more than one in me and I like to be watched. These rooms are for use if someone doesn't want to be watched, it's just you and whoever you're with. It's dark and I think it's the big guy who grabbed me. At least I hope it was him. He was following behind me. He flicks a switch on and sure enough, it's him. He has a bare chest showing all his pecs; he has a leather studded cuff around each wrist and leather fringed arm cuffs covering his biceps, these are usually worn to hide any distinguishing marks like tattoos, if he needs to hide this much he doesn't want to be known. That's fine with me. I look down at his body, really taking him in. He has tight leather shorts on, showing his rock-hard cock that's just peeking out of the top of them, touching his belly button. I can see the moisture on it and I lick my lips, watching as it twitches. He has no hair on his chest, but he has a trail that runs down from his belly button and disappears into his shorts. I want to run my tongue down his bare chest to his cock.

I walk up to him, smiling as I strut. I stick my tongue out and I lick down his front. I move over to each nipple and bite them, then carry on down his chest, crouching, until I swipe the top of his cock with my tongue. He breathes in as I do this a couple of times. I then start to pull the shorts down, it's easier than I thought. The hardest part is getting them over his thighs, the muscles are so huge. I take them off him and untie his black boots and take them off. His cock is bobbing up and down with the movement. I look up his body and what a fucking sight. I'm crouched with my legs spread wide, and I start to play with my pussy while licking my lips. I stand up and sit on the edge of the bed, pulling him to me. Standing in front of me like this, I lick his cock like a popsicle. He's oozing cum out of the end and I lick it all up while watching his face. He puts his arms up behind his head and exhales, puffing his chest out. I take his cock into my mouth and he starts to thrust in and out. I play with it, holding the base with one hand and squeezing tight. I have him between my legs, which are both stretched on either side, wide. As I bob his cock in and out of my mouth, I start to play with myself again with my other hand. He watches me closely. He brings his arms down and tears the tit pasties from my nipples and pinches each one between his fingers. I like it rough. He takes his cock out of my mouth with a loud pop and he kneels down in front of me. I'm still playing with myself and he watches exactly what I do. I put my heels on the edge of the bed, spreading wider still. He then joins in with my hand. I play with my clit while he starts to stretch me open and inserts two fingers. In and out he takes them right to the edge then back in again. He pushes in as far as he can and curls his fingers inside, he finds the spot. I freeze and grab his hand, making him stop.

"Stroke me, just there, stroke, that's it, right there, ah fuck me," I shout as I explode all over his hand.

He pumps in and out and with his other hand he plays with my clit. I scream out my release. He bends his head to between my legs and he laps up my juice as it squirts out everywhere.

"Fucking hell, that's hot, baby," he says, nuzzling his nose inside me as I lower my legs.

The next thing I know, he kneels up and takes his cock in his hand. Finding my pussy, he rams it into me. I freeze, bringing my legs back up to either side of me with my stilettos digging into the bed. I spread my thighs as wide as I can to take in his body as he gets as close as he can to me, trying to ram all his big, fat fucking cock into me. I shuffle to the edge to make it easier for him. I put my arms under my knees and I lift my legs up, giving him all the access he needs, taking the crab position. He thrusts it in good and hard and stays in there rotating and rotating. He licks his fingers, then sticks them up my ass. He starts to pump with his cock and his fingers, in and out, over and over, he's like a machine.

I watch him closely, licking my lips. I think about *my love* in this moment, thinking of him doing this to me. He used to love sticking it to me everywhere and anywhere he could. I look to my shoes he bought me, I don't take them off often. I feel the big guy getting harder as he gets more frantic. He takes hold of my legs and puts them over his shoulders, almost lifting my ass off the bed. That's it, he explodes, and boy does he come, hard and fast, so fast it leaks out everywhere. The one thing about this guy, he is not selfish, he's shooting his load but then plays with my clit while thrusting to make me come again. I do, with not as much squirt this time, but enough. I scream out with my release. He pulls out when he's finished, and he leans down and licks me dry, including his own cum. He then crawls up my body and he kisses me hard. Kissing isn't usually allowed in the club, but I let him, and get into it with him as he plays with my tongue in his mouth.

I have flashbacks to Igor, remembering back to when he took me to his home in LA and our first kiss.

Age Fifteen

I had the most amazing time in Paris. The next day he took me shopping again then some more sights including a museum where there was a world-famous painting that everyone has heard of, everyone except me. To be honest, it was just a weird, miserable-looking old woman. I personally didn't see what the fuss was all about. Igor thought it was so funny. I enjoyed walking around the museum as it was the first one I had ever been in. Once we finished, we headed straight to the airport to board his plane. At least I knew what to expect this time, but it didn't make it any easier. It still scared me. He kept hold of my hand during takeoff and then once we were able to move, we had a lovely dinner, then he took me to the bedroom. He told me to sleep, that he would sleep with me. I couldn't believe it. Only I slept in my clothes under the comforter and he slept in his clothes on top of the comforter. We were woken up to have breakfast just before we landed.

On the drive from the airport to his house, I was in awe of everything around us. It was all so big, the trucks, the cars, the buildings. I was truly showing my age, jumping up and down on the back seat, trying to look at everything, pointing out all the different things to Igor, like he's never seen them before. He just smiled and laughed at me, watching my joy. We arrived in a high-rise area where I couldn't even see the tops of the buildings. Igor flicked a switch and the top of the car moved.

"Now you can see. Here, stand on the seat and pop your head out of the roof."

I smiled at him and climbed up. "This is unreal, Igor. Come, have you seen this?"

He laughed. "Of course I've seen it, I live here."

The car pulled up outside a really, really tall building. I had to crane my neck to try to see the top. All around were buildings just like this.

"What, you live like here, here? This isn't a house. I thought we were going to your house?"

"I don't have a house here in the city, I have a penthouse."

I look down to him, frowning.

"A penthouse is what they call an apartment that is usually on one floor with no levels. Except mine does have levels, with being a penthouse. A penthouse is the very, very top of the building and my penthouse takes the complete top floor of this building." He points up to the roof.

I look up to where he's pointing. I gape.

"You mean I'm going to stay right up there, right at the very top? I can't even see the top. It will be like living in the clouds. What if I'm scared up there?"

"Now why would you be scared? There's nothing to be scared about and when I'm not there I have staff and guards who are there constantly, so you will never be alone. You said you like reading, I will make sure we stock up on any books you need and I will get a tutor in for you to learn English. You will need to speak English living in America, you will need to talk to people and you can't speak Russian like we do."

Hmm, I never even thought about it. With speaking to a Russian constantly and anywhere we went in Paris, he spoke to them in French. I didn't have to do anything. I suppose now I will have to.

"We need to see what level your education is at. How long is it since you dropped out of school, my angel?"

I think about it.

"It must be three years. Papa had his accident, so Mama had to go out to work. I had to drop out to look after my sisters. Mama said I didn't need an education because I would get married and have a family. Looking after my sisters was my education, she used to say." I just shrug my shoulders. The car door opens and he jumps out. I'm still sticking my head out of the roof.

"Come on, Svetlana, time to see your new home."

I climb down and out of the car. He takes my hand and leads me through some doors that go around, you have to be quick to jump on or get trapped. He drags me in with him so I don't get trapped then pushes me out with him holding my waist.

"Guess you need to get used to a few new things, huh?"

I nod, all wide eyed at him. He walks me to the back and we head into the elevator. We used these a couple of times in Paris so I know what they are now. He's holding my back to his chest by my waist. I lean into him as I watch the arrow and floor numbers go by quickly for each floor we pass. He's right, all the way up to the top, the very top. The doors open and he pushes me out, still holding my waist, walking behind me. There's a man standing by the doors. Igor greets him. I think he called him Mavra? I just smile at him as Igor pushes me gently forward. He moves me through the place and I don't know where to look. My head is whipping backward and forward and side to side, trying to take everything in. This place is enormous.

"Am I really going to live here, in this place, with you?" I run from his hold to the windows. I place my forehead on the glass and my hands on either side of me and try to look down. It's a long, long way up here. "Do these windows open at all?"

He shakes his head, scowling.

"Good thing, that would terrify me. Look, Igor, you can see for miles and miles, it's huge out there, all the buildings, and it's so busy, so much traffic I noticed as we were driving here."

He laughs again, then takes my hand to show me the rest of the place, including a bedroom which is as big as the room I had in his house in Paris. He gets me to open the double doors and I freeze.

"Wow, look at all this stuff. Whose room is this, why am I looking at all their stuff?"

He comes up behind me and places his chin on the top of my head, wrapping his arms around my waist.

"This is your room and this is all for you. I had my personal shopper pick me out all the trendy clothes for a sixteen, nearly seventeen-year-old. I hope you like them. By the looks of it, there is everything from dresses to skirts to jeans and lots and lots of tops. I suspect the island in the middle will have all your new underwear in them."

I don't know what to say as I gaze around the room, I see shelves of shoes and sneakers and purses, just so much. I'm crying, I wipe at my face. He's going to think this is all I do, cry at everything. He turns me in his arms and lifts my chin up.

"Thank you, Igor. Thank you for everything you have done and are doing for me. I don't know how or why this is happening, but I'm beyond grateful to you. Never in my wildest dreams could I imagine anything like this. Thank you," I whisper to him, hugging him tight.

He holds me for a few minutes then pulls back from me.

"One more thing, I think it's here."

He walks to the island in the middle and on top is a bag. He grabs the bag then walks to me, grabbing my hand and we sit on the bed. He empties the bag onto the bed and out falls a white box. I have no idea what it is. He opens the box and turns it upside down and a cell phone falls out. I gawk again.

"This is for you. It's an Apple iPhone. I know you don't know what that is now, but believe me, you will. What sixteen-year-old isn't a whizz after ten minutes with one of these? Here, let me show you how it works, the basics and if I'm not mistaken, it should already be programmed in with two numbers."

He shows me how to turn it on and off and sets it up with a code that we both know, then we have to do what he says is face recognition. He says I'm sixteen, and he needs to be able to access it also. Then he shows me my contacts, there are two, him and another number. He dials the number, looking at the time on his watch. It doesn't pick up, so he presses the green button again. This time I hear a voice saying hello in Russian. He passes me the phone, pressing another button. I hear the voice again, only it's loud so we can both hear. I freeze and look at Igor. He nods to me.

"Mama, Mama, is that you, oh Mama, I miss you so much."

I hear her laugh at the sound of my voice. She shouts for everyone to 'come quick, it's Lana on the phone.' I hear lots of noise and shouting. I hear them shouting my name.

"Oh my goodness, I miss you all so much. I hope you are all being good for Mama and Vidana. I can't believe I get to speak to you."

Mama is ecstatic, as are my sisters. I can hear little Zoya running around shouting, 'Lana, Lana.'

I laugh to Igor. "I think she's looking for me in the room. I miss them so much."

He leans forward and wipes the tears that are streaking down my face. I wipe my snotty nose on my sleeve. He gets up to get me some tissues.

"Mama, how are you all. Have you moved? Silly me, it's only been two days. How's Papa? Is he home? Can I speak to him?" I see the moment I mention Papa, Igor freezes, passing me the tissues. I look to his face and it's like stone. I know it's the mention of my papa.

"No, Lana, he is not here," Mama says.

"He hasn't been home since before you left, Lana, he's missing. No one has seen him," Vidana is telling me, but Mama is telling her to shush. She tells them all to say goodbye to me and leave the room.

"Mama, where is Papa? Is he still at the bar?" I watch Igor, his face hasn't changed. He turns and leaves the room but he leaves the door open. "Mama, do you know where he is?"

"No, Lana. No one has seen him since he stayed at the bar the day you left. Don't worry, he will turn up at some point. When he does, I will let him know you can phone us now. Igor put this phone in the bag he gave me. I hoped it would be so I could speak to you. How is he treating you Lana? Has he said anything to you?

I'm shaking my head no, forgetting she can't see me. I go on to tell her all about staying in Paris in his big house and all the clothes he's bought me and about where I am living. I tell her how happy I am and how he is really looking after me. We speak for a few more minutes. I say my goodbye, promising to call her again soon, just as Igor comes back into the room. He looks a little better than he did when he left. I'm upset Papa is missing but I don't tell him that. I don't want him to be upset every time I mention him. I get up and walk to him, hugging him tight to me.

"Thank you, Igor. I know I keep saying it but I don't know how else to show it."

He kisses the top of my head.

"Come, we have some food waiting for us. You need to get used to the time difference. You will be a little off the next day or two. It is called jet lag. It is ten hours difference between here and your mama's. You will need to remember that when you want to speak to her. It is now, erm…" He looks at his watch and I can see him working it out. "It is six thirty a.m., it is very early for them, are they all early risers?"

"Yes, we were always up at six a.m. so Mama and I could get the others ready and dressed and porridge made." I smile, thinking about them.

He takes my hand and leads me to the dining area where there is a lot of food set out for us. I don't even know what some of it is. There is a mixture of Russian food and American food. He has me tasting the burgers, hot dogs, fries, and the good ole American mac and cheese. We laugh and I really like the mac and cheese. We sit in the lounge, me drinking Coke by the can and him drinking vodka. We chat, he asks me about school and where I was up to, he then informs me I have a tutor coming in two days to start giving me lessons. Great, just what I need. He is right though, one thing I must do is learn English. He looks at his watch.

"Right, young lady, I think you need to go to bed. I know you don't feel like it, but it is now nine thirty p.m. This is where you need to get your body clock adjusted to the big time change. If you have trouble sleeping, which I suspect you will after devouring three cans of Coke, then I suggest you read one of your books. Oh, that reminds me, come with me first."

He gets up, and I follow. He walks into a room and there are bookcases on three walls, all full. He walks over to a section.

"These are for you. My personal shopper got me the most popular young adult books and also books for your education."

My eyes go wide. Books, so many books. I spot my favorite book, *Twilight*, but next to it there are four more, I grab them.

"Oh my goodness, Igor. This is my favorite, I've read it so many times but I wasn't sure if there were any more yet. You have four more of them." I squeal and start to flick through the one I picked up. I groan and slam it shut and put it back on the shelf. He scowls at me. "It's in English, Igor. I cannot read it unless it is in Russian. It will take me forever to learn English and be able to read them." I sulk, pouting, sticking my lip out and he laughs loud at me.

He pulls my bottom lip slightly then lets it go. I furrow my brow at him and cross my arms over my chest. I immediately see his eyes go to my tits, which I have now pushed up with crossing my arms. He looks away quickly, he actually looks embarrassed. He starts to walk toward the door when he stops and turns.

"Well, that gives you more of an incentive to learn English. You are young and will pick it up very quickly. Now, bedtime."

I still have my arms crossed as I skulk out of the door. He's standing with his thumb at the corner of his mouth. I lean up on my tiptoes and kiss his cheek.

"Thank you, again. I feel I will be thanking you for a long time and you will get sick of it soon. Good night, Igor."

He smiles at me, bowing slightly to make it easier for me to reach his cheek.

"I will not be here when you wake in the morning, as I have meetings to attend to. Polina will wake you and she will have your breakfast ready for you. I have told her to do you a mixture of Russian and American so you can try different things. She will do all the cooking for you, so let her know what it is you like. You will also see another lady around that is Daria. She cleans so she will no doubt be picking up after you. I am not sure what time I will be back. If it is late, do not wait for me. Maybe watch some television, one of them will show you how it works, you will learn English faster that way. Good night, Svetlana, sleep well, my angel."

The next few weeks passed by so quickly. I never left the apartment, not once. The tutor came in for six hours a day, five days a week. I learned a lot, I had nothing else to do. Igor was out working all the time. He even went away on trips, but like he said, there were always people around. One stipulation he had was that I was not to leave the apartment under any circumstances. That was great for a while but it started to annoy me that I couldn't go outside. It was something I was going to ask Igor about. I wanted to go out and explore LA. I wanted to go out and see people of America, see what the young teenagers like me actually did and what they were like. I would be sixteen in the next week, fake seventeen to Igor. I wanted to start my plan to seduce Igor ready for my birthday, but it's like he is avoiding me. How can I do that if he isn't around me? One good thing is that my English is really good. I started reading *New Moon*, I can't wait till I can read faster and move onto the next one.

The day before my fake seventeenth birthday and Igor isn't home. I feel so sad, he's away, and I have no one around me. I've spoken to my mama a few times over the last few weeks and Vidana. Mama hasn't told me, but Vidana told me Papa has gone. He isn't coming home. I didn't know what she meant, so I pressed her. She told me the man at the bar told Mama that Papa stayed that night but then Mr. Ustrashkins visited him and that he didn't see Papa leave, but he was not seen again after that. I want to ask Igor about it. If he was the last person to see Papa, then where is he? It upset me that Mama was moving without him. How would he know where she moved to? How would he see my sisters again? I was confused.

Mama was so excited, telling me that she found a beautiful house for them all in a really nice neighborhood. It had five bedrooms and was enormous. Zoya and Klara, being the youngest, would be sharing a room, but it was big enough for two beds. The others would all have their own rooms and Mama and Vidana's rooms had their own bathrooms, just like mine did here with Igor. I was really excited for them all, the fact Igor kind of bought me from Mama so it would give them all a better life, it made me so proud I had done this for them, the fact I wanted to do it was beside the point, I would have done it, anyway. Mama was so pleased it was working out with Igor. I didn't tell her I was mostly alone and hardly saw him.

Whenever I do see Igor, I'm so happy and just smile at him all the time. Sometimes he comes back home really unhappy and I don't speak to him, choosing instead to stay in my room. It is best to keep away from him when he is like that. He is not nice when he is like that and he scares me. The first time he came home angry I felt sure he was going to hit me, he never did, but he got into my face when I asked him would he be home tomorrow.

"It's none of your fucking business when I am home. You are a little girl, do not ever fucking question me, do you hear me? E.V.E.R.," he shouted, spelling the last word out to me.

I recoiled at his venom but he just continued spewing right into my face. I felt his spit on my cheek, but was too afraid to wipe it clean. I tried to step back, but I stepped back into the hall table.

"If I want to stay away and screw someone, then I will, Svetlana. You are a pathetic little girl. Never ask me if I am going to be home, if I'm not here, I'm either working or fucking. In fact, you know what, the only reason I don't bring my current fuck home is because of you. Well, it's my fucking home, so I will bring who I want back to fuck. You can just put your earbuds in if you don't want to hear. Now fuck off out of my sight before I fucking do something I will regret."

I ran to my room, crying my eyes out, but relieved he didn't do anything. I stayed in my room, never daring to venture out. I don't know if he told Polina or if she heard it, but she brought me some food before she finished for the day. I was embarrassed to look at her. I felt like I was a burden to her and everyone. Even the next day, it was the afternoon before I ventured out of my room, I did so gingerly in case he was around. He wasn't. Luckily.

It is my birthday tomorrow and he is not around again. If he does not come back, then I will go out on my birthday. I will be sixteen. He cannot keep me locked up forever. I used to go out on my own back home and it was more dangerous there. So much poverty in my village, men treated women like they were objects and thought they could do what they wanted with them. Maybe that is what Igor thinks also, with coming from the same town.

Waking up, it's my birthday. Finally I am sixteen. I dive out of bed and run to the living area to see if Igor is around. He's not there, so I knock on his office door. Nothing. I see Mavra.

"Have you seen Igor today, Mavra?"

"No, he didn't come back last night. I'm not sure when he will be back. He doesn't tell me, I just guard the elevators for him."

He looks at me a little weird, I look down realizing I'm in a short nightdress. I forgot to put my robe on with being excited about my birthday. I see the problem, this nightdress it is slightly see-through. I turn quickly, he was looking at my tits then his eyes wandered to my pussy area. Fuck, I don't have any panties on either. It's a good thing Igor wasn't around, he would have scolded me for being out of my room like this. I skulk back to my room to jump in the shower and get dressed. I guess it's just me on my birthday. Well, if he's not around, I'm going out. I don't care what he says.

As I come out of the bathroom drying my hair with a towel and one wrapped around me, I notice a big orange bag sitting on my bed with a card on top. A present. OMG, he remembered. I open the first orange box from inside the bag and there are some new jeans. They feel amazing. The tag name is the same that is on the box, there's another box and inside is a T-shirt also with letters LV and some little star-shaped flowers. It's nice, but I'm not sure what it stands for and then there's the third box with some new sneakers with the same letters on them and again a little star floral design all over them. They are lovely. I put them on, but they are like a lot of the other stuff in my wardrobe. I open the card excitedly and it says 'Happy Seventeenth' on the front and inside it says 'Love Igor' but I doubt he wrote it. I'm sure it is not his writing.

I dry my hair, it's gotten really long now, I need to get it trimmed, maybe I will go to a hair salon today and have it all cut? Maybe get a new color on it, I'm sick of the boring brown hair, I put it up in a high ponytail at the top. I still feel like a little girl. I want to be a woman. I want women's clothes. I want to wear makeup like I see in the magazines he has delivered for me.

I head to the kitchen for my breakfast. I still only have porridge, the odd time I will have a pancake with syrup. Polina is there puttering around as usual. She smiles when she sees me and hands me a card.

"Is Igor back home? I had a present on my bed when I got out of the bathroom." She turns away from me to get my drink, a can of Coke, even for breakfast I have a can of Coke with my porridge.

"No, he's not home, dear. I put them on your bed as instructed," she says, still with her back to me. I think she's a little embarrassed.

I open her card and I see her writing matches the one on Igor's card. It makes sense now. She turns to me with my breakfast, only it's not porridge. It's an all-American breakfast with bacon, scrambled egg, sausage links, hash browns, and orange juice. Not what I wanted, but I think she's trying to make it special for me. I eat it anyway. She putters about while I eat. I wonder if she knows.

"Polina, thank you for my card and breakfast."

She smiles at me.

"Do you know if Igor will be coming home today?" I ask. Surely he would tell her if she has to cook dinner for him or not.

She turns away from me again, this time cleaning something. "No, he didn't say to make him any dinner tonight."

Great. But if I want to get my hair done, how do I do that with no money or buy makeup with no money?

"I would like to get my hair done and buy some makeup for my birthday, but I don't have any way of paying for them. Could you lend me some money, I promise I will pay you back?"

She looks to me with sympathy on her face. She nods then walks out of the room. I don't know if I offended her or what happened. I finish my orange juice and get up to get another can of Coke. I turn around just as I see Polina coming back into the kitchen. She hands me an envelope.

"Here is five hundred dollars. I have been saving money to try and bring my daughter over from Russia. You can borrow this as long as you pay me back, Svetlana. Do you promise you will pay me back?"

I throw my arms around her.

"Thank you so much, Polina. I promise, no matter what, I will pay you back. I don't know how much it will be to have my hair done or to buy makeup, but thank you."

Just then I think about what she just said.

"How old is your daughter? I didn't know you had a daughter in Russia? Have you not asked Igor to help you?"

She shakes her head and scowls at me. I'm not sure how to take that. Her daughter must be older. Polina looks a lot older than my mama. Just then I start to cry, it just hit me, it's my birthday and my mama always tries to do something special for each of us on our birthday. Polina takes me into her arms. I don't know if she knows why I am crying, unless she can guess.

"Shhh, Svetlana, it is your birthday, sweet girl. I know you miss your mama and your sisters. I am sure they will all speak to you later today when they get up. Remember, it is still the middle of the night back home. Don't be upset. You remind me of my daughter when she was your age. She is now forty-five and I have two lovely granddaughters who are eighteen and twenty-two. They still all live back in Russia. My daughter was in a bad marriage but she has finally escaped from that, which is why I am saving up money. She wants to come and live here, in America, with me. I am so happy she wants to. No, I will not ask Mr. Ustrashkins for money to help.

That is not who I am. Now listen. I know you are not to leave, but it is your birthday and I see you want to get done up nicely. Maybe I can ask one of the guards to escort you. What do you say? I will also distract Mavra from his post so you can go."

Hmm, I don't want anyone with me. But if I don't agree, she will not help me. I agree and tell her I will be back in twenty minutes. I just need to get myself sorted out and get my purse to put the money in. She nods and walks out. I head to my room, grab a purse, put the money inside, and head to the elevators.

As I get there, I see Mavra is not there. I run to the doors and press the down button just praying they open, they do, and I move quickly, pressing the button to the ground floor. The doors shut and I'm moving. I'm nervous. What if there is a guard waiting when the doors open? I start to panic. Moving around the box, I feel like it's getting smaller and smaller. Just then it stops and the doors open. I sigh out in relief. There doesn't seem to be anyone around who would stop me. I move quickly to the doors that move.

I'm out on the street and moving quickly but not running. I don't want anyone to think I'm running from someone. I go up and down streets, I'm watching everyone around me, looking at what they wear, how they have their hair, how much makeup the women wear. I watch the ones I think are about my age. Some of the girls wear such short skirts and low tops. They have on lots of makeup and their hair's all nicely done. I near a park and I see some others who look like most of the people back in my village. They look a little dirty with clothes that are too big and hang off them and are dirty and torn. There are a lot of people like that. I walk around and through the park.

I come into an area where there are stores. I see a big store that has perfumes in one window, then there are purses in another window, then clothes on mannequins in other windows. This looks like where I want to be. I step inside and I am straight into what looks like the beauty department. I walk around in awe of the place. I know Igor took me into stores in Paris, but they were exclusive little boutiques as he called them.

I start to look at the makeup on one of the counters, picking up different items. A lady comes to ask if she can help me. I tell her I want to get my hair done and I don't know anything about makeup. She takes me to the salon in the store. They can do my hair straight away, she tells me once my hair is done to go back to her and she will do my makeup and show me some simple things to do and use.

Wow, what a helpful lady.

Nearly three hours later and my hair is done. It looks amazing. I head back to the lady at the makeup counter and she sits me down and shows me some makeup by putting it on me. I don't recognize myself once she's finished. I end up buying everything she used on me. I still have a hundred dollars left.

I head to the lingerie dept and I actually buy myself my first ever sexy set. Wow, I feel so grown up. A lady tells me they have a sale rack on one of the floors and that I may find something on there to wear. I head up and after looking through all the racks, I find this gorgeous gold dress. It is very short. I have never put anything on this short to wear outside. It also has no back and the front is a deep plunge. The lady at the counter asked if it was for me, and I nodded. She frowned at me.

"Is this a little too old for you to wear? Will your parents be okay with you wearing this?"

I scowled at her. "That is none of your business. I have the money to pay for it and my boyfriend will love it."

She took my money and I left. I'd had a nice day up until that point. I thought I looked a lot older than my sixteen years with my new hair and makeup. She was rude. There was so much I wanted to buy, but I didn't have the money.

I left the store with my bags and I actually felt great when I kept seeing myself in other store windows that I passed. I even got some flirty looks from men and boys as I passed them. I turned a corner, realizing I didn't know my way back to Igor's apartment. I was lost, having never been out before. I walked down different streets. I couldn't even find the park I saw. I started to panic. I didn't know what to do. I didn't even know the address of the building, so I couldn't ask for directions. I felt like a fool. Why the fuck didn't I take note of where I was walking? Stupid fool. I was so engrossed in watching people instead. I start to panic as the streets start to get more residential. I've been walking for a while now. I turn and try to head back toward the stores.

I'm walking when my cell rings in my purse. I only switched it on when I left the store. I forgot it was off all day, it's not like anyone phones me anyway. I look and I only have two numbers listed, Igor's and my mama's. It's neither of them. I answer it anyway.

"H-h-hello?"

"How many times have I told you to never, ever, leave the fucking apartment."

It's not his usual number.

"Are you there, Svetlana? Fucking answer me."

"I'm out," is all I snap at him.

I hear him growl, but it sounded loud. I pull the phone away from my ear and look at it. I notice the time is five fifty. I've been out all day.

"It's my birthday, Igor, in case you had forgotten, and I wanted to get out instead of being locked up all day on my own, on my special day."

"I don't give a fuck what day it is, Svetlana. You never leave the fucking apartment unless I know about it. Do you hear me?"

He is really loud.

"You are not my papa, I can do what I want, IGOR, so don't fucking shout at me like a fucking little kid. I am not a little fucking kid," I shout back at him through the cell. I am so angry with him. I know he's done a lot for me, but, well, it doesn't mean he can keep me prisoner in that place.

"Turn around."

Huh, what does he mean? I have the cell to my ear and I turn around, he's standing right behind me. I pull it away from my ear and gulp hard. I feel my face going red. He's going to rip into me. I can see how angry he is.

"Do you even know where you are?" he says, passing the cell to a man standing next to him. It's one of his guards, I can't remember his name but I've seen him with Igor a few times. That's why I didn't recognize the number. I still have the cell in my hand by my side. I look down to the ground. He moves closer and lifts my chin up. He gets into my face. "Do. You. Fucking. Know. Where. You. Are?" he says quietly but sternly at me.

I shake my head. Do I admit I was lost? How did he find me?

"How did you know where I was?" I say timidly.

He takes his cell from his pocket and waves it at me.

"I can trace you through this. That way I know exactly where you are. I check it a few times a day usually. A lot of the time you don't have your cell switched on. I didn't think anything of it at first until your cell pinged on a couple of hours ago and I saw you were not at the apartment. Polina told me you wanted to treat yourself. I got it out of her what you intended to do and how she gave you the money. Yes, I do know it's your birthday. You had a gift from me, didn't you? It doesn't excuse your behavior and I know you are lost. I have been following you for the last hour. I wanted you to realize what you had done and how stupid your actions were. Now come." He turns and walks to the car waiting just behind him.

I don't move. I stand my ground. He turns to look at me.

"Get in this fucking car now before I put you over my shoulder and throw you in." I wouldn't put it past him to do that. "Oh, and one more thing, if you ever swear and shout at me over the phone again, you will know what punishment is."

"Stop treating me like a fucking stupid kid, Igor. I am sixt... seventeen, I am a grown woman. You need to start treating me like one." Holy cow, where is this coming from? I watch his face go from anger to quizzical to amusement.

He stands with his legs apart, putting his thumb up to the corner of his mouth like he does. I love it when he does that. He saunters back to me and leans down right into my face. He quietly whispers, "Stop acting like a fucking stupid kid, and maybe I will show you how a real woman gets treated."

Woah, what does he mean by that? I know I want to find out.

I get in the car, buckle up and try to squash as far into the corner as I can, trying to stay away from him. He gets in and laughs. We head back in silence. It's a good thing he is with me because you need a special card in the elevators to get to our apartment. I hadn't realized until just now. I stay in the corner of the elevator, not speaking and not looking at him. He stands on the other side. I can feel his eyes boring into me. I'm getting all hot, just the two of us in here, but I'm angry with him and this ride is taking forever. Finally the doors open. I move with lightning speed to get out and away from him. I walk around into the apartment and freeze.

There are balloons and banners all over the place but it's not those that have me floored. Standing there is my mama and my five sisters. I drop my bags and I fly into my mama's arms, crying my eyes out. She hugs me tight to her. My sisters all crowd around and hug me. We are just a big mess of tears. Polina appears wheeling a trolley which has a huge cake on it and everyone starts to sing "Happy Birthday" to me. I look at Igor, who is standing there, thumb at his mouth, smiling at me. I mouth 'thank you' to him. He did all this for me. I don't know what to say. My heart melts for this man even more. I love him.

The evening goes by too quickly. All of us talking and laughing and there is music playing. Zoya and Klara are asleep in one of the spare rooms. Apparently there are a lot of spare rooms and my mama and sisters are all staying here for two whole weeks. I am so excited. Igor stays with us all evening. He wanted to be a part of this. He took me to his office at one point, I thought he was going to scold me again but he didn't. Instead he gave me a present. It had a little card attached to it. I read it.

Svetlana, you are a beautiful young woman,

You deserve this beautiful gift.

Happy sweet seventeenth, my angel.

Love Igor.

I couldn't believe the words. In his writing as well. I opened the box and gasped at the beautiful necklace inside.

"Did I also mention how stunningly beautiful you looked, before the ugly crying, of course. I love the new color of your hair, it suits you. Not so much all the makeup, maybe it's a touch too much."

He's holding my face in his hands as he tells me this. I try not to cry. I love this man with all my heart. If my mama and sisters were not in the other room, I would ask him to take me here and now. He takes the necklace from the box and puts it on me. He hands me another box, which has a matching bracelet, and then another with matching earrings. They are all green. He notices me looking at them closely.

"These are real emeralds. I wanted them to match your eyes. Now with your hair being blonde, they stand out more on you. I do like the new color, but I did like the long brown hair also. This new shorter blonde style makes you look older. You are beautiful, my angel."

He leans down and he kisses me. Not on the nose or the cheek but on the lips. I put my head up to reach him, I don't know what to do. I keep my eyes open this time and notice he has his closed. He's cradling my face in his hands and kissing my lips. He parts his slightly and sticks out his tongue. He gently pries my lips apart with it and then inserts it into my mouth. He opens his eyes and sees me, startled, staring at him. He smiles but starts to move his tongue around my mouth, playing with mine. I join him, playing with his. He starts to move his lips and I copy him. Before I know it, he is kissing me deeply and I just go with the flow. I have butterflies in my tummy, hundreds of them, and I get prickly feelings all over my body. He moves his hands from my head and wraps his arms around me, pulling me tight into his body. I can feel something hard sticking in my tummy, my nipples are also hard like pebbles. He must be able to feel them.

He suddenly breaks away from me and pushes me slightly. I look at him, confused. He looks hurt and in agony. He turns away from me.

"I'm sorry, Svetlana. That should not have happened. Please, can you leave? Go and enjoy your time with your family. I shall make sure you spend every day with them while they are here. You will have my guard with you at all times when you are out, but I have a woman coming each day to take you all out and spoil you all in LA. Now leave."

Wow, what a turnaround. I mean, I had the desired effect on him that I wanted, but then to throw me away like that. It hurt. He's turned his back on me. I leave the room, closing the door behind me quietly, and go back to join my family. Although I'm upset, I am elated I got what I wanted for my birthday. My family and my man. I will get him one way or another. I can wait and bide my time until my family leave but I am not going to rush their time away. I want Igor to be my first, to take my virginity. I want him to have it, I will offer it to him on a platter if need be, and I will make sure I accomplish that.

Five

Svetlana
Present

I'VE THOUGHT OF NOTHING BUT MY LOVE SINCE MY ENCOUNTER with him in his apartment. I yearn to be the one to look after him, to make sure he has everything he needs. How can she do that when she is running his business and rushing to meetings, leaving him constantly? I would say to hell with the business for now and just take care of him. That's all I want to do. It's my life's mission to get back with him and be his rightful queen. To knock her of the pedestal once and for all. I will conquer.

She hasn't had me back up to the apartment since my encounter with him. I think she is jealous that we have this connection. She heard me speaking to him, yet she never said a thing about me calling him *my love*. She's just making sure we don't see each other anymore. She knows he wants me, and she's scared he will toss her aside for me. It's never been about her. The only reason he put me in the basement those couple of times was so he could come and see me. Trying to show her he is the one in charge. She is not in charge of me and never will be. As soon as he realizes it is me he wants, I will put her in the acid vats myself and get rid of her. I just need him to give me the nod, I will bide my time.

We've found a building to set up the refuge. She has made me the project manager. She trusts me that much, the fucking fool that she is. We found the building together, it's not too far from where we live. Now she's left me to it. Maybe so I could prove myself, and I now have a team of people working at getting it fit for habitation so we can start to rehome those that need it. I have to say she has kept her word and helped me with my drug problem. For that I am grateful, but it was when she told me about

Igor that made me really change. Apparently, he loathes anything to do with drug users. I've been clean for two whole weeks now. It was a real struggle in the beginning. I did relapse a couple of times, but when she told me that about Igor, that he said it was all self-inflicted and he had no time for druggies, it made something click inside me. He's on board with the project. He thought it should be geared more to those sexually abused rather than druggies. Poppy told him that most of the druggies were sexually abused and they needed the help to get off the stuff and get away from their abusers. That changed his mind, and he was in full agreement then. I'm not too sure what changed his mind. She didn't tell me that part.

We only really talk on the phone. I haven't actually seen her for weeks now. She is either with him in the apartment or off on trips or meetings. Sergei has told me she is earning quite the name and reputation in the Bratva. Now they all accept her as Igor's second, even the godfathers have accepted her. When Sergei told me that, I hurt him bad. How could they accept this American bitch? How could the Bratva let an American bitch sit in on the deals. Surely it should be a Russian woman. Surely it should be me.

Sergei and I were at the motel when he told me, just normal boring fucking. I ask him questions while arousing him, I need as much info as I can get. When he told me this about her being accepted, well I flipped mentally, but I literally flipped him over and started to ram first my fingers, but then almost my entire hand, into his ass. I was ramming it in there hard, thinking of her sitting with the godfathers. It should be me sitting with them, doing *my love's* business. Me sat by his side, me being the fucking rightful queen, not her, the fucking bitch. I didn't realize I was being so aggressive with Sergei, he was crying like a baby asking me to stop, that it was hurting him.

Fuck, I didn't even realize he was crying, but I didn't fucking care either. I started playing with his cock at the same time, pulling it so fucking hard. He didn't know what he wanted and in the end, he actually enjoyed it. Once he came everywhere, I removed my hand from his ass, it was a bit bloody, maybe I was too hard on him, so what. I'm so angry, I can feel my blood simmering under the need to inflict pain, I feel I need this. I took the hairband from my ponytail and I wrapped it round and round the base of his cock, it was bulging at the end. I bent and bit it, hard, he screamed out and grabbed at my hair. I could see the hairband was tight. His cock was turning purple and blue. With me licking it, he forgot the pain. I put his cock in my mouth and I sucked and bit all at the same time. He didn't know if he was in pain or in ecstasy. He was pulling my hair hard each time he thrust until he was coming in spasms down my throat in no time.

"Wow, didn't know you liked that kind of stuff, Lana. I didn't even know you knew about doing anything like that," he was saying as I was trying to take the hairband off his cock. It was a struggle and I was starting to panic at the size his cock was getting, and the color it was changing to. Eventually, I managed to remove the hairband, and he was in a lot of pain, but I was starting to loath having to go through this with Sergei, I just needed the information from him. He told me that Poppy had gone away for a couple of days on a trip to New York. Somehow, I needed a way into the apartment. I had to see Igor and speak to him again, to find out exactly what had happened to him. I needed to be the one to help him, to make him realize it is me he wants.

When we got back to the building, Sergei went in first, but I asked him to wait at the elevators for me. I needed his key card to the penthouse, it was my only way up. I told him I needed to see Igor, to sign off on some paperwork for the building construction on the refuge center. He was unsure at first if he should let me up. Under instruction, no one was allowed up there. I played him, telling him if I didn't get it signed off then there would be a big delay and neither Igor nor Poppy would be happy about it and it would all be on his head. He agreed to wait for me.

I walked out of the elevator, expecting Mavra to make me turn right back and send me away. What are the fucking chances he wasn't sitting there? I breathed out a sigh of relief and headed round to the living area, quickly, before he returned. I didn't see Igor. I knocked on the office door and waited. There was no answer. I tried the door but it was locked, typical Igor. Moving away from there I checked the kitchen. Nothing. I went down the hallway to where I knew his bedroom was but he wasn't in there either or he didn't answer when I knocked, trying the door and again it was locked. I was confused as to where he could be. I know there are rooms that are locked that I never had access to, so I walk along and knock on all the doors and nothing.

I suddenly see a huge man I don't recall seeing before. He emerges out of one of the doors. I'm not sure who he is, but he's ripped like my big guy at The Hex Club. He's as tall as him, has the same hair color and he even looks like him. His eyes look very familiar. He has on sweats and a tank top. The tank top is loosely hanging and I can see his pecs are prominent, just like my big guy. I cock my head, really looking at him. Is it him? There are too many similarities. This guy has tattoos that catch my eye on his biceps. One looks like a wolf and the other is a lion. My big guy at the club always wears leather cuffs over his biceps. He eyes me suspiciously, then his eyes widen as though recognizing me.

"Who are you? Where is Igor?"

"It's you, how, why are you here? Why are you in Mr. Ustrashkins' apartment? Are you his wife or girlfriend? Is that it?"

What does he mean 'it's me?' I must look confused.

"The Hex," is all he says. I was right. It is him. Oh my god, what are the chances? My eyes nearly pop out of my head, and my mouth hangs open for a few seconds. Then I wonder where Igor is.

"Shhhh, don't say that. Where is Igor?"

He looks slightly confused.

"I'm working with Mr. Ustrashkins. I'm his personal trainer. I've been helping in his rehabilitation. He's just getting changed upstairs and I will go and bring him down when he's ready. Part of my job is to make sure he is getting in plenty of protein and nutrients for his recovery. I'm just about to make him some lunch. Are you waiting for him to come down, I take it your not his wife then, are you a girlfriend?"

I look at him and it's the first time I have seen his whole face. He is fit as fuck. No wonder we've spent the last few weeks in the solo rooms fucking each other's brains out. I can't get enough of him. If I didn't have *my love*, he would for sure be my interest. I've started to have feelings for him. I search him out each time I go. He suddenly crosses his huge arms over his enormous chest, and I lick my lips. He raises an eyebrow. I scowl. I shake my head. My words won't come out. I'm too busy looking at his beauty. I shake myself out of it.

"No, I work for the Ustrashkins, I am not his girlfriend," I grit out to him, not that it's any of his business. We fuck, end of. He's smiling at me now I've told him no.

"Would you like to go up and see him or wait for him down here?"

I know Igor would hate me appearing out of nowhere. I didn't even know there was an upstairs. I lived here all that time and never knew. I head to the kitchen with the big guy following me. I open the fridge to take out a can of Coke, only there isn't any. It's all water in here. It was just instinct, forgetting I don't live here.

"Hey, I'm Ryker, nice to meet you, finally."

Finally, we've been fucking for a long time. But I get what he means.

"I'm Svetlana. Most call me Lana, even though I prefer Svetlana."

He holds out his hand to shake mine. Is he for real? I've had his cock everywhere and he's now holding out his hand. I raise my brow at him and he raises his back, jutting his hand farther out to me. I take it and shake it firmly.

"Nice to meet you, Svetlana. Would you like to go out on a date with me?" He smiles at me, showing his perfect white teeth and that mouth that has done so many amazing things to me.

Go on a date with him? That's a bit backward. But I must admit I want him. Here and now. He's making me all hot and wet, standing smiling at me with that goofy look on his face. He's adorable, and now I have a name to go with him. How will this work at The Hex? We are anonymous there.

"What is it, what are you thinking? I can see your mind ticking over, your face moves perfectly as you think. You are running through so much, I see the way your eyes change. One second they are deep and dark, the next they are light and starry. Tell me what has you confused."

Just then I hear a buzz. He looks at the watch on his wrist.

"Hold that thought. I have to get Igor. Are you staying to see him?"

I must look startled. Just then, Sergei comes into the kitchen. Great, just what I need. They greet each other, then Ryker moves away and goes to get Igor from wherever he is. I'm getting myself worked up. If he brings Igor here, I am sure he will tell me to fuck off and embarrass me in front of Sergei and Ryker. I don't want that. I also don't want Ryker or Sergei to talk about me, that's the last thing I need, I also don't want all three men I've fucked in the one room. That would be weird. But what I do want, most of all, is to see Igor. I don't know if I should flee or stay. Flee.

"Sergei, can you let Igor know I would like to see him, alone, at some point when he has time to sign some documents. Then you can let me know when is convenient for him?"

He just nods. I turn to leave just then I hear him.

"Svetlana, what the fuck are you doing here. What have I told you? How many fucking times do I have to tell you?"

I turn slowly, my eyes widen at seeing him in the arms of Ryker. He's clinging to Ryker's neck. Ryker has hold of him around the back and under the legs. I am shocked. Why is Ryker carrying him? I can see the look on Igor's face hardening each second I stand here. I need to leave before he starts on me in front of the others. I just can't seem to move my legs, it's like I'm glued to the spot. I can't take my eyes off him, I must look pityingly at him, at how helpless he looks in Ryker's arms. He looks small, he looks gaunt and older, he looks broken. My poor love. I just stare, I know I should leave.

"Answer me, Svetlana. What the fuck are you doing here? Sergei, I told you no one, under any circumstances, be allowed in here. Where's Mavra, why the fuck didn't he stop her? Leave now, Svetlana, before I throw you out the fucking window myself."

And here I die of embarrassment on the spot. I feel tears escaping down my cheek. I don't move to wipe them away, I don't want to bring attention to it. Why is *my love* being like this, why does he act like this when I know it's me he wants?

I see the frown on Ryker's face. He looks down to Igor and scowls. Igor doesn't look at him, he can't take his eyes off me.

"LEAVE, NOW," he shouts, startling me.

I turn and run to the elevator. I feel the tears streaming down my face. I press the button and the door opens straight away. I don't turn around, I stand facing the back wall and wipe at my tears. I feel the car dip. Someone has come on with me. Why didn't the door shut right away? I don't want to see any of them. I don't know who it is. I hit floor nine where my suite is. Suddenly there are hands rubbing up and down both my arms. I don't know who it is. I'm scared to turn around. I know who I want it to be, but that's an impossibility seeing as though it looks like he can't walk.

"Hey, baby. I'm sorry he spoke to you like that. I shouldn't have let you up there. I knew it was a bad idea. He did say no one at all was allowed up. I just left him with Ryker to come see if you were okay."

I don't turn, he's the last person I want comforting me. Why couldn't it have been Ryker? I could do with a good fuck to relieve all this tension I have. The doors open. I turn to make sure it's my floor, then I walk out. I don't speak to Sergei, I just leave him there. That was the most mortifying thing ever. Three men, two I am currently fucking, one I want to fuck so badly, but he was the one who shot me down, yelling at me to get out. I lay on my bed crying, always fucking crying. I can't get the picture of him out of my head. He doesn't look like my strong, protective love. He looks so weak. I need to know what is wrong with him. Why was Ryker carrying him? I know he's been in a wheelchair. Does that mean he can't walk? Where is upstairs? I never knew there was an upstairs in the penthouse, I never went upstairs. She must know every part of that place now. She pretends to be his queen. She's only there for the power. I wonder how long she will be gone for, maybe I can try again. One thing about me is I never give up.

Age Sixteen—Fake Seventeen

The day of my fake seventeenth birthday was one I would never forget, my very first kiss and with the man I loved. It was the best birthday ever. I loved spending time with my family. Those two weeks flew by. I didn't see Igor much during this time, only if we were home on the evenings he sometimes joined us for dinner, only to show his face to Mama. Deep inside, I was looking forward to my family going back home, and I felt guilty for wanting that, but I wanted Igor more. I wanted him, I was determined to get him one way or another. I never give up, it's one thing he soon learned about me, I was relentless when I wanted to be.

The week after my family left, I asked Igor if he could try to trace my papa. Mama was still upset he just disappeared. She could accept he left us all, but wanted to know where he was to give her closure. He agreed. I hardly saw anything of him. The following week he came home early a couple of nights. The first night was great. We sat and had dinner together, he asked me how the visit went and did we get to see all of LA and I told him all about it, it was the first chance we had to really talk.

The next night was nearly a week later. When I realized he was going to be having dinner with me, I quickly went to my room and I got cleaned and changed. I wanted to make him think I was beautiful like he did on my birthday. I put on my tiny gold dress, the one I bought on my birthday but never got to wear. I dress it up with the emerald jewelry he bought me and I apply a little makeup, not too much. He seemed to think I had on too much for my birthday, I do my hair, leaving it down and straight. I put on some high-heeled shoes, these are amazing, they are see-through so it looks like you are walking on air. They make me taller.

I saunter into the dining room. He doesn't look up from his phone. I cough to try to get his attention. I very slowly walk up to his side of the table and I sit on it right next to him. I cross my legs and lean back with my hands on the table behind me. I watch his face turn slightly when he realizes I am here. His eyes rake up my long slender legs, all the way up my front, getting wider and wider until he reaches my face where I'm smiling so hard at him. I see him gulp, then he smiles and his eyes soften.

"Svetlana, what are you doing, angel?"

Well, isn't it obvious? Wow, men can be so thick at times. Leaning back like this has my chest sticking out in front of me and with the dress being open at the front right to my navel, well, let's just say it's hard for him not to look back down my body to there, taking me all in. I feel empowered by the look on his face. I can tell he wants me. He licks his lips, his pupils dilate. He has the look of lust written all over him. His hand moves from his lap and he places it on my bare knee. He squeezes it.

"Go sit on your chair, Svetlana. Polina will be in to serve dinner any second now and I don't want her feeling uncomfortable with you dressed like this." He smiles, waving his other hand up and down my body. He then pats my knee, telling me to shoo.

How patronizing is that? Oh my god, I'm offering myself to him, here on the table and he pats my knee and tells me to shoo. I am so angry. I climb down from the table and walk round to my side, only it's a cocky walk, swaying my hips and ass as I do. Showing him what he's missing out on. Just as I sit, Polina arrives. We sit eating and talking. I try to be sultry, pouting my lips and licking them, batting my eyes, trying to make him want me. He can't stop looking at me. I know he wants me as much as I want him. When we finish eating, he gets up from the table and slowly walks round to my side. He sits next to me with his ass on the edge of the table and his arms crossed over his chest, with his thumb up to his mouth. He just looks me in the eyes for a while. I smile at him, pouting and batting my eyes again as I stare into his lovely blue eyes. He reaches out and strokes a finger down my cheek. I lean into his touch, closing my eyes as I do.

"Svetlana, you are beautiful, my angel, but this" —he points to me, then him—"is not happening. I see what you are doing here, but let me be clear, we... will... not... be... anything. Do you understand? Now, not to upset you but I have a date arriving very soon," he says, looking at his watch then back at me. "I do not want you around when she gets here. Please go to your room and stay there. I certainly don't want her seeing you dressed like this."

He motions to my body with his hand. I'm in shock. He's got someone coming here, he never brings anyone here, not that I've ever seen.

"So, get what you need, cans of Coke, water, food and take it to your room and stay there for the night. I don't want to see you while I am entertaining. Are we clear on that?"

I'm dumbstruck, I can't acknowledge him. My brain is trying to take in what he just told me. I blink and look up to him.

"You're bringing someone here, where I live, to fuck her. You want me to stay out of the way, to lock myself in my room so you can fuck her here." I point to the table and the rest of the room, I'm so angry. "You need to bring someone else to fuck, when you have me here, just waiting for you to say get naked. In a heartbeat, I wouldn't hesitate, yet you don't want me. You want to fuck someone else here where I can listen to you fucking." I scream the last word at him.

He leans right into my face. I have tears streaming down my cheeks. He grits his teeth. I can see his jaw tensing, and I can see his hands balled into fists. He suddenly slams one down hard on the tabletop, making me jump.

"Stop fucking swearing at me, you're a kid, Svetlana. I will not fuck a kid. Get it out of your head. You are stunningly beautiful, but I'm too old for you. Do you understand me?" he snarls at me but he doesn't raise his voice, he doesn't scream at me, and he doesn't really seem that angry. He looks conflicted.

I rise from my chair slowly, jutting out my chest as I do. I very gently rub my chest on his arm while maneuvering around him. I hear his intake of breath. I smile to myself because the victory is mine in a small way, knowing he wants me. I saunter, slowly, into the kitchen where I grab what I need to take to my room. I can feel his eyes boring into me, watching my every move. I walk like I've seen the models do on the catwalks on the TV, I want him to be sorry.

I've been in my room for almost an hour when I hear voices. Has she just arrived or has she been here a while and I just didn't hear them? Then I hear it. Definitely fucking noises, even though I've never been fucked. He starts shouting, she starts screaming, she's shouting louder and then oh my god's a lot. I hear slapping noises and him grunting.

I cry, sitting on my bed, listening. I feel like a little girl. He's belittled me. My mama was married younger than me, yet he thinks I'm a kid. He makes me feel like a kid. I'm a woman. I will show him. I will make him sorry. I put on headphones and listen to music, he put a music app on my phone. I can't bear to hear what he's doing, it's killing me not to walk out of this room right now to watch them. To learn what he likes. But to see him fucking someone other than me will kill me. I get under my comforter, listening to my music, and pretend it's not happening.

Weeks go by and I've hardly seen him. We haven't had dinner since that night, it's him staying away, I'm sure of it, but I've heard him a few times since, fucking. It kills me every time, wishing it was me. He's resorted to leaving notes by my bedroom door, telling me to stay in my room. I know that's when he's bringing someone back. I've left him notes by his door, asking for money to go shopping and asking when we are having dinner together again. I want some money. I want to be able to go out and buy things instead of being locked up here all the time. He never acknowledges my notes, but today for some reason he's left me an envelope with a card inside. I've never used a card before, I've seen them, I mean, I've seen Igor using one when we were shopping. His note tells me if I go out shopping that one of his men will be with me at all times to make sure I am safe. That I can use the card, it's mine and there is no limit on it, I just show the card or give the card to the sales assistant and when prompted type in the numbers 0524. Never, ever give these numbers to anyone and shield with my other hand when entering them. I can also just sign my name if they ask for that. It's then I realize the numbers are my birthday, May 24.

I'm giddy. I run to my bathroom and get ready as quickly as I can.

At the elevators, Mavra stops me.

"Miss Svetlana, I have to call a guard before you are allowed in the elevator. Mr. Ustrashkins' orders."

Great. I lean against the wall, waiting. Just then a man appears and oh my god, he is stunning. I can't take my eyes from his face and body. I stand up straight and walk up to him.

"Are you to guard me?" I ask him. He just nods. "Can you speak?"

He cock's his head to one side, then nods again.

Great, he looks good but he may be a little dense.

"Russian or American?"

He tilts his head slightly again and I see his eyes turn to slits. He has to answer me.

"Russian," is all he says in a very deep voice. I press the button for the elevator which opens straight away and I walk in. I turn to face the doors, watching the giant of a man walk in. I lick my lips and eye him from head to toe. He presses the button for the ground floor. My mind is too occupied to do that simple task. What if... yes, I'm going to do it.

I head out to the front of the building. I roughly know where everything is now, when Mama was here we went out every day. I'm going back to the department store. I want to buy some clothes and some sexy lingerie. I peek behind me a couple of times, just to check the giant is around. He follows me but keeps at a distance. I go through the same routine I did on my birthday. Get my hair done, back to brown, buy some really sexy sets of lingerie, new dresses that are not on the sales rack and some shoes. I then go and get my makeup done before heading out. Using this card is so easy. I spot a shop I don't remember seeing before. It's a lingerie shop. I head inside and browse around. I see the giant outside. I want to play.

I open the door and tell him to come inside. "What is your name?"

Again he tilts his head slightly but he has to answer me when I talk to him.

"Rasputin." That's all he says and looks away. He looks around the shop, and I watch his face as he takes everything in.

I wander to the back where there is a door that says adults only. I think I pass as an adult, so I open the door and walk in. I stand with my mouth almost touching the floor, the room is all dark and red, there are whips and other things hanging up, but what I notice is all the very sexy lingerie, not like out front or in the department store, no this stuff is real sexy. There are mannequins wearing a lot of it and holy cow, I want some of it. I have no idea what you call them. There are red ones that are all frilly and lacy, and black leather ones and black shiny ones. They are wearing all kinds of briefs, but most of them don't have either a back to them or a front to them. Easy access, I guess. There are boxes and boxes of gadgets that I have no idea what they are for. Some of them are rubber penises, there are lots of rubber penises in all sizes, shapes, and colors, all lined up on the wall being displayed. I must look shocked. An assistant comes in and asks if she can help me. I turn and I must look embarrassed. I see her squint her eyes at me.

"How old are you, miss? Do you have any ID on you?" Maybe I don't look old enough. But I lie.

"I'm twenty-one?" I search in my purse as if looking for ID, I make sure she sees my card, I know it's a special one from the reaction when I bought my clothes. "Rasputin, I don't seem to have my ID on me. Do you happen to have it?" I wink at him standing by the door.

He reaches inside his jacket pocket. He obviously doesn't have any ID for me.

"No sorry, ma'am, I must have left it in the penthouse."

I see the assistant eyeing Rasputin up and down. She just nods.

"Okay, I believe you. Sorry for asking, but we have to be careful. This area is for adults eighteen and over. Please, if you need any help or have any questions, I will be more than happy to help." She leaves the room.

"Rasputin, can you come in, please, and shut the door behind you."

I have no idea what I am doing but I have nothing to lose. He comes in and closes the door. Again I watch his face as he takes in the room. He doesn't seem embarrassed like I was. Maybe he knows what most of this stuff is for. I pick up a box. I compose myself before turning to face him.

"Have you used any of these things before, Rasputin?"

He coughs and nods.

I use my best girly voice. "What is your favorite to use? What would you recommend for someone like me?"

I smile at him, and look all innocent and timid, putting my finger into my mouth. I watch him, watching my movements. I slowly pull my finger out, making a show of sucking it. I have no idea where this comes from. Maybe it's those books Mama let me read. My finger pops out of my mouth and I look at him sheepishly. He eyes me suspiciously, wondering if I'm being serious or not.

"Well, Rasputin, what would you recommend for a girl like me?"

I see him blush. Got you. He's so easy.

He gulps and looks around the room, not moving. He points to the wall of rubber penises.

"I think they are a good start if you are new to this stuff. Then when you have a boyfriend you can come in here together and choose what you would both like to try together. What is good for one person may not be good for another."

I love his deep husky voice. I want him to speak more. I take hold of a red lacy thing, full of ties. It obviously goes around my body as it has cups for my tits. I also pick up some red lacy panties to match, only these are not complete panties, they are open at the front.

"Would you say these will suit me? Maybe if I try them on, you could give me your opinion?"

I smile seductively at him. Licking my lips, I can see he's getting hot in this little room with me showing him this stuff. He has a little sweat on his forehead. It doesn't take much to get this giant hot it seems. I don't give him a chance to answer me. I head straight into the changing room. I strip and hold the lacy thing to me. I have no idea how to fasten this thing up. I wonder if he will come in and help me. I manage it, I fasten all the eyes up then twirl it around the back. Wow, I look amazing in this even if I do say so myself. My tits are big anyway, but this thing pushes them right up and makes them look huge. I open the door. Rasputin is standing there with his back to me.

"What do you think, Rasputin? How does it make me look?"

He turns. I don't think he realized I would hardly have any clothes on. He swears and looks down immediately. Do I look that bad? Way to kill a girl's confidence. I just stand there looking down. He covers his eyes with his hand and lifts his head.

"Please, cover yourself up, Miss Svetlana. If Mr. Ustrashkins knew you and I were in a room together like this, he would kill me. I must leave this shop and wait outside for you." With that, he turns and practically runs out of the room.

I shut the door and admire myself in the mirror. I think I look fucking hot. I'm getting this and the panties. I read the label, crotchless panties. They will do. I also pick up a box which reads vibrator, it's one of the rubber penis things. I don't know if I will ever use it but it can't harm to have it. I will read up on these things on the laptop back home.

I leave the shop, smiling. Rasputin is waiting for me outside. He won't look at me. He's all embarrassed. I'm going to see if he wants to have a coffee with me at home and maybe make him something to eat. Try and time it for Igor coming home. Not that I ever know when or if he's coming home. I want to see if I can make him want me by being jealous. I wonder why Rasputin said Igor would kill him?

"Hey Rasputin, what did you mean by Igor would kill you if he saw us like that?"

He turns and scowls at me.

"Nothing."

Liar, but I know he won't tell me. I want to stall going back home, so I head into a restaurant and order some lunch. Rasputin comes in but doesn't sit with me. He eats at a table farther away from me, but where he can keep an eye on me. I take my time, reading on my phone while eating. Once finished, I want to do more shopping. I go in and out of different stores, I don't buy anything else apart from some cuff links I found that I really liked and a pocket knife key ring. They were platinum and very expensive. The sales assistant said platinum was the best to buy, I want the best for Igor. All this expense is way beyond what I am used to. I've never had money. I know it's not a problem for Igor but it's new to me. The gifts I bought him are close to two thousand dollars. He might go mad at the amount I spent today.

I slowly walk back to our building. I walk through the park nearby and take a seat, just watching people going about their business. Some are totally oblivious to what's going on around them. I look on my phone to see what time it is, it's only two twenty. I feel like it's later. I'm not hanging around until later. I will go back and call on Rasputin later on, get him to come to the apartment thinking I'm going out again. Maybe I will go out again. It's then I realize my tutor will be waiting for me. I dash back, not even bothering with Rasputin. I fly into the apartment just as Loretta, my tutor, is about to leave. I apologize and we get straight into it.

Igor didn't come home for dinner. I ate alone, again. My plan is foiled. I will just have to wait patiently.

It's weeks again before I have dinner with Igor. It feels like months since my birthday but then I guess it is with us now nearing Christmas. He seems to be working all the time and if he isn't working, he is out with some whore or bringing one back. Again, the number of times I've had to listen to him fucking, it makes me so mad and so sad. I'm beginning to despise him for it. How insensitive is he? He knows how I feel about him, yet he insists on bringing whores back so I can hear them fucking. I was in my room as usual after my tutor left. She says that I won't need tutoring, that when she breaks for Christmas that will be the end. I am fluent in English now and I am at the top of my level for everything else. She was going to send the report to Igor. He suddenly appears at my door, leaning on the doorjamb, thumb in mouth with legs crossed.

"Do you want to join me for dinner, Svetlana? It seems to have been a long time since we last had dinner together."

I didn't hear him at first. I had my earbuds in. I startled when I saw movement and him standing there. He raises his eyebrow at me.

"Well?"

Huh, I look at him like he's stupid. Well, what? He asks me if I want dinner with him. I just shrug, not letting him know that my tummy is in turmoil at the sight of him standing there or that I'm excited he wants to have dinner with me. I get changed. I know he likes me to dress nicely for dinner. I put on one of my new buys. It's not a sexy dress like the one I bought on my birthday, this one covers me up at the front. It's emerald green with lace all over the front, the back dips right down to my ass, but he won't see that. It is short, I mean, right up my thigh short but again once I'm sitting down, he won't see that either. I don't put on any makeup and I put my hair up at the sides, it's still not as long as it was after having it cut on my birthday.

I walk into the dining area where he is standing at the windows with his back to me. I sit down and wait.

"What is wrong, my angel?" he asks, walking toward the table.

I don't speak. He sits on the table next to me. I wish he would just sit in his chair and stop calling me angel.

"My name is Svetlana," I spit out. I didn't mean it to sound so hostile, but hey, I'm mad at him.

He leaves me alone here all this time, he doesn't do anything with me, like take me out. He fucks whores where I can hear. At this point, I want to go back home. He takes my chin and turns my head to look at him. God, he's perfect. I love him so much that it hurts.

"Hey, what is your problem? Why do you speak to me with such venom?"

I shake my head out of his hold and just shrug.

"Svetlana, speak to me. Never hold in what is wrong, only ever tell me the truth, never lie to me. People who lie to me get punished."

My head shoots up to him. Is he serious? He frowns at me. "Now, what is wrong?"

I gulp, he said don't lie.

"You are never home, and when you are, you fuck whores. I have to sit in my room and listen. Do you know what that's like? Knowing the one person you want in the entire world doesn't want you. Instead he would much rather avoid you and make you sad by letting you hear him fuck others. What if I was fucking Rasputin, and you heard it, how would you feel about that?"

I see his look go from sympathy to hurt to wild anger. Oh fuck. I move my chair. I think I need to leave. That look is murderous.

"Are you fucking him?" he growls at me through gritted teeth.

I just shrug. I'm not denying nor confirming it, therefore I am not lying to him. I start to get up but he's quick. He stands in front of me and straddles my chair. Placing his ass on the table, he pulls the chair in toward him so I am between his legs. I gulp as my face is at his crotch level.

"I asked you a question. Now fucking answer me," he grits out.

I lift my chin again to look at him, only this time he pinches it. I can feel the tears start to form in my eyes and I want to wipe them away, but I can't with him holding my chin. He lowers his face down to mine. I feel his breath on my lips, and I close my eyes. I can't take him being this close. I don't speak. He licks my lips, and I instinctively open my mouth. Before I know what's happening, he is thrusting his tongue into my mouth and kissing me with such angry passion. He's hurting me. I'm kind of scared and I want to get out. This isn't like that first kiss on my birthday. He was so tender with me then. This is harder, kind of frantic. I don't respond. It takes a minute before he realizes I'm not moving my lips and am trying to force them closed. He pulls back and looks at me.

"Isn't this what you want? I thought you wanted me. Has that changed now you are fucking Rasputin? I will see him gone. He will not work for me or anyone else."

I stare at him. Oh god, what have I done? I shouldn't have mentioned Rasputin, but it seems to have worked. I shake my head, and he frowns.

"I'm not fucking him, or anyone, for that matter. Not that you would know. I'm not a whore, Igor. I don't just fuck anyone, although I've spent more time with him than I have with you in months. I thought you brought me to America to help me? Yes, you've given me a beautiful place to live and yes, I can have what I want more or less, except you. But I'm bored, Igor. I'm bored out of my head. I read a lot now that I have my phone, and I speak to my mama and sisters, but at this point, I would rather be back home with them. The most I've seen of LA is when they were here back in May, it's November, it's nearly Thanksgiving here, whatever that is, but it's Christmas next month. I am bored, Igor. Even my tutor is finishing because there is nothing more to teach me. I need to do something, anything, give me something to do, didn't you mention me modeling? What about that?"

Way to rant at him.

He gets out of my face and sits back slightly, still on the table and still straddling my chair. He puts his thumb to his mouth, he's thinking. I watch his face, I see his brow crease, he seems to have more lines than he did, his eyes are slightly darker than the vibrant blue they are, but he is by far the most beautiful man I have ever met. I love him so much. I don't speak. I sit watching him. Watching the different emotions on his face. One minute it's like he's had a brainwave then he'll shake his head, then think again. Polina appears and coughs. I look at her and she's holding two dishes. I smile at her and nod and raise my eyes at him. He hasn't acknowledged her.

"Thank you Polina, Igor was just going to move to his side of the table," I say, looking at him.

He turns his head and sees her standing, holding the dishes.

"Sorry, thank you, Polina."

He heads to his side of the table. We eat in silence. He watches me all the time. I know he's still thinking.

"Okay, what would you like to do if you are so bored? I can't have you doing anything with my business. You are far too young for that. Maybe I can get you to help me with some girls I have down on the ninth floor. Just like you, I have brought abused girls back here from Russia. They stay on the ninth floor, a lot of them don't speak English, what about if you start to help them, teach them English, take them shopping and…"

"Yes, yes, I'll do it. Anything to do something. Yes, a million times." Oh my god, I will have other girls to speak to, Russian girls at that. "Why are you only just telling me you have other girls here?"

He looks up just as he is about to put his spoon of soup into his mouth.

"They only arrived last week. I didn't know what I was going to do, to be honest. I got them out of bad situations, like you were in, but I have no idea what to do with them when I rescue them. With you, it was easy. You were to stay here, with me, but I can't have my apartment overrun with adolescent girls. It's bad enough with one and knowing what to do for the best. I'm not really cut out for what to do when they are rescued. It's where I was two weeks ago. I was back in Russia. By the way, I could not find your papa."

My eyes water with tears. One, he just thinks I'm an adolescent, and two, my papa is missing. I put my spoon down and push my dish away. I don't want anything else.

"Please excuse me, Igor. I do not feel very well. I need to go to my room." I get up and leave. I lay on my bed, crying.

The next thing I know Igor enters my room without knocking, or at least I didn't hear him knock. He lies on the bed behind me and pulls me to his chest. He cradles me for a while as I cry. I wish it wasn't that he felt sorry for me. I wish it was because he loves me and wants to comfort me. I wish it was because he wants me like I want him. He doesn't see how caring he is. I grab hold of his arm that is wrapped around me and I kiss his bicep, he's changed into his casual clothes, which usually means he's not going out again, and his arms are bare. I just lay there hugging his arm, silently crying. I must fall asleep. When I wake up in the morning, I am in my bed, still in my dress and Igor is nowhere to be seen.

Six

Svetlana
Present

THAT SECOND TIME, HE THREW ME OUT OF HIS APARTMENT AND embarrassed me in front of Ryker and Sergei. I called Sergei and asked him to see if Igor would see me to sign the papers. He came back and told me Igor said 'fuck off and go to hell'. Why is he treating me like this? What have I done so wrong to him? I have never done anything but love him. I have always obeyed him and done everything he asked. Maybe I should open up and tell him all about what Andrey and Ivan did to me, about the drugs and the abuse, how they raped me constantly along with all the others he threw away. Maybe he would take pity on me, that his men did that to me after he threw me away.

It's been weeks again since seeing Poppy, we speak on the phone a lot but she never comes to see me, she's even taken to visiting the refuge when she knows I'm not there. I don't understand why they both treat me like this. All I'm guilty of is loving Igor. I'm on my way home when I remembered I left my plans at the refuge. I return to collect them, it's looking amazing now. I know lots of girls will love it here, we've thought of everything to make life happier for them and to help them. I'm just in what will be the communal room when I hear the front door open. I turn around, a little on edge. No one should be here now, it's after seven. I hear a voice shout.

"Hello, is someone in here?"

I recognize it, Poppy. Should I hide? No, she knows there is someone here with the door being unlocked.

"In the communal room, Poppy," I shout back, being all friendly.

As I turn, she's standing there staring at me, and I drop the papers in my hand as I look at her. Oh my fucking god, she's pregnant. What the actual fuck, when did this happen because looking at her she is very pregnant, not just pregnant.

"Oh my god Poppy, look at you, when did this happen?"

I walk toward her, trying to act happy, but inside I'm tearing apart. My heart feels like it's shrinking like a shriveled prune. It hurts like fuck. She's having his baby, I can't believe it, why her? It should be me. I want to stab her in the tummy, kill it. It can't be, they can't be having a baby together, no it must be someone else's, it has to be, she must be screwing around.

"Svetlana, did you hear me?"

Her voice breaks through my thoughts. I didn't realize, I have my hand on her huge tummy, but I see now that I'm pressing on her. I look up to her.

"Sorry, what did you say, Poppy? I'm just so shocked."

I drop my hand immediately. Why would I want to touch it, I want to rip her open and cut it out. What if I do that here, there are no cameras yet, no security. I could leave her for dead with her baby cut out. They would just think a rival got to her to teach Igor a lesson.

"Lana, you're miles away."

She's talking again, breaking my thoughts on ways to cut it out.

I want to be the one to carry his baby, me, not this bitch. She suddenly grabs my wrist. I look at her face. She's angry. "What are you doing? That fucking hurts, Lana, twice you've put your hand on my tummy and pushed hard. What's your problem?"

I shake my hand from her grasp. I didn't realize I had done it again. I just want her to die, I want that thing in there to die. I look into her face. She doesn't look hurt but angry. I step back. If she feels threatened I know she will have a gun on her, it's her way now.

"What is your problem, Lana?"

"I'm sorry, Poppy, I'm just in shock, you're not just a little pregnant there. I didn't think it had been that long since I last saw you. You never said anything, you never told me, not even on the phone on our calls. I thought we were friends Poppy, I feel hurt." I fold my arms, not realizing I'm cradling my tummy until I see her eyes lower to them.

She cocks her head to the side and squints at me, she's trying to read me, trying to see what my problem is.

"I'm sorry, I just haven't seen you to tell you. It's not a conversation for over the phone. Why are you so upset that I'm pregnant? What aren't you telling me? I can see you're in turmoil over it. Did something happen to you, Lana? Let's have a drink and sit down. I want you to talk to me."

Fuck, what do I tell her, that I want her and that thing dead? It should be me. Or… yes, a perfect plan. She heads to the kitchen area. I follow behind, thinking about pushing her over. Letting her fall on her tummy, squashing it, then pouncing on her back to make sure it's dead in there, and then knocking her out, smashing her head on the concrete floor. I can picture it all in my head so vividly, like it's happening. The blood from her smashed face everywhere and blood seeping out between her legs from the crushed fetus. I stand, smiling down at her body, laughing. Then he will finally be mine.

I'm standing in the doorway to the kitchen, there is a small temporary fridge in here, just to hold cold drinks for the workmen. She bends down but struggles to grab the water bottles from the bottom shelf. I don't move to help her. She grabs two and turns to hand one to me. I take a step toward her and take the held-out bottle from her hand. I have vivid visions in my head of ramming the bottle down her throat as she takes a sip, then taking a knife and stabbing her in the stomach, over and over. I have to shake these images away before she pulls me on my distancing again.

There are a few fold-up chairs scattered around the room. She pulls two out and sits on one. She struggles with that as well. I wonder if she drove here herself, she might have Steve or even Sergei out in the car. Shit, I couldn't hurt her, or it after all.

"Do you want to tell me what your problem is with me being pregnant?"

She glares at me with her hard, 'don't fuck with me' face. She pulls her purse onto her lap. It was hanging down the side. I know she will have a gun. That's how the big woman rolls now. Thinking she's something special.

"Lana, you're staring at my tummy again and looking like you're way out on Mars somewhere. Please talk to me. Did something happen to you when you were younger? I know you told me your papa was good and never did anything to you, but the way you are acting is kind of scaring me. It's making me think you were once pregnant. What happened? You know you can tell me. We help these girls, remember? Igor has told me all about your role in helping the girls he saved from being abused. What happened?"

She leans forward and squeezes my knee to get my attention.

"I was pregnant once, Poppy. It just hurt seeing you like this. Hurt, like I said, because you didn't tell me when I thought we were friends. But also, please don't be angry when I ask, but is it Igor's baby?" I watch her face as I ask, and her eyes go wide and angry.

Yep, it's his baby and here it comes.

"How dare you, Lana, how dare you ask, you know he is the only love of my life. I would never cheat on him. Of course they are his."

My eyes spring open wide. 'They' as in more than one. Fuck, that's why she's so big. I feel the tears flowing down my cheeks and I wipe them away.

"What's wrong, tell me?"

I don't speak, I have a lump in my throat, I wipe away the falling tears.

"Lana, fucking speak to me now."

She's getting angry. She asked for it.

"He made me kill our baby. He said he never wanted children. Now, here you are with however many are in there. You're going to play happy fucking family when he never wanted that. He specifically told me he would never be a papa to anyone. He would never put them through the life he has to live, in fear, daily, always looking over his shoulder. He made me kill our baby. Igor fucking killed our baby." I shout the last bit at her, and the Oscar for best actress goes to Svetlana Baranov-should-be-Ustrashkins.

Yay, yay, whoop, whoop, I cheer in my head as I let the tears pour out of my eyes. I feel I should stand and take a bow, but instead, I hang my head after I see the utter shock and disgust on her face.

"He did that. He made me kill it. I have regretted it ever since. He said he would kill me and it if I didn't get rid of it. The man you love did that to my unborn child." I carry on in a whisper, not looking at her, just laying it on thick. I heave a couple of times with sobs.

I hear her move. She comes to me and cradles my head to the side of her tummy. I fucking hate it, being near that thing or things in there, but she's a fucking sucker, I want to stab her tummy now, make her lose them.

"Svetlana, I had no idea. He's never told me and neither have you. I'm so sorry you did that, but—"

"He fucking did it. I didn't have a choice. It was either kill it or be killed," I shout at her, cutting her off and startling her. I hang my head back down and wipe at my nose and eyes. I stand up and look at her. "I hope you're both happy."

I move away and head out to the front. I hear her shouting for me, but I don't stop. I see her car outside, Sergei is standing by it. He starts to walk toward me.

"Don't, Sergei, she's coming out," I snap at him and head in the direction of our building.

A few minutes later the car is beside me, the window is down and she's asking me to get in.

"I want to walk and get some air, Poppy. You go home, I'll be fine."

The car moves off in the direction of home. Yep, the award for best actress most certainly goes to me, and not for the first time either.

———

Age Sixteen—Fake Seventeen

He's been gone for weeks again. He wasn't even here for Christmas. I got a couple of presents from him, which was a watch, an expensive one with diamonds, also a laptop of my own and an iPad. His note to me said the iPad would come in useful when I started helping the girls. That hasn't even happened yet. I still haven't given him the gifts I bought ages ago, the pocket knife and the cuff links are still wrapped up. I put them under the Christmas tree, the one that suddenly appeared one day, expecting him to be home. I ended up having Christmas with Polina, Mavra, and Rasputin.

Rasputin has come round to me now, he's been out with me each time I wanted to go out somewhere. Some days I took an Uber and just told them to drive anywhere. That did not go down well with Rasputin. That first time, because he couldn't get a car fast enough to follow me. I was on my own for the day, well most of it and I loved it. The car took me to Malibu Beach, I sat for hours on the wall watching families having fun in the sand. All the people on roller blades, skateboards, and bikes, riding along the path, the men in the fitness area. Well, I sat watching them for a long time. I grabbed something to eat and when I looked up, Rasputin was standing with his arms folded, scowling at me. Fuck, he found me. I remembered Igor told me he could track me with my phone. That must be how Rasputin found me. I hadn't put my phone on until a little while ago. I just held out my wrap to offer him a bite. I actually saw a slight lift of the lip there. Maybe I'm breaking him in.

So Christmas Day it was just the four of us. I didn't know where Igor was and I didn't ask. Luckily I had gotten gifts for the three of them and Polina got me a gift. It was a beautiful scarf she made herself. The other two I bought them key rings. I went back to that jewelry shop and bought them expensive ones. I figured it was good to spend Igor's money. The presents I bought for Igor stayed under the tree until it was taken down and he still hadn't returned home. Then on New Year's Eve, I was sitting in the living area watching the TV, we were on the countdown to the new year. There was an hour to go when in strolled Igor. I jumped out of my seat and ran to him. I jumped into his arms and wrapped my legs around his waist. I almost sent him flying. He just managed to keep on his feet. Just then a woman came waltzing around the corner from the elevators. She tripped and grabbed his arm, straightening herself before she fell. She was drunk and by the looks of him, so was he. I looked into his face. He smiled at me.

"Ah, there she is, my angel. What are you doing up? Isn't it past your bedtime?" He leaned forward and kissed my cheek.

"Who is this, Igor? I thought we would be alone. I didn't know your sister would be here."

She was not Russian, she was Polish. She had a different dialect from us. I scowled at her.

"I am not his sister," I snapped at her. She looked at the two of us. I didn't unwrap myself from him. I let him hold me up with his arms under my ass. I clung to his neck.

"Then who the fuck is she and why is she wrapped around you?" He slowly lowered me to the floor. She still had hold of his arm, glaring at him, wanting to know who I was. Me, I was angry, that's who I was right now. It's New Year's Eve and he hasn't been home for weeks, well not that I heard or saw him and now he turns up with her. I roll my eyes at him.

"What's wrong, angel, why are you mad?"

I cross my arms over my chest, making my tits nearly pop out of the shirt I had on. I watched his eyes widen as he noticed.

"You've been gone forever. You missed Christmas. Thanks for the gifts, by the way, then you come home on New Year's with another whore on your arm. Now I'm gonna have to listen to you fuck all night, great start to the fucking new year for me. I want to go home, Igor, back to my family. I can't live like this anymore." I'm shouting at him as I turn and walk away to my room.

He speaks but I don't actually listen. In my room I put the TV on mute so I can watch the new year be counted in and put my music on loud. I'm on my bed, so angry with him, and yes, crying again.

Waking in the morning, still fully clothed on top of my bed, I remember him coming home with yet another whore. I must have crashed. I didn't see the ball drop in New York. I'd never seen anything like it before, so I wanted to see what it did when it dropped with all those people around. The one other good thing was not listening to him fucking the whore. I check the time, it's almost ten, it's later than I thought. I think I was just feeling homesick yesterday after speaking to my mama and sisters when they phoned me at midnight their time. Pretending everything was great here was hard, but I couldn't let Mama worry about me. They are all happy in their new house. I told her Igor couldn't find Papa. In truth, she didn't seem to care. My sisters are all settled into their new schools but Mama did tell me she was having trouble with Vidana. She said she was a little bit promiscuous with the older boys in the neighboring school. I had no idea what that meant and had to look it up after our call ended. Vidana had been caught twice with boys around the back of the building. Well I knew what that meant. She's only fourteen as well. The little minx, I need to have words with her. Yes, it all made me homesick.

In the kitchen I sat having some scrambled eggs that Polina had made for me. She's been showing me how to cook. She sees how bored I am and she's been showing me the basic things. I used to cook a lot at home for my sisters but it was mainly easy stuff. I don't ask her if Igor is around, I am so angry with him, then I hear the noises from his room. After eating my breakfast, I run to my room to retrieve the presents I had for him and I leave them outside his bedroom door. I hear the loud noises but not from his bedroom. I turn and follow the noises, it's one of the other bedrooms, his fucking room, I presume. The noises are so loud, I lean my ear to the door to listen. There are grunts, and she's panting and squealing.

"Right there, don't you fucking stop, Igor, that's it, that's the spot, flick it, more, harder, pinch, fucking do it, Igor, that's it, oh, oh, ah, ah, yes, yes, yes arghhhhhhh."

Then she shrieks so loud, like a fucking witch on helium. I then hear him grunting, I hear slapping. Is he hitting her? Then he's shouting angel, angel, fucking hell, angel, I want you. He huffs and huffs, then silence. He's calling her angel. I never want to hear him call me that ever again. Not after this. The noises start up again. I put my hands over my ears and run back to my room, where I put my music on loud to drown them out. My door flies open, the whore is standing in my room practically naked, she has the dress from last night around her waist with her tits hanging down, on show, I'm glad my tits aren't that droopy.

"Turn that fucking shit off. How can I fucking come with all that noise?" she shouts at me.

He appears behind her with just a towel wrapped around his waist. The look on my face must say it all as he grabs her shoulders to move her out of my room.

"If you weren't fucking like rabbits so loud I wouldn't have to have my music on to drown you out, get out of my room, bitch. I didn't say you could come in here telling me what to do."

She gets free of Igor's hold and she flies for me on my bed. Just as she's about to hit me with her fists, mine fly up right into her nose. It's hard, my hand throbs. Igor is there, dragging her off my bed. There's blood pouring from her nose, she tries to cover it with her hand.

"She's broke my nose, you fucking bitch, I'll kill you."

I laugh because she can't speak properly, it's funny to me. Igor drags her out of my room. He's furious. But not with me, with her.

"I told you to leave it. It's none of your fucking business what goes on in my home. Who the fuck do you think you are storming into someone else's room demanding shit? Get your fucking stuff and leave now before I do something I regret."

He's mad, real mad with her. She crossed a line. He pushes her but not in the direction of his room, but toward the living area. I think he's pushing her out of the apartment. He won't care if she's naked or not, she doesn't mean anything to him. Closing my door, I turn my music off. He appears in his towel just before I shut it completely. He's still mad, but not at me. He smiles sheepishly. I don't give a fuck. I'm leaving here for good. I was looking on the internet to buy a ticket back home last week, but wanted to see him first. Now it's a no-brainer, I'm booking the ticket today. I shut the door in his face.

He knocks but I don't answer and unless he just storms in like usual, I am not opening the door for him. I search for flights back home, grabbing the credit card, I input all the details and buy a one-way ticket. I could only get a flight for next week, something to do with the holidays and being so busy. Well, it gives me a little bit of time with Polina, she's been like my surrogate mum. I hear a faint knock, again, I ignore it. It might be Polina but she would shout my name. Another knock, but louder. Again, I ignore it. Then my door opens, no storming in but standing at the door. I look up and he's standing in his suit, which means he's going out, but he has my presents I left him in his hand.

"Can I open them in here with you, please?" he asks softly.

How can I ignore that? It pulls at my heart. I should hate him for everything, but I don't, it's crazy. He's just been fucking a whore, yet I want him more than ever. I nod gently. He moves over and sits on the bed. I scoot back so I am sitting against the headboard with my knees pulled up to my chest and my arms wrapped around my legs. I rest my head on the top of my knees.

"Angel, I'm…"

"Don't ever call me that again. My name is Svetlana to you," I grit out with such venom in my voice. No way, not after calling that whore his angel.

He flinches. I've never seen him do that before. I must have hurt him or he was surprised at the hate in my voice.

"Svetlana, I'm sorry about earlier. She's gone now, for good. She had no right to come in here like that, and way to go, kid, with the right hook. You did break her nose."

I don't smile but I flinch when he calls me kid and yes, my knuckles are bruising nicely from that punch.

"Angel, please forg—"

"I said, don't call me that. You don't get to call me that ever again, not when you call your whores that as you're ramming it into them."

I see the puzzled look on his face.

"I heard you, 'angel, fucking hell angel, I want you angel,'" I mimic him from earlier.

He looks embarrassed. What the hell, does he think I'm deaf or something? He looks down at the presents in his hands. He plays with the tag on one, then turns it over. I forgot what I had written, and I just realized. I move, trying to rip it from the present, but he stops me. He reads it aloud.

"Igor, Merry Christmas. Glad I get to spend it with you. Love always, your angel." I bury my head in my hands, too embarrassed to look at him.

He doesn't say anything. I hear him unwrap the gifts. He takes my hands away from my face.

"Thank you, angel. I love them. I will use them always."

I don't shout at him for calling me angel, yet again. But he must see the look on my face. All I picture when he calls me angel is that whore who was here earlier. He gets up and kisses the top of my head and leaves.

I'm packing my case, the one I went and bought yesterday. Rasputin asked me why I needed a case. I just told him to put some old clothes in to get them out of the way. He bought it. It's only a small case. I'm not taking everything with me. Igor bought all these things, even the stuff I did buy was with his money. The jewelry and shoes and purses all stay. I just pack the basics, even my sexy lingerie that I never got to wear. It all stays. I spent a lot of time with Polina yesterday. I haven't seen Igor since New Year's Day when I broke that whore's nose. I'm sad, I'm leaving the man I love, the man that sees me as a child. It will never be, as much as I wanted it. New Year's Day was the last straw for me. I phoned Mama this morning and told her I would be home, that I was getting on a plane tonight. She was shocked and wanted to know what he had done to me. I put her at ease, telling her he had done nothing, but I was lonely and bored because I never saw anyone. She was worried he would want the money back. I don't think she wanted me home, in case he took the house from them.

My case is in my room and I'm sitting in the kitchen talking to Polina. I don't know how I will leave without Rasputin being on my tail, but he will just have to follow me to the airport. I was able to draw a couple of hundred dollars on the credit card. I just needed a little cash to see me through getting home. I then left the card on my pillow in the bedroom with a thank you note to Igor. Just for giving me the opportunities he has and that I would be forever grateful to him. I only have fifteen minutes until my Uber arrives. I need to say goodbye to Polina and Mavra.

Just as I jump from the stool, I hear him.

"Svetlana, where the fuck are you? Svetlana, answer me." He is so irate, he storms into the room, his face deadly, his eyes bore into mine. "Where the fuck do you think you're going?"

I jolt back at the rage penetrating me from his body and voice.

"Fucking answer me. I've just left a very important meeting after first getting a text to say my check-in was open for my flight to Moscow and then a call from your mama, frantically telling me you're going home, that she didn't have the money to give back to me." He stands with his hands on his hips, right in front of me, bearing down. "Well," he bellows at me. I see Polina leaving out the corner of my eye. Great, now I'm scared. "Fucking answer me, Svetlana?"

I cower and sit back on my stool.

"I told you I was leaving," I quietly tell him. "There's nothing here for me, Igor. I'm grateful for the opportunities you have given me but I'm bored and lonely." I don't shout, I don't want to fall out.

He paces in front of me. First, he's rubbing his chin, then he's running his hands through his hair when he stops to look at me. I don't know what to make of him, he's angry, really angry, but he's conflicted also, he stops in front of me.

"I don't know what you expect from me. I can't have you with me when I am working, it's too dangerous, you're too young."

Here we go again, everything boils down to my age with him.

"Your tutor gave you glowing reports. What about going to college? Is there anything you would like to do there?"

I hadn't thought about it really. College never entered my mind. What would I do?

"What did you expect of me when I brought you here, angel?"

I wince at him calling me that again. He notices. He stands in front of me and takes my head to his chest. I'm crying yet again.

"You are my angel. I will always call you that. The first time I saw you, I thought you were an angel sent to me. I wanted you, I wanted you bad, but it's your age that stops me. When you heard me fucking and calling out angel, it was you I was thinking about. It's always you I think of when I fuck anyone. I do it more to think of fucking you. I wasn't calling her angel. I was saying I wanted you, my angel. I can't get past your age. It breaks my heart, it's why I stay away for so long. Every day gets you closer to eighteen. I can do eighteen. I know a lot of Russian women get married very young, but it's hard for me to get past that. It is not the way in LA, I think of that and think eighteen is for the best."

He pulls back and tilts my head to look at him. He smiles then lowers and kisses me softly on the lips. He cradles my head back to his chest.

"Please stay, go to college, or I will get you set up helping the other girls. They are younger than you, some a little older, but you could help them. I promise, in a few short months I will make love to you. When you are eighteen, angel."

Oh my god, I don't believe what I am hearing. He wants me. He actually fucking wants me.

"I love you, Igor. I have since the first moment I laid eyes on you. I know you think I'm a kid, a silly little girl, but I'm a woman. You need to stop letting age dictate to you. Back home, I would probably be married with a baby by now. Are you just saying these things to keep me here? Although, for what reason, I don't know. I just get so lonely. I'm used to a family around me, looking after my sisters. I've helped Mama raise them all."

I'm still being held to his chest. I wrap my arms around him and hug him hard. He wants me, but he keeps fucking other women. I know he said it's me he thinks of but if he truly wanted me then why not wait? Why not spend time getting to know me? Why? I pull back slightly and look up to him.

"If you want me, Igor, then wouldn't you just wait until you can have me, get to know me, not sleep with anyone else?" He frowns at me as if that's the most absurd thing he's heard. Not to me, it isn't.

"I tried that for the longest time, but it was over a year until you turned eighteen. That's a long time for a man to be celibate, angel. I gave up. I know I should have waited, but I couldn't. Fucking those other women helped me stay away from you. I know it's not right, I do, but it was all I could think of for my own mind, my own sanity. I couldn't and wouldn't go there with you. I vowed that day we left Russia, I would not touch you. I failed at that, and believe me, Igor, does not fail at anything. But you, I failed with because I kissed you. That only led you on more and made me want to ravish you. I don't know if it's the old saying you always want what you can't have." He smiles down at me.

"But you could have me, Igor, it's only you stopping yourself. I've wanted you. I've told you before, but you just ignored the fact."

We hug for a few minutes until my cell starts buzzing on the countertop. I pick it up, it's my Uber. I turn it to show him.

"My ride is waiting on me, to take me to the airport."

He looks horrified.

"Don't go, angel, please stay. We only have a few more months to wait. I promise I will be around more and I promise there will be no other women. We can get you working and helping the other girls."

He lifts my face up and leans in to kiss me. I kiss him back. He opens my mouth with his tongue and deepens the kiss. I can feel he's getting hard down there. I feel it pressed against me. I break the kiss and look down to his penis. Am I brave enough to touch it? I want to. I've never touched one before, let alone seen one. He notices me looking and steps back. My phone buzzes again. He raises his eyebrow.

"What are you going to do, angel? Stay or leave?"

I pick up my phone and I cancel the Uber. I turn the phone to show him and he pounces on me, kissing me hard. He holds my face in his hands and devours me. My tummy is doing somersaults, my heart is beating out of my chest. I'm sure he can feel it. He wants me. I feel like the luckiest girl, no woman, alive.

I phone Mama and tell her I've changed my mind and I'm staying, she's relieved. I'm really upset she only thinks about the money and is not interested in me. Igor orders me to get my glad rags on, that he is taking me out to dinner. I squeal with delight.

"Is this like a date?"

He thinks for a minute.

"Yes, it is. Now shoo, I'll make a reservation so you don't have long to get ready."

I run to my room. I don't know where we're going. I don't know what to wear. I'm already showered so I need to do my hair and some makeup. I get them done in no time, then I just sit on the floor in my closet. I have dresses and trousers and shoes surrounding me. I've tried on so many different outfits but have no idea what to wear. I'm sitting here in one of my new matching bra and panties sets that I bought a while back. They are red lace and the bra is strapless because I tried on some strapless dresses. I don't hear Igor enter my room, but I feel him behind me. He sits down on the floor and puts his legs on either side of me.

"What's wrong, angel. Why are you sitting here in all this mess?" He points around to the mess on my floor.

"I don't know what to wear. I don't know where we are going. Do I need to dress up in a nice dress or in something more casual? Help me, Igor, I have no idea, I've never done this before."

He pulls me back so I'm against his chest. He is being very loving. I like it, but it also makes me nervous.

"We are going to an elegant restaurant so I would wear a dress. Nothing too sexy, not that I'm complaining about that, but we need elegant, not trashy."

I feel hurt at that. Is he saying my dresses are usually trashy? I look up into his face and scowl at him.

"Are you saying my dresses are trashy? Don't you like the ones I wore here to dinner?"

He kisses the tip of my nose, smiling down at me.

"I love the ones you wear here, so much so that every time you walk in the room I just want to rip them off you. Now here, what about this one? It's quite chic, off-the-shoulder so the bra you have on goes perfectly but it doesn't let everything you have hang out and it's not too short but short enough."

Wow, he's a fashion expert as well. I did try the dress on he picked up and loved it but wasn't sure it would fit.

I get up off the floor, taking the dress with me. He moans as I get up, so I turn to see what is wrong with him, he's staring at my ass. I bend over in front of him and wiggle it slightly. He groans but suddenly grabs my hips, pulling me to his face, and he bites my ass. Not hard, and then he nuzzles me. I feel quite embarrassed, but yet I feel quite emboldened that I can make him groan like that. I laugh out loud at what he's doing, but I don't stand up, I just let him do it. The next thing I know, he's pulling my panties down with his teeth and exposing my ass to him. I go to stand, but he stops me by putting his hand on my spine and putting pressure on it to keep me bent. He nibbles my bare ass cheeks and then starts to lick them. Once or twice his tongue ventures to my ass crack. I try to stand again when he does this, but he stops me.

He pulls my ass right into his face and he puts more pressure on my back, making me bend over farther. I'm now bent right over in front of him, I put my hands on the floor to stop me from falling. I look between my legs at him, I can see his body, he has on sweats and I can see his penis is sticking right out and it does strange things to me, like his tongue now. I notice my panties are now down by my ankles. When did that happen? I feel mortified. He's groaning and making funny noises all the time, licking me. His tongue wanders down my ass crack then suddenly it's flicking at my private parts. Oh my god. As soon as he does that, I jump, trying to get away. He holds my hips so I can't escape.

"Stay, angel, just a little taste. I've been wanting to taste you for so long. My willpower is nonexistent. Please, just this once, just this time. Then we wait."

I don't know what I'm supposed to do. I read a few things about this in the books and the women in those books seem to love it. It's not sex, so he's not breaking his own vow. He flicks more and more with his tongue. I start breathing heavy, the sensations all over my body are what? I don't know how to describe them. I feel sexy, that he wants me like this, I feel wanted, I feel kind of dirty. Is this normal? Is this what happens. I start to move with his tongue. He suddenly puts it inside me and moves it around. Oh my god, then a hand suddenly leaves my hip and appears under me, he's touching me, he's now using a finger on me. I want to get away, I want to leave, I don't know if this is right, but then I don't want to leave, and I want him to touch me more. He's flicking my clit with his finger and his tongue is licking inside and out. I hear the noises and don't know if the wet is from his mouth or if it's from me.

I start to move more, I nearly fall. He stops what he's doing. Then I feel as though I'm falling backward. He's laying down and taking me with him. My ass is now on his face, but I get a great view of his bare abs and the line of hair that I can see leads from his navel to inside his sweats. The sweats are gaping at the top, and I see the tip of his penis poking through. I lick my lips. I know in the books the women suck the cocks. Maybe if I lay down his body and just have a taste. I don't know what will happen though. Am I brave enough to do it? I'm thinking about it when he pushes me slightly forward. Not a hard push, but enough for me to lose my balance and fall across his body. My head is right there at his crotch. He spreads my legs wider and pulls my private parts right above his mouth. He licks and licks while he kneads my ass cheeks. I very gingerly move his waistband down slightly. I run my finger over the top of his penis. He breathes in and stills for a second. It's all wet, I can see the moisture coming out of it. I lick my finger to taste it. It's not disgusting but it's not that nice either. I'm starting to rub my private parts more on his face the more his tongue is moving inside and out. He flicks and sucks on me down there, this feels like, I don't know what, but the feelings all over my body are making me want more. I start to grind down on his face harder. I start to pant. I feel my whole body tingle with excitement. I take the plunge and I lick his penis. He inhales sharply again, pausing for a second before continuing the onslaught of sucking and licking. I like that I do that to him. I lick more, lowering his sweats just a little bit more to free it.

Wow, it's huge, that won't fit in me anywhere. If I stick that in my mouth, it might make me gag.

"Angel, suck my cock, put it in your mouth and suck with all you have. I can't get enough of the taste of your pussy, you are so fucking sweet." He breathes out into my pussy.

I grind away on his face and I lick his cock before I put it in my mouth. He spreads my pussy open more to give him better access and then his tongue is inside me again, while he rubs at my clit with his thumb and his fingers play in my folds. I love what he's doing.

I get brave and I take more of his cock into my mouth. I put my hand around it and it feels so smooth, it's like silk, I never would have thought that. I start to grip it harder but I don't want to hurt him. I bob up and down as I suck at him. Then I get brave and I move my hand to his balls. They are weird. Not sure why they are called balls, it's just a sack with what feels like two eggs in it. I play with them and he starts thrusting up with his hips into my mouth.

I feel his cock near the back of my throat and I start to gag. Oh god, I don't want to throw up. How embarrassing would that be? I soon forget about it with what he's doing to me. I don't realize I am bobbing up and down harder, sucking harder with my hand back on the base of his cock, pumping away. I feel my body start to shudder and I feel like I want to explode. I don't know if it's because I want to pee or what, but all the sensations are making me lose it. I'm grabbing and sucking, he's flicking, sucking and thrusting and together we both explode. I lift my head up just in time before it shoots all down my throat and I throw up, I scream out at the top of my lungs with my face up to the ceiling, he screams out "fucking hell angel, fuck, fuck" as he thrusts and thrusts. I look down and watch all his wetness spewing from the tip of his cock. I hear him lapping away at all the wetness in my pussy. I have stars in my eyes, I'm breathing like I've just been running, faster and faster the more he licks me. I'm doing a funny kind of dance on him with my back arching then straightening, up and down. I'm panting and the sensations all through my body are like electric shocks over and over. I feel like I don't want it to stop, but then I do all at the same time. I have my eyes open, facing the ceiling again but everything is white. My head is buzzing as he continues the onslaught on my pussy.

I need him to stop, I try to get off him but he holds my legs so I can't move, I'm wriggling around, trying to get him to stop but I don't want it to, fuck I don't know what I want. I let him finish and before I know it I'm screaming out again.

"Fucking hell Igor, I need you to stop, I can't take any more, please stop."

He stops right away.

"Oh don't fucking stop, oh fuck I don't know."

He laughs into my pussy. I feel the vibrations all over me. I wriggle, then I look down and I see he has cream all over his tummy. I bend and I lick it. It's actually not too bad, I could get used to it. I lick his cock which starts to rise again. I lick his tummy and navel, sticking my tongue inside to clean it out. I then lick down his cock to his hair and I lick him clean. He's doing the same to me. I feel him lick down my inner thighs. I move off him and collapse on the floor beside him. I still have my strapless bra on but somehow my tits are popping out of the top of it. He moves beside me and leans over my face, he notices my tits and he smiles before kissing me hard, thrusting his tongue in and out like he was in my pussy, then he moves down my face to my neck then to my tits. He nibbles first one then the other, then he sucks them both in turn.

"I need to stop now before I do something I will regret later. But angel, you are so fucking sweet. I don't know if I can wait until May. I know one thing, you will be my supper every night."

He smiles at me, then he gets up. He stands over me with his cock stuck right out over my head. I can see how hard he is again. He starts to play with himself. He straddles my body with his feet on either side of my shoulders. I reach up and play with his balls while he starts pumping his cock hard. I then use my other hand and I start to play with one of my tits, pinching and squeezing it, he's watching as he starts to pant harder and harder, I squeeze his balls, playing with them in my hand, I never would have thought the cock or balls would feel so silky. Before I know it, he's squirting all over my face.

"Open your mouth, angel," he shouts. I do, and he fires it straight down my throat.

I swallow with each thrust and take it all. I don't know what possesses me but I start to play with my pussy while his juices are squirting into my mouth. It just seemed like the automatic thing to do. I don't know why, and all these feelings are amazing. They make me want to cry. The next thing I know I'm screaming yet again and he dives on me to lick it all up. He's on the floor between my raised legs and he's lapping at my juice and my fingers. Fucking hell. What is this man doing to me?

An hour later we are sitting in a restaurant in a hotel where everyone seemed to know who he was. People were coming up to him, shaking his hand, wanting to talk to him. A few times he had to tell people he would catch up with them another time. He was out enjoying his date. That got me a few funny looks, especially from the women. I suspect most of these women want him. Who wouldn't? I mean, when I look at him sitting here it's like a different man. He commands the room and the attention by just being him. His posture and everything about him. His stunning looks with his blond curly hair and dazzling blue eyes, and charisma. Not forgetting that. I feel so proud sitting here with him, that it's me he wants, and it's me he was licking dry just an hour ago. I can feel my cheeks getting red just thinking about it and thinking about how I acted.

"What are you thinking about, angel? I can see the blush on your face. Are you thinking about my supper tonight?" He winks at me, and I must be scarlet sitting here.

I take a sip of my Coke, always Coke for me.

"You look beautiful with that glow on you. That dress is perfect, see I know my stuff." He smiles at me with a cocky, know-it-all smile.

We head home, arm in arm, up to the apartment and this time he comes to bed with me. I become his supper, he didn't lie, each night he was home he made it to my room where I would be woken by him having supper. Life couldn't be more perfect right now.

Seven

Svetlana

Present

I HAVEN'T SEEN POPPY AGAIN FOR A FEW WEEKS. SHE MUST BE READY to pop out those brats she's having. Maybe she's had them. Surely Sergei would have told me if she had. I scolded him when I found out she was pregnant. He should have told me. He said he didn't know, that I didn't know, and found it very strange as I worked with Poppy. I've been fucking Sergei still, even though I've had enough of him and was determined I was going to finish it. But I wanted to find out more about her being pregnant. The useless shit that he is, doesn't even know when she is due. I need to arrange to meet her, use her going on maternity as an excuse.

I'm having lunch with Poppy today. She rescheduled on me for another week when I phoned her but I said we needed to discuss things before her maternity started. She agreed, albeit reluctantly. Walking to the restaurant I'm meeting her at, I start to have palpitations. I think it's the thought of seeing her again and her having *my love's*, babies. I stop, I can feel myself starting to get short of breath, now I'm near, I'm not sure I want to see her. I may do something to her. I'll be in a restaurant with knives around me.

"Svetlana, hey are you okay? You look a little pale there. Do you want to postpone lunch?"

It's her. Where did she come from? Then I see her car, with Steve behind the wheel. She looks worried. I must look in a state.

"Hi Poppy, I'm fine. Honestly, I just had a funny turn. I feel okay though."

She furrows her brow at me. Doesn't she believe me? The restaurant is only on the next block, so we walk the rest of the way. Well, I walk and she waddles.

"How are you doing Poppy? You look ready to burst there. How long till they are due now?"

She laughs at me.

"It can't come soon enough. I'm so tired all the time. I spend so much time sleeping at the moment. It's why I haven't seen you since that night at the refuge center. I need to come with you to see how it's coming along again. Is it nearly finished?" She hasn't told me when she is due still, evading my question.

"Yes, I would say the next month it will be finished. We had a couple of problems with some of the fixtures, but I sorted them. It's looking so good. Just all the interior finishes to do now. You need to come and see it before they make an appearance."

We enter the restaurant and are seated straight away.

"Here, let me look." I pull out my phone and go to the calendar. "When can you stop by the refuge?"

She pulls her phone out and looks through it. "I am only doing a couple of meetings this next week. I've cut back a lot with these due any time now."

I act surprised. "What date are they due?"

She rubs her tummy and straightens her back

"Four weeks tomorrow but my OB-GYN doesn't think I will go full term. She thinks they will be here any time now. Most twins don't go full term. I can't wait for them to be here. I know Igor is more excited than I am."

Wow, that hurts. He's excited and they are due after my birthday which means she could have them on my birthday. How ironic would that be? She notices the look on my face.

"I'm sorry, Svetlana, it's another reason I haven't seen you since that day. I saw how painful it was for you. I haven't said anything to Igor about it. He isn't in the best of places yet, but he's getting there. I think these two coming along has done him the world of good and the last thing I want is to upset him about your past. I know that's insensitive of me, but I have to think of him and these two little ones."

I must look bad, I feel bad. Them having these babies is killing me inside. Igor never wanted babies, I can't understand how he now wants them.

I bet they have at least one boy, everything falls into place with this bitch, why does she have it all and I couldn't have anything? I feel sick. I rush to the bathroom. She comes in, following me.

"Look, do you want to forget about lunch? I know it's hard. We can do this once they are here, and I can come out and meet you. If you can't accept it, Svetlana then the only solution would be for you to move on. I trust you and don't want to lose you, but I can't have this being a problem for us either. Igor and my babies are my life and I would kill to protect them. Please tell me you can manage this, I don't want to lose you."

What an insensitive bitch. How dare she? I was here long before she was. What I wouldn't give to knock her on her ass now and kick the shit out of her tummy. I smile, it's fake, but I do it anyway.

"Not at all, Poppy, I'm sorry. I just need to get used to it. I know he's moved on with you, it's just hard, after what I went through. I promise we are good."

Age Seventeen—Fake Eighteen

The last five months have flown by. I'm fake eighteen tomorrow and I am so excited. Igor has stayed with me in my room almost every night he's been home. Most nights he just holds me. We have come close to sex a few times but he always manages to stop just in time. How he does, I have no idea. I beg him sometimes, but he never does. We've been out a few times to shows and different restaurants, it's like being out with a celebrity each time. We never get any peace. I think this is the reason he prefers staying in. I've started helping the girls rescued from Russia. The state some of them are in breaks my heart. To know they have been sexually abused and some are so young, it makes me so angry. The whole ninth floor of the building is just for the girls. We have a Russian counselor who comes in daily to help them. Igor makes sure I have enough money to buy them the clothes and other things they need. I tutor them daily, teaching them to speak English so they can get by. I help them get ready for school, college or university, and some I help to find jobs. Igor makes sure they all have US IDs like I have, so they can be classed as legal and he is down as their ward for references. I've loved having something to do each day. It passes the time while waiting on Igor to get home.

I'm going out tonight with Igor to celebrate my birthday. I don't know where we are going. It's a surprise. He took me shopping for a new outfit and honestly, I'm in love with it, he chose it. It's a purple high-low dress, it's to the floor at the back, then up at the front to mid-thigh. It's strapless with a v cut not too low in the front and straight at the back. It's very flowy and silky. I'm just having the finishing touches done to my hair and makeup by the stylist Igor brought in when he appears in my room.

"Leave us," he orders the stylists.

They've finished anyway. I say goodbye and thank you to them. I stand up. I have my dress on, and now I'm all ready for our date. He stands staring at me with his thumb to his mouth.

"You are the most beautiful woman I have ever seen. You look stunning in that dress, but there is something missing."

He saunters over to me and kisses my shoulder, then my cheek. He pulls out a gift from inside his jacket and hands it to me. "This is your gift. I know it's not your birthday until tomorrow but well, you need it tonight."

He smiles and hands me the gift. I sit on the chair and unwrap the beautiful purple velvet wrapping with a bow to match, to reveal a beautiful large square purple velvet box. I open it slowly and inside is the most stunning diamond pendant necklace. I gasp at it, examining the beauty of the color.

"It is a rare Siberian purple diamond. Only one percent of diamonds mined are ever this color. Here, let me put it on for you."

It shines bright, it's not a big diamond, just a petite stone on a platinum chain. I love it. It goes perfectly with my dress. I hold the pendant as he places it on my bare neck. He leans down, kissing along my shoulder to my ear.

"Thank you, Igor. It is beautiful. I will wear it with pride and make sure I look after it, if it is rare." I get up and kiss him.

"Right, let's get going or we will be late for the reservation." He takes my arm and leads me out of the building to the waiting stretch limousine.

"You are treating me like a princess tonight." I laugh as he holds the door open for me and helps me inside the car. He runs around and gets in on the other side.

"No, not a princess, you are my queen."

I glow, I can feel my skin getting prickly from the warmth of his words. He holds my hand the entire journey, every now and then he lifts it to kiss the back of it. I love him so hard, I know it's not an infatuation and although he never says it, I'm sure he loves me. He treats me so good, ever since New Year's Day he seems to have made it his mission to prove himself to me. I move close to him on the back seat and lean in to kiss his cheek.

"Thank you, Igor, *my love*, for everything." He leans in and kisses my lips gently. Staring into my eyes.

"You never have to thank me for doing something I want to do, angel."

I smile at him. We travel for about thirty minutes. I have no idea where we are. We pull up at what looks like a hotel in the middle of nowhere. I look at him quizzically. He laughs.

"This is an exclusive club, for members only. It is a hotel and spa with a five-star restaurant. Only the best for my queen on her birthday."

He gets out and walks round to my door. I see him shoo away the concierge, just so he can open my door. He takes my hand, helping me out of the car. As soon as I stand up he puts his other arm around my waist, pulling me into his side. I smile up at him. How can he want me? He walks us into the club, ignoring all the hellos from people, he only has eyes for me. He walks us past everyone, straight to the elevators. He obviously knows where we're going. In the elevator, he faces me and takes my head gently in his hands and leans down to kiss me. He's very gentle, trying not to mess up my makeup, but right now I don't care. I pull him into me and deepen the kiss. The doors open and there is cheering on the other side. I stop kissing him and look out at all the people standing there clapping and cheering. I'm shocked, it's my family, my mama, who gives me a very slight knowing nod, Vidana, Dominica, Iskra, Klara, and even little Zoya who is so much bigger now. My hands fly up to my face as the tears stream down my cheeks. Igor hands me a handkerchief to dab at my eyes. I try not to ruin my makeup.

I rush out and hug them all. There are a few people, including Polina, Mavra, Rasputin, and some of the older girls I have been looking after. Andrey and Ivan are with us anyway. They drove us here. No matter where we go, they are always with us. I turn to Igor, who is standing by me with his hand on the base of my spine. I kiss him again.

"Thank you so much, Igor." We look deep into each other's eyes and I see the slight nod of his head.

The night goes by quickly. Mama tells me they all arrived yesterday, and they were staying in this hotel. In fact, everyone is staying the night here, including Igor and I. I feel so much love from everyone. This is the best fake eighteenth I could ever have imagined. A huge cake is wheeled out, it's five tiers full of candles and sparklers. I blow them out and everyone sings "Happy Birthday" to me. I'm glowing. We spend the evening talking with everyone, we have music we dance to until it's time for bed.

We are staying in the Emperor's suite, it's on the top floor but takes up the whole floor. He carries me into the suite, kicking the door shut behind us. As it's my birthday and it was a private party, I was allowed to drink champagne. I've never had it before and I think it went to my head. It made me very giddy. I only had one glass, Igor didn't want me to have any more. He wanted me to be sober, to enjoy my night. I have my arms wrapped around his neck as he carries me into the living area. There are floor-to-ceiling windows, it's not a high building but I can see the lights on the balcony. As soon as he puts me down, I move to the bifold doors and open them. I hear the ocean straight away and feel the sea breeze. I stand at the railing, looking out. My dress is billowing out behind me until I feel him press up against my back. He cages me in, putting his hands on the rail on either side of me. He kisses my back and my shoulders and starts to lick up to my ear.

"You were amazing tonight, my angel. I watched you glow with the love in the room for you. I found it hard to take my eyes off you and speak to anyone else. Happy eighteenth birthday, angel."

I turn to face him, and he devours my mouth. It doesn't take long to get heated, and he's unfastening my dress. It slips to the floor. I break the kiss to step out of it.

"Fucking hell," he says loudly. I stand and look around to see what is wrong. I don't see anything. He grabs my hand and pulls me back into the suite.

"What is it, Igor, what's wrong?" I ask, worriedly.

He turns to look at me with hooded eyes.

"Stand right where you are, don't move," he orders. His voice is a bit shaky. He steps away and he stands staring at me. He slowly rakes in my body. As he does this, he starts to undo his tie, throwing it onto the floor. Next is his jacket, again thrown to the floor. Then he slowly starts to undo his cuffs and then the buttons on his shirt. I move toward him. I want to help him get out of his clothes.

"No, don't move," he says firmly, his eyes still raking me in. He pulls his shirt from his trousers and discards that with his jacket onto the floor. Igor never drops his clothes on the floor, ever. He is so tidy.

"What is wrong? What did I do?" I see his face soften.

"Oh angel, there is nothing wrong, believe me. Everything is perfect, you are the epitome of perfection standing there like that." He gestures to my body. I look down.

Oh, I forgot I was wearing the new purple lace corset with crotchless panties that I bought to go with the dress. I haven't even worn the first ones I bought months ago yet. I wanted to feel sexy for him, and tonight I have never felt more like a grown woman than I do right now. Standing here in front of this beautiful man, who I love with all my heart, and having him look at me with such love and adoration. I feel powerful, just from the fact I put that look on his face. I feel I could command anything of him right now and he would do it.

I drop my dress to the floor from my hand and I put a finger into my mouth and suck it provocatively. His eyes narrow to slits and he breathes out. He unfastens his belt, then his trousers, and they fall to the floor. He steps out of them and kicks them to the side. I let my finger pop out of my mouth. I stretch both my arms above my head knowing my tits will pop out of the top of the corset by doing so. I watch his eyes widen as they do. He goes to take a step toward me.

"No, don't move," I command of him.

He stops and raises his eyebrow. I look to his tight white boxer briefs. His cock is rock hard, but it's restricted in them. I put my finger back in my mouth and I suck it, like a popsicle. I let it pop out of my mouth again, but this time I slowly move my hand down my body, between my tits, down to my crotchless panties. I move each leg in turn to spread them, and I start to play with my clit while he watches. He only lasts a few seconds before he falls to his knees right in front of me. He takes my finger and puts it in his mouth.

"Hmmm, angel, you taste divine. I think it's suppertime."

I know what that means. My finger pops out of his mouth and he's nuzzling my crotch, sniffing, then he starts to lick my clit. I spread my legs to let his head gain access and he's inserting his tongue inside my pussy. I start to move on his face. I hold his head in place, putting pressure on it to make him lick and suck more. He stops, rises up to his feet and lifts me up as though I don't weigh anything. I'm not the smallest person, even though he towers over me, but he does this with such fluidity, I feel like I'm weightless. He brings my pussy to his face. I wrap my legs around his shoulders and he holds my ass, squeezing it as he does, and flicks at my clit with his tongue before inserting it into my pussy. Oh my god. I hold on to his head, pushing it harder into me. I try to thrust on his face, using his head as leverage. He may drown in there, but I'm so close to coming I don't fucking care right now. I explode on his tongue, screaming out my orgasm. It doesn't take much. He laps and sucks it all in. I let go of his head and he looks up to me with a glistening mouth and the biggest smile on his face.

"That was a delicious appetizer. Now for the entree."

He slowly pulls me away, and I slide down his body slowly. He sucks on my tits as he lowers me to the floor in front of him. He smiles down at me before he bends to take a tit into his mouth while squeezing and rubbing the other one. He starts to move us. I'm going backward at this point. I trust him to not let me trip on anything. He alternates between each tit. We end up in the bedroom. I feel the bed behind my legs. He doesn't let me sit just yet. I have my hands around his waist, and I've managed to pull his tight boxer shorts down to free his enormous cock.

"Angel, I'm going to make love to you for the entree. Do you think you're ready for this?"

Is he for real? It's all I've wanted these last few months. Since knowing him just over a year ago, it was always him I wanted to take my virginity. I still remember what Mama told me in the back of my head about Papa. That if he asks, Papa never actually had sex with me, he just played. He's never asked me any details. I hope he doesn't tonight. I'm pulling on his cock. I wrap my hand around the base and I start to pump him. I let my tit pop from his mouth and try to lower to his cock but he stops me.

"No, not yet, angel. First, I want to feel inside you with my cock. Then you can suck him later, for dessert."

I nod. He slowly turns me and starts to undo my corset.

"As much as I love you in this, I love you naked and want you naked now."

He throws it to the floor. He turns me to face him and gets on his knees in front of me. He licks at my pussy again, then suddenly tears the crotchless panties from me. So much for them, one use only.

"As inviting as they are, and we will get you more so we can play in public, they are in my way right now."

Whoa, what does he mean about playing in public? I'll ask about that later. I watch as he steps out of his boxer shorts.

He lifts me up and carries me to the side of the bed where he lays me down gently. He climbs on top of me and just stays raised above me, stroking my forehead, rubbing his nose on mine and looking deep into my eyes.

"You are my angel. Don't ever forget it. I want this to be special. I want you to empty your mind of anything that came before us. Take this as you giving me your virginity. Do you understand what I am telling you, angel?"

Oh fuck, I need to tell him. No lies, he always says no lies.

"You will be my first, Igor. You will take my virginity."

He pulls his head back slightly, looking confused.

"Please don't ruin the moment. I will explain later. But you are my first. No one has ever had a cock in me before. Please make love to me, Igor, I'm more than ready."

I can see the turmoil on his face. He wants answers but I don't want to ruin the moment. I lift my head up and kiss him. At first he doesn't respond. I put my tongue in his mouth and start to duel with his. I reach down between us and I play with his cock, with him not on me but holding himself up with his elbows on either side of me, I can play with it. I grab him and gently try to pull. He starts to moan in my mouth, and he starts to thrust slightly with his hips. I've got him. I spread my legs wide and bring my knees up, he raises up onto his knees between my raised legs. He pushes my knees farther to the sides and I adjust my feet. He looks at my pussy. I've never been so exposed to anyone in my life. He spreads my pussy lips with his fingers and leans in and licks and flicks at my clit.

One thing he hasn't done before is insert his fingers inside me, only his tongue. While he licks at my clit and I start lifting my hips to get more friction, he brings his fingers into play, he plays in my folds then slowly he inserts a finger into me. Oh my god, it goes deeper than his tongue, he pushes it all the way in. The feeling of him sucking my clit and then inserting a finger is amazing. I jut my hips up more, raising my ass off the bed. He then pulls his finger out and sits up. He puts the finger to my mouth.

"Here, taste how fucking sweet you are." He places the finger in my mouth and I suck it. He then lowers his head to my pussy again. This time it feels like he has two or maybe three fingers inside me. Fucking hell, he's scissoring his fingers in me, then he hooks them around and oh my god, I thrust up harder and harder and he laps at my juices.

"Right there, Igor, don't stop, oh my fucking god, Igor, oh god."

He stops. I'm panting hard. I put my arm over my eyes. I feel so excited but so frustrated. I didn't come, he didn't let me come, he stopped just as I was on the cusp of it. I move my arm.

"Why did you fucking stop? That is so cruel, Igor. So, so cruel. I was a second away from exploding."

He lays back on top of me and kisses me hard. I can taste me on him again. Then he puts his three fingers into his mouth and licks them like popsicles. This is so fucking erotic.

"That was the idea, angel. I didn't want you to come like that. I needed to get you as wet as I could so when I enter you, it shouldn't hurt you so much, when I break you in, unless my fingers just broke you in and you didn't feel any pain." He smiles at me and wiggles his hips.

I feel his cock on my pussy. God, I want him so bad. I understand, this is what Mama said about breaking my hymen. She said the first time hurts. He reaches down and he takes hold of his cock, never taking his eyes off mine. He starts to rub his cock on my clit and in my folds. Each time he gets near my hole, I try to thrust up to get him to enter me.

"Be patient, angel. Let's just enjoy the feelings."

He kisses me. He pulls back to look into my face again. He wants to watch my reaction. I wonder if he wants to make sure I'm not in pain. He plays again, only this time when he's rubbing in my folds I don't thrust up and he puts his cock slightly where my vagina begins. He lets go, leaving it there and he places both arms at the side of my head, stroking my hair.

"Are you ready, angel?"

I nod. "As ready as I will ever be, Igor, I want you so bad."

He gently starts to move, pushing bit by bit into me. This is fine, but suddenly he thrusts. He holds my head as I freeze and stop breathing. I close my eyes. It hurt, it was like a small tear but it wasn't so bad. I breathe again.

"Open your eyes, angel."

I do and look into his beautiful blue ones.

"Are you okay?"

I nod and smile at him. He smiles back and then he starts to move. He's slow at first, just moving gently and rotating his hips. The sensations are bliss one second and hurt slightly the next. He's looking deep into my eyes with so much lust in his hooded eyes, he has his arms around under my arms and his hands on my shoulders, he's using them as leverage as he starts to thrust harder. The feelings inside are overwhelming, my body is singing, I feel him hit that spot. I put my arms under his and grab on to his shoulders. I lift my head and try to kiss him. He gives me a kiss, but he breaks it. He wants to watch me. I feel my face contorting into so many different expressions. I'm panting hard as he hits the spot over and over. I dig my nails in, trying to lift my hips to get him closer. I lift up and bite his shoulder and I scream out as he slams into the spot over and over. It goes on forever. I wriggle, wanting it to stop but wanting it to never stop.

"Look at me, angel," he commands and I do.

I can't smile, my face must look a mess, it's contorting with the feelings of ecstasy, I must look in pain, but it's not pain, this is fucking amazing. I smile as I come down from my high. He's still thrusting away inside. I lay back down, panting, trying to get my breath. He smiles and kisses my lips hard as he raises himself above me with his hands on the bed. He starts to thrust harder, gyrating his hips. I feel hurt and upset. He didn't come. Am I doing something wrong? I feel myself start to go again. Oh fuck, what is he doing to me? I don't think I can take anymore but I don't want to tell him to stop, he needs to come.

He starts getting harder and harder, deeper and deeper, if that's at all possible. I close my eyes and arch my back up and I bring my knees up, holding them off the bed, bringing them toward my chest, spreading myself as wide as I can to get him deeper in there. He bows down and bites on my tits as he thrusts inside me. He then moves, sitting up slightly and holding my raised knees for support, he brings my legs up, putting them over his shoulders. Ah, he gets even deeper this way. He thrusts in and out harder and harder, bringing his cock right out, only the tip inside, and then thrusts in hard. His balls are slapping against my ass as it's lifted off the bed. He's panting hard and getting faster and faster with each thrust. Before long, he's like a madman thrusting and thrusting like his life depends on it. I'm about to explode yet again when he blows, and boy does he blow, I feel myself constricting his cock as he pumps and pumps his cum inside, his head is raised to the ceiling and I can see the ecstasy on his face as he grunts and moans.

"My angel, fucking hell, my angel," he says over and over, he's still jutting away and I go for a second time.

I scream out as my vagina grabs his cock, squeezing it tight. He collapses on top of me. He's panting so hard into my neck. We are just a ball of sweat and cum. My hair is stuck to my head and Igor's is stuck to my face. We lie there, trying to bring our breathing under control. I wrap my arms around him and hug him tight to me. I'm crying, like a fucking baby, I cry, and I don't even know why. I think I'm just so overwhelmed with all the feelings and the love I feel for this man. I vow to myself I will never let him go, I will do whatever I have to, just to stay by him, to be his queen.

He pulls back and looks down into my face with such adoration. He wipes away the tears with his thumbs and he leans down and kisses each of my eyelids.

"Did it hurt bad, angel? I'm so sorry." He looks anguished.

I shake my head. "No Igor, it hardly hurt at all, just a slight tearing pain at first, but that soon disappeared with the ecstasy you made me feel. I don't know why I am crying. I guess it's all the feelings and emotions I feel right now. All the love I feel for you, it's so overwhelming. That was the best experience of my life, Igor. Thank you." I lean up and kiss both his eyes. "I just feel so different. I don't know how to explain it. I love you, Igor. I love you so much it scares me."

He pulls me up and I sit on his lap on the bed where he holds me, stroking my back. He never tells me he loves me but that might just be the way he is. I cry more because I think he doesn't love me. We get cleaned up in the shower together. I did bleed and he wanted to make sure I was okay. Then we cuddle back in bed.

I'm woken up in the best way possible, with Igor inside me.

"Good morning, my angel. How are you feeling?"

"Hmmm, with you inside me, it's the best feeling in the world."

It's not long before we are both screaming with our orgasms. We meet my family in the restaurant for breakfast. Igor had a case of clothes for us both brought during the day. He is so thoughtful. We spend my birthday with my family enjoying the facilities of the spa and the pool and we all end up on the beach where the club has organized a BBQ for us. It's the best time of my life. I have my family here and I'm in the arms of *my love*, who I will never let go.

It's been two months since my birthday and my world is falling apart right in front of me. Just because I peed on a stick that he thrust into my hands twenty minutes ago. Since my birthday we have not stopped making love or fucking hard. It's been day and night like we can't get enough of each other. I know I am naïve, but I never once thought about getting pregnant. I had no idea about contraceptives. He should have been the one to sort that out, knowing it was all new to me. I'm standing in my bedroom next to my bed with my hands over my ears. I have my eyes screwed shut and I'm humming to myself. He's trying to get in my face, he's screaming at me, waving that damn stick around like a lunatic. Suddenly my hands are yanked away from my ears and he pulls my head up by my hair to look into his screwed-up face. The venom he is spewing has me terrified.

"What the fuck, Svetlana, you stupid bitch. Why the fuck didn't you tell me you weren't on the pill. Fuck. You did this on purpose, didn't you? You said you would never let me go, well listen to me and listen to me good." He's spitting in my face, trying to get the words out. His eyes are normally the brightest blue, but they are dark and menacing. The lines on his face are visible with the hatred he has emanating from him.

I squint, I can't move my head. He has me held tight by the scalp.

"You will get rid of it or I will get rid of you both. Do you hear me? I don't want a baby, I never want a baby and especially not with you. You silly little girl. You decide what it's going to be, it or the both of you? I will personally oversee either choice. You will never trap me like this, ever."

He throws me to the floor and throws the stick at my face. I'm stunned, shocked, numb. I have never seen him react like this to anything. He's been so loving and attentive. I really don't know this man. I know he's dangerous. I've heard the whispers and Mama told me to be careful. I sit on the floor, holding my tummy. I'm pregnant. I'm having a baby, or not, if he has his way. I can't let him take it from me, no way. It's mine. The stick says I am eight weeks pregnant. If that is true, it must have been the first time he made love to me. It was meant to be from the start.

I sit for a while on the floor, rocking with my knees up to my chest. I try to think about what to do. I'm not getting rid of my baby and if he doesn't want it then I will get away from here. Maybe if I give him a couple of days he will change his mind, he may realize he wants us both, that he does want a baby with me. If not I could go back home to Mama. He will find me, I'm sure of it. I need to leave LA and go somewhere else. He has my documents in his office. I need to think about this hard. Try to plan a way.

I don't see him for nearly two weeks. He's stayed far away from me. The longer he is gone, the more I am starting to loath him and the way he treated me. I have been tutoring the girls on the ninth floor and just walked back into the apartment from the elevator when I hear it. The screaming and the panting. I stand still, frozen to the spot. There's no screaming, it's stopped. Then I hear slapping and grunting, I listen and I hear the heavy breathing, then I hear a woman scream out again, she's screaming in ecstasy. I follow the sounds. They are coming from one of the other rooms. I approach the open door. I see him thrashing into the ass of a woman who is bent over a chair, he's like a man possessed. There's no chanting or anything, just grunting and heavy breathing. He's facing the door. Her head is down, so she doesn't see me, but she will if she looks up. She has long red hair, her hands are palm down on the floor to steady herself and stop him from toppling them over. He sees me right away, standing there watching, he sneers at me, giving me a cocky smile, his eyes bore into mine, he looks evil, he thrusts harder and harder with me watching. She screams out for him to stop, but he doesn't, he's too busy watching me and my reaction. I'm standing crying, the tears streaming down my face, watching him from the doorway.

"You fucking bastard," I shout at him.

The woman looks up on hearing my voice. Her eyes bore into mine. I recognize her from somewhere but I'm not sure where. I'm standing holding and rubbing my tummy without realizing it. I see his eyes watch my movements and he snarls again.

"Fucking get out of here, bitch, you will never have my cock again."

He stops what he's doing and he pulls out of her. He slowly walks toward me holding his rock-hard cock in his hand, he's making a show of playing with it, lifting it up in my direction. He stops by the woman's head. He still faces me, stroking his cock and thrusting into his hand, all the while keeping his eyes on me.

"Take one last look, Lana. You will never see it again. Do you want one last lick? Come on, don't be shy. I know you're not shy. Just one last lick, one last taste of what you will never taste again. Look good and hard, whore."

I scowl at him. He then lifts the woman's head and making sure I can see, he rams his cock into her mouth. He moves her slightly so I get a side view. She uses her hands and plays with his balls while sucking on his cock. He's ramming it so far down her throat, all the while watching me. I look down to my tummy, then back up to him.

"This baby will survive, but you will never know it. Go to hell, you fucking bastard." I turn and walk away and head to my room. I hear him come just as I shut my door, I hear him shout angel. I slide down the closed door and cry.

Why is he being like this, he wanted me to see that. He had the door open, knowing I would go and see what was going on. I knew he was in that room, that's his fucking room. The room he used to fuck anyone he brought back. I have never even been in his actual bedroom. Now that I think about it, he's always just been in here with me. Strange man. I don't even know why he is against children, it's not like we discussed it or anything. The reaction though when he found out, he was so vile. He must have a good reason. Maybe if I could just talk to him, if he opened up we could get through this. I sit there for a long time, just thinking about what to do. I'm going to leave. I have to. I can still hear him going at it and it's killing me. I get up and walk into my bathroom and shut the door. My heart is breaking. I truly thought he loved me. I need to see if Mavra or Rasputin know of anyone that can help me. I have to take the chance, to save my baby and me.

I need money. I need to go out and get some cash from his card. If he sees huge withdrawals, he will know I'm up to something. I have to bide my time here. Try to avoid him at all costs. It's been two days since our last encounter and luckily I think he's gone away. Polina has no instructions to make dinner for him anytime soon. I will do my tutoring with the girls and go out for fresh air and draw out money. I do this for the next ten days, withdrawing two thousand dollars a day. Each day I think he's going to come for me. I didn't ask Mavra or Rasputin for help. I don't have anyone I trust. They all work for Igor, not me. Once I leave, I will make a larger withdrawal. I need enough to survive out there. I need a nice place to have my baby. Then, well, I don't know what will happen.

Igor has only been back once and although I didn't see him, he never came and asked me about the money. I was on pins the entire time he was home. I'm going to make my move when he is next out of town.

I went about my normal duties each day. He came home for a few days on the run, not on his own either, he was fucking all the time, I don't know who with or even if it was the same woman, we never spoke except one time. He opened my bedroom door, without knocking, and stood there naked, letting me see him in all his glory. I didn't look to his cock. I didn't give him the satisfaction of seeing my tormented face.

"You have an appointment on Friday at a private clinic. I have left the details on the dining room table. I figured you wouldn't have done anything about it, so I took the initiative. I will track you to the clinic. If you do not go, then your choice is made."

My eyes are wide staring at him, he's serious. I feel the tears cascade down my face. He sneers at me, then slams the door shut. Fuck, I need a plan now, before Friday. I don't sleep at all. I wait until I think he's left for work before I go out of my room and to the kitchen where Polina is puttering around.

"Hey Polina, is Igor around?" I want to check he's gone before I venture anywhere.

"Good morning, Svetlana. No, Mr. Ustrashkins will be gone for a few days now. He left early this morning."

I smile and inwardly smile with relief. This is my chance. I'm going to leave tonight. I go about my business as normal. I have dinner with Polina in the kitchen, then say good night and go to my room. I leave my door open so I can hear if there is anyone around.

Later on, I wheel my case out to the living room and hide it out of sight, just in case someone comes in. I have on my sneakers and sweatshirt and have my coat under a blanket I lay on me while I sit on the couch reading. If anyone came in, they would just see me reading. I listen very carefully for Mavra to move. He has to have pee breaks. As soon as I hear him, I turn my phone off and shove it down the side cushion on the couch. Igor is not going to track me with that. I very quietly get up and I grab my case and tiptoe to the elevators, peeking around the corner to make sure Mavra has gone. I creep to the elevator and press the button. The door opens immediately and I sigh out in relief. Just as the door starts to close, I see Mavra appear. He looks shocked seeing me. I plead with my face and shake my head slightly, I put my hands together as if praying, telling him silently not to do anything. He rushes toward the door, or he at least tries to make it look like he rushes because he lets the door close. I silently thank him. I put my head in my hands and I take deep breaths, just praying the elevator doesn't stop until I reach the ground floor.

As soon as the doors open, I rush out and I flag down the first cab I see. Rushing to get in. I tell him to go to the nearest train or bus station. On the way, I tell him to stop at an ATM. I withdraw ten thousand dollars. With the other twenty thousand I managed to withdraw, this should be enough for a while. I won't be using the card again, so I drop it down the storm drain before getting back into the cab. He dropped me at Union Station. I bought a ticket for the first train as far away as I could get. It was to Phoenix. I'm curled up on the seat trying to sleep but everyone that passes me scares me in case it's Igor or one of his men. It takes me hours, I have to get off and get Greyhounds then back on the train. I buy a guidebook of the US and look for places far from LA that I could hide out. I also bought myself a new cell. I wasn't going to call anyone, not even Mama. I don't trust she wouldn't tell him where I am. Her being scared he would take the house away from her. I can at least use it for the internet and the time.

I finally make it to Phoenix, I book another train from there to Dallas, only this time I get a sleeper cabin so no one can disturb me, and it's nearly a day to get there. I still don't think it will be my final destination. I need to get farther away. I would cross over to Mexico if I had my passport with me but I don't so I can't go there or Canada, I have to stay in the US. I have a fake driver's license, it's the only thing he let me carry with me. I'm so tired when I reach Dallas, but I need to keep going. I book another train from Dallas to Houston. This is only a four-hour journey, then from Houston to New Orleans. After traveling for two days, I decide to stay for a little while. I stay for a couple of days, but I live in fear. He's bound to know I've gone and I'm terrified he will track me down. I don't know anyone and have no one to help me. I decide to move on from New Orleans. I don't feel right here, back at the station, and I book another train to Atlanta. I think I want to head to Florida. It's hot there and who knows I may be able to get on a boat to somewhere else if I don't need a passport, I'm sure I will need one though.

I made my way to a place called Anastasia Island where I was lucky enough to rent an apartment right on the beachfront. I paid cash upfront, so they were not interested in my details. I paid for ten months altogether, it was a lot to pay in one go but I didn't want my name anywhere, so I gave them a false name and handed over eight thousand dollars. That left me plenty to live on. I will just be frugal with my money. I can do that, I came from nothing. From a family who struggled to feed eight mouths.

I have been here for six months now and I'm due to have my baby any time. I've lived in fear nonstop, thinking Igor would find me, but so far nothing. I hope it stays that way. I miss him so much. I've been thinking about our last times together and not really understanding why he was so mad. One thing I thought of, was did he find out my real age. I know it was a tricky point for him, age, it didn't bother me. But he said he could never have sex with anyone under eighteen. As I was only seventeen on my fake eighteenth birthday, if he found out, that would have sent him over the edge. I didn't know what the fuss was about until I started to research one day sitting on my balcony, but in California, the consensual age is eighteen, so he was doing right by making me wait, that way he could not be prosecuted for statutory rape. He did however in the eyes of the state of California sexually abuse a minor because of all the sexual acts we did leading up to my fake eighteenth birthday. If he comes after me now, I have ammunition. I will tell him I will have him prosecuted for statutory rape. That I lied, and I was only seventeen when we had sex, but I was sixteen when we first started to fool around. I would be able to prove it with documents from my mama and the fact I'm about to give birth before my eighteenth birthday.

I still have to make up my mind about what I am going to do. I've thought about this nonstop. Do I give my baby up for adoption? Do I try and raise my baby alone? Do I go back to Igor with our baby? At this point, when I am so big and just want it out, I am leaning toward adoption. I am selfish, I know, but he made it clear he didn't want a baby and I don't think I can do this on my own. I know I helped Mama raise my sisters, so that isn't the problem, but when I run out of money and need a proper place to live, I won't be able to afford anything nice and will end up living in some run-down place, like back home with Mama. I can't go back to living like that and especially not bringing up a baby like that.

I love Igor.

I need Igor.

I want to be back in his arms. I can make him want me again, I'm sure I can. I can be his queen again.

PART IX

Igor

Eight

Igor
Present

I DON'T REMEMBER MUCH ABOUT BEING SHOT. I REMEMBER BITS OF it, like Poppy getting me to my doctor but then nothing until I woke up with her resting on my bed one night. Turns out the doc got the bullet out that was lodged in my spine, but I was paralyzed from the waist down. Me, fucking paralyzed, a cripple. How could that be? I couldn't be paralyzed. I was the fucking Pakhan, the godfather of all the USA. They wouldn't accept a cripple as a godfather of one territory, never mind all of them. I was fucked. My life was going to be over, I may as well put a bullet in my own fucking head right now.

Why does she stay by my side? I'm no good for her. If I can't make love to her then I'm sure she will eventually leave me anyway. She may as well just go now. I don't want her sympathy, or anyone's for that matter. I tried my hardest to push her away. I was mean to her, so fucking mean, but she gave as good as I gave her. She never let me wallow in self-pity for long. She was hard on me and in truth, it was what I needed to get me out of the depression I had fallen into. I just felt my life was useless, that I was no good to anyone. At one point I let myself into my ammunition room, when I knew Poppy was out with Svetlana, and I sat there with a gun in my hand. I hammered it on my legs, trying to feel something, but there was nothing. It was no use. I was of no use. I pointed it at my head six times in all, then put it in my mouth twice. The pussy that I am, I just couldn't pull the fucking trigger. I kept thinking to myself that a Pakhan can't do this, this isn't what we are. It was when I heard Steve shouting my name that I put the gun away and wheeled out of the room, making sure it was locked behind me.

Andrey and Ivan are the only ones that know, no, knew what was in this room, apart from Poppy. I am not ready for Steve to see what I have, he's a good man, but he's not fully Russian, his mama was American, and his father was Russian, I have made him and Sergei my keepers—guards. They watch over me and Poppy no matter what, giving their lives for us. I have two spies, Rasputin and Maks. They oversee all the Brigadiers—the captains. Each Brigadier concentrates on a different area. One will deal with arms, the other drugs, one just security, another money laundering, and so on. Then I have Bratok. These are the Brigadier's soldiers. Then we have a bunch of Boyevik, these are the newbies, the errand boys, we use them as lookouts, informers and light security until they are either recruited as Bratok or tossed aside. Steve's father worked for my father. I know he has always been loyal and he was the one I trusted to look after Poppy when she arrived. Steve and I were like brothers when we were younger, but drifted apart after papa died. It makes me think of Andrey. He was my best friend as well as my keeper, the only friend I had.. He helped me out more times than I can count when I first became the Pakhan. We were like brothers, but I know there was a side to him I didn't know. Like I always tell Poppy, never trust anyone completely.

How she hasn't left me I will never understand, but she tries everything she can to get me motivated to start up again. The thing that got me going was her being pregnant. I couldn't believe it. When she told me at first, I think I went into shock. She was a little worried. I didn't speak, then I broke down. I fucking cried and hugged her, holding her tummy to my face. How could this be real? I was a bad man, I had done bad things, yet this amazing woman who was trying to help me was also carrying my baby. I clung to her and told the baby I would be there for him no matter what. I would be the best papa ever. She'd given me a purpose, she'd given me something to aim for so I could be the best for my family. Me with a fucking family. I never wanted to have children. I was too afraid to bring them into the life I lived. Once you are in the Bratva, the only way out of it is death. I will automatically put any sons I have on that road, but I will protect my family for as long as I have breath. I will not teach any of my children the way of the Bratva until they are old enough to decide if that's the route they want to choose. That way, unlike me, they will have a choice. I am the Pakhan. I can change the rules. I will not let them live as Dimitri and I did.

I found out a lot about my father not long before he died. It was at my hands he died. No one ever knew that. It's a secret I will take to my grave. He was not a good man. I found out Dimitri and I had different mothers, which we never knew. I always believed we had the same mother. The woman who we both thought was our mother was, in fact, not either of ours. We still loved her as our mother, we didn't know any different. She was good to us. We were devastated when she died. That was another story. We were told she died of cancer, it wasn't true. My father killed her, he slowly poisoned her to make it look like an illness. He wanted her to suffer.

After our mother died, Dimitri said he didn't think something added up. We were both still young teenagers. I was just fourteen and he was eighteen. He was the one that found out the truth, that father had her killed. We confronted him. He said she was cheating on him. I knew it was the other way around. I'd seen him with countless women. It was then we both started to dig around, we had lost all trust in him. Dimitri came to me one night. He had papers on our births. He snuck into Papa's office and found them in the safe. He guessed Papa's code for the safe. Dimitri was Papa's second-in-command. He would take over from Papa one day. I loved Dimitri. That's when we found out we were half brothers and neither of us to the woman we called mama. There were no names on the documents about our birth mothers. We both started digging around, talking to people. We found out Papa was into sex trafficking. I was dumbstruck. I never knew he was into that. I knew about the drug trafficking, the arms deals, the money laundering, but not sex trafficking. It repulsed me to think he was into that.

When Dimitri found out, he marched into Papa's office and demanded he tell us who our mamas were and asked him if we were actually his children. He laughed at us, telling us not to be absurd. Dimitri pounced on him, hitting him in the face. Our whole lives had been a lie. Papa was able to fight Dimitri off and I grabbed him to stop him from attacking Papa again. I wanted to hear what he had to say. He told us our mothers were just whores who tricked him. He only fucked Dimitri's mama once. She came over with a lot of Russian women that he had brought over, promising them new lives. He proceeded to tell us she caught his eye one night when he'd had too much vodka and he took her hard that night. She was there for anyone to take in the club he was in. He thought he used a condom, but he was too drunk to know for sure. But one stipulation of the girls at the club was that they were all on birth control. He still never knew how she got pregnant. The DNA test proved Dimitri was his. He had her killed after she gave birth.

With my mama, however, he had fallen for her. She was fourteen when he moved her into his apartment. She was another one of his girls, brought over from Russia, full of promises for a better life, only that life never materialized for almost all the girls. He says my mama fooled him, telling him she was on birth control already. The fool believed her. As soon as I was born, he killed her for trying to trap him. I had no choice but to kill him after hearing all this. I was told he was the reason Dimitri was killed, that it was him that set up the sting, telling everyone it was a rogue Bratok who killed him. Finding out about the sex trafficking, It's why I will have nothing to do with sex trafficking and I try to rescue anyone that suffers sexual abuse. These girls were given false hope and promises. They were all pumped with drugs and used to make money in all his clubs. I only ever thought he had the one club, but no, they were scattered throughout California. When I took over, I found out he had twenty-nine clubs in total. Full of Russian girls and boys used for sex. It repulsed me.

When I took over the reins after I killed Papa, I wanted full details of all the clubs and everything that went on in them and how they operated. I needed the information so I could shut them all down. I was outraged. Most of the girls and boys that were brought over were young. I found out there were some as young as four. There was a fucking huge market for the young ones. I was disgusted, I was sick, physically. I had the club managers run through everything in detail with me. They were vile pieces of shit. The club here, near home, I spent a week there, seeing what went on. I don't know how I stuck it out for that week, or how I didn't kill every punter who entered that club.

Part of this club was for the elite. I mean politicians, rock stars, rap stars, film stars, big industry billionaires and so on. They used the club a lot for whatever their tastes were. My father started importing young Russian boys. They were in high demand with the elite who were prepared to pay big bucks for them. I mean big, big bucks. If they didn't want to use the club which happened a lot, some of the big clients didn't want to chance being seen, they would pay for so many girls and boys to be taken to where ever they requested. Sometimes just to be used by them in a house they owned. I found out some of the elite owned houses no one knew about, just for this purpose. A lot of the times the kids were to be used by multiple people at parties. Again they paid huge bucks for these privileges. Privileges. They are sick fucks, these are not privileges.

They took them at all ages. The girls had to be spotlessly clean, and if they had reached puberty, they had to be clean-shaven. The boys had to be spotless but not shaven, they were then paraded naked in front of the partygoers who proceeded to pick which ones they wanted, to be used by individuals or groups and then taken to different rooms to be used as the partygoers pleased. This is what the managers told me. I was physically sick over and over.

Seeing it in the clubs was bad enough. I wanted to see the other side for myself, I used a latex mask I'd had made for me to cover my identity, and I helped escort girls and boys to a house in Malibu on an exclusive estate, I wanted to see who and what went on. I couldn't stay and watch as they paraded the naked kids around like cattle. These kids weren't drugged beforehand, some people didn't want them drugged at all, they wanted them alert, terrified, and screaming for mercy. Some drugged them just enough that they were lucid enough to know what was going on, but didn't put up a fight. I hated it. When the parade started and people started to choose, I couldn't let it go on. I stopped that party. I couldn't let these kids be used ever again. Let's just say it didn't go down too well until I took my mask off and they realized who I was. I had some of my men with me, and they made sure no one kicked up a stink. One unlucky person did, he was a young singer, one who was well known and he thought he was above everyone else. A cocky little bastard who was stoned, and he tried to charge at me. I knocked him out before he could do anything, breaking his nose in the process.

After that house party, where I wanted to kill every fucker there, I bought a tall ass building which was part hotel and part business office, my current home. I turned a floor into a home for all these girls and boys and I made sure they were all looked after by caring people and never used again. They were given new lives. I had counselors, teachers, and caretakers there to look after them all. It was a lot but I felt responsible. My papa organized all this and knowing my own mama was brought over to be used like this was enough.

I wanted to burn every club to the ground. I executed all twenty-nine managers and whoever was second-in-command and instead I turned all twenty-nine clubs into adult-only clubs. My new clubs are full every night. They are for age twenty-five and above, it's consensual sex with different rooms for different purposes. They are a huge hit, no one pays for sex, no one demands sex or is entitled to it, everyone has a voice and a choice, the only payments are to be a member of an elite club. Let's just say my annual membership fee is high, but there are always people willing to pay. I only allocate so many memberships so we have a waiting list at each and every club.

Nine

Igor
Present

POPPY TOOK OVER RUNNING MY BUSINESSES, WITH MY GUIDANCE, courtesy of an earpiece hidden in her ear so she could hear me and repeat what I said, a microphone hidden in a small pendant necklace so I could hear what was being said, and a camera hidden in a brooch pin she wore, it was a stunning platinum and diamond dragon brooch pin. Plus, with my intel on everyone she had to meet up with, she rocked it. If something didn't go well or I told her not to trust someone standing there, she shot them with no hesitation. She became a killer, but she took to it so easily, like a bee to nectar. She gained herself a name. Mrs. Poppy Ustrashkins was becoming a woman no man messed with and I couldn't have been any prouder of her. I heard they had started calling her the dragon lady because of her brooch.

She's gone for a meeting with the godfathers, they're going to vote on letting her stay and run my businesses, if they reject her it could be over for us both. If they reject her, I will wage an all-out war on the lot of them. No one messes with me. I am Igor fucking Ustrashkins, god of all godfathers, king of all Bratva, the name that brings fear to many, even the top dogs of the criminal world. Cross me and your life's over. Well, for everyone except one person. I never understood why I had a sweet spot for her. I could never fathom out what it was that Svetlana had, that I just couldn't shake. Don't get me wrong, I wouldn't touch her or anyone now, not a chance. I have my angel, my Poppy, my fucking queen by my side. What a fucking woman. I knew she was strong the moment I saw her in the park, and she gave chase after Svetlana tried to steal her bag. She caught her, and she gave her what for, but then she let her go. I watched it all play out. I knew I wanted Poppy from that moment, for myself. I watched her walk into the park that day. She sat and watched everyone around her, taking in all her surroundings and the people around her. It was when she brought that cup of Jell-O out of her bag I knew she was alone and didn't have anywhere to go. I gave the nod to Svetlana to get her on board.

Svetlana almost screwed that up. If Poppy had taken the hint and left, I would have taken Svetlana to the basement and tortured her before putting her in the acid vat. I should have done it a long time ago. She was the only other woman, well girl as she was, that I knew I wanted. If things had gone to plan, she would have been my queen one day. I remember that first day I saw her, I knew I wanted her, but she was so young and I knew I couldn't have her. I was surprised when she told me she was nearly seventeen. Her mama confirmed it to me, so I took it at that. I couldn't wait till her eighteenth birthday.

———

I was fucking anyone I could, one, to try to make me forget the young Svetlana back in my apartment, and two, because if I didn't, I would probably take her when I knew I couldn't have her yet. The problem was, everyone I chose to fuck had similarities to Svetlana, and when I was fucking them, I was imagining it was her. When I started taking them back home to fuck, I knew it would upset her, but I needed it to. She was coming onto me and dressing like she was older and it was fucking with my mind. The problem was, it didn't discourage her. If anything, it made her more determined.

On her seventeenth birthday, I tried to stay away. I arranged for her family to come over so she wouldn't be alone, but I couldn't do it. I had to be there with her to celebrate. I made a big fucking mistake when I had her in my office giving her the emeralds I bought for her. I kissed her, I couldn't help myself and if it wasn't for her age, I would have fucked her there and then regardless of who was in the apartment. I wanted her so badly. I made her leave me and go back to her family. I saw her to the door and then I locked it as soon as she left. I had to fucking rub one out there and then in my office because all I could think of was her squashing those huge globes of hers against my chest and her nipples were rock hard, just like my cock. I wanted to dip and bite them hard. Then I would have fingered her until she was screaming my name. Yeah, to rubbing one out in my office with everyone on the other side of the door, that was hard, literally.

I was a bastard to her at times, but I was trying to distance myself. She could be a little firecracker when she wanted to be. I loved it that day on her seventeenth birthday, she had gone out shopping and gotten herself lost. I was following her, of course, I had to make sure she was safe. I found it so funny and again, I just wanted to take her back home and fuck her. She had a real go at me and it made me so hard. She'd changed her hair color that day, which I liked but it meant each woman I fucked from then had to be blonde.

I used to stay away from my own apartment just so I wouldn't fuck her. I stayed at the Dimitri a lot. She didn't know about the Dimitri and I never took her there. I wanted to a few times, but thought better of it. In hindsight, I'm so relieved I never did take her there. Some days when Rasputin informed me he was out guarding her, I would finish whatever meeting I was in, or project I was working on, and I would follow her. I was sad and mad for this girl. She was a beauty. I know I could have anyone I want, and I do, except her. She is the one I can't have and I don't know if it's because I can't have her that it makes me want her more.

I will never forget the first time I saw her. She was tall and voluptuous, had long brown hair and green eyes that bore straight into my soul. The day I took her from Russia, I had just killed her papa. He stayed in the bar that night, like I told them, but when I went to see him earlier, to find out exactly what he did to Svetlana, he was sitting drinking again. I was so angry when I saw him as I walked into the bar. He has a family to support yet he's sitting here drinking, not giving a fuck about his family, and he's a pedophile. I walk over and sit opposite him. I lean over and quietly tell him to finish his drink and then follow me out of the bar. He just looks at me.

"Fuck off," he says, leaning forward and quietly saying it right to my face.

That just sealed his fate. He clearly doesn't know who I am.

"Do you not know who I am?" He looks at me like I'm shit and then takes another swig of his vodka. "Let me introduce myself. My name is Igor, Igor Ustrashkins."

I watch the realization dawning on his face. He slowly lowers the glass from his mouth and lifts his head to look at me.

"The, Igor Ustrashkins, how do I know you are him?" He has the balls to ask me.

"Well, if you come outside, you will find out. I am going to get up and leave. You will finish that vodka and you will leave this bar of your own free will. If you tell me to fuck off one more time, I will cut your hand off here and now so you know who I am. Follow me out and I will be waiting down the road in my car. If you are longer than five minutes, I will come back for you and drag you out. Do you understand me, Vlad?"

He nods slightly without looking at me and I see him gulp as he raises his glass with a shaky hand. I stand and pat him on the back and leave. I head to my car just down the road. This area is shit, it's so run down no one will even pay any attention to me or him. I wait. I watch my clock in the car and wait. I'm just about to go and get him when I spot him in my rearview mirror.

I get out and open the passenger door for him. He walks to me slowly.

"Hurry up, old man, I don't have all day. I have a princess to rescue." Once he reaches me, I push him in and close the door. I start the car and drive.

"Now, tell me Vlad, what is it you do exactly to your little girl?"

He looks over to me, I can see the shock on his face.

"Yes, I know all about you Vlad, but I want you to tell me exactly what you do to her, then tell me if you think it is normal. Does she have any siblings at home?"

He doesn't speak.

"Answer me," I shout. It startles him.

"Yes, I have six girls altogether."

Fucking hell, this is going to be worse than I thought. If he does things to them, well, his death is going to be slow and painful.

"And," I say, looking over to him. I pull the car up at a building next to an old disused mine shaft. All the mines are closed around here now, it's why there is so much poverty. I turn in my seat to him, waiting. "Tell me what you do to them?"

I grab his head and smash his nose on the dashboard. He cries out as his hands fly up to hold his broken, bloody nose.

"I won't ask you again. I will take your silence to mean everything you do is bad and I will fucking kill you now, slowly. Get out of the car."

He turns to me, he's crying, the big fucking weak, pathetic bastard. What, does he think I'm going to have sympathy for him? I don't think so.

"I didn't do anything. I don't know what you're talking about. I love my girls." He's pinching his nose, trying to stop the bleeding. Great, I don't want blood in the car.

"OUT," I shout at him.

I watch him slowly open the door and step out. I wait to see if he makes a run for it. He just stands there with his head down. I get out, grabbing my little bag from behind the passenger seat, my tools.

"Walk into that building." I nod, he moves slowly, I follow behind pushing his back to make him walk faster, he trips and goes down. "Get the fuck up, you pathetic piece of shit."

He doesn't move. I move to his side and kick him hard, he falls on his side and curls up into a ball, crying.

"You big fucking shit, get up now, or I'll just do what I have to here and now."

He moves back to his knees and slowly rises. He's a big man and could easily have a go at me, but he doesn't. I'd be able to take him no problem, you would think he would fight back, especially if he wasn't guilty. That solidifies it more for me.

He walks into the building, the door is hanging off. I suspect kids have been in here messing about. I walk inside, then move to look around. There's not much here. I move to the doorway on the other side to look through there. I hear him moving and turn, he's fleeing out the door. Here we go, he's not going to get far. I run to the door and he's just by the car.

"Stop where you are or I will shoot you now."

He stops.

"Turn around and walk back to me."

He does slowly. I have a gun pointed at him. I'm not going to use it, this would be too good a death for him, too quick and easy. I motion with the gun to get back inside. He walks past me. "Move over to the doorway and through into that room."

Once in the room, I look around, there's an old desk and chair in here. These will do, although they are falling to pieces.

"Sit on that chair," I order him.

He slowly lowers himself onto the old wooden rickety chair. I move in front of him. "Now, this is the last time I will ask you. What do you do to your girls? I heard you saying you will slap Lana's bare ass. Do you do this to them all and what else do you do?"

He winces but shakes his head.

"Just to Lana. Only a couple of times to Vidana and none to the others." He hangs his head but doesn't elaborate.

I look at my watch. I need to get this done. I have people to see and places to be, one of them being at his house later on.

"You know what? There is one thing I will not ever tolerate, and that is abuse of a minor in any form. When I heard that and she confirmed it to me, my mind was reeling. I was thinking all sorts of things. In my mind, no child abuser should ever be allowed to live. I am fortunate, when I come across one, I don't have to abide by the law, I am the fucking law and I kill them. That means this is your end. You know what I do to pedophiles?"

His eyes are wide, he has blood all around his nose and mouth. He's crying again. Yeah, pedos are weak.

"Stand up and take off your jeans."

He looks up at me, terrified. I take out some gloves from my little tool bag and put them on, then I pull out my hunting knife. His eyes go wide.

"What are you going to do to me?"

He's terrified. I can see his jeans getting wet down the front as he pees himself.

"Well, most pedos use their cocks, so I am going to let you suffocate on your own cock. Now take off the jeans."

He shakes his head vigorously.

"I won't ask you again. Stand up and take off your fucking jeans, NOW," I shout at him.

He grabs the seat of the chair on either side of him and grips it tightly, trying to anchor himself down. Yeah, like that's going to fucking help. I walk up to him smiling. I slowly bend and slice. His fingers, on the one side, are no longer gripping the chair, they are on the floor. He screams out, blood is dripping onto the floor. He lifts his hand up and holds his wrist with his other hand, the blood is dripping all over.

"Now are you going to stand up and remove your jeans, you know, while you still have one useful hand?"

"YOU FUCKER," he screams into my face.

I grab his hair, lifting him to his feet. I take the knife and before he sees what's coming, I jab him three times in quick succession in his side. Enough to break the skin and puncture him, but not actual stab wounds that would kill him, just hurt and make him bleed. He bends over to the side, placing his fingerless hand on the stab wounds. He looks to me. I motion with the knife to his jeans. He slowly uses his good hand to unfasten and then slide the jeans down his legs. Good, now he's cooperating. I pull out a belt from my bag and shove his shoulder hard, making him sit back down. I take his hands and tie them with the belt behind the chair, threading the belt through the slats in the back of the chair first. I know he will kick out when I grab his cock.

"Kick off the jeans," I tell him and he slowly uses each foot to remove them.

He's really trying my fucking patience here. I bend down while behind the chair and I slice both his Achilles tendons in quick succession. He screams out. At least he can't kick me now. The blood starts flowing from the open wounds, fast. I need to hurry; I need him to suffer. I use the knife to cut at his briefs and then lift his cock. Maybe do something different. I slice at his ball sack and nearly cut it off in one swipe, but it takes two. He's screaming loud. I hold it up, showing him. His eyes are starting to droop.

Oh no, fucker, you will not die just yet.

I push his head back, exposing his throat to me. I slice down his neck deep into his trachea, not across. I don't want to slit his throat. I open the cut wide and I push the ball sack inside, blocking his windpipe, and I keep my hand over the hole so the sack doesn't blow out. Now he can't scream. This is good. I usually cut off cocks to shove down their throats. I watch as his face starts to turn blue. He's struggling to breathe, his nose is broken so he can't breathe through that. I stare into his eyes, watching the life draining from them. He had green eyes, they are dark and getting darker by the minute. I wait and wait, not letting go of his neck. With the blood loss and this, he doesn't last long. I take great pleasure in my smiling face being the last face he ever sees.

From my little bag, I take out my small can of lighter fluid and pour it on him, then light him up like a firecracker. I stand right back near the doorway, and I watch as his skin burns and crisps to nothing. He got what he deserved. The family will be better off without him, and I don't have to worry about him doing anything to Svetlana's sisters. Yes, they will mourn him, but time will heal them.

I spend the rest of my day sorting out what I came here for, trying to sort the new routes for my next shipment to the States, then I drive to Svetlana's. She's so happy to see me. We are leaving and on our way to Paris in no time. I gave her mama two hundred thousand dollars, which in Russian Ruble was an immense amount of money, and I promised a monthly allowance of two thousand dollars for them. I will pay this until the girls have grown up, as long as things are still good with everyone and the family is safe. I made an oath to Larisa, Svetlana's mama.

I wanted to fuck Svetlana on the plane. I put her into the bed and then laid on top of the comforter so I didn't do anything. I watched her sleeping all the time I was there by her side. I stroked her face, telling her how I would look after her and that she had nothing to worry about. She was so beautiful and peaceful. I hope she never finds out what I did to her papa, although she should hate him for what he's done, but she was upset he wasn't there to say goodbye to her. I got her out of there as quickly as I could to distract her. I can never understand why a child still loves a parent that does unthinkable things to them.

We had a great time in Paris. I loved the expressions on her face at everything that was new to her, which was practically everything. I couldn't help but keep holding her hand or just touching her. She was happy and it made me feel happy. I don't remember the last time I was happy. It's been so long. Once we got to LA, it was great at first. I was working most of the time, but I was finding it harder to be around her. I wanted her so much. We never did talk about what her papa did to her. Each time I hinted at it, she changed the subject. Maybe it's too raw for her to talk about. I never pressed for the details.

I decided the best thing I could do was fuck other women. I thought by doing that it would change how I felt about Svetlana. It didn't and only made me want her even more. After her seventeenth birthday, it got harder. I know I could have her. In Russia, I could have had her a long time ago. We are not in Russia, and I will not go down for statutory rape.

Ten

Igor

THE NIGHT BEFORE HER EIGHTEENTH BIRTHDAY, AND I COULDN'T wait to take her. I know I was breaking the law leading up to this day, a lot, by us both having oral sex. But my god, she tasted good. Once I got that first taste of her that night in her closet, there was no going back. She was like a drug I needed every night. I'd had countless women, tasted countless women, but there was just something about her. I beat myself up at first, she was still seventeen, although it wasn't sex it still didn't feel right. But as the months passed, I started to not care. She felt for me the way I felt for her. How could that be punishable? We came so close to sex on so many occasions. I would stroke my cock up and down her pussy, playing around with her clit with him. I even placed him at her entrance a few times but I managed to stop myself thrusting inside. How I will never know.

As my phone buzzed to tell me it was past midnight and she was officially eighteen, I entered her for the first time. She was tight, but it made me want her more. The tighter the better. I eased in gently until I thrust hard. I felt the tear as she froze In my arms. She told me she was a virgin. It confused me. I thought her papa fucked her. She said she would explain to me. At that point, I didn't fucking care. I was in, buried deep inside her tight pussy and it felt like heaven. I stared down into her face, giving her a minute before I continued to move. I made love to her, the fucking came later, but I knew or I thought I loved her.

It didn't take long for my world to come crashing down. How the fuck did that happen? We were nonstop fucking and making love. I couldn't get enough of her and she couldn't get enough of me. No matter the time of day, even in the middle of the night, one of us would wake the other up the best way we knew how. It suddenly dawned on me one day that she didn't seem to have had a period for a while. I started to panic because I had never used condoms with her. I just presumed she was on birth control. What an ass I was. I bought some pregnancy tests and marched home.

"When did you last have a period, Svetlana?" I asked as soon as I walked into the apartment. She scowled at me.

"Well, hello to you too, Igor. Did you have a nice day?" She walked up to me and kissed me on my cheek.

I pushed her away from me. I was feeling sick. "Just answer the fucking question, Svetlana. When was your last period?"

She stood back, frowning and trying to think. She shrugged.

"I don't remember. It must have been a while ago. I never thought about it. Why?" Is she for fucking real right now? Why? What the fuck. I open the brown paper bag and I throw the boxes at her. She flinches, then bends to pick one up. I see the look on her face as she reads what it is.

"Pregnancy test, what do I need this for? I'm not having a baby." She threw the box at me. Is she stupid or just playing me?

"You don't remember your last period. I didn't use any condoms. Are you on the pill or any other form of birth control?"

She shakes her head. I start pulling on my hair and move away from her, just in case I have the urge to reach out and grab her neck. I pace by the windows. I rub my hands over my face, trying to compose myself and not lose it with her. I turn, but I can't hold it in.

"Go and fucking pee on those sticks now. You did this on purpose, didn't you? This is what you wanted all along. Me, and this is you trapping me?" In three strides, I'm in her face. Towering over her, I bend and pick up the boxes and shove them into her arms. "Go now before I do something I will regret."

She looks terrified, but she doesn't move. I grab her arm and I drag her to her room and march her straight to the toilet.

"Sit and fucking pee," I yell at her as I unbox the sticks one by one. I grab a glass off the side and pass it to her. "Pee in here and we can dip them in."

She's sitting on the toilet but she still has her bottoms on. I pull her up by the arm and then I yank her bottoms and panties down and uncenremoniously push her back down onto the toilet. I place the glass in her hand and bow down to be in her face.

"PEE," I scream at her.

"I can't just pee on demand. I don't want to go. I'm not pregnant, I can't be."

I take the glass and the other one from the vanity unit and fill them both up with water, and I take them to her.

"Drink these, they will make you pee."

She doesn't move. I place one on the floor and then tilt her head back, squeezing her cheeks on either side of her mouth to make it open. I pour the water down her throat, making her drink. She starts to splutter and spit the water out.

"Fucking drink it now or so help me God, I will get a hose and feed it down your throat to force water into you."

I see the tears flowing down her cheeks. I'm in such a rage I feel nothing for her. She's like the others, like my father said, trapping us by getting pregnant. I don't want a kid. I don't want to bring anyone into this fucked-up world and live like this, especially not by someone trapping me. She's crying hard as I pour the other glass of water down her throat. She splutters again.

"Are you ready to pee yet?"

She nods, she's terrified. I give her the empty glass and I watch her place it under her. She's trying to force herself to pee. I wait and wait, eventually I hear the trickles. I thrust a stick at her.

"Pee on this as well then into the glass."

She does, then passes me the stick and the glass of pee. I move over to the vanity unit. I read the box so I know what to look for. I got the best tests, four of the same one, they are digital so it will say pregnant on it. It should only take two minutes.

I couldn't stop looking at the one she peed on. To distract me, I dipped the others in the glass and lined them all up on the counter. I felt her behind me but she didn't speak or touch me. Then it appeared. The word I was dreading PREGNANT—8 weeks. I hung my head. I could feel myself burning up inside. The rage was about to take a hold of me. I didn't want to be like my father, but that was exactly what was happening. My hands were gripping the countertop so tight, I felt I was going to break the marble top.

I looked and watched as each test one by one said PREGNANT. I turned, ready to do what, I don't know, but she wasn't there. She knew she must be pregnant, she's gone. I pick up a stick and storm into the bedroom. She's standing by the bed with both arms folded over her tummy, as if protecting that thing inside.

I move around to her and start yelling in her face. She screws her eyes shut and puts her hands over her ears so she can't hear me. She's humming. What the fuck? Humming some Russian tune. I pull her hands away from her ears and grab her hair to hold her face up, so she looks at me. I wave the stick in her face.

"What the fuck, Svetlana. You stupid bitch. Why the fuck didn't you tell me you were not on the pill? Fuck. You did this on purpose, didn't you? You said you would never let me go. Well, listen to me and listen to me good."

She's crying, but I can see she's getting angry herself. I am almost nose to nose with her.

"You will get rid of it or I will get rid of you both. Do you hear me? I don't want a baby. I never want a baby, and especially not with you. You silly little pathetic girl. You decide what it's going to be, it or the both of you. I will personally oversee either choice." I let go of her hair, throwing her to the floor and throwing the stick in her face. I leave, not looking back.

I go to the Dimitri. I don't want to be anywhere near her. I can't believe she has done this to me. She's like a naïve child. I take some blame. I should have checked she was on birth control. I never have sex without a condom, but with her, I felt I didn't need it. I just thought she would be the one and we would have a long, happy life together. Did I really think that shit? I'm fooling myself. She's young. I've always had my doubts about her age, but with her mama saying the same to me about her age, I didn't think any more of it. I'm going to do a check on her, get Andrey to follow up on her with Larisa. Send one of our men over there to get it out of her. But as a ruse, not to threaten her. See what he finds out about the ages of her children.

I've been screwing women the opposite of her for nearly two weeks. I've been trying to get her out of my head, but it's been a struggle. Each woman I screwed, I just closed my eyes and imagined it was her. I've started to loath her because she tricked me. I just keep playing it over and over in my head. I want to hate her. I also did some research on abortions, the test said she was eight weeks pregnant, which means it must have been when I took her on her birthday. The first time or thereabouts, we fucked so much it could have been any of those times. But we need to get the abortion sooner rather than later. I'm going back home, but not alone. If she's still there, then tough shit, she doesn't own me, and I will screw who I want.

She's not home. I take this woman to one of the rooms, and I leave the door wide open on purpose. I grab a chair and put it right in view of the door. I make quick work of getting this one bent over the chair. Svetlana could come in at any time. I'm facing the door, so I see when she arrives. I want to see the look on her face. This one is a screamer, that's good, the more noise the better. I'm plowing into her from behind, she's already had one orgasm and wanted to get up but I wouldn't let her. I just carried on gripping her hips and plowed as hard as I could into her. My balls are slapping her as I do. I sense the second Svetlana is there and I look up and look her right in the eyes. I sneer at her giving her my best 'fuck you' face. I thrust harder and harder. The woman is saying something, but I don't hear what she says. I see the tears flowing down Svetlana's face. I hate it. I hate seeing her cry, but I sneer more and give her my ecstasy face even though it's fake.

"You fucking bastard," she shouts loud over the grunting noises.

I just smile but then I look to her holding her tummy and it makes me snap, I'm so fucking angry.

"Fucking get out of here, bitch, you will never have my cock again."

The woman I'm fucking looks up at Svetlana. I can't see her face so I don't know what she's doing but Svetlana looks at her. I remove my cock from the woman. I don't even know her fucking name, but I don't really care. I hold my cock and pump it as I move toward Svetlana. I smile at her as she watches me. She's staring at me as I pump away with my own hand.

"Take one last look, Lana. You will never see it again. Do you want one last lick? Come on, don't be shy, I know you're anything but shy, just one last taste."

She watches me as I lift the woman's head. Making sure she can see exactly what I'm doing, I ram my cock into her mouth. I stop and position us so Svetlana has a side view of watching me ram it in. I look to the woman who is sucking me hard. I smile at her. She starts playing with my balls and I start to pant, turning to Svetlana so she can watch me come. I thrust deeper, all the while watching her expressions change from hurt to anger, to lust, to sorrow, to shame. I look at her, still stroking her tummy, and it riles me up so badly. I grab the woman's hair and get as deep as I can. She's good, she can take it all, no problem. I'm not far from exploding. I want Svetlana to watch me come. I watch as she looks down to her hand on her tummy, then back to me.

"This baby will survive, but you will never know it. Go to hell, you fucking bastard." She turns and disappears.

That fucking annoys me, and I want to chase after her. No way is that baby going to live. Just then the woman bites down on my cock and I look to her, that's all it takes. I shoot my load down her throat, screaming and shouting my release as I do, prolonging it on purpose, being louder on purpose, calling out angel, on purpose, hoping Svetlana hears me.

I stayed at the apartment after getting rid of the woman. I worked in my office, had dinner, then went to bed. I didn't hear Svetlana. I didn't see her. I wanted to go into her room to comfort her, just instinct I suppose, but then as soon as the images of her rubbing her tummy pops into my head I just want to go into the room and drag her to a clinic for an abortion. I left early. I couldn't sleep and I needed to get away. I looked up some clinics, but I needed private, exclusive. I didn't want this getting out. I found one and made the appointment. It's for the week after next. I will drag her there myself. If I tell her about the appointment, she won't go on her own. I'll coax her there on the day, and once there she won't have any choice, I told her I'd kill her.

I went back to my apartment to get some files I left. This is fucking stupid, it's my fucking apartment. I should just kick her out, tell her to get a room on the ninth floor. Why should I have to stay away? I don't see her. I have dinner on my own. Polina left as soon as I was sorted. I didn't ask her about Svetlana, I knew she was in her room. I heard the TV when I stood at her door, debating if I should go in or not. I put my forehead on the door and stood there, listening. I didn't hear her at all. I moved to my room and slammed my door. Just so she knew I was home in case she hadn't realized. I left early the next morning, yet again. I just can't sleep with her there.

I've been back a couple of days. I even ran into her a couple of times but we didn't speak. This is fucking stupid.

I've just walked into the kitchen and she's there holding a mug and talking with Polina. She looks terrified as she looks at me. She freezes. I stand and scowl at her. This is my fucking kitchen. I'm not leaving because of her. I stand and make her feel as awkward as I can until she gets the hint and leaves the kitchen. Why isn't she wearing baggy things? I can see the little bump over her tight leggings, surely other people will notice. Her tee was also tight and short, her tits looked huge to me. I can't possibly be the only one to notice. Once she leaves the kitchen, I stand thinking. I get a drink. Fuck this, I go to her room, I don't knock, I just open the door.

"You have an appointment on Friday at a private clinic. I have left the details on the dining room table. I figured you wouldn't have done anything about it, so I took the initiative. I will track you to the clinic. If you do not go, then your choice is made." I glare at her.

Fuck, she's crying again. I actually don't feel anything for her as I stand glaring at her. This is the first time I've not wanted to take her into my arms to comfort her. I scoff, then slam the door shut so I don't have to look at her sat there anymore. Fuck, why did I tell her about the appointment? Never mind, I've told her I will track her. She will probably not take her phone but Rasputin will be with her and I track him so I will know where she is by him. If she doesn't do it, then I will do as I said, I will kill her and put her in the acid vat which will kill them both.

"FUCK, where the fuck is she?"

I storm into her room and check around. Everything looks okay. Her clothes are still in the closet. I run to my office, fucking run. Like, who the fuck am I? I check the CCTV footage and I see her with a case, then sitting on the couch. I watch as Mavra leaves, probably on a bathroom break, and she runs with her case to the elevators. I watch him come back and notice her in the open elevator. He stands staring for a few seconds then runs to try to stop the elevator from closing, he's too late but also he was too fucking slow. I march out of my office.

"Mavra, why the fuck didn't you stop her?" I grab his shirt and get into his face. I'm in such a rage. She can't get far, she doesn't have any mon— FUCK. I let go of him, shoving him to the floor before he has a chance to speak. I log into the bank and see the withdrawals each day then the big one last night, she's got thirty thousand. Fucking hell, why didn't the bank inform me? Why didn't I think to fucking check it. Dumb piece of shit. She could be anywhere. I've tried her phone, but it's switched off. I bring the tracker up to track. I have this new device that can track even when it's switched off. It's here, in the apartment. I follow the directions. I find it stuffed down the side of the couch. I throw it hard across the room and watch is smash to pieces against the wall. I put Andrey to work trying to find her, checking the airports. I'm sure with that money she will try to get a flight back home. I phone Larisa.

"Hello."

"Do you know where she is? Has she been in contact with you?" I shout over the phone to her.

"No Igor, I have not spoken to her. Why? What has happened? Where is she? Is she safe? Is she?"

"I don't fucking know but I will tell you now, if you hear from her you tell me straight away, if I find she turns up there with you and you don't tell me, I swear I will kill you all by burning your fucking house down. Do you hear me, Larisa? You know not to mess with me." I hear the quiver in her voice.

"I swear to you, Igor, I have not heard from Svetlana for a few weeks. I never worry, I know if she needs me she will phone me. She has not phoned me. If she turns up I will call you straight away, Igor." She sounds terrified.

Good, if she is, she will tell me. While I'm on it.

"Larisa, you better do as you say. I have men everywhere. Have you been having a good time with Tomas lately?"

I hear her intake of breath as she realizes.

"Yes Larisa, he is one of my men. I want you to tell me the truth to my next question. If you lie or I find out you lied, I will burn your house down with all your children in it. Do you understand, Larisa?" I hear her crying.

"Yes, Igor," she whispers down the phone.

"How old is Svetlana?"

Nothing, she's silent. I think she's hung up on me until I hear her sniffle.

"If I have to ask you again, La—"

"She's seventeen now. She was seventeen on her last birthday."

I drop the phone.

"FUCK, I fucking knew it," I scream into the air. I pick the phone back up. "You let me fuck a seventeen-year-old. You practically sold me your fucking fifteen-year-old just so you could get a nice house. What kind of fucking mother are you? You going to do that to all your girls, sell them to the highest bidder? You're as bad as that fucking husband of yours, Larisa, you deserve what he got."

I turn the phone off and slam it on the desk. I probably just cracked the screen. I sit down in my chair. Placing my elbows on my desk, I put my head in my hands. Seventeen, fuck, she could get me sent down for statutory rape if she goes to the police. She has proof, she's carrying my fucking baby, she could tell them I raped her, held her here, and used her. She could spew so many lies. What the fuck have I done? The baby's DNA will prove it, no backhanders will get me out of this one. They will lock me up for years, just what all my rivals want. This could ruin me. I need to find her, I have to find her. She could actually be my downfall.

Eleven

Igor

I'VE HAD EVERYONE SEARCHING FOR HER. NOTHING, SHE'S JUST vanished. I traced the cab driver who picked her up using all the cameras available to me, he told me he dropped her off at the Union Station. Using cash, I have no way of tracing which train she boarded. I found out which trains left around the time she arrived, but there were over ten that night. She could be anywhere. I still have her passport so she can't leave the country, but it's a big fucking country and unless she uses the card again to purchase something, I don't know where she is. This is fucked up. I've not been able to concentrate and more people have died since she disappeared than needed to. I haven't done anything to Larisa, and the only reason I haven't is because she has five girls relying on her. I can't do that to them. That would make me as bad as the parents they had. I may bring them all over here at some point, but that depends on what happens with Svetlana.

It's been eight months since she vanished. I haven't been able to find her, not a fucking trace of her. With all the resources I have, you'd have thought I could find anyone, and I usually do. But not her, apparently. Larisa swears she has never heard a peep out of Svetlana. I believe her because she's terrified every time she speaks to me, and my men are watching her. I also believe her because she has never once mentioned a baby or anything about Svetlana being pregnant, and I certainly have never told her. There's been nothing, no sightings of her anywhere. I wonder if she's even alive. If she is I'm sure she will have kept the baby, there will be proof out there no matter what. She will always have that hold over me if she didn't terminate it. It will have been born by now. The week I thought it would be due was a bad week for me and for anyone who even looked at me the wrong way.

I couldn't shake it, no matter what I did or who I buried myself in. I just had this strange feeling all week. I hoped to God she hadn't given birth and that it was just me feeling a little sorry, but no matter what, I did not want a child. I swore I would never have children.

I was surprised at how easily I got over her. I thought I loved her. Turns out I didn't, I thought she was the one, turns out she wasn't. I think when I found out her real age it all went out the window. I cared for her more than anyone else before her or after her, but I think it was more of an infatuation, because I knew I couldn't have her until she was the right age. What a fucking joke that was. But she was also the first one I personally rescued from an abusive family. Yes, I helped all the girls and boys my asshole of a father used for sex trafficking, but Svetlana was the first I saved. I wonder sometimes if she is alive or dead, not being able to find her has been hard. I never thought anyone could escape me. I always thought I could find anyone. But when there is no digital footprint for someone it turns out it's difficult. I even started looking at the births around the time I thought it was due. But how the fuck can I pinpoint her in all the hospitals in the States without even knowing the actual date or where she is? That would take forever if she's using a false name. I give up.

It's been a year since she disappeared and I still think about her. Nowhere near as much as I did, but well, I would just rather know what happened to her. I've also had the fear of being arrested for underage sex hanging over my head. It's a fucking nightmare. I've never met anyone since. I just fuck random women when I feel like it. I go to my club, The Hex. I don't indulge in the activities I just watch. I have every right to just walk around and see what is going on. I would never participate there. I don't need to.

I don't believe my fucking eyes. I've just walked into my building, heading home after a fucking horrendous meeting with a potential Romanian client, when I look up and see her standing there. I stop dead in my tracks and put my thumb to my mouth and stare at her. I have so many mixed feelings running through me right now. One, she's fucking beautiful. Two, I fucking hate her. Three, I want to fucking kill her. Four, I don't know what. I just stand staring. It's definitely her, I would know her anywhere, she looks good. One thing I do notice is she's on her own. No kid in tow. I start toward her and I see the fear on her face the closer I get. She's rigid, her shoulders are tense, one hand by her side, the other grabbing the strap of her purse tight. I notice how white her knuckles are. She doesn't know how I will react to her. She's right to be afraid.

"Svetlana," that's all I say, standing right in front of her, bearing down on her, trying to make myself bigger than I am. Not that I need to, she's tall but not that tall. She's changed her hair, it's shorter, I like it, she looks older.

"Igor," is all she says with a quivering, timid voice, not looking at me.

I grab her by the throat and push her up against the wall. I get right into her face and don't speak, I just stare at her terrified wide eyes. I want to put so much pressure on her throat right now, to watch the breath leave her, but I release her. There are too many people around. I grab her arm and pull her along to the elevators. I don't let anyone else in the car with us but instead of going up I swipe my card and hit the unnamed button under the car park level button. She hasn't noticed until she feels us going down instead of up and she suddenly looks to the panel and then up to me. I smirk. She looks terrified.

"Don't say a fucking word," I snarl at her, gritting my teeth.

She's shaking, I still have hold of her arm, I can feel it through my hand. I stare down at her, but she looks down.

"Look at me."

She doesn't move. I grab her chin and pull her head up to look at me. I see tears in her eyes. Here we go. I give zero fucks about her and so give zero fucks about the tears. They do nothing for me anymore. I don't have the urge to comfort her, I want to rip her fucking head off.

"You need to know, I…"

"I said don't fucking talk. Not until I'm ready for it." I grab her cheeks and squeeze hard. "You will talk when I ask you to talk and not before, do you understand?"

She tries to nod but I have hold of her too hard for her to move her head. We reach the basement, the doors open and I grab her hair and drag her out. I take her through a few security doors until I'm happy with the room I pick. I shove her into the room and shut the door. I leave her there. I go to the security room and tell Sergei to cut all coms for the room I'm about to enter. I watch as he does. I grab two bottles of water and march back to the room. It's a dark, bare room. It's like an old cell.

Entering the room, she's standing in the middle with her arms wrapped around herself. She looks up at me, it's dark but with the light from the hallway I can see she's still crying.

"Cut the fucking crocodile tears, Lana, they won't work on me."

She swipes them away. I put the bottles on the floor outside the room and bring the chair in that I carried down here. I throw it down.

"Sit," is all I say. I'm so fucking angry.

She doesn't move. She has her head hanging again and she's rubbing her arms.

"I said fucking sit, NOW."

I make her jump. I have no patience for her right now. She moves slowly and sits on the chair, I notice she looks to the open door as I move around her, I wonder if she will try to make a run for it? I doubt it, she saw the security doors we came through, she must know she would never get out. I stop behind her and I grab her short hair and pull her head back and I look down into her face. She's not crying now and from the looks of her, she's angry. I watch as her lips turn up and she smirks at me. The bitch is playing me. I let go of her hair and walk to stand in front of her. She looks up, smiling at me. I backhand her face hard, knocking her head sideways. She slowly moves her head round to look at me, she wipes at her lip which I can see is bleeding but she looks menacing, she was terrified earlier but now she's cocky as hell.

"What's so funny, Lana, you think you can just turn up here and everything will be hunky-fucking-dory? Where have you been?"

She licks her lip, trying to be provocative. I have to remember she's still just a kid, she'll be eighteen now.

"Around." One word. She obviously came back for a reason.

"Did you run out of my money? Is that why you're back, to try to get more money out of me? Do you have any idea who I am, or what I can do to you?" She glares at me.

"Of course I know who you are Igor, you're the love of my life and the father of my child."

I freeze at her words. She sees it and smirks again. I need to play it cool.

"So where is this child? I don't see it here anywhere. You got rid of it, Lana, I know you did. Are you here then just to try and get money from me?"

I watch her eyes squint as I say this, she's wondering if I know the truth or not. I don't of course, but she doesn't know that.

"You know I have people everywhere, Lana. You know I can find anyone or anything I want to, don't you?" I now sneer at her, playing her. I can see her thinking.

"If you did, Igor, you would have come for me sooner. You know nothing. You don't have a clue about our child, you don't even know what sex it is. That, I will never tell you. I have not come for money. I have come back for you, Igor. You are *my love*."

I laugh out loud. She really thinks after everything she will be *my love*. I would rather take her into the other room and throw her into the acid vat. In fact, I grab her by the hair again and drag her out of the room to the room just a few doors down. We enter, I shout at the men to clear the room. They are in hazmat suits. I try to protect my men. I grab a mask for myself because the fumes in here are off the charts. They all leave and I drag Lana over to the stairs. I pull her up, she's trying to scratch at my hands to let her go, but I don't give a shit at this moment. The fumes are getting to her. She starts to cough and tries to claw at her throat.

"Now tell me why you are here, or so help me, I will throw you into this vat and watch you burn and shrivel away to nothing, I will watch as your skin peels off, then your flesh from your bones, I will watch as your hair falls out and your face peels until it's just bits of flesh hanging there and your eyeballs melt away to nothing, you will scream until you can't make noise with all the pain and flesh being burned from your bones. TELL ME." I'm holding her over the edge of the vat. There is a little bit of acid and I lower her hand to it and watch as her skin smokes and burns. She screams. "Okay, Igor, please, I love you. I came back to be with you. Not for anything else."

"What about the child?"

"I got rid of it like you said, Igor. I couldn't love it, I wanted you and only you."

"Then why did you wait so long to come back? Why did you not just come back once you got rid of it? It's been over a year, why now?" I lower her even more.

Her face is not far away from the acid. I know she is struggling to breathe. She coughs and claws at her throat more. I can see she's tearing her flesh doing so. She shakes her head.

"I can't," she coughs more "speak" then she coughs again. I drag her down the steps and this time to the room next door. One of the torture rooms with a torture chair in it. She's coughing a lot. She holds her hand to her mouth and as she pulls it away, I see the splatter of blood she's coughed up. That room can be deadly just being in it for a few minutes, never mind being held over one of the three vats in there. It's why my men wear suits. I lost a few men In the early days, I found out my father lost a lot of men in that room, he didn't give a shit and just tossed them into the vats. I protect my men now. I throw her onto the chair, I restrain her with the leather wrist straps, I don't want her grabbing any of the implements to surprise me with while I fetch the bottles of water from outside the first room she was in.

Once back in the room, I untie her. No need to restrain her while I'm here. I pass her a bottle of water and she snatches it out of my hands and glugs the lot down.

"You fucking asshole, why did you do that? I told you I was here for you. I love you, Igor. I always have. I want you. I was afraid to come back. Finally, I built up the courage. I ran out of money and got evicted from where I was staying. I'm sorry, Igor, I'm sorry for leaving you." She's crying again. I have no feelings for her. I don't trust her. She lied about her age. I'm not going to let on that I know.

"Why would you stay away so long if you loved me? It doesn't make sense, money or not. You know money means nothing to me. If you loved me, you would have come back as soon as you got rid of the child. Why would you wait? You're lying to me Lana, you know I hate liars."

She looks me straight in the eyes.

"I do love you. I promise I am not lying to you. I was scared. I realized it was you I wanted more than any child, so I got rid of it like you wanted. I did it for you."

"But you wouldn't wait for over a year if you wanted me, Lana."

"It's fucking, SVETLANA," she shouts at me and I can't help it. I back-hand her again. Her lip opens more and blood pours from it. She licks at it, the tears flowing down her cheeks. "I was scared of this, Igor, of what you would do to me. Turns out I was right to be scared." She's lying and hiding something, I know it.

"Have you spoken to Larisa?" She looks at me, trying to gauge what I'm after. She shakes her head.

"I knew you would contact her, and I didn't have a phone. I wanted to come back so many times. I was so scared. I thought after taking your money you would surely kill me. I needed the money to get rid of the baby."

I know it costs a lot, I don't know what to believe.

"Are you going to kill me Igor, was I right not to come back all that time? What a fucking idiot to finally come back." She hangs her head, and she cries again. I see her shoulders moving.

I still don't believe her. I pick up some pliers. She hears me move and lifts her head to watch me. The only way to get the truth from anyone is to torture them. I know this better than anyone. I'm Igor fucking Ustrashkins and I will not be made to look a fool or weak for anyone.

"What are you going to do, Igor?" She looks terrified as I walk toward her with the pliers.

I restrain her hands with the cuffs again. I don't want her lashing out at me.

"Igor, what are you going to do, please Igor, I love you, please don't do this, I'm begging you." She's crying hard.

"Tell me the truth, Lana, because I don't believe a fucking word coming from your mouth. For that, you will lose your teeth, one at a time. If you continue to lie, I will cut your tongue out. Now tell me the truth. Why has it taken you over a year to finally show your face, no bullshit about running out of money." I grab her hair, pulling her head back so she looks up into my face. "I will count to three. On three I pull the first tooth. One." I pause and wait. She starts wailing.

"What do you want to know?" she shouts.

"Two."

"I told you everything." I open her mouth with the jaw jack. I reach inside.

"Three." I grab on to one of her molars at the top and I twist and turn until it comes out.

She's trying to shake her head, but it's no use. I have a knee on her lap, pressing against her chest and her head held right back, any more and I would snap her neck. She screams out as I pull the tooth out and blood splatters everywhere as she spits at me. My suit will just have to go in the trash. I step back, looking at her. She's stopped crying and is thrashing about in the chair. I wait for her to stop, she's panting, out of breath. "One," I say again and watch as her eyes go wide.

"Okay, okay." I wait a second.

"Two."

"I had the baby, I gave it away, I put it up for adoption. You will never find it. I want you, I only want you, and I realized I couldn't kill my baby, so giving it away was the next best thing. I ran out of money because I gave the new parents ten thousand dollars. I only want you Igor, not the baby, I don't care about the baby."

Finally, I knew she wouldn't terminate it.

"Three." I grab her head again and go in and pull a molar from the opposite side this time. She screams out as I do it.

"I told you the truth, you bastard. Why did you do that?" She's now crying again.

I shrug.

"Simple, you lied to me, you're lucky it wasn't your tongue. Never, ever lie to me." I see her eyes go wide. "I want to know where you were all this time. Where you lived and what you did. I want to know the truth about everything." I watch as her expression changes. She has that smirk on her face again. Is she fucking playing me still? "One."

"No, no. Okay. I was in a place called Anastasia Island, in Florida. I've been there all the time."

"Two."

"You hurt me one more time, and I swear to God, Igor, you will be sorry. Do you think I would finally come back here without a backup plan? I didn't know if you were going to kill me or not. I had a backup plan. If I disappear, you will be arrested for statutory rape." She smirks at me. I fucking knew it. I knew she had something planned.

"Speak."

"I was seventeen when you fucked me, Igor. I was seventeen when I had the baby. I know the law and you will be put away for statutory rape.

I found a lawyer, and I gave him an envelope to keep for me. It is not to be opened unless I don't check in with him every month. If I don't check in, then the instruction is to hand it to the LAPD. In the envelope are the details of the baby, where it is and both mine and your names, our dates of birth and our addresses and so on. Along with DNA from you and me. I took your toothbrush when I left and placed it in a plastic bag and sealed it. They have all the evidence they need."

Is she fucking lying again? How do I know it's true?

"If you're lying to me yet again, I won't give a fuck and will kill you, regardless. I can buy my way out of anything. You should know that, LANA, your threats don't scare me for one minute. Do you think some fucking snotty little girl will ever get one over on me? I'm the fucking Bratva, Lana, that's who I am. I have cops all over the US in my pocket. You will never get one over on me. Now I want the fucking truth, One." I grab her hair again and put my knee on her lap. She shakes her head vigorously.

"I'm not lying, Igor. It's the truth. I swear to God, I swear on our baby's life. I swear on my own sisters' lives. It's the truth." I move as though going to pull another tooth as she cries, "It's the truth, it's the truth, it's the truth" over and over. I shove her head back and stand in front of her.

"If I find you lied, like I told your mama, I will not only give you a fucking slow death, but I will burn your mama and sisters' house to the ground with them all in it." I get right into her face. "Don't think I won't do it, Lana, I've killed so many people, what's a few more." I see the horror on her face as I tell her I would kill her sisters.

"I am not lying, Igor. I have told you everything. I love you, Igor. I came back for you, to be your queen like you said."

I walk out of the room but just as I do I look over my shoulder at her.

"Do you think I would go anywhere near you after this? You're delusional, Lana. You're a stupid, naïve, little girl. I did care for you once, Lana, but not anymore."

I walk away, leaving her there tied to the chair. I stop at the security office and tell Sergei to leave her tied there with no food or water until I say so. I leave. I need to get on this before it takes me down. I need to find all the lawyers on Anastasia Island and get that envelope, no matter what. I can't have her hold this over me forever. She will ruin my life with it. I need to decide what to do with her. She will stay down here until I have that envelope.

Now that I know where she was, it was easy for my hackers to search out the CCTV footage. There were only a couple of law firms, so it wasn't hard to track which one she used. I sent Andrey and Ivan to do their worst on the lawyer. I am pleased to say I have the envelope. It only took three days from her telling me about it to obtain the envelope. I have left her in the basement for those days, only giving her minimal bread and water. I had Sergei move her to one of the white rooms and put a small cot in there for her. I enter the security room and tell them to cut all coms to her room. This is for us to go through, not anyone else. As I enter, she looks up, but she doesn't move.

"I am not scared of you, Igor. You will not harm me anymore. I know you."

I scoff at her as I slowly pull out the unopened envelope from inside my suit jacket. I see the moment she realizes what I am holding.

"How, no way, you could not get that. You're bluffing, Igor."

"Yet you know exactly what I'm holding."

I start to rip the envelope open, watching her as I do. I pull out a piece of paper, which does in fact have all our details on it, but it also tells me the baby is deceased. The baby who she named Sabina Ustrashkins, a girl, died during childbirth. I look up to her. I see the sorrow on her face, and I'm sure mine matches it. Now I have a name for the baby. I feel a deep pang in my chest, I feel a loss. That was my baby. I move over and sit next to Lana, still holding the papers. I look to her, I see that her shoulders are moving as if crying. She sniffs. I pull her into my side. I suddenly feel sorry for her. She went through all the trouble of disappearing to give the baby a chance, yet the baby died anyway. She's a young mother who lost her baby. I let her cry into my side. I still feel responsible for this young girl I'm comforting. I let the papers fall to the floor and I bring her to my lap and stroke her back as she cries into my chest. I feel a sense of remorse.

We stay like that for a little while, until she calms down, I don't suppose she has been able to mourn her loss with anyone else. This must be why she came back after all this time. I could see she had changed. She is angrier than she used to be, but I now know why. I feel regret for torturing her, but if she had told me the truth in the first place, then it would not have happened. She didn't tell me the baby died. I suspect she was going to hold this over me for some time so she could stay here with me. There is no us anymore. That ship sailed the moment I found out she was pregnant and solidified it when I found out her true age. I will not throw her out onto the streets. I could not do that to her. I place her back on the bed next to me. She looks up, she looks a mess, but then she's been down here for four days with no clean clothes or even a wash, with dried blood on her face.

"You should have told me the truth, Svetlana. You tell me lie after lie. I cannot abide by lies and you know this, yet you continue to do it. I will not turn you away, you can stay here..."

She throws herself at me. She tries to kiss me but I hold her back, she looks hurt.

"No, Svetlana, you will not stay with me. There will never be an us again. I was going to say, you can have a suite on the ninth floor and it is yours for as long as you need it."

I see the hurt on her face. She looks down. I lift her chin up to look at me.

"You burned that bridge by lying about your age, Svetlana. You are far too young for me. You will stay on the ninth floor as I said, in a suite. I want you to care for the other girls and also teach them English like you used to. You will now work for me. You will do as I ask you to. Is that understood? No more lies, ever Svetlana, you've seen what I can do, and next time I will not hesitate."

She's looking into my eyes, and I see the sorrow. In her head, she's lost me and a baby, but I also know she is very manipulative.

I take Svetlana to her new suite, it's the biggest room on the ninth floor. I will make sure she has what she needs, I will pay her for working for me. She is now an employee. I need to tell her what working for me means, so she is under no illusions. Seeing how easily the lies come, I could never trust her again. She needs to know this. We enter the suite, and I sit her down on the couch. I sit on the table in front of her and lean in to take hold of her hand.

"Svetlana, we are never going to happen again. You need to understand this. Tell me you understand."

She looks me in the eye and gives a slight nod.

"You are now an employee of mine. You need to know." I take a deep breath. "The only way you leave my employment is by death."

I see the realization on her face of what I'm saying. Her eyes go wide. I see the tears pool in the corner of her beautiful green eyes. I take her face in my hands.

"Tell me you understand, Svetlana. I need to hear you say it. If you don't want this and you want to leave, you are free to go now, but only now, you cannot stay and decide in a few weeks or months that you want to leave."

"I understand, Igor, I want to stay, I have nowhere else to go." I sigh.

"Yes, but you may not like it. In my employment you do as I say, with no argument, no matter what it is, do you understand? You are not Svetlana, the girl I used to fuck. You are just my employee. There will never be a repeat of us. I know you want that. I'm telling you now, it will never happen. You've lied to me and tried to blackmail me. Those things are unforgivable and you are very lucky you are still alive. No one else would ever survive one of those things, never mind two. I need to hear you say you understand."

She nods and looks down.

"Say it, Svetlana. You need to swear an oath you will stay employed either until death or until I let you go, if I let you go. Your oath is your word and no matter what, it cannot be broken. In Bratva, oath is everything."

She nods again.

"Say it."

"Okay, I swear an oath to you, Igor. I will work for you and do as you want. I will earn your trust again, Igor. I promise I will. I want you. I came back because I want you. I love you, so fucking much it hurts in here." She hits her chest over her heart with her palm.

"We will never be, Svetlana. I never trusted you, and I was right not to. Don't be fooled, don't think you will worm your way back into my apartment or onto my cock. It will not happen. You fooled me once, never again. From now on you do as I say and when I say it. You have sworn an oath to me."

I get up, ready to leave the room. She jumps up as soon as I stand and throws her arms around my waist and hugs me to her with her head on my chest. I just stand there. I don't put my arms around her. I don't show any affection. She means nothing to me now. She is an employee who will do as I ask. I step away and remove her arms from me.

"That will be the last time you ever touch me, Svetlana. Any time you try to do that again, I will break your arms. Do you understand me?"

She doesn't look at me but nods. I leave the room.

I tell Andrey and Ivan no one is to touch Svetlana, we are not together but I want her respected until I say otherwise. They both agree. I send her some money to buy some clothes with as I threw all her stuff away. With the money are instructions for her duties for now. I will make use of her in other ways, but for now, she teaches the girls and boys that are here, getting them ready for a new life from now on.

Twelve

Igor
Present

THE MEETING WITH THE GODFATHERS WENT WELL. THEY accepted Poppy as my stand-in. They were told it was only temporary, that I would be back at the realm soon enough, but that I would have Poppy by my side. When she told me she was pregnant, I paid for the best doctor to come see me and was elated there was an operation I could have to replace the two damaged discs in my spine, and I should hopefully walk again if I had the operation. I didn't waste any time. He had me on the operating table a day later. It was fucking hell, I had to have caregivers at home to help me, it was so fucking embarrassing, but Poppy couldn't do it. She was pregnant and getting bigger and bigger every day.

I've been training hard, real fucking hard, pushing myself to the absolute limits. The twins will be here soon and I am determined I want to be able to walk, I want to be a good papa and chase them around, playing horses on my hands and knees with them on my back, teach them to play ball or maybe taking them to ballet classes, who the fuck knows. We don't know what we are having, we wanted to leave it as a surprise. I just know I want to be a normal papa.

Ryker is my personal trainer, and he's been really tough with me. I told him right off to ignore any of my rants and to make me work. That if I threatened to kill him, to just ignore me, I wouldn't do it, or I hoped I wouldn't do it. I've been swimming a lot with him in the pool with me, trying to get my legs to work. He trains me in the gym next to the pool, it's all been upper body work, for now, I'm almost as ripped up top as he is, let's just say Poppy is enjoying it. The fact I can now lift her up to my face with no problems, even heavily pregnant, gets her going like a madwoman and she rides my tongue like there's no tomorrow. Her hormones are really kicking in the closer she gets to having the babies. Ryker has been working my legs for me. The first time I moved them on my own, I cried like a fucking baby. I had to call Poppy to come home quickly so I could show her. She cried along with me.

It's been the toughest few months of my life, with the surgery and therapy on my spine, and Ryker working me hard. I can now move my legs on my own. They are getting stronger and stronger. Ryker is increasing the weights on my ankles each day, making me lift them until the sweat is pouring from me. He gets me out of the chair and has me standing at some parallel bars he had installed. I started off slowly. One foot wanted to move, but the other didn't. Each day got better and better. I was not a quitter, although there were so many times I told him to fuck off. He just ignored me, like I told him to, he's a good guy. I eventually was able to shuffle my feet, one in front of the other. Until now, I could stand on my own but only with the help of a walking aid. Poppy doesn't know the progress I've made. I want to surprise her.

I was ready to show Poppy the other day when fucking Svetlana was standing in my apartment. Ryker came to get me from the gym and she was standing there, staring at me in his arms as he brought me down the stairs. I felt like a pathetic, weak man in the arms of another man, holding on to his neck for security while he brought me down. I was so angry. If I had a gun, I would have put a bullet straight between her eyes. I yelled at her to get out, she was just standing staring at me. I could see her trying to work out why I was in the arms of another man. The look of pity and sorrow on her face made me so fucking mad. If I could, I would have thrown her out the fucking window. She ran away crying. I could sense Ryker looking down at me. I looked at him.

"What? Don't fucking tell me who can and can't be in my own fucking apartment. Or who I can fucking yell at," I yelled at him.

He shrugged and placed me in the wheelchair. He went to sort out my food while I wheeled to the dining room and sat by the table waiting. I was so fucking angry right then. No one, except Steve and Sergei, knew about my paralysis. She's not stupid, she'll work it out. Why else would I have been carried by a grown-ass man. Ryker puts the food down and just stands there. I look to him and raise an eyebrow.

"If that's how you treat all your employees, then I sure as hell am glad I'm not one of them. You made her cry, Igor, for god's sake. Why were you so mean to her? Svetlana is a lovely girl."

I look up at him and eye him suspiciously.

"How do you know her?"

He looks a little taken aback at the hostility in my voice. He starts to move away.

"Answer my fucking question Ryker, how do you know her?"

He turns back and comes to stand by my side again.

"Not that it's any of your business, but I've known her for a while. Well, I didn't know her name until we just met here. I thought maybe she was your wife or girlfriend when I saw her standing there when I came down. It kinda made me mad. We've been fucking for a long time now, but…"

"You've been fucking but didn't know her name?"

He raises his eyebrow at me. He better explain.

"I can talk to my employees any way I fucking want to. Especially Svetlana. Now why didn't you know her name?"

He stares at me, crossing his arms over his chest, thinking if he should tell me or leave. I glare at him, giving him my death stare and I see him gulp slightly. He grabs the straps of his wifebeater with his thumbs pulling them together.

"We belong to a club, a sex club, and we always seek each other out to fuck. You don't know who is who in the club. You could fuck anyone, but we always look for each other. Please don't tell her I told you. She would kill me."

"Are you talking about The Hex?"

I watch his eyes widen. He nods at me.

"How do you know about that place? Don't tell me you used to go, oh god I bet you've fucked her haven't you. Just when I thought I really found someone I liked." He rubs his hands over his face and through his hair.

"No, I didn't use to go there to fuck. I own the fucking club, and I had no idea she had a membership. Svetlana and I go back a few years and she's worked for me a long time now. I can't stand her, yet I still seem to be protective of her. I can't believe she's a member. I'm surprised you are too. It's not exactly cheap to be a member there."

"Oh shit, please don't let her know I told you. I just asked her out on a date but then you buzzed and I brought you down and you yelled at her so she never agreed. I'll have to wait to see if she's at the club later."

I don't answer him. I eat my lunch and he leaves. It's not long before Poppy arrives back. She's getting so big now, it won't be long before the babies arrive. I don't tell her yet about me walking. I'm not in the mood after what happened earlier. Instead, she sits on the couch with her feet in my lap and I massage them for her. I watch as my queen falls asleep, she's exhausted, she needs to start cutting back on work. I know she has the refuge center she's setting up with Svetlana, plus the meetings. I'm going to cut back on all the meetings now. I think it's time I went back out there and did them from my car. I need to let my rivals know I'm still around.

It's been a few weeks and honestly, I think she's ready to pop. I canceled all her meetings, I still haven't shown her I can walk and I'm still getting better at it each day. When Ryker told me about Svetlana being a member of The Hex, I got onto Karol, my club manager, and asked for the information he had on Svetlana. He told me she had been a member for some years now, that it was Andrey who gave her a life membership. I couldn't fucking believe Andrey would do that and not tell me. Why would he do that and not tell me? I wanted answers but only she could give them to me. I'd asked Ryker when the last time was he was at the club with Svetlana, and I got the video footage from that night. I couldn't believe it when I saw her. I knew it was her straight away, but fuck me, she looked stunning. She was in a PVC catsuit that you could clearly see was crotchless and bottomless and titless. She had on those fucking red shoes I had bought her. I never even knew she kept them. I watched her saunter about the club and I watched as Ryker followed behind her. She knew he was there, it looked like a game they played. Most people wore masks at the club. It wasn't mandatory but most wanted to stay anonymous.

I knew it was her and him. They danced provocatively together. I watched as he bowed down, taking her tit into his mouth. I then saw his hand wander down and watched as he fingered her during the dance. She unzipped his leather trousers and pulled out his cock. They were in the dance room where anyone could join in. One woman tried to take over, pulling his cock until Svetlana hissed at her and she moved away. So Svetlana really had a hot spot for Ryker. I watched as they did this dance with each other. He would turn her around so her ass was on his cock, and I watched as he thrust into her. She bent over right in front of him, spreading her legs wider as she reached underneath her, either to play with her clit or play with his balls. I found myself getting fucking horny watching them. I could feel my cock starting to rise. This wasn't a new feeling. It happened often with Poppy, only she didn't realize it wasn't the Viagra doing it anymore. Why wasn't I telling my queen all this stuff? I need to let her know.

I watched this play out. I saw another man come and stand in front of Svetlana as Ryker was hammering into her ass. She lifted her head to see who it was. I think she maybe knew him. She took hold of his cock and started to suck on it. Ryker hadn't noticed, but when he did, he pulled her back up to face him, essentially pulling the cock from her mouth. He was being possessive. He picked her up, so she had to wrap her legs around his waist, and I watched closely as he entered her pussy slowly. I was fucking hard now. I felt so guilty. Poppy was out meeting Svetlana for lunch. I would hear anyone arrive from the ding of the elevators. I had to get my cock out, and I rubbed and pulled on my cock, watching these two go at it. I felt terrible. This was the woman I hated, but in fact, it could be anyone I was watching because you couldn't see her face. Only I knew it was her, Svetlana, the one I have never had as a woman, only a girl.

That made me feel sick. I stopped stroking and pulling my cock, and he deflated. I still watched them go at it. She had now let go of his neck and was leaned back. He was holding her by the hips, thrusting inside her. That same guy came back and put his cock in her mouth. She grabbed it and sucked on it like a popsicle. Ryker was not happy. He twirled her around in the opposite direction, then lifted her back up, taking her tit into his mouth. He now grabbed her by the ass and was fingering her ass while thrusting up into her hard. She started bouncing down on his cock, and then they both exploded. I could see the circle of people that had now surrounded them. Some were pleasuring themselves while watching, some were pleasuring the person standing next to them, and others were cheering as Svetlana and Ryker were frantically riding out their orgasms in front of everyone. That was fucking hot to watch. The best thing about it was, I didn't feel an ounce of jealousy. I thought I had a pang of it when I found out Ryker was fucking her, but I was wrong. I really didn't care who she fucked.

The twins are due any day now. Poppy is home constantly. I have had a few meetings for which I had Steve wheel me to the car, making sure the coast was clear before helping me into the back seat. I don't get out of the car, but I'm letting my team and my clients know I'm back for business. Once the twins are here, both Poppy and I will go to meetings together. We will have nannies to help with the twins. I haven't left her for the past week, just in case she goes into labor. I want to be there. I am not missing a minute of this.

Last week when she came home from her last meeting, it was an easy meet, she didn't have to kill anyone, I asked her to phone me when she was on her way up to the apartment. I waited for her as the elevator doors opened. I was standing there with open arms. She stopped and gasped. She ran to me. Well, waddled would be a better word, and slowly, but she managed to stop herself from jumping into my arms. We held each other so tight, she cried like a baby and I joined her.

"Where's your chair, Igor? I can't catch you if you fall, baby."

I smiled and took her cheeks to kiss her hard. She kissed me back, it started to get heated. My cock was rock hard.

She looked down. "Have you been taking Viagra without me being here?"

I laughed hard and nearly toppled over. I turned slowly. This was my first time not using a walking aid. I started to shake thinking if I fell she couldn't help me, but then Mavra appeared back at his post. I grabbed her hand and started to slowly take steps.

She stopped and gasped. "Igor, you're walking. You're doing it, oh Igor. I'm so proud of you right now. You've done it, you've defied the doctors who said you wouldn't walk." She hugged me tight and started crying into my chest. I hugged her back, leaning down to kiss her head.

"Мой ангел, my angel. I did this for you and for them," I say, patting her tummy. "I want to be the best papa to them. I want to be the husband you married. I have been working hard and no, I have not taken any Viagra for a while now. This is all you, you do this to me. My cock is working again because of how fucking sexy you are. Now come with me to the bedroom so you can ride to your heart's content."

We walk very slowly to our bedroom. What would normally have taken me a minute carrying her takes me ten minutes without carrying her. I'm wobbly and she keeps hold of my hand and arm as we go. My cock deflated, it took that fucking long, but once I was lying on the bed with a naked Poppy mounting me, he soon sprung back to life.

We've been at it countless times a day for the last few days now. I am currently laying on the bed with my gorgeous angel, riding me hard. I have her by the ass cheeks helping lift her up and down, she's huge and struggles sometimes. We both exploded together. I then lift her to my face where I proceeded to lick her. I stick my tongue inside her and she starts riding my face like there's no tomorrow. She's really grinding down hard on my face, it's getting hard to breathe, but I want her to have this. I spread her ass cheeks and stick a couple of fingers in there. The next thing I know, I feel like I'm drowning. My face is soaked. I can't quite comprehend what's happening, I try to breathe, try to catch a breath, my mouth is full of water, I try to gulp in air but I can't, I feel I'm going to suffocate and drown all at the same time. I try to lift her up off me, she screams out.

"Fuck, Igor, fucking hell."

It's not an orgasm scream, it's a blood-curdling scream. I gently lift her from my face, taking deep breaths as I do. I slowly sit up and lower her to my chest. I look at her face, her eyes are closed, screwed tight, and she's holding her tummy. She screams out again. It's like a blood-curdling scream. Panic starts to set in. I look at her pussy, I can see how wet it is, and it looks like it's open slightly and what looks like water is all over me.

"Мой ангел, what is it, what's wrong, angel? Speak to me, what the fuck is wrong."

She opens her eyes and bursts out laughing. I think hysteria is setting in. She grabs both my hands with hers, intertwining our fingers. I hold her up with them. Was the orgasm that good? She is laughing so hard until her eyes go as wide as saucers and I see the pain and worry on her face. She suddenly squeezes my fingers so fucking tight and digs her nails into my hands.

"My fucking water broke, you asshole. Don't just sit there. We need to get to the hospital." She lets out another ear-piercing scream.

Fuck. I can't move that fast. I slowly pry my hands from hers then lift her gently to the side of me so she can lay on the bed.

"Wait there, don't you move, just wait. It will take me a while to get dressed and get some clothes for you. There is no way either of us are going out naked."

I lift both my legs one by one to place my feet on the floor. Luckily my walking aid is next to the bed, just in case I needed the bathroom. I rush, well as fast as I can go, to the closet. I grab a towel to wipe my face, get dressed and grab clothes for Poppy, throwing them over my shoulder. I watch her as I move back to the bed. Her eyes are closed and she looks as though she is sleeping. I reach her and lift her up by both arms and swing her round to me.

"Here, put this over your head, lift your arms, baby."

She does, she's quite lethargic. It's just a maxi dress that will cover her up while we get her to the hospital. I phone for Steve who comes rushing into the room, bringing my wheelchair with him. I sit on it and put Poppy on my lap. He grabs her hospital bag and wheels us both out. It's quicker for us to drive to the hospital than wait for an ambulance to arrive. Sergei is waiting with the car running as we get to the basement car park.

It's been a bad few hours, Poppy was having problems with the babies. She was worn out and in so much pain with the contractions. They took her to the operating room when they were ready to pop out. I was with her, in my chair, the whole time. I stayed by her head, stroking her. I stood up so I could see what was happening and also try to keep her calm. It didn't work. She ripped holes in my hands and cussed me like a sailor. She was going to cut my cock off and feed it to someone. I couldn't make out who. I was trying not to laugh at her. The first one arrived. A boy. They held him up so we could both see him then took him to be cleaned. He didn't like that, he screamed the place down.

"He sounds just like his mama," I joked and she screamed as she started to push baby number two.

The baby got a little stuck and they had to help it by cutting her vagina so they could get it out quickly. Ouch. I bet that's going to hurt when the drugs wear off. They hold baby number two up for us to see. A boy. I have two fucking perfect boys. I cry, as does Poppy and as do both babies. I hug her hard, kissing her head.

"I am so fucking proud of you, мой ангел." I always call her my angel in Russian, she has always loved it. "You are amazing, the strongest woman I have ever known."

They bring the cleaned-up babies to us, both of them swaddled and both being quiet. They put one in her arms and the other in mine. We just stare at each of them. I can't tear my eyes away from each of them and Poppy. They ask me to leave while they just clean Poppy up and put in the stitches she needs. All I think is, well, she won't be riding my cock for a while. I know, not the best thing to be thinking after your boys have just been born.

They put her and the babies in a room and there is a cot for me so I can stay over. There is no way I would be leaving. I paid extra for the big private room for us all. I helped her try to feed them. Baby two didn't want to latch on, but baby one was straight in there. Like father, like son, I thought to myself. Poppy is worn out completely but she keeps waking and just crying. The nurse said it's natural, hormones or something.

Little Dimitri Igor, baby number one, and Nikolai Igor Ustrashkins are now a month old. The time has flown by. Poppy is nearly healed, thankfully, because she is driving me crazy, wanting my cock all the time. Great for me because I get to come but not so for her. I have had Ryker here each day making me walk. I can walk well with the help of a walking aid. I don't mind the aid, I feel it makes me badass. It means I can walk around carrying one baby while Poppy has the other, she tries to feed them one after the other rather than together, getting them into a routine. They are good boys. I melted when they were first put into our arms. I couldn't believe the love I had for them immediately, it's like my life is for them and Poppy only.

I will protect them all whatever the cost.

PART X

Svetlana

&

Igor

Thirteen

Svetlana

I HAVE JUST FOUND OUT THE BABIES WERE BORN LAST WEEK. I CRIED my fucking eyes out. They are back at the apartment playing happy fucking families, while I'm here in this seedy motel room fucking the most boring man there is. He's just told me they had the babies last week, he's only just telling me this now? I've seen him since last week. Why is he just telling me now? I've had it with him. This will be the last time. I don't need him for anything. He told me the babies were both boys. I left him there, I walked slowly back home. All I could think of was my baby.

I was crying when I got to my bedroom and I've now been holed up here for the last few days. My eyes are puffy, my head is hurting and my heart is broken. I've just looked at my phone and I have a few missed calls from Poppy. Great, just what I fucking need. I press dial on her name.

"Oh hey, Svetlana. I wanted to let you know I had the babies last week. I thought it best you hear it from me. Two healthy little boys. Dimitri and Nikolai, I would love for you to come and see them, if you would like to of course. I also have some news for you. How is everything with the refuge? When will the first girls be moving in? Do we have a date yet?"

Wow, she sounds quite chirpy but then she would be with *my love* and what should be my babies. The fucking bitch.

"Congratulations to you both, Poppy, that's amazing news. I trust you and the babies are all well?"

She goes on and on about them. She's an insensitive bitch, she knows what happened. I told her he made me get rid of my baby. Yeah, he will deny it and probably tell her it died In childbirth but it was still all on him. Once she's finished rabbiting on, I hang up. I can do this, I'm going to go and visit them, I promised I would and take all the pictures of the refuge with me, now it's completed, I just hope I don't crack when I see the babies for the first time.

I head out to buy some baby things, I need to go with gifts to show no hard feelings. I don't know if *my love* will be there, but I need to worm my way in somehow. I get some baby boy balloons, two each of everything, I buy lots of little boy clothes, some teddy bears and then some bits for Poppy, my best friend. Yeah, right. I feel such sorrow shopping for the babies, such emptiness, but it's for *my love* more than anything else. I head home laden down with gifts and I ring the apartment for them to let me up as I don't have a card for the elevator to take me up there. Once I reach the penthouse, I struggle through the elevator doors. Someone suddenly grabs the falling gifts from my arms. I look up and it's Ryker. I smile at him until I see Igor standing next to him, glaring at me.

"Thank you, Ryker," I say, glaring back at Igor.

"Who the fuck let you up here?" Igor scolds me. I glare daggers at him, ignoring him and not speaking as I head round to the living area.

Poppy is sitting with one of the babies on her breast. The other is in a bassinet next to her. I return her huge smile, she's glowing, the bitch. I put the gifts on the coffee table and set the weighted balloons down. I lean in and kiss her on both cheeks. We've done this the last few times we've met, it's friendship, it's what friends do and as we are now 'best friends' I felt we should do this too. The baby on her breast has finished and she is just taking him off when she holds him out for me to hold. I hesitate, gingerly opening my arms. She places him in them. I take him and wind him a little before I cuddle him, sitting down on the couch next to Poppy. I feel a tear slip from my eye as I look down into his beautiful face. He looks just like *my love*.

"This here is Nikolai, he's the demanding and greedy one. He always wants feeding. Dimitri here is a little angel," she says, lifting him out of the bassinet.

We each hold a baby, Igor's babies, and my heart tears open. This should have been Igor and me, not her. Why her? He is *my love*. I am his rightful queen. He told me on my fake eighteenth birthday I was his queen. Another tear falls as I look into his beautiful little face. He has a little squashed nose, his hair is blond, he looks adorable. This could have been me with our baby and Igor next to me. The tears slip out, trailing gently down my cheeks, Poppy notices.

"Oh Svetlana, I knew this would be hard for you. I'm sorry, I'm just so in love with them. I didn't think. Please forgive me. If this is too hard, I understand. Thank you for the gifts, that is so thoughtful of you."

I shake my head.

"It's okay, Poppy. They are beautiful, they look just like their papa with a mix of you. I am happy for you, truly I am," I lie through my teeth.

Another Oscar awarded to me for lying. I want her to think I'm okay with this. I want to get close to them. Become their aunty Lana.

"It reminds me of my sisters. I used to look after them all with my mama, to help her out. There were six of us in the end. I miss them. I spoke to Mama for the first time in a long time last week and she is upset. She says Vidana is missing and has been for a while. She was a little frantic about not hearing from her. I didn't tell her about the video of the Iranians, Poppy. I know you were getting your men to look into it but that was so long ago. I fear she is now dead." I watch her face turn pale. She is, I know it. "Poppy? What is it?"

"Our men have been looking. They had a lead a couple of months back but nothing came of it. We do have another lead, but I didn't want to get your hopes up. It was why I was asking about the refuge being ready. I'm hoping Vidana will be one of our first to use it."

I take in a deep breath. Is she serious or is she just saying that? I stare at her, not wanting to believe it.

"It's a good reliable lead, Svetlana. I am hopeful. It is what I wanted to tell you when I said I had some news. We have a man in our custody. Igor has him secured and we are going to work on him. I promised you we would find her and we haven't stopped looking. We think he is ready to talk, we may have her and many others for the refuge."

I put my hand to my mouth to control the sob that escapes. She shuffles over to me and comforts me, putting her arm around my shoulder. We sit there like that for a while. How ironic. The woman I hate and were both sat here holding *my love's* babies, and she's talking about rescuing my sister. I actually feel a little admiration for this woman. She knows I was with Igor. She knows I still love him and that I was pregnant with his child, yet she still wants me around and helps me. Maybe I have got her wrong, or maybe it's just these babies screwing with my mind.

I don't stay too long. I don't want the wrath of Igor again if he returns. One thing I did notice, he wasn't in a wheelchair. Just as I leave I decide to ask Poppy. Why not? I have nothing to lose.

"Poppy, if you don't mind me asking, what happened to Igor? I noticed he was out of his wheelchair. Is he okay now?"

She eyes me suspiciously. I know what Igor always says, never trust anyone and she's right not to.

"He just had a fall and ended up with a couple of slipped discs in his spine. He needed to take it easy for a while, with no walking. He is much better now, thank you." With that, I leave. I don't believe a fucking word of it. I go back to my room. I want to go to The Hex, I need a proper fuck. I know Ryker is out with Igor. I will just find someone else.

In my room I put on the new outfit I bought, it's a black corset full of studs, and my tits hang out over the top, the panties I have on are again crotchless, I hate having to undress in there, I always end up losing my clothes. I have on garters and patterned stockings and, as always, my red shoes which Igor bought me.

I'm in The Hex, it's really busy today. I walk around as usual. I have people groping me as I do but no one has caught my eye yet. I still look for Ryker, even though I know he's not here. I don't see anyone that even looks like him. I need someone tall and ripped to satisfy me. I grab a water and I sit at a table watching what's going on. I have a new red mask on today that covers most of my face, I've had a few men, and women, come and sit with me for a little while, but this woman who has just sat next to me is hot as fuck. I'd say she rivaled me. She sits right next to me, putting her elbow on the table and leaning her head on her hand to face me. She has beautiful green eyes and her lips are the brightest red lips to match her flame-colored hair that is cut in a mullet style. It suits her. She has on a red corset, only her tits are contained inside, not like mine. She raises an eyebrow at me and looks at my tits. I know what she's asking. I just nod very slightly. She moves closer still, then bends her head and flicks a nipple with her tongue. I push my chest out toward her and she starts to lick, then suckles on my tit, then moves over to the other one. She's so gentle the way she does this.

I lean my hands back behind me on the booth bench, jutting my chest out more. She alternates between each tit, she's looking at me, watching me closely and I'm watching her closely. We don't speak.

She carries on doing this for a few minutes, then her hand starts to caress me down my front until she's at my panties. She looks up into my eyes. I nod again slightly, giving her the go-ahead. To my surprise, I lean in and I kiss her on those full red lips of hers. She reciprocates until we're all dueling tongues. Her hand is at my tummy, she's very gently and softly caressing my belly button and lowering her fingertips over my panties to my pussy. My thighs are tight together at this point but as soon as I feel her finger slip between them I instinctively open them wide, giving her full access. She smiles on my lips and I smile back. Her fingers fondle around my pussy and my clit, very softly caressing me down there. She gently inserts first one finger then another and starts to move them inside of me, hooking around, trying to find my G-spot. Oh god, I love the feeling of her, I've never let a woman near me before, I always just wanted a cock but she's good.

I start to feel her tits through her corset, gently squeezing and kneading them, I spread my legs as wide as I can, then I feel a tongue flicking at my clit, it's not her tongue as that is currently dueling with my own, I don't really care at this point. I move my hand down to her pussy. I had no idea she was naked down there until just now. There are fingers already playing with her clit, it's not her fingers. They are currently inside me and on my tits. Someone is obviously under our table joining in. I start to feel myself getting close, I have her fingers inside, with her nails gently scraping me, but it adds to the feelings of arousal, and then the mystery tongue flicking and sucking at my clit.

I insert my fingers into her pussy, something I have never done to another woman before, only to myself. It's nice, it feels like mine but different because it's not me I'm doing it to. The other fingers that are on her clit join mine inside her, our fingers dueling in her pussy, she starts to gyrate on them, then her hand leaves my tit and she's pushing our fingers farther inside her, I do the same with her fingers in me. I grab them and gyrate, pushing them farther into me. The tongue is still sucking and flicking my clit and lapping at the cum dripping out of me. I want to taste her, I want to taste a woman. I pull my fingers from her and I twist my body around and bend my head to her pussy.

She still manages to keep her fingers in me, I take a lick at her pussy, it's difficult at this angle but I can just about do it. I try to get my tongue inside her, but I can't quite reach without breaking all other contact with each other, so I suck and lick at her clit, replicating what's being done to me by the stranger. We're both thrusting up, trying to get more friction from each other, both panting. I suck and suck as the stranger's fingers work her inside. It suddenly happens, she explodes, screaming out with her release, keeping hold of the fingers inside her, thrusting and thrusting, I'm lapping at her cum as it's squirting out of her, it tastes sweet, not as bitter as a man's cum, similar to my own.

I'm that excited doing this to her, with her working her fingers and the anonymous tongue at my clit, that I follow her and explode myself, screaming out my own release. I'm being pumped by her and sucked dry by the stranger as I writhe in my seat. This is fucking hot. My first time with a woman. Don't get me wrong, I've watched women on women plenty of times. I always thought about trying it, but I just always thought I wanted cock more than anything. We are both now forehead to forehead, panting and looking into each other's eyes. She licks around my mouth and I do the same to her. The anonymous person under the table seems to be licking both our pussies clean, alternating between them. I smile at this beautiful woman and she smiles back. We don't speak at all.

The stranger under the table has now stopped. I have no idea if it's a male or female. I turn my head to the side, still against this woman, and watch as Ryker emerges from under the table. I'd know his eyes anywhere. I'm kind of annoyed it's him, but elated it's him all at the same time. I feel a pang of jealousy that he had been finger fucking another woman while sucking on my clit, but I enjoyed it all. Maybe we should explore this woman more in one of the private rooms. I don't know what I want right now. I do know I need a good fuck, and I'm glad Ryker is here. I get up and take hold of the ties on the waistband of his leather trousers. I pull him along and enter one of the private rooms. Sometime later, fully satisfied from Ryker, we leave the club together. We have never done this before but he asked if

I fancied something to eat, besides him, of course, the cocky bastard that he is, but I agreed.

It's hot out in LA and I'm walking along in a long raincoat, granted I don't really have much on underneath so I'm not really that hot, but I get funny looks as we walk along. Ryker got changed into jeans and a plain black tee. He has his leather trousers, cuffs, and mask in his backpack. It's a really weird setup we have, we've been out on one date since I had my embarrassing run-in with Igor in his apartment, yet we've fucked constantly at The Hex. Our first date was just a get-to-know-you date. We didn't even kiss good night at the end. Ryker wanted to keep what we did at the club separate from our normal lives. I'm not sure how it's going to work, but he's the first person since Igor that I have felt anything for. We didn't speak about Igor on that date, neither of us brought my encounter up. I know he will want to know if we continue this.

"Svetlana, do you want to go home and get changed before we get some food?"

He looks sympathetically at me. I don't know why. I scowl at him. Is he embarrassed by what I have on?

"It's okay with me you staying like that, it's just I see the way people are looking at you in that coat and I know you can't take it off in the restaurant, not unless you want every man in the place ogling you, that is."

I see what he means. We aren't far from home.

"Okay, home is just up ahead. Let me stop in real quick and get changed. I agree, I don't think I can take my coat off in public." I laugh and he laughs with me. We approach my building, and I see the look on his face. "Do you want to just wait out here or in the lobby? I won't be long."

He looks kind of angry.

"You live here, but this is where Mr. Ustrashkins lives? I thought you said you were nothing to him, that you just worked for him?"

He's angry with me. He thinks I've been lying to him. I smile.

"I do work for him and yes, I also live here, in the building. I live on the ninth floor. I've always lived here since coming over from Russia."

He smiles back at me and blows out a breath in relief. I don't think I'm ready to tell him yet. I rush up to get changed and leave him in the lobby. When I come back down, I see him standing talking to Igor. Just my fucking luck. I never run into Igor down here, yet here he is. They only headed out a few hours ago. I didn't actually ask Ryker about it. We never talk about anything in the club, it's strictly sex as though we are strangers. I stand where I am, watching them both. I don't want Igor to be pissed at me again, not that I've done anything wrong. He can't be mad at me for walking in the lobby. I live here. Watching them together, I can see why I am attracted to Ryker. They are a lot alike. I find I'm gravitating more and more toward Ryker. I go to the club more in search of him and I do want us to take this a lot further and go out more and find out about each other.

I'm lost in my own little world thinking about Ryker when I notice Igor looking at me. I see the anger cross his face. He cuts his conversation with Ryker immediately and he hobbles over to me using a walking aid. I smile as he approaches, but I'm scared shitless he's going to scold me again.

"Hi Igor, how are you?" I smile at him, he doesn't return the smile, instead he squints his eyes at me.

"Ryker tells me he's waiting on you, that you're going out on a date."

Why is he angry about that? It's none of his business who I date. I look past him and see Ryker standing with his hands in his front jeans pockets, watching us. I see the quizzical look on his face. I nod and look down.

"Well, have a good night then."

I look up to him, startled.

"I thought you were going to scold me for some reason. You didn't answer my question either. How are you doing, Igor? Poppy tells me you had a spinal injury. Oh, and congratulations on the babies by the way. I saw them when Poppy asked me up. They look like you, Igor. Our baby would have looked like you."

"Don't even fucking go there, Lana. Our baby is dead. You've had plenty of years to get over it," he grits out at me with a disgusted look on his face.

I don't understand the hatred he seems to have for me.

"Don't look at me like that. I told you when you came back, there was nothing between us and there never would be. You've tried to screw my life up too many times. It's a good thing I have a strong woman in Poppy standing by me. No matter what Lana, you could never walk in her shoes and do what she does."

I feel the tears slipping down my cheeks. He leans into my ear so no one around can hear.

"Turn off the fucking waterworks because they don't work with me. You're lucky Poppy likes you and wants you around. If I had my way, I would have done away with you a long time ago. Now move out of my way."

I stand, shocked at the venom in his voice.

"How can you be like this with me, Igor? I love you. I always have and I always will. I have only ever loved you. It should have been me Igor, not her, ME," I shout at him. I'm so angry with him.

He looks startled at first, that I would actually answer him back.

He leans back into my ear. "You ever raise your voice to me again with people present and I will drag you down to the basement by your fucking hair, and you know what goes on down there. Do you understand me, Lana?"

He leans back to look me in the face and I look straight into his eyes. He smirks at me. My hand is itching to slap him, but I know he will do as he says and kill me.

"What should have been you?" he asks.

I gulp but stay staring straight into his eyes.

"I'm your rightful queen. It should have been me standing by your side with babies. Not her," I grit out and turn to leave before he has a chance to say anything else.

I don't look back as I walk up to Ryker who has moved closer to where I was standing. I don't know if he heard any of that. He looks at me, cocking his head to the side slightly and looking worried. I wipe at my eyes.

"You ready?" I ask angrily, walking past him.

If he follows then we are on for a date still, if he doesn't I'll just grab a coffee and come back home. I don't turn. I don't want to know if Igor is there or if Ryker is following me. I just walk. I'm almost at the coffee shop when someone grabs my arm. I'm ready to swing and punch whoever it is, it's Ryker. He holds his hands up as though in surrender. I don't know if he was behind me all this time or if he just caught up to me now. I must look a mess. Walking here just thinking of the hateful way Igor looked at me. Like he wouldn't spit on me if he passed me in the street. He hates me. I could see it in his eyes, and the venom coming from his words. I think he would actually kill me if he could. If Poppy would let him. I still don't know why he has this kind of hate for me.

Ryker must see the look on my face. He steps close to me and takes me into his arms, holding me to his chest. I didn't realize I needed this so badly. I cry into him. He strokes my head, holding me close. He whispers, "Hey, do you want to talk about it?"

I look up into his face. I search it, he's being sincere and genuine. I nod.

"Do you still want to go eat or would you prefer to come to mine where there is no one around?"

I raise an eyebrow at him.

"Just to talk, Svetlana." He smiles at me then leans down and kisses the tip of my nose.

"Okay. Are you sure you want all this shit though?"

He scowls at me.

"It's not shit, Svetlana, to be there to support someone." He's a little annoyed I even asked that.

"Okay, let's go."

He grabs hold of my hand and starts walking. I have no choice but to walk with him or be dragged along.

"It's a bit of a walk or we could get an Uber. I also need to stop and get some food for us. I don't have much in right now."

He surprises me. I can't believe he isn't taken.

"Ryker, do you live alone?"

He turns to look at me. He hesitates before answering. "Yes."

That's it. One word and he hesitated and looked away when he said it. Hmm, something's not right here.

"I'm okay with walking, by the way. Have you always lived on your own?"

He doesn't turn to look at me this time and he doesn't say anything. This stinks. If he has someone, then I would rather not waste my time.

"Ryker," I prompt him.

He stops and hangs his head, letting go of my hand.

"Hey, look I'm sorry I asked, but if you're with someone, I would rather know now."

He slowly starts to move again and I just stand there, not moving, watching his back. It takes a few minutes before he turns, realizing I'm not following him. I tilt my head to the side and he mirrors me. He stands with a wide stance, putting his hands in his front pockets. I don't move, neither does he. People walk past us and between us, not giving a damn. We stand staring like this for what feels like an age. I'm waiting for him to explain and he's waiting for me to walk to him. I cross my arms over my chest and watch his eyes narrow as I do. He slowly walks up to me.

"Look, I don't have anyone. I haven't had anyone for a while now. I was in a relationship, she died and I don't want to talk about it out here. If you need to know, I will tell you when we get to my apartment. It's not something I blurt out to strangers." He turns and starts walking again.

Ouch, that hurt. It's not like we haven't fucked a thousand times. I would hardly say we were strangers. I know we don't know anything about each other. But isn't that the whole point of these dates? I like Ryker. I mean, I really like him.

I catch up to him and I link his arm. He looks down to me and smiles. We walk in silence for a good twenty minutes.

"How far is it till we get there, Ryker?" I ask, thinking we should have taken that Uber. He smiles down at me and out of nowhere he stops and holds my head in his hands and bends slowly to kiss me. It's the first kiss we've had. I know we fuck, but we never kiss. He pulls back.

"Sorry, I just needed that. Come on, it's not that far now. The mini-mart is just up this road and my apartment is about a three minute walk from there." He takes my hand and we walk a little quicker. He seems to be in a hurry now.

Entering the mini-mart, he grabs a basket. We walk around and he places lots of things into it. It's full and looks heavy. We head out and he's right, his apartment is not far. It's not a bad place, a tall building, it's not shabby and he is on the sixth floor. His apartment is surprisingly feminine. With pillows and throws on the couch, there are plants scattered around, and there are pictures on the walls. He even has ornaments and candles scattered around. It's tidy. This is so weird. I stand just looking around while he puts his stuff away in the kitchen. It's open plan with just an island as a partition between the kitchen and the living area. I turn and he's watching me take it all in. I smile.

"This is not what I expected from a man. I thought it would be very minimalistic, but wow, this is nice. Very feminine." I walk to see who the photos on the wall are of.

There are a few that look like they might be his family. On the unit underneath these, where the TV stands, there is a picture in a frame of Ryker hugging a woman who is looking up into his face with so much love and admiration. They look happy and in love. I pick it up to take a closer look. I feel him move up behind me.

"That was Danni," he says quietly. "She died just over two years ago now." I hear the sorrow in his voice. I want to ask him questions but then don't want to push him. "We were married."

I turn to look at him. I still have the picture in my hand. I look at the sadness in his eyes. He loved her. I can see it hurts him. I look at his finger but don't see a wedding ring. He notices, he pulls out a chain around his neck and there are two wedding bands on the chain. I've never noticed this before, he's always naked from the waist up in the club and I don't ever recall seeing the chain before.

"I don't wear them in the club. I can see the confused look on your face."

"What happened to her? I can see you love her." He plays with the bands, then turns and sits on the couch. I follow and kneel next to him.

"She got sick. We didn't know what was wrong. We were childhood sweethearts, lived near each other, went to school together, fell in love. We were voted prom king and queen, everyone thought we would last a lifetime, so did we. I went to the doctors with her. She was scared. She kept on bleeding when we had sex. It turned out she had cervical cancer. The fucking big C killed her. She was so young, cervical cancer killed her so fucking young." He runs his hand over his face and through his hair. He doesn't look at me. He leans his head back and looks up to the ceiling. I reach over and take his hand in mine and stroke the top with my thumb, soothingly. He doesn't look at me, and it's a few minutes before he continues.

"It was aggressive. By the time she went to the doctors, it had spread to her bowels and bladder. They were going to operate, but she was having trouble breathing and was in pain. She had so many tests and scans, it was too late for her, it had advanced to her lungs. We did hospice care at home, not here. She wanted to stay at her parents' house and we lived there for three months. That's how much time she had. We got married as soon as we realized we didn't have much time. It was beautiful, in her parents' back yard. We were married for seventy-three days before she passed away in my arms." I feel so bad for him, I can see how much he is still hurting. I place the frame down gently on the table and I scoot closer to him. I see tears on his cheeks and I take his head and lower it to my lap where we stay for a while not speaking, but with me stroking his hair.

He turns on his back with his head in my lap and he looks up to me.

"You remind me of Danni in some ways. Not your looks, but your personality. She could be a little firecracker at times and I've seen that in you." I stroke his forehead, then lean down and kiss it. He smiles. "Tell me, Svetlana, what is your story? What do you have to do with Igor? I cringe every time he treats you the way he does. It makes me want to punch him to shut him up. I know that wouldn't be a good idea, not with him being who he is."

I look away, still stroking his forehead. I look out of the window to my left. Do I tell him? How much do I tell him? Igor always says never trust anyone.

"It's okay. We can save that for another day if you don't want to talk about it now. I understand he is our boss and although we know each other intimately, we don't know each other at all. We can take this slowly."

I look back to him and nod slightly, smiling at him.

"Okay, then what are you going to cook for me?" He smiles, gets up, kisses me on the lips then wanders into the kitchen. We spend the night eating, drinking, and telling each other about our families and growing up. I never mentioned *my love* all night.

Fourteen

Igor
Present

EVERY TIME I SEE HER I WANT TO REACH OUT AND WRAP MY HANDS around her throat, squeezing the life out of her, watching her eyes bulge out and hopefully pop, watch as she takes her last breath. I don't know how it went from loving her to loathing her with a passion. I suppose passion is the operative word. I think I was in love with her, but it's nothing like what I feel for Poppy. With Poppy, I feel she is the oxygen that I need to survive, to breathe, to live. Svetlana, I think it was more lust than love. I couldn't have her so I wanted her more, but then when I could have her I couldn't get enough of her, until the day we found out she was pregnant. Then I wanted to rip her open and kill them both. I hated myself for thinking like that, but at the time I never wanted a family. I loathed my papa in the end, and I didn't want to bring children into this world to end up loathing me. I think having your own child loath you has to be one of the hardest things anyone could take. She lied to me about so many things, I can never trust anything she says to anyone. I tried to warn Poppy, I've told her I don't want Svetlana around and if I had my way, I would have killed her a long time ago. Poppy wanted to give her a chance. She said there was something about Svetlana. She was a lost soul and needed someone to capture that soul. It's bullshit if you ask me.

When I saw her today laden down with presents and balloons for my boys, my fucking babies, I flipped. I wanted to throttle her there and then. If it wasn't for the fact Ryker was with me, I think I would have done. I don't know what she's playing at, visiting my babies. I see the look in her eyes when she's with Poppy. I see the hatred hidden, the false façade she has going on.

No, she is one person I would never trust. I'm just on my way back to Poppy and my boys when I see Ryker in the lobby. He sees me and comes over.

"Hey Ryker, did you forget something? We don't have another session today, do we?"

He looks a little pissed, but I don't know why.

"Hey, no we don't. I'm just waiting for someone."

I raise my eyebrow at him. Who he fucks is none of my business. He's being a bit guarded with me, and now I want to know. I know he works for me and I've talked about hiring him, to keep my men in shape, get him on my books. I like Ryker, he's a good guy and I don't think I would be standing here, granted with a walking cane, if it wasn't for him and his hard ass, not taking any of my shit. Not many people get away with talking to me the way he does, but then I know it's for my own good.

"Who?"

He furrows his brow, looking into my face, then his eyes narrow slightly. He knows not to mess with me. He's seen me with my men, he knows I'm someone not to be messed with, but he doesn't know exactly who I am, unless he's been asking around. He widens his stance slightly, putting his hands in his front pockets, then very slightly tilts his head. I see it, I see everything. He's standing, bracing himself ready for war.

"Svetlana," is all he says.

He must see the look on my face, the hate that suddenly flashes over it. I straighten up, lifting my cane as I do, not needing it to just stand here. It helps me stay balanced when walking. I see his defenses go up the moment he recognizes the look on my face.

"We have a date, I just want to get to know her, I like her."

I scoff at his words.

"Hey, you can fuck who you like. I don't give a shit, but just be warned about her. She is not to be trusted. She lies. A lot."

He shrugs but relaxes at my words, knowing I'm not going to do or say anything. We talk about my next session until I feel her eyes on me. I know she's there. I turn and glare straight into her eyes. What the fuck. I leave Ryker standing there and walk over to her. I don't want to see her or talk to her, it gets harder every time, thinking of killing her.

"Hi Igor, how are you?"

How does she actually have the nerve to speak to me and try being nice to me? What a stupid bitch she is. I just want to leave before I do something, like kill her.

"Ryker tells me he's waiting on you, that you're going out on a date."

She looks beyond me, probably looking at Ryker, who I have no doubt is watching us. Good.

"Well, have a good night then." I go to move but she steps to the side to stop me.

"I thought you were going to scold me for some reason. You didn't answer my question either. How are you doing, Igor? Poppy tells me you had a spinal injury. Oh congratulations on the babies, by the way. I saw them when Poppy asked me up. They look just like you Igor, our baby would look like you."

"Don't even fucking go there, Lana. Our baby is dead. You've had plenty of years to get over it."

God, she's still delusional. She looks at me sympathetically.

"Don't look at me like that. I told you when you came back, there was nothing between us and there never would be. You've tried to screw my life up too many times. It's a good thing I have a strong woman in Poppy standing by me. No matter what Lana, you could never walk in her shoes and do what she does."

I see the tears slip from her eyes as she takes in what I am saying.

"Turn off the fucking waterworks because they don't work with me. You're lucky Poppy likes you and wants you around. If I had my way, I would have done away with you a long time ago. Now move out of my way."

"How can you be like this with me, Igor? I love you. I always have and I always will. I have only ever loved you. It should have been me Igor, not her, ME," she shouts at me, looking into my face.

The bitch actually thinks she can speak to me like that in public. I lean down and get close to whisper in her ear.

"You ever raise your voice to me again with people present and I will drag you down to the basement by your fucking hair, and you know what goes on down there. Do you understand me, Lana?"

She looks me straight in the eye as I stand up tall in front of her, I sneer at her with contempt.

"What should have been you anyway?" I want to know what she's talking about.

"I'm your rightful queen. It should have been me standing by your side with babies. Not her," she spits at me with so much venom in her voice as she turns to leave before I can do or say anything more to her.

I watch as she walks past Ryker, he's standing watching us both, I see the look on his face, it's a 'what the fuck' face. I raise an eyebrow then turn to head up to my wife. I need to be with her, she grounds me.

Poppy is asleep when I get to our apartment, she's in the bedroom with the two bassinets. I try to be as quiet as I can, I don't want to wake any of them. I know Poppy is struggling with breastfeeding so she gets sleep when she can. We've been lucky that both boys sleep pretty much the same time. I quietly look into each bassinet and the love I have for my boys is unreal. Who would have thought you could instantly fall in love with something you don't know. They are a part of me, they are my flesh and blood. I've sworn to Poppy on so many occasions that I will do everything to protect them. These precious little boys are going to depend on me to guide them. I will make sure I guide them through life, I vowed I would.

I leave them, grab a coffee, and head to my office. I know I loathe Svetlana, but ever since the video we saw of Vidana with the Iranians, I promised I would find her and bring her here. Not for Svetlana but because she was caught up in something that had nothing to do with her, it was all about me and the Iranians getting revenge on me. I feel guilty she was caught up in it. My men have been trying to find her. We knew she was still alive at one point, but now we are not so sure. My informant told me she was being kept alive to use as leverage against me, that Farhad Javid was not the leader I thought he was. He was a soldier in an arms cartel. I have the cartel name, at least from my latest intel, who is in my basement. When the nanny arrives later, Poppy and I will be going down to see how the interrogation is going. We believe the man we have is much higher up in the cartel, higher than Farhad was. We will try to extract what we can about finding Vidana.

The babies wake up, I hear them both crying, I have a baby monitor I carry around with me. I try to get to them before they wake Poppy but by the time I get to the bedroom she already has Nikolai feeding from her breast. I move over to Dimitri who is still in his bassinet crying, I lift him out and sit next to Poppy on the bed. She looks worn out. I know she is tired from having to keep feeding the babies all the time. She refuses to have a nanny full time because as she tells me no one else can feed them. I have some baby equipment on the way. Who knew there was a pump where she can pump out her milk and that way I can help feed them? I envy my boys. I have to wait until nighttime when we are in bed together before I can have some milk. She says I'm soothing when I suck her tits, because I'm gentle. I cherish her. I'm always gentle. I can't wait until we can make love for the first time in what feels like forever. We had plenty of sex but to actually make love, not since before I was shot, what with me being in a wheelchair and then with the babies arriving just as I learned to walk. I need to be in her soon though.

FUCK, the nanny let us down last night. Poppy has been trying to find a new one for us as ours is currently unavailable as she is in hospital. It took forever to find her. Vetting nannies is harder than you think. We've had no luck and we need to get to the basement to carry on with the next stage of the interrogation. Every hour that passes is an hour Vidana could be killed if she is still alive. Poppy just told me that Svetlana is on her way up to watch the babies. I have no words for her. I just sit behind my desk staring at her.

"Be nice to her when she gets up here, Igor. She's doing us a favor, remember?"

Is she for real? Trusting Lana with my boys. The woman has an unhealthy obsession with me and is mentally unstable in my opinion. She told me herself just yesterday that it should be her here with my babies. Fuck.

"No, Poppy. Just no. The woman is unhinged. I do not trust her with my babies." She's glaring at me like I'm the crazy one. I can see the anger on her face.

"Yes, Igor. She's used to looking after babies and we know her, one of us extremely well," she snarls at me.

Fucking hell, she's mad at me now. I rub my hands over my face and through my hair.

"I would rather you stay here and leave me to the interrogation then. I DON'T FUCKING TRUST HER," I shout, making her jump.

She has Dimitri in her arms and he jumps at her jumping and then starts crying.

"Now look what you've done. Do not shout at me, they can sense when we are angry and it scares them. Never shout in front of them again and curb the fucking language around them."

I laugh, actually belly-splitting laugh. She huffs and walks out of my office. I spend the next two hours trying to find someone else to look after the babies. Polina is not around as much, but she is too old to look after two babies. One is hard enough. I know Lana helped raise her sisters, I know she can look after them, but I don't want her near them or me, but definitely not near them. I don't know her mind and what she may do. She lost her baby in childbirth, granted years ago, but still, you never know what that does to a woman mentally. I have no feelings regarding that situation at all. Harsh I know, but in my mind, she tried to trap me, then finding out about her age. That just screwed with me.

I know it was years ago now, but I need to follow up on that. She threatened me with a letter and statutory rape, something I never told Poppy about. Maybe if I tell her, she will kill Lana herself. I need to find the birth and death certificate. I've asked Lana a few times to show them to me but she never did. I left it as it was. The baby was dead, so no need. But something has been playing at the back of my mind ever since my boys were born. I remember when she came back, she told me she got rid of the baby, then she told me it was adopted and then it died in childbirth. She couldn't seem to make up her mind, Lana just seems to be a compulsive liar. What if she lied and it didn't die? What if I do have a kid out there somewhere? If I do, and she is capable of leaving it to return to me, she is certainly not right in the head to look after my babies.

Poppy has just walked in on my conversation with yet another agency to send over some resumes for nannies. She frowns at me, standing there with her arms crossed just under her tits, giving them a lift. Not that they need it with the size they are. My eyes automatically go to her tits when she does this. I lose concentration and just tell the agency to email me the resumes and I will follow up on them. It doesn't help this situation, but we need to get it sorted. I end the call and lick my lips.

"You are so fucking hot, Mrs. Ustrashkins, I want to fuck you bent over this desk. It's been forever since I have been able to even consider doing that, мой ангел."

I stand and walk around to perch on the edge of my desk and reach out to pull her into my arms. I know she's pissed at me. I start to kiss her neck, it works, she gives me access, I then move around and down and kiss along her collarbone, then dip to her tits. I fucking love the globes they are at the moment. I am gentle with her as I move her top away and unfasten the nursing bra. I know it's not sexy but she's fucking sexy enough. I very gently kiss and lick her tit, taking her nipple into my mouth and very gently suck. I know she gets so sore and tender with feeding the babies which is why I am as gentle as I can be. She moans. I move to the other side and do the same there. I know it's too soon for sex but I want to taste her. I slowly unzip her jeans. I slide them down over her hips, still sucking and drinking her milk. I need to make sure it's only tiny amounts, the boys need it more than me. I pull away and I turn her gently so she has the desk to her ass. I lift her up. I need her to stand up on the desk so I can get to her. I can't kneel down yet with my injury. I help her out of her jeans and panties. I get her to spread her legs. This is where I belong, between her legs, worshiping this amazing goddess in front of me.

"Igor, we can't have sex yet, it's too soon. I need time to heal from the deliveries."

I smile up at her. "I know, мой ангел, I am desperate for a taste of you. I will be so gentle with you, I promise. If I do hurt you, you must tell me to stop. Okay?"

She nods and she looks nervous. I smile at her as I put my mouth to her pussy, maintaining eye contact all the time. I swipe my tongue out, getting a taste. She's wet and ready for me. I very gently use my tongue to move to her clit, I flick slowly then swirl my tongue around it. I watch her all the time, she's panting and biting her lip trying to not make a noise. I know she gets very vocal when we are in the thick of it. She likes to scream. I have the baby monitor on my desk, so I move and shut the office door.

"There, no need to suppress the noises I fucking love."

She smiles at me as I lower in front of her again and carry on with my tasting session. She has stitches still which I stay away from, I don't enter her pussy, I don't want to inflict any pain on her so I stick to licking, flicking, and sucking her clit. She's grabbing my head, trying to get more friction. I refuse to let her do that. I don't want to hurt her. I go wild on her clit, my hands are on her ass kneading it, and before I know it, she's squirting all over my face, trying to suppress her screams as I lick her dry.

"I fucking love you, мой ангел. So fucking much."

I help her down and she sits me in the chair while she takes my cock into her mouth to return the favor. I'm just blowing my load when the penthouse phone goes. We ignore it until I'm sucked dry, and it rings again. I'm annoyed when I answer it because it disturbed us and I'm out of breath.

"What?" I shout down the phone. "Fuck," I say and press the button to let her up.

"What's wrong, who was that?" I scowl at her.

"What time did you tell Lana to be here? You could have fucking warned me."

I see the look go from anger for shouting at her to amusement because she knows I'm angry Lana is the one that disturbed us. Just then we hear the elevator door ping open. We both get dressed and walk out together. I have my sweats on. I have them hanging low and I make a show of straightening my cock out as Lana steps round the corner. I see her looking at my hand and what I'm doing, and her mouth falls open. I kiss Poppy hard on the mouth.

"Hmm, I can taste us mixed together. Thanks for sucking my cock and letting me taste you, мой ангел."

I swat her ass playfully as she scowls at me, knowing exactly what I'm doing. I look to Lana as I walk past, heading to my room for a shower. I make a show of licking my lips and around my mouth, I take a finger and wipe around it and suck it, as though still tasting Poppy. I see the look of hurt, sorrow, embarrassment, and then anger wash over her face. I smirk at her, knowing full well I got to her. I turn and walk backward, carefully using my cane.

"My queen, I won't be long. Then we can get going. Unless you want to join me in the shower?"

I playfully raise my eyebrows. She squints her eyes at me, annoyed. I wink at her then turn my back and whistle as I go. The babies are in our room still. Poppy wants them with us for the first few months so she can feed them easily, which I have no problem with. I open the door quietly as I don't want to disturb them, I tiptoe into the bathroom and take a quick shower. Entering my bedroom after my shower, again quietly, so as not to wake the babies, I stop at the door. Poppy is just picking Dimitri up and Lana is standing with Nikolai.

They both turn to look at me as I cough. I'm standing naked in the doorway to MY fucking bedroom. I watch Lana take me all in, keeping her eyes on my cock, she licks her lips. I scowl at her, Poppy turns to see what I'm scowling at. Lana quickly diverts her attention to my baby, she has MY fucking baby in her arms and my heart starts pumping fast, not because it excites me, no, it fucking terrifies me. I can feel myself getting all worked up. I move without realizing, and I take Nikolai from her.

"Get out of my fucking room, now," I shout in her face, still naked but I don't give a fuck, it's not like she hasn't seen it before. I see the hurt on her face as she turns to walk out.

"Lana, wait. Here, take Dimitri into the living area and I will be right behind you with Nikolai." Poppy passes Dimitri to Lana after I just took Nikolai from her. What the fuck. Lana takes him and walks out of the room, slowly. She shuts the door and Poppy turns on me.

"What the fuck, Igor, Lana is here to look after them. Of course she's going to hold them. Give her a fucking chance, will you? She's doing us a favor, not the other way around." Nikolai starts to cry in my arms. I hold him up to me and rock him slightly, whispering for him to shush. I turn and scowl at Poppy. Very quietly and in a hushed singsong voice so as not to upset Nikolai.

"What the fuck, Poppy, I don't care. It fucking terrifies me she's here to look after my babies. I don't know what she will do to them. She's unstable, I told you this."

She laughs at me, she actually fucking laughs at me. I scowl at her.

"You are so funny when you are mad but trying very hard not to speak mad. I should have you hold one of the boys constantly. It might calm you down, stop you shouting all the time." She thinks this is funny, I don't. I hand Nikolai to her.

"Well, you can stay here and I will go deal with the situation in the basement on my own. I just thought it would have been good for us, doing something together, you know, something we haven't done yet." Again I say this in a hushed singsong voice. She laughs. I scowl, she leaves. A few minutes later I'm in the closet getting dressed when Poppy walks in. She gets changed. We both like to wear our suits when on business, no matter what that is.

"Where are the babies? You've left them both with her, haven't you? Fuck, I don't like this, Poppy. It fucking terrifies me and you know nothing ever terrifies me."

She strokes my cheek.

"I trust her. I don't know why. She's trying to redeem herself and let's face it, what we are doing is for her sister anyway. She won't hurt them, Igor. If she hurt them she knows she would pay with her life. I've already told her this. We are friends now. She'll be coming up more as we finalize the finishing touches on the refuge. It will be ready to start helping girls very soon. You know I would never put our boys in danger Igor, trust me."

I still don't know. I do know that if Lana did hurt them that Poppy wouldn't hesitate to kill her. Poppy doesn't know Lana like I do. She's definitely unhinged.

Poppy makes sure Lana has everything she needs. I stay in my office, I'm too riled up about leaving them with her. I would prefer Poppy stay here. I'm going to demand she stay. I don't fucking care. I hear them talk through the baby monitor, I hear Poppy telling Lana we won't be long but this is something we have to do to help find Vidana. Lana is so thankful that we are doing this. Listening to them, I think Poppy may be right. Maybe she won't do anything to the babies because we are after all helping find Vidana, but this is Lana we are talking about. She only cares for herself and what she wants.

We are on our way down to the basement. I tried to demand she stay but she just laughed at me. Standing in the elevator car, we don't speak but we hold each other close. I don't know what I would do without this woman, it's unbelievable how she and now the boys have become my whole life. We head to the room the Iranian cartel guy is in. He's tied up by his wrists above his head and hanging naked. I can see he's wet. My men have had cold water dripping on his head for hours. He's also got no toenails, and he's got slash marks across his torso. I see blood on the floor. He's not given much up yet but we need to press on with this as time is precious. I have a picture of Vidana, it was a still taken from the video they showed Lana, they sent it to her phone as a reminder.

"Do you know where this girl is?" I ask as he is lowered to floor level, even though he can't stand on his feet.

He doesn't look, I grab his hair and show him the picture. He screws his eyes shut. I let go and move over to my table of instruments. I grab two claw-like implements, these are eyeball cages. They pry his eyes open, keeping his eyelids pinned up. I try to place them in his eyes. He starts to struggle, Poppy has a pole, it's like a cattle prod, it electrocutes. She stabs him with it. His body jolts for a few minutes, then he stills. I place the eye-openers on him.

"Now look at the picture. Do you know where she is being held?"

He has no choice but to look, but he doesn't speak. Poppy comes back, but this time she has a knife. She slashes at his chest in a quick crisscross, not too deep, but deep enough to open his flesh and bleed. She moves away and comes back, opening her hand she has salt. I love this woman. She starts to rub the salt in the open wounds. He screams out, then she gets bleach and splashes his torso in that.

"Мой ангел, can you grab me the penis cup please?"

He would look startled if his eyes weren't pinned up. Poppy passes me a cup.

"Now this little thing here is full of bleach. It has a rubber seal on the top so I can put your cock in there and no matter how much you move, it will not come off. It has to be removed by hand, and unfortunately as yours are above your head, that's not going to happen anytime soon. This isn't your normal toilet bleach, this is industrial strength bleach, in fact, this is what they use to clean crime scenes. Now putting your cock in bleach is not recommended by the medical experts because, well, let's just say your cock will burn and start to dissolve. Now are you going to tell me where this girl is being held? This is your last warning before the cock gets bleached?"

I laugh at him and Poppy joins in. I lean over and kiss her. I know it's not professional, but this is making me fucking hard having her here doing this with me.

"Fuck you, asshole," he shouts.

I turn back to face him, grabbing his cock as I do and wedging it tightly into the little silicone cup. He screams out at the burning sensations. I wiggle the cup around a bit making sure his cock gets a good soaking. I know this will burn like hell as the bleach travels up his urethral meatus, or his pee hole as most call it. I personally couldn't imagine the pain of it. He squirms as he feels the burning. He starts to shout and tears cascade down his face. One because his eyes are pried open still and also because the bleach is burning.

"You ready to tell me where she is yet?"

He doesn't speak.

"Come on, мой ангел, let's get a drink and let him think about it."

She moves forward and pokes him with the cattle prod a couple more times. I have Sergei raise him up off the floor, and we leave him hanging there for about thirty minutes. When we return, I ask him again if he knows where she is. He tells me to fuck off.

"Time to get serious. Sergei, lower him." I move up to him. "Okay, have you heard of the three wise monkeys?"

He stares at me. He doesn't speak.

"Just in case you don't know, we have the first monkey who cannot see, the second monkey who cannot speak, and the third monkey who cannot hear. As you are not speaking, I will do the first one on you. That way once I've popped the one eye, you may speak before I do the second eye."

I move over to the table and walk back with a huge syringe, it's good I have his eyes pinned open, it makes this easier. The syringe is full of water with a little bit of bleach, just to add to the pain, the idea is that I keep blowing the eyeball up with liquid until it gets so big it pops, rendering him blind in that eye. He screams out as I put the syringe right into the front of his eye, into his pupil. He tries to move his head, but I have Poppy hold it still from behind. I smile at her with all the love and admiration I have for her. My heart melts when she smiles back. I've emptied the one syringe and am now on my second, he's screaming as the liquid starts to fill up his eyeball. I watch the bulbous eye getting bigger and bigger, three syringes full and his eye is now huge and looks ready to pop. The eyeball is already a sack of gel-like fluid and adding this liquid with no outlet just forces the eyeball to lose its shape and the only thing it can do is stretch. It doesn't look very pretty. Once it bursts, without surgery to replace the cornea, lens, etc. he will be blind in that eye. Just a little bit more. There it goes. It pops and the fluid and gel spill out all down his face. He screams loud. I wait until he stops.

"Now you have one good eye left, it won't last for long unless you tell me where she is." I hold the picture of Vidana up to his good eye. He still doesn't say anything. This is going to take longer than I thought. I don't want to ruin his good eye until later. I have something I want him to see. The next stage is his hearing. I have to leave the tongue until last otherwise he won't be able to tell me anything. I'm going to call it a night and we can come back and finish him tomorrow.

"Let's move onto your hearing. The saying is 'see no evil, hear no evil, speak no evil.' All three senses will be gone by tomorrow night unless you tell me what I want to know."

He watches me with his one good eye, the other one looks a mess. I pick up an earphone. It's a state-of-the-art inner earphone, used to play music, of course. This one is modified. I place it in his right ear. It was his left eye I just popped so I change to his right side. I superglue it inside his ear so even vigorously shaking his head will not dislodge it. I move to the sound box and I play a siren into the earpiece. It's very high-pitched and reaches two hundred decibels. Leaving it playing overnight will damage his eardrum and inner ear, leaving him deaf in that ear and who knows it might make him a little crazy by the morning.

"Sergei, can you please raise him above the floor and turn the light directly on his face?"

We leave him in the stark white room, hanging by his wrists and a florescent light shining close to his face from above. He has one popped eye, the other pried open, high-pitched sirens playing on one ear, and a plastic suction cup stuck on his cock. I turn to look at him as we leave. Hopefully that will change his mind by the morning. I take Poppy's hand and we head back up to the apartment. I've been anxious and wanted to get back as quick as we could, wanting to check on my boys and get Lana out of my place. God knows what she's been doing while we've been gone.

As we enter the penthouse, I hear Lana moving around.

"Everything been okay, Mavra?" I ask as we exit the elevator.

"Yes, sir, all quiet. Even the babies have been quiet."

That disturbs me. I rush around to see Svetlana, I hate actually calling her that now, which is why I now refer to her as Lana. I know she doesn't like it, she's standing in the living area with Dimitri in her arms, asleep. I look around and don't see Nikolai.

"Where is he?"

She knows who I'm referring to. Poppy walks past me, shaking her head. She heads to our room. Lana follows Poppy, I follow her. I watch as I see Poppy tucking the swaddle around Nikolai, and Lana places Dimitri in his bassinet. I sigh out and rub my hand over my face. I'm not up for this shit. I head to the closet and let Poppy see Lana out. I don't speak. Once I've changed, I head to the living area. Fuck, why is she still here. All I wanted was a nice glass of wine and to sit with my wife for an hour. I need to wind down. I've started walking better now and use my cane mostly when I am away from the apartment. I try not to use it much inside. I use the furniture to help keep me balanced, Lana fucking notices.

"Hey Igor, so good to see you without your cane. Looks like you're on the mend. Poppy was just filling me in on the guy you have to try to find Vidana. I am so grateful to you both." I scoff at her. I don't speak and walk back to my bedroom. One thing I fucking hate is she's been in here. No one except for Poppy ever set foot in this room. Now I feel it's tainted. I can't wait to fucking move. We will be moving soon into a huge house in the Hollywood Hills. It can't happen soon enough.

Fifteen

Igor
Present

"**O**KAY, LET'S GET THINGS STARTED. YOU READY TO TELL ME where this girl is yet or do I have to do more damage?" I lean into his left ear so he can hear me. The other ear still has the pod glued in. I need to cut it out. I get a scalpel and not so gently cut the ear pod out. I lean into that ear and whisper.

"Tell me where she is or I will kill your wife and your three daughters."

He doesn't move. I move to the left ear, repeat what I said in his right ear, and I get a reaction. Good, he's deaf in his left ear.

"Yes, I know you have a wife and three daughters, in fact..." I hold up my phone and I show him the picture of all four of them on their knees with their heads bowed down and you can see the tip of a gun pointed at them. He starts to move, trying to get his hands free, but it's no use. He's not got the energy to do much.

"Right then, let's see if you're willing to talk now."

I pull the suction cup off his cock and what a fucking mess. His cock is white, the skin is all burned and peeling, and it's practically withered to nothing. I motion to Poppy. She stabs it with the cattle prod. He doesn't move, he's lost all feeling.

"Now then, your cock is useless. You have one eye and one good ear. Are you ready to lose the other eye and ear, because once you decide not to speak, the tongue will be the last to go? Before I take your other eye, you can watch your family being executed. The choice is yours."

I had Sergei lower him to my eye level. I have a feeling he's going to talk.

"Okay," he says.

I let Poppy take over.

"Tell me where she is. I need the exact location. Once our men have her safe, we will let your wife and children go. We will show you proof of life. If we don't get our girl then they will die. Do you understand?" He nods his head. He's that weak he struggles to lift it, I lift his head up by his hair.

"Answer the lady," I shout at him, hitting his torso with my cane.

"Yes, I will tell you where she is. Please let my family go."

"Not until we have our girl in safe hands and you have given me everything I need to know." I glare at him then strike him again with my cane. "Tell me now, the sooner you tell me the sooner your family is set free."

He finally talks. He tells us she is in America already, that she is in New York. He gives me the location address and I leave the room to call my men to go and locate her and any others that are being held there. They were to contact me when they go to the location and then I would video connect to their bodycams to watch it play out. I returned to the room, I'm surprised when I walk in and I see Poppy standing there with a knife, she's cut off his big toe on each foot. I raise my eyebrow at her.

"He called me a whore, so I cut off his toes." She shrugs.

I laugh at her and walk over and kiss her forehead. I look at him.

"You ever call my wife a whore again and I will kill you and your family, regardless of the information you gave up. I want your full name and I want the names of everyone in your cartel. I need everyone who is higher up than you, starting with the name of your cartel and who runs it."

His good eye, which is still clipped open, stares straight at me. He shakes his head,

"I cannot do that. They will kill me if they find out it was me who gave them up. They will kill my family, torturing us all."

I laugh at him.

"Isn't that the predicament you're in now? I don't see you have much of a choice right now. The difference is, I have you and your family currently. I could help you all disappear so your cartel doesn't find you."

I see him mulling this over in his mind. He nods.

"My name is Pedram. I am a Captain of the Darvish Cartel. Alborz Darvish is the Don of our cartel. He is a very dangerous man. He will stop at nothing and no one. He usually gets what he wants."

"As do I."

My cell rings and I head out to answer it. I go to the security room and watch the bodycams of my men as they raid the address I gave them. We already had intel she was in New York which is why they have been quick to respond. It's a run-down house, in the middle of a row of houses. Fuck they need to be quiet. I watch it play out as they stealthily but efficiently kill each guard at the house. There are rooms with futons on the floor, they are filthy, as is the entire place. There are some girls my men help to the waiting vans outside. They are being very careful not to make noise to attract attention from nosy neighbors, good. Once all the girls are in the van and the house is set alight they drive to a secret location, not too far away. They take the girls out one by one. I watch, I see her, Vidana, it's definitely her. I tell my men to ask her name. She confirms her name is Vidana. I sigh out with relief. She looks a lot older. Her hair and face are dirty and a mess with cuts and bruises, she was so young the last time I saw her here, for Svetlana's so-called eighteenth birthday. I should be furious with them all for lying, but kids will do that for their parents. I tell my men to get them cleaned up, feed them, and then bring them all back to me here to LA, to the new refuge. I counted fourteen of them. I hope this refuge is big enough to house them all.

I need all the information on the Darvish Cartel from this guy. I told him I would let his family go so I contact my guy who has his family. I take my phone to Pedram and show him his family being released unharmed. He cries with relief. He's a mess. I usually kill all the informants I have down here but if he gives me the information I want, I will take him and release him far away from here. I will not protect him or his family. I did not give him my word, I just said I could, not I would.

He gives up all the information I need. I do one more thing. I let Poppy cut his tongue right down the middle. He won't be able to talk for a while until it heals at least and then he will have to learn to talk again. It will also be so painful, but once healed, he will be fine. Just my mark, he's an informant.

I'm glad this is over with, now we can concentrate on moving house. I will still have this building and the penthouse for when we need to be here, which will be a lot, but I will have the solitude of a house for just my family and no one else around. I've had renovations done on the house with a safe room for us and state-of-the-art equipment installed, Poppy and I discussed the basement use. Let's just say she wants a soundproof playroom, and not for the kids. Oh no, she wants this for the two of us to play in. My wife can be quite kinky when she wants to be. I love her so much and I can't wait till I can make love to her, then give her a good fuck.

We're heading back up to our apartment, it's lunchtime and I'm anxious to get back to the boys. Poppy had Svetlana looking after them again. And I fucking hate it. You know I don't trust her so I had my cameras recording all the rooms, apart from our bedroom, because I refuse to have a camera in there. I'm going to play them back and see what she gets up to while we are not there. We step off the elevator and there's no Mavra, that's strange.

"Where's Mavra?"

"Probably on a toilet break, Igor, he's allowed to go pee, you know."

She's right. We walk round to the living area and there's no one around, I look to Poppy, panic written all over my face. She squeezes my arm.

"Stop, Igor. They are more than likely in our room. Lana may be putting the boys down for a nap, although they will be hungry now. I need to feed them."

There's no noise from anywhere. I rush as fast as I can, which isn't very fast using a cane, to our bedroom. It's empty. What the fuck.

"SVETLANA, SVETLANA." I come out, shouting her name, over and over, going from room to room. Nothing. I see the panic on Poppy's face. Fuck, if she starts to panic, there's no hope for me. We search all over.

"Igor, come here," Poppy shouts at me, she's in the room next to my office which we had cleared out for their double stroller and car seats and all the other stuff babies need. I rush to her. "Their stroller is gone. She must have taken them out. I told her they hadn't gone out yet, that I was waiting on their inoculations before I ventured out. She knew that. What's she doing?" She's going into a panic. "What if she's taken them out without protection? Where's Steve, I know Sergei's in the basement."

I pull out my cell to phone Steve. I have four missed calls from him and there's a text.

Steve – Babies out with Svetlana, I am with them just so you don't panic. She said she tried to call Poppy to let her know.

"Fuck, I shout again. Have you got a missed call or any messages from Lana?"

She pulls out her cell and nods. She has a voice message, she puts it on speaker.

"Poppy, sorry, I called a couple of times. The babies were both crying. I couldn't get them to calm down. One would calm, then the other would start which then made the other one start, again as you can hear. I found the stroller and decided fresh air would be good for them. I know you said about the vaccinations, but in Russia, we take our babies out straight away. I am sorry."

There's a text message.

On our way home. Both babies are flat out asleep. They needed the motion and the fresh air. See you soon.

Just as the message finishes, the elevator pings its arrival. We both rush round. Mavra is back on his seat, and as the elevator door opens and Lana comes out backward, pulling the stroller, I grab her by the hair and pull her back hard. Poppy grabs the stroller. Next, I have Lana by the throat, pinned up against the wall. I may still be in recovery but in this instant, I feel nothing, just rage for her. I look to Poppy who is checking both boys, she looks to me and nods with a slight smile. I turn to Lana. I can see the terror on her face as it starts to get red with the pressure I have on her windpipe, stopping her breathing.

"You ever pull a fucking stunt like this again and I swear to God I will fucking kill you. It will be a slow, painful death. Do you hear me?"

She grabs my wrists, trying to make me let go, but she is no match for my strength.

"Do you hear me?" I shout, putting more pressure on her throat.

I feel her try to nod, but with the hold I have on her neck, she can't move her head. I suddenly let go, dropping her, and she falls to the floor. She puts her hand to her neck and gulps, trying to take in air. I walk away, leaving her and checking on my sons. I need to see they are okay. Poppy has Dimitri in her arms where he is sucking on her breast. He must have woken at me shouting. He seems very content. I check on Nikolai who, to my surprise, is awake just lying there. He usually cries for his food first. I pick him up to make sure he's okay. Lana appears out the corner of my eye. I turn my head to her.

"Poppy told you they have not been out yet and wouldn't be going out until they were inoculated. You disobeyed her, that is unacceptable, no matter what you thought. Get out of my sight. I don't ever want to see you again. You will not set one foot in this apartment ever, do you hear me?"

I look to Poppy, letting her know I have spoken and she is not to disobey me on this. I am still the king of my empire, no matter who is beside me. Maybe I give Poppy too much leeway. She nods slightly at me, letting me know she understands. Lana is still standing there. I don't turn to her.

"Leave, now," I shout. Nikolai starts to cry at my deep, angry voice. I see Poppy frown and Lana leaves the room. Steve coughs. "What?" I snap at him.

"Igor, look, the babies were stressing her out. Mavra called me to come down. One baby is hard enough to look after but when there are two."

I turn my head slowly to him, he's fucking justifying her taking them out.

"I'm sorry for speaking out of turn. I just want you to know it was my idea. I'm not sticking up for her but she tried everything to get them to settle. I tried to help. They were having none of it. We figured they were hungry and we didn't know how long you two would be. I've helped my sister with her kids and the best thing is motion and air. She didn't want to take them out. She fought me, saying you would both be upset. We thought we would have been back before you but obviously we weren't. I'm sorry but it's me you should blame, not Lana."

I'm glaring at him.

"Leave us," is all I say and turn back to Nikolai, who needs my attention. Steve wouldn't stick up for Poppy, not unless she was screwing him as well. Maybe I chose wrong having Steve as my second. He never forgive me for having Andrey and Ivan and not him. He still thought we were best mates but that was when we were kids. He told me when I picked Andrey that it should have been him by my side. I dismissed him. We were close once, but a lot has happened since then.

Poppy feeds Nikolai while I get Dimitri's diaper changed and look him over to make sure he's okay. I notice a slight bruising on his arm. I take him back to Poppy and ask if she knows how he got it, she has no idea, she never picks either of them up by the arms and neither do I. We are the only ones that have looked after them, until Svetlana. I take Nikolai to change his diaper and look him over. He too has a bruise on his opposite arm to Dimitri. How strange, they are in the same place, but opposite. I show Poppy. She's puzzled, as am I. We settle them down. It doesn't take long before they are both asleep, one on me, the other on Poppy. I love this life. I turn and smile at her.

"I had my cameras running the whole time she was with them. I'm going to watch it later to make sure she didn't do anything. It just baffles me about the bruises."

"I know, Igor, let's watch them before we jump the gun. There may be a perfectly good explanation for this. What? I don't know, but let's see. They are good and content. Look at them in our arms. I love them, and you, with all I have, and if anyone hurt any of you, they would have me to deal with. I am a wife and mother before anything else. I would kill for the three of you. But we need to listen to why, before jumping the gun. If there is one thing I've learned from getting my revenge on Blaine, which I now regret, it is to think about things logically and the consequences that come from it. If I see she hurt them, then there is no question."

She's right and I know it, but deep down I want Lana to have done something, not to hurt my boys, god no, but so I can get rid of her once and for all.

Vidana and the other girls will be arriving tomorrow. Poppy has been with Lana a few times since we discovered the bruises on their arms to discuss the final details for the refuge and to meet with the city department to get it signed off. She asked Lana did she know how the boys ended up with bruises on their arms. She said she had no idea, she hadn't noticed any bruises when she changed them. We played the videos and there was nothing to say she harmed them. That doesn't mean she didn't harm my boys. She could have done it in the one place there is no camera, our bedroom. But then she wouldn't know there was no camera in there, would she? Something doesn't sit right with me here. I know she lies through her teeth. I should also have copies of the birth and death certificate from Lana's baby. I need that proof.

Now I'm out and about I have a meeting to go to this afternoon. I have to fly to New York to meet the other godfathers. I don't want to go, but I have to show them I am still in charge and let them know that Poppy will be my second no matter what, I will fly back tonight so I am here tomorrow when the girls arrive at the refuge. Poppy told me Lana is coming over to go through some last-minute things before the girls arrive, that they would have dinner in our apartment, mainly because we still don't have a nanny to look after the boys. I don't like that Lana is getting too cozy. Coming to my apartment and even having her around my boys has me on pins. Not after what she said the other day. It worries me she will do something to either Poppy, because I know she thinks it should be her by my side, or my boys because she is jealous it's not our baby.

Poppy hasn't told Lana that Vidana will be arriving tomorrow with the girls. We both agreed it best not to say anything just yet until we knew the situation with her, it's taken a few days to get the girls to us, because I didn't have the documents to be able to fly them all so they had to be driven. I hired a couple of RVs to bring them, so they could be comfortable at least on their journey, it's a long drive. They needed to rest. I had a doctor and a few nurses travel with them because some of these girls have been pumped full of heroin and God knows what else for so long and they will be going cold turkey. I needed professionals with drug addiction skills to travel with them.

My meeting with the godfathers went well. They actually said they had heard great things about Poppy and how she has been handling the business. They were impressed with her and had no qualms about her staying by my side to run my sector with me, especially as I was still theoretically in rehabilitation. It was kind of a nothing meeting, but a necessary one.

It was three a.m. by the time I got back home. I stayed in the living area, I didn't want to wake Poppy or the boys. If I heard them stir, I could then go to bed. I settled on the couch to have a drink. I have other rooms I could use but once I sat down, it didn't take me long to fall asleep. I'm woken up by a hand on my chest and another palming my cock.

"Нmm, мой ангел, that feels good. Are the boys still sleeping?" I don't open my eyes. I have no idea how long I've been asleep or what time it is. I'm enjoying this too much. "One of my favorite ways to be woken up, as you know," I mumble, still half asleep.

My shirt is unbuttoned halfway and she undoes it the rest of the way, pulling it out of my trousers. She then unzips them and her hand goes inside to my cock. I lift my pelvis up so she can move my trousers away. I still don't open my eyes, I let her do what she wants to me. She kisses and licks down my chest slowly, getting nearer to my rock-hard cock. Her hand is wrapped around him now, she's pulled him from my boxers. I thrust up into her hand. She's just reaching my navel, licking down the hair toward my cock. I stroke her head. I freeze. That doesn't feel like Poppy's hair. Hers is silky smooth, this is coarse hair. I'd know Poppy's hair anywhere. My eyes fly open. I can't believe what I'm seeing. She has the nerve to look up to my face and smile, just as she's about to put my cock in her mouth.

"What the fuck are you doing, bitch? Why the fuck are you in my apartment?" I shout at the top of my voice as I shove her shoulders away, hard, before she puts my now deflated cock anywhere near her mouth. "Lana, you fucking whore." I push her firmly again, this time in the chest.

She flies backward and hits her head hard on the table. The lights go on and I see Poppy standing there looking at me with utter disgust on her face. She's disgusted with me? What the fuck, like it's my fault.

"What the fuck is going on, Igor, why the fuck are you naked with her at your feet?"

I know what it must look like, but now I'm so fucking angry she would even think that. I look to Lana now the lights are on and she's naked.

"FUCK," I yell and kick out at her limp body. I see blood on the floor under her head. Good, I hope she's fucking dead. I turn to Poppy.

"I was asleep. I thought it was you. What the fuck is she doing in our apartment in the middle of the night?"

She glares at me, she doesn't believe me. I stand up and move over to her, tucking myself back into my trousers.

"I didn't do anything. I swear to God I was asleep on the couch. I didn't want to disturb you or the boys, I fell asleep here. If you think for one minute I knew it was her, I swear, Poppy, I will walk out right this fucking minute."

I see the conflict on her face.

"What am I supposed to think. I come in here and see you and her naked. What the fuck, Igor."

I don't fucking believe this. I run my hand through my hair. I walk back over to Lana, I lift her head up by her hair and I slap her face to wake her up. I don't care if she has a head injury or not. I need her awake.

"She's not dead," Lana murmurs, but there is a lot of blood coming from the back of her head.

"Stop it, Igor, she might need to go to the hospital."

She walks over to me and I watch her stumble a little, she crouches down next to Lana. I just told her Lana did this to me while I was asleep and she's worried she may need the hospital. She needs the fucking acid vats, that's where she needs to go and now. I can't even comprehend what's happening right now. Why is Poppy worried about her when she nearly had me fucking her mouth? She should be ripping her hair out and gouging out her eyes. I stand up and step back. I rub my head, not sure what's going on. I hear the babies start to cry. I leave the room and go see to them. If Poppy thinks I had anything to do with this when I didn't even know the bitch was here, for fuck's sake, it's not like she had to walk home or anything. She lives a few floors down. I don't understand why she's here. I pick Dimitri up and place him on our bed and then do the same with Nikolai. I then get on the bed and hold them, one in each arm. I look down into their faces. I really look at them. I see myself in them definitely and I also see Poppy. They both have her nose, but they have my coloring. I love these sweet boys so much. They are actually calming me down.

I must fall asleep with them in my arms. I'm being shaken gently. I slowly open my eyes. I look into my arms. My boys are still there asleep. I shouldn't have fallen asleep with them like this. I could have easily dropped one and rolled over, suffocating him. I startle at my thought.

"Hey, what's wrong? It's okay."

Poppy is trying to comfort me. I must look startled. She takes Nikolai out of my arms and climbs on the bed next to me holding him. I remember earlier. I look at her and she smiles. I frown. She accused me of what, I don't know, but she acted like it was all my fault.

"No, it's not okay, Poppy. You practically accused me of being in on whatever the fuck that was. I was asleep. I had no idea she was even here. Why was she here exactly? She fucking nearly had me fuck her mouth. She had my cock, Poppy. I feel violated. I thought it was you until I touched her hair, then I knew something wasn't right and I opened my eyes and pushed her away." She looks at me sympathetically.

"I do believe you, Igor. I'm sorry, I just couldn't understand what was happening."

She believes me, but I'm pissed she could even think I did something wrong like that. I watch her yawning, she looks really tired but I'm angry.

"I would never touch another woman, never, Poppy, and you know that, and especially not her, whom you know I hate with a passion. Where is she, by the way? I hope you fucking killed her for doing that."

She smiles at me but it's not a real smile, it's more of a grimace. She yawns again, she's struggling to stay awake.

"What is it?" I ask, getting really pissed off.

Just then Nikolai wakes, he needs feeding. We swap babies and she feeds him.

"She's gone back to her apartment."

"What, what the fuck, Poppy? Why? She should be in the fucking basement for doing that."

"I know. I just kind of feel sorry for her. I know she's never gotten over you. I know she hurts and with the babies…"

"Hold on, what about the babies?" She looks sheepish.

"I know about her being pregnant with your baby. She told me you made her get rid of the baby. I just feel she's had a bad time and made some rash decisions. That's all."

I rub my free hand over my face, rest my head back, and look up to the ceiling. That woman has caused me nothing but problems. I breathe out, trying to compose myself so I don't lose it completely here. I have to say, I'm really struggling.

"First off, yes, I wanted her to get rid of the baby, but she disappeared, just vanished and I never knew what happened, only what she told me, that it died in childbirth. I really don't believe a word that comes out of her fucking mouth. She lies nonstop. She fooled me, Poppy. She told me she was sixteen when I brought her here and her mama confirmed that. I was a fool and I should have checked her birth certificate. She was only fifteen. The day I fucked her on her so-called eighteenth birthday was in fact her seventeenth birthday. I didn't know this until later on. I've felt so bad about it ever since, even now. I feel like a child molester, Poppy. It was statutory rape here in LA. I've felt dirty about it ever since. You have no idea what that feels like. She threatened me when she came back, saying she would go to the police and that she had evidence she had a baby at age seventeen. I got the evidence, which was a letter from a law firm, but I have never known the truth about the baby. She told me three different stories and I still don't know the truth." I look at her. "I didn't want a baby with her. She trapped me. She did it on purpose so she would always have me. I didn't want children at all back then. Not until you. I swear, I always used protection but she was the only one, until you, that I never did. I thought she was on birth control. Poppy, it's my biggest regret in my life, ever wanting her. I've hated her ever since. I just, I don't know, maybe I felt sorry for her or thought she could ruin me by claiming statutory rape, which she threatened me with multiple times. But I swear to God I would never touch her or anyone else. You and now these two are my life. I would die for you all."

She leans in and kisses me without disturbing either baby.

"I know you would, and I do believe you, baby. We will sort her out tomorrow. Okay?"

I nod and we swap babies so Dimitri can get his feed. Poppy is tired, I can see, but she seems a little off. I don't know what it is. I watch as she falls asleep feeding Dimitri. I shake her. She startles and looks to Dimitri.

"Oh, I don't know what's wrong. Ever since I woke up earlier I've just felt funny, so tired, I could just fall asleep anywhere. That's scary. I've never fallen asleep while feeding the boys. I just can't keep my eyes open. I feel like I've been drinking, all I had was a glass of wine with Lana. I just don't feel quite right."

Dimitri finishes and I lay them both down. I turn around and Poppy is flat out again. I get in and pull her to me. Tomorrow, I keep saying that to myself, tomorrow we will sort her out.

Sixteen

Svetlana

OH FUCK, I JUST COULDN'T HELP MYSELF. I WENT TO GET A GLASS of water before I put my plan into action and I saw him lying there asleep on the couch. I wondered if they'd had words and that's why he was on the couch. She told me he wouldn't be home until tomorrow. My plan went straight out the window seeing him there. I stood staring down at him. *My beautiful love.* I watched him for ages, watching his chest rise up, then lower. I was mesmerized by him. His eyes were fluttering under his lids. He must have been dreaming. What if he came home and she had a go at him and told him to leave? I wouldn't put it past her. All she cares about are those babies. That should have been me. I would never kick him out, never. I love him so much, I even feel some kind of love toward his babies, I could love them as my own, I have no doubt, but then they won't be around long enough. I will just be there to comfort him and it will get rid of her.

I've already had them both on my breast. Not that there was anything for them to take but it felt good, it felt normal, natural, because they are *my love's* babies. I've had them to my breast three times now and I know they will get used to suckling on me. I read about breastfeeding and if you don't have any milk apparently if a baby suckles on you it stimulates your breast to produce milk, that's what the article on the internet said, anyway. I will give it a go each time I sit for them, if there is another time. I even managed to have them suckling on me last night. Poppy fell asleep. My doing, of course with a sedative in her wine, part of my plan. I helped her to bed and then I sat in the living area and let the babies suck on me. I had one on each breast and I loved the feeling. I sat there with my head back on the couch, just letting them suckle.

She asked me about bruises on their arms when we were having dinner. I think it was when I grabbed them both out of their bassinet and put them on the bed. I had one in each hand, gripping their arms so they didn't fall. It was better than them falling, wasn't it? They might have damaged their heads. Besides, it was the only way I could carry two screaming babies at the same time. I flung them onto the bed, not hard but it was difficult with the two of them. I think I should have just done one at a time. It's not like I was going anywhere. I didn't tell her that though. I just played dumb.

I'm now back in my room. My head is bleeding from a cut and it's banging and my ribs are killing me. I'm not sure why. I remember someone lifting my head up by nearly ripping my hair off my head. I think he pushed me off him and that's why I hit my head. He must have gotten excited at the thought of fucking my mouth or he wanted to fuck my ass and was pushing me off so I could bend over for him. That must be it, it was an accident. Maybe Poppy kicked me while I was on the floor. That must be why my ribs and side hurt so much, the bitch. He must have stopped her from laying into me. He knows it's me he wants, it's me that's his rightful queen, not her. I can taste him in my mouth still. I smell his musky cock on my hands as I breathe it in. I wanted him so badly, and I know he wanted me. She told me to leave. She was so pissed, shouting at me to get the fuck out of her home. She's a jealous bitch. She said we'd sort this out tomorrow.

I'm lying on my bed with a towel wrapped around my head so I don't get blood on my pillow. I refuse to wash my hands. I can't help but keep sniffing where I was holding his cock, I keep licking my lips, remembering kissing and licking down his chest and swirling my tongue in his navel. The smell of him was driving me wild. As I stood there looking down at him I took his hand and inserted his fingers into me, I played with my clit with his fingers then moved his fingers in and out of me, it wasn't long before I came all over his hand. I licked his fingers, I was hoping he would wake and fuck me, he didn't, I wanted a taste of him.

I can picture what would have happened if he had not gotten too excited and pushed me away. He would have had me on my knees in front of him, first to suck his cock and play with his ass. He loves that. Then he would have bent me over the coffee table, he would have got on his knees behind me and he would have spread my ass cheeks wide open and licked at my pussy

204 | LYNDA THROSBY

and then stuck his tongue in my ass. He would have then played with my clit and pumped his fingers in and out as he did the same with his tongue in my ass. He would have just brought me to the edge of orgasm and then he would have rammed his cock in me so hard the table would have moved with the force of it. Then I would be on all fours while he thrust into me like a madman possessed, because he missed me so fucking much. I would have screamed with my release. Then *she* would have come and watched as he rammed into me until he was screaming with his release. He would have looked at her with contempt because it was me he was fucking.

I scream out with my orgasm at the images and thoughts of what he would have done to me. It felt so real, it was me finger fucking myself. I was wishing he would come to my room and do it to me. I'm soaking and now my juice is mixed with his musky scent yet again. We are reunited.

Waking up, the memories of Igor and me pumping his cock come flooding back. I slept well, all things considered, because I don't know what's going to happen to me today. My head is still hurting. It's the big day, the opening of the refuge and we have some girls arriving. I need to get there and make sure the new staff turns up and that all the rooms are ready for them. I'm actually excited about this. The thing worrying me is Poppy and Igor and what I did last night. Worrying about what they are going to do to me, if anything. I was only trying to pleasure *my love*. He can't be fucking her straight after the babies. He needs it, he has needs and I can take care of them. He needs to be looked after, and I'm the one who should do that. Maybe they will understand and let me do that for them. I just want to get this place set up and try and avoid them although it's going to be difficult.

I thought they would arrive here early to make sure it was all set up but they didn't, it was Poppy on her own. I wanted to see him. She didn't mention last night, she just kept it very professional as we walked through everything to make sure it was perfect. She was off with me, being very stern. The communal area for the girls was a great comfortable place, with a huge flat screen TV. They will love it here and if they don't then there is something wrong with them and maybe they will need to be asked to leave.

The idea is they get help here for drug and sex abuse. It will take time and some longer than others. Once they are rehabilitated they either get a free flight back home or Igor gets them paperwork to stay in the USA, like he did with me, and they can either go out on their own or they can stay on the ninth floor for a little while longer until they are good to leave. We still have plenty of shared rooms on the ninth floor but it depends on how many we take into the refuge. We can have a maximum of thirty girls staying here at any one time. The place is huge and they all get their own bedroom. What Poppy envisioned has come to fruition, and I have to admire her for this and wanting to help all these girls. I still think there is more to her story and I doubt I will ever find out about it.

We just got notice the RV homes will be here within the next hour. I have the kitchen staff working away to prepare a hot meal for them, we are keeping it simple with soups and fresh bread along with good old American mac and cheese. Some may not have had a proper meal for some time and they will need building up slowly. I'm not sure where these girls have actually come from or why they are in RVs. I don't know if they are American or from other countries. I have some bilingual staff on hand, just in case. If there are nationalities we don't have an interpreter for, then I will make sure we bring someone in. It's all systems go as we just wait for their arrival.

I'm sitting in the office with Poppy, still waiting. I don't want to be alone with her. I don't want her asking about last night, but I know it's inevitable.

"Lana, while we have a minute, do you want to explain about last night and what that was with Igor?"

She tilts her head. I can hear the slightly authoritative tone in her voice mixed with a little anger. I don't look at her. "Lana, now would be a good time before Igor gets here."

Oh fuck, I didn't think he would be coming. I look at her. I need to play dumb. I frown at her.

"I don't know what you mean, Poppy. I woke up this morning with a banging headache and a bad cut on my head, but I had no idea why. I remember me being at your place having dinner, to discuss things for today but that's it." I lie through my teeth. It just came to me to pretend the bang on the head gave me memory loss. One for the win, I think.

She tilts her head more, squinting her eyes at me.

"You're telling me you honestly don't remember anything after us having dinner?"

I shake my head and wince as though in a lot of pain.

"You don't remember us in the living area, sitting, having some wine, the babies asleep in our arms?"

Again, I shake my head, more gently this time. "I don't remember Poppy, honestly I don't." A tear slips from my eye as I put on my really sad face.

"Poppy, when—" someone shouts at us, the RVs have arrived and saved my bacon.

I shoot up and run out the door, wanting to leave this conversation behind us. I hope she doesn't bring it up again. I'm standing at the door just as the first girls walk through. Poppy welcomes each one as do I. They are taken to their rooms by our staff to be shown around before being brought to the dining room. I head to the kitchen to see how things are going, leaving Poppy to greet the remaining stragglers. I make sure all is done as the girls start arriving into the dining room. Some of them are in such a state, you can see their faces so thin and pale and gaunt looking. Most of them have long hair that looks like it's seen better days. They all need to be groomed and pampered. They each come to the serving station and I help dish out the soup and warm bread and mac and cheese. I feel sorry for them, they are all so young. I would say some are very young teens, if that. It's horrendous actually seeing them like this. I'm not sure I understood the devastation of it. How the hell do they come back from being used like this? I think my drug problem pales into insignificance looking at these girls.

I'm happily smiling and serving the girls when I feel like I'm being watched. I look up and I see Igor standing in the doorway, glaring straight at me. He looks angry. He motions with his finger for me to go to him. Oh shit, here we go. Deny knowing anything, I chant to myself as I walk in his direction. He turns and walks away, I guess that means to follow him. I stay behind him, not speaking or acknowledging him. He walks to my office and holds the door open for me to enter before him. Fuck. Inside is Poppy sat at my desk, but there is someone else sat in the chair opposite her. I smile nervously at Poppy.

"Svetlana," is all she says and the girl sitting in the chair turns around slowly and stares into my eyes.

My hand flies to my mouth, trying to hold in the sob that escapes. I cry in disbelief that Vidana is sitting here in front of me. She doesn't smile back, she stares at me as if trying to fathom out who I am. I rush to kneel at her side. I grab her hand and kiss the back of it, I stroke her cheek but she still looks blank.

"Vidana, it's me, Svetlana, your big sister. Oh Vidana, I thought you were dead. Thank god you're here."

She doesn't acknowledge me or say anything. I turn to Poppy.

"Thank you so much for finding her and bringing her here. I can never repay you or thank you enough."

I'm crying so hard while holding Vidana's hand. I turn her face gently toward me and I move the lank hair from her face and put it behind her ears. The eyes that stare blankly into mine, they are dull and lifeless. She has dark circles around her eyes, making them look bruised. I can see scars on her face as I run my hand gently down her cheek, probably from being hit. She looks lost, like a shell of the girl I knew. I don't know if she will ever come back from this. I want to take her home with me so I can look after her, but I know this will be the best place for her, and I will be here every day. She looks hollow and skeletal, it's been nearly a year since I last saw her on that video. God knows what she's been through in all that time. I don't know how she's still here. Poppy gets up and moves around to us.

"Vidana, sweetie, come with me and let's get you something to eat."

Vidana doesn't acknowledge her. Poppy takes her hand, looking at me as she says this. What's she doing. I get up to go with them.

"Not yet, Lana. Igor wants a word with you."

I scowl at her then turn and scowl at him.

"I want to stay with Vidana."

He frowns and shakes his head, glaring at me. Poppy leaves, taking Vidana with her. Vidana doesn't say anything as Poppy leads her out, it's like she doesn't know me. It upsets me. I stand facing the door, watching them leave and waiting for him to speak. I don't turn to look at him, I'm too scared. Suddenly he grabs my hair and pulls my head back for me to look up into his face, he's nearly ripping my hair out and he kicks the door shut.

"You are so fucking lucky you are still standing at this moment in time. If I had my way, you would be in the basement in the acid by now. God knows why Poppy stopped me last night. I don't get it. You fucking try anything like that again, and I will slit your fucking throat and rip your head off. Do you hear me?" he spits out into my face. His voice is pure venom and I'm scared fucking stiff of him right now.

I have no doubt he would kill me. He's a dangerous man. He lets go of my hair and shoves me hard in the back. I fall forward, grabbing on to the chair to stop myself from falling. I stand up tall, trying to show him he's not affecting me when inside, I'm shaking like Jell-O. I don't turn. I don't want to look him in the face.

"I don't remember anything. Poppy asked me earlier. I don't remember anything after we finished dinner. I don't know what I did or how I ended up with a big cut in my head. I can only presume I did something wrong and you or Poppy hurt me." My voice is quivering, I'm trying to act unaffected, but I can't stop my voice or my body from shaking.

"You so much as lay one finger on me again, and the breath you take as you do will be your last. Do you fucking hear me, Lana?" he shouts and I jump as he's standing right at the side of me as he does.

I just nod slightly.

"I've not finished with you, but you need to do your job for now. Get the fuck out."

I leave the room, almost running. I just want to get to Vidana. I spend the rest of the day getting her settled into a room. She hasn't spoken at all. I have to move her to sit or stand, she's non-responsive. I've been told this is normal and she will probably be like this for some time.

Poppy has been great with me lately. It's been two weeks since I last touched *my love* and I haven't seen him since. I have a lot to do at the refuge. I try to spend as much time as I can with Vidana. I see her throughout the day and then I spend the evenings with her which is my own time. She still hasn't spoken to anyone. I rang Mama the day Vidana arrived, once I got back home and she cried hard, thanking the gods and Igor. Igor can do no wrong in Mama's eyes, she's always telling me to keep him sweet no matter what the consequences are. Poppy has still had me in her apartment but only when Igor is out and she makes sure I leave before he returns. I've also been asked to look after the babies a few more times. They are still having problems with finding a suitable nanny. It suits me just fine. I've been able to have the boys to my breast a few times now and although I still don't have any milk coming from my breast, they are always so content to suckle on me.

I haven't seen much of Ryker these last few weeks. I haven't even had time to go to The Hex with spending all my time with Vidana. He understands but he's asked if he can see me tonight. I will spend some time with Vidana and then leave early to spend time with Ryker. I've missed him, if I'm honest, and I could do with a good fuck. The problem is, we don't fuck on dates, we do that in the club. Maybe I can get him to change his mind later. I lay Vidana down on her bed to tuck her in.

"Thank you," she suddenly says as I give her a kiss on the forehead to say goodbye.

I stand back and crouch in front of her.

"Oh, Vidana, you never have to thank me. I love you, my sweet sister. Can you tell me how you are feeling? You are looking so much better, sweetie."

She has her eyes closed and doesn't look at me.

"I'm feeling okay," she says with a shaky voice and struggling to get the words out.

She hasn't let anyone see to her as such. The counselors, nurses, and doctor have all been taking care of her and talking with her but she doesn't speak to anyone. They haven't been able to get her hair done. Apparently as soon as anyone even tried to touch her she would freak out on them. She lets me touch her and has since the day she arrived. I hold her hand, kiss her head, stroke her cheek, and she's never once freaked out on me. I won't push her now, but I will see if she will let me do her hair and help her feel better. She's at least been eating and her appetite has improved, she's on medication for her withdrawal from whatever drugs she was on but that is only temporary. She hasn't let anyone near her body to examine it and she stays covered up in big baggy sweaters, even if it's hot as hell some days. She hides away. The tears slip from my eyes with her speaking.

"Listen to me. We will fix you, Vidana, no matter what it takes. Do you hear me? Mama is waiting patiently to speak to you. I told her once you are up to it then she can FaceTime you. But only when you are ready. You let me know when you are ready for anything, do you hear me? My sweet, sweet sister. I am so sorry you have gone through all this, I will help you any way I can."

She finally opens her eyes and looks straight into mine.

"It's all his fault, Lana, it's all his fault. If he hadn't wanted you, Papa would still be alive, and I would still be a young girl enjoying her life in Russia. Never dreaming anything so vile could be done to me. It's all on him." The venom in her shaky voice scares me.

I know she's talking about Igor, I know that's *my love*, but I guess she's right. I give her another kiss and leave her, telling her I will see her tomorrow, as usual. I walk back home slowly, thinking about what she has said. She's right, if he hadn't had been in the bar at the exact same time mama sent me to get Papa, none of this would have happened. I wouldn't be hurting because the man I love is married to someone else. I wouldn't be hurting because he's playing happy fucking families with his twin boys. I wouldn't be hurting for our child right now. I hurt every fucking day and he has no idea. Maybe Vidana has made me realize. Maybe I should hate him instead of loving him, maybe I should do something about it. If he tries anything, then the first sign I get of him taking me down to the basement to kill me, I will put my plan into action. The plan he knows nothing about.

Seventeen

Svetlana

I'VE SPENT A LOT MORE TIME WITH RYKER THE LAST FEW WEEKS and I crave him. I think I'm falling for him. He's told me he's fallen for me and he asked me last week to not go to The Hex again. He said the only reason he was going for the last six months was because of me. He only wanted to see me. We actually made love that night for the first time, that's when he asked me not to go again, it wasn't the raw fucking we normally do, it was him being loving and looking me in the eyes as he thrust gently inside me. We both stared into each other's eyes, holding on to each other tightly with our release. It's the first time I have ever felt loved by anyone. I always thought Igor loved me but making love to Ryker like this, I now know it wasn't love on his side. He wanted me because he couldn't have me, then he discarded me the moment he found out we were expecting a baby. He became a monster.

My feelings for Igor are changing. I thought it was me that was supposed to be by his side, but now I'm beginning to realize it was never going to be me. I've been so naïve all this time.

Vidana is doing so well. Ever since she first spoke, she's come out of herself more. Mainly with me. There was one time she had come to see me in my office. Poppy was there, and Igor appeared to pick Poppy up. It was the first time I had seen him since the day Vidana arrived. As soon as Vidana saw him, she flew for him. She jumped on him, wrapping her legs around his torso tight. She had his head in her hold and started clawing at it, screaming it was all his fault, everything was his fault. She wished he had never come into our lives. Poppy and I tried to pry her from him. It took a lot, but with our help, he managed to get her off and pushed her away. She fell onto the floor. She sat snarling at him, showing her teeth.

"Get her the fuck out of here before I do something she will regret," he shouted, looking at me while wiping blood from a scratch on his face. "I think maybe you two should be put down like the rabid dogs you are." He snarled as I took Vidana out of the office and back to her room.

"What the fuck, Dana, why did you do that. If it wasn't for him, you'd probably be dead. Mama and our sisters would still be living in that shithole we grew up in and, and…"

She cocks her head to the side.

"And what, Lana?"

I very nearly slipped up.

"And I wouldn't have fallen in love."

"But you're not with him and from what I just heard he doesn't want you either."

"I know, and I'm okay with that now. I always believed it should have been me by his side, that I was his rightful queen, not her, but I've found someone else. Someone who I've fallen for hard. I didn't even realize I had fallen for him until recently. I just want to be with him all the time. He makes me feel special and loved. Igor never made me feel loved. Special yes, he treated me well, but that wasn't enough and I've only just realized that. I will introduce you to him soon. When you're better, we can move away from here and start over together. Would you like that, Dana?"

She looks at me but doesn't say anything. I sit on the chair next to her bed, she's sat on the bed against the wall.

"What do you want to happen when you are better, Dana, tell me?" She shrugs.

"I don't know Lana. I was thinking of going back to Mama, you know? I just don't know. I don't know where I've been this last twelve months or so. I don't even know how long I've been gone. I think I block it all out. I feel so old, like a lifetime has passed me. I just feel deflated and lost. I'm sorry for attacking him but I still think all this is down to him. I just want to kill him and I know he's helped set this all up and I am grateful they found me, but I still hate him, Lana. Why does he walk with a cane now? What happened to him?"

"We will work it out, Dana, once you are back to full strength. Staying here is best for you now. You get all the help you need, then we'll talk about what you want at the end." I smile at her and lean forward to take her hand. "As for Igor, I was just told he had an accident and hurt his spine. I don't know what is true. It's not like they tell me anything." I shrug again.

We sit talking for a while until I leave. I'm meeting Ryker again soon.

Just as I start to head out, I hear my name being mentioned. It's Igor. I stop and listen. I think he must be talking to Poppy.

"They have to go. I can't go on like this. Lana is bad enough to keep around. But now, having Vidana fucking attacking me like she did. She's lucky I didn't smash her head against the wall. I just don't think I can do it anymore. I know you've formed a friendship with her, but I've had enough. Especially after what she did to me that night, then denying all knowledge of it. As soon as I get those documents I'm waiting for, so I know for sure, I will have the final word on what happens."

I move quietly away. I have tears running down my face. I need to leave before they see me and know I heard them. He hates me so much, I will always love him but now I need to go into protection mode, especially as Dana is now involved and I have to protect her.

It's been a few days since I overheard them talking about me. Poppy has been her normal self with me, and I haven't seen Igor. I'm not sure what documents he's after. I know he asked me a long time ago about the birth and death certificates for our baby but I never got them for him and he never asked me again. I know my time here is coming to an end. I just don't know if it will be the end of my life or just for me to move on. I need to sort this out. There is no way he is going to kill me. I've made a few phone calls and am waiting on a return call from Mama. I'm putting things into motion. Dana is doing far better than I ever thought possible. I honestly thought there would be no coming back from what she must have gone through. She's far stronger than I gave her credit for.

I've told Ryker about Igor and me. He wasn't very pleased, but he said he suspected there was a history between us from Igor's reaction to me. He said he couldn't understand why Igor kept me around all this time though, especially if he had such distaste for me. I didn't tell him I always thought Igor still loved me and I didn't tell him about our baby, I left that part out.

Ryker asked me to move in with him. Move away from the ninth floor. I was shocked, I didn't know we were to that point, but I declined. I used the excuse of not being able to live in another woman's apartment. That I felt I would be disrespectful to his wife by doing that. I just suggested we move into our own place. He agreed with no hesitation. I think I have fallen in love with Ryker. I say I think, because it doesn't feel like the love I had and still have for Igor. I think he will always be the love of my life, no matter what happens.

I'm in my room, it's late. I was at the refuge till late, talking with Dana. I am just about to get into bed when there is a loud banging. It scares me. There is only me in the suite, but then I hear it again. I move slowly to the door just as it flies open. I scream and jump back. Igor stands there looking murderous. He moves toward me like an animal stalking his prey. The look on his face terrifies me.

"Igor, what is it, what's wrong?"

He doesn't speak, he just moves closer to me. Suddenly he grabs me by the hair.

"Igor, you're hurting me. Please let me go. What's wrong?" I plead with him, trying to get him to release me.

I grab his hand to try to pull him off me but he doesn't let go, he pulls harder. He starts to drag me out of the room, I try to grab hold of anything I can to stop him from taking me.

"Please tell me what I've done? Don't do this, Igor. I love you, please don't do this."

I fear for my life. He's so angry, I don't know why. He drags me down the hallway to the elevators, I know straight away where he is taking me. The basement. I've been there a few times, I don't want to go back. I hate it.

"Igor, please just tell me what I've done, don't take me down there, please don't. Igor, you love me, I know you do. I love you Igor, please stop, please let's talk."

We are in the elevator descending, he's let go of me and pushed me to the floor. I'm crying and cold. I only have a short sleeping tee on. I try to pull it over my knees as I sit up and bring my knees to my chest, wrapping my arms around my legs. He can't see anything and it's not like he hasn't seen it before, anyway. I look up to him, my face streaked with tears.

"What have I done now, Igor?"

He glares down at me but still doesn't say a word. I watch as his nostrils flare, his eyes are a lot darker than the usual bright blue they usually are and he is so angry.

We reach the basement and he moves toward me. I scurry backward, backing myself right into the corner. I hold on to the rail that runs around the elevator, I hold on for my life. He moves over and grabs my hair to pull me up, I fight him, I don't care if he rips it off my head. I don't want to go into one of his torture rooms, or the acid vats.

He's a lot stronger than I could ever be. Even with a walking cane, he only needs one hand. He pulls me hard but I grip on tight. He takes his cane and he raps my knuckles hard with it.

"Ouch, you fucker, leave me alone, I don't want to go with you, let me go, Igor let me go, please."

I think he broke my hand. I automatically let go of the rail and he pulls me by the hair and drags me out of the elevator so I can't grab hold again. I'm still on the floor, trying to grab the base of the hair he's pulling to try to ease the pain, then I grab hold of the elevator doors before they close and I hang on to them. They shut on my hands and I have to let go.

He drags me upward to make me stand. I don't want to walk, but he's going to rip my hair out if I don't. He still never speaks this entire time. We pass through his security doors, only the one lot and he opens one of his cells and throws me in. I am face down on the floor, he straddles me and lifts my head up using my hair.

"Look at me, you fucking bitch."

He spits in my face, I have my eyes screwed shut. I don't want to see his monstrous face, I've never seen him like this before.

"OPEN YOUR FUCKING EYES, NOW," he screams into my ear.

I open them and I'm sorry I do.

"You are going to die a very slow death. Do you know why, bitch?"

I shake my head as best I can with his grip on my hair.

"You hurt my boys. Nobody hurts my boys, ever."

My eyes fly open wider. "I haven't touched them."

"Don't fucking lie to me. I have had enough of all your bullshit lies for far too long. It ends tonight. I saw what you did to them. I saw you put my boys to your tits, you sick evil bitch, and I saw the way you held them both by the arms. Holding an arm of each baby in each of your hands, my boys were dangling at your sides like rag dolls. They are human fucking beings, NOT DOLLS. You bruised them, you could have ripped their arms out of their sockets, you sick bitch."

I stare at him, he has to see the fear on my face. How did he see me? He wasn't there.

"How, you weren't there. I only held them like that to get them from one place to the other. It's hard with two of them. I didn't mean it maliciously. Igor, please believe me."

I think it's futile trying to plead with him. He has made up his mind.

"What about all the times you had my boys to your fucking tits. Do you know how sick that is? That is crossing the line. They are not your babies, you do not put them to your tits. That to me is sexual abuse of a minor. That is so far out there you deserve to suffer."

I'm crying hard.

"Igor, you have it all wrong. It was nothing sexual. They loved suckling on my breasts. I thought because they were your babies and I love you so much, it was okay to do that. It was not for pleasure. I felt closer to you having your babies suckle on my breast. Igor, you have to believe me."

He shoves my head hard and I bang my forehead on the floor. The cold tiled white floor. This is one of his white rooms. I know some of the tortures that go on here. Sergei has told me. I wonder if he's around, if he will help me. He loved me. He will help, won't he? Maybe Poppy will come and help me again like she did last time. I need someone to help me. Igor is going to kill me. He lifts my head and I spit at him. I could see it was blood. I didn't realize I was bleeding. He lets go of my head. I stay head down, listening for movement. I'm shaking with fear and cold. Someone will help me, right?

Eighteen

Igor

I HAD A HUGE ARGUMENT WITH POPPY, ALL OVER SVETLANA AND her sister. Her fucking sister attacked me and scratched my head. She would be dead if it were anyone else. Poppy defended them, again. I don't know what it is with her, why does she keep defending Svetlana? It's not like she has to prove she's queen anymore, she is the fucking queen, and both men and women fear her. Svetlana obviously hasn't seen that side to her, yet. There's still time. After Vidana scratched me, we were in our room when I told her they had to go, and soon. She turned on me, telling me Vidana needed a lot more time to get herself better before being turned out and that Svetlana has been fantastic with the refuge and really thrown herself into it.

"I don't get why you are always sticking up for her. I told you how she lied and what she did to me. Yet you're always on her side. Why?" She stared at me.

"She reminds me of me. I just have a soft spot for her. I know she lies, I do, but they need a chance."

"How many fucking chances can one person have?" I shouted at her. "Svetlana has had a million more chances than anyone else I've ever known who has wronged me. I'm sorry, мой ангел, they have to go. I think you are too attached to her. What have I always told you, don't trust anyone."

She didn't speak to me for the rest of the night.

I still don't have all the documents I've been waiting for. My man managed to get the birth certificate which names me as the father of a female unnamed. My firstborn was a daughter, I knew this but have never thought about it since. I don't know why I feel so bad. Maybe it's having the boys, imagine never meeting them, I never got to meet her. I know I didn't want the baby, but seeing it written on paper that I had a little girl has me choking up. I must have softened a little with having the boys. I hate Svetlana, she put me through this. I need the death certificate, I suspect there isn't one. I truly believe I have a daughter out there somewhere. If that's the case, and she left that little girl somewhere instead of looking after her like a mother should do, then I despise her even more and I will make her suffer. Poppy and the boys are asleep, I came in to do some work before I headed to bed, but all I can do now is stare at the birth certificate that has just landed in my inbox. I'll show Poppy tomorrow.

Sitting at my desk working, I click on the CCTV icon by mistake. I have never watched any of it back, apart from the day Svetlana took the boys out without telling us. I decided to flick through it from the times Svetlana stayed to look after the boys. I had a hidden camera put in our bedroom, I swore I would never do that, but with Svetlana in there, and wandering around our place, I thought it best. I don't know why I have never watched it before, knowing how much I distrust her. I flick through, and I'm horrified at the images I see. At first, I had to zoom in because my brain just wouldn't compute what it was seeing. She has my boys sucking on her tits. It disgusts me. My blood boils at the images, it's sick. Who does that to babies that aren't their own? I pause it. I don't know if I can watch. Is she really trying to feed them or is this some sick sexual thing? I carry on flicking through and I see that each time she's been with my boys she's done the same thing. Every time she has them sucking her tits. I feel physically sick, I feel rage, I'm boiling, ready to blow.

I watch the night she almost sucked my cock. I was clearly asleep, I must have honestly thought I was dreaming or it was Poppy. I watch as she undresses right in front of me. She stands there naked for a good five minutes, watching me. What I didn't know was that she took my hand and had me stroking her pussy. I watched as she widened her stance and she took my fingers and stuck them inside her. She was moving up and down on my fingers, making sure they stayed there, moving them in and out of her. I suspect she was playing with her clit as she exploded. She didn't scream, so she didn't wake anyone up, her other hand flew to her mouth to muffle any scream, but her body was shuddering and shaking with her release. I then watched as she lowered herself to the floor next to me. She sucked the fingers that had been inside her. Then she undid my shirt and trousers. I watched her take out my cock as she kissed and licked her way down my chest. I have to stop, I don't want to watch it. I feel violated and disorientated from what I'm watching. My jaw is tight, my mouth is dry, and I feel like something is creeping all over my body.

I get to a part in the bedroom where she took both boys out of the bassinet's but she had one in each of her hands, grabbing each by their arm. They dangled at the side of her like rag dolls. She did bruise them, she did that to them. I found again where she did exactly the same thing, only she made sure there was clothing on their arms so as not to bruise them. The fucking bitch. She helped her mama bring up her sisters. Is that how she handled them? She could have ripped their arms out. There's one time she had them dangling by the arms and flung them both onto the bed like dolls. I freeze it, then rising from my chair, I start to pace my office. I bite down on my knuckles to stop myself from screaming. I press play again. This time I stand up and my face is closer to the screen. It looked like one of them hit his head on the edge of the bed before landing in a funny position on top of the bed. My blood is boiling with rage, I'm now grinding my teeth and my pulse is quickening as my heart beats out of my chest at the anger I feel. I want to rip her fucking head off. I watch as she sat on my bed then dragged them both by a foot to her, placing them on her tits while laying back on my pillows. I pause on the image, she's smiling. She's sick. That's it. I look at the time, it's late. I don't give a fuck what time it is. She's going to pay for this. She's sick in the head. She hurt my boys. The anger I feel, because I swore I would protect them. Yet here she is in my own home, hurting them.

I march out the door, grabbing my cane, which I still fucking hate using, slamming my office door behind me. Fuck, I don't want to wake any of them up. I'm just seething, thinking of what she did. I take the elevator to the ninth floor. I can't get the images out of my head of her harming my boys and making them suck her tits. It plays on a loop over and over and I have a rage in me I've only ever had once before. The time

I killed my father. This rage is worse because I let that happen to my boys after I told Poppy over and over I didn't trust her. It's all my fault. I should have demanded she not look after them. I give in too easily to Poppy. Before I know it, I've stormed into her suite, slamming the door open then nearly ripping her bedroom door from its hinges. I have her by the hair, dragging her to the elevator. She's pleading with me but I don't speak and my heart pounds. I've never felt like this before a kill, I just want to harm her as much as I can. I have no words right now.

I'm in a white room in the basement after dragging her by the hair here and I lay into her, I'm right in her face yelling at her for what she did. She's been begging me to let her go. Like fuck I will. She's going to die, no matter what. I push her head and watch as it smashes on the hard-tiled floor. Good, I hope she broke her nose. I move around and crouch down in front of her, lifting her head again. I see blood coming from her nose and a split on her forehead. Good. She spits in my face, there's blood as I wipe it away, I slap her hard across the face. I leave the room. I want to get some instruments and put a new clean tee on. This one has her fucking blood on it now.

I return to the room and she's tucked herself into the corner, like she did in the elevator. I put my cane against the wall and I grab her hand, dragging her to the center of the room. I raise her up and I clamp first one hand in the shackles hanging from the ceiling then the other, I move over and press the button which raises her feet from the floor. I move and stand in front of her. She spits at me again and then kicks me in the chest. I grab her ankles and hold them tight.

"You fucking bitch. Do you think you're leaving this room alive? Well, maybe barely alive, just so you know the pain as I throw you in the acid vat."

She fights me to try and get loose. I grip her tighter. I let her wear herself out and then I break her big toe on each foot by bending them right back. She screams out in pain. I see her eyes go to the door and I turn to see who is there. It's Sergei, he's looking annoyed.

"What is it, Sergei?" I've had my doubts about him for some time. I know these two are or were fucking. If he tries anything, then I will kill him too.

"I Just wanted to let you know Poppy just rang down to see if you were here."

"That's fine. Now leave."

He doesn't move. I look at her, looking at him pleadingly, wanting him to rescue her. Like fuck that will happen. I turn to look at him and raise an eyebrow.

"I said now leave, unless you want one last fuck before she dies."

His eyes go wide. He knows not to mess with me as do all my men. He says nothing as he turns to leave, giving her one last sympathetic look. She kicks out at me again with my head turned. I punch her in the stomach to wind her and then in the face. Her head snaps back. I move away and grab my cane. I walk back to her and I crack right across her shins with the cane. I know that will fucking hurt. I look at her face, she's crying as she looks at me with blood now pouring out of her nose, but the look on her face is one of pleasure. She smirks at me as her tongue comes out to lick at the blood.

"Got something to say now?"

"Let me go, Igor. I'm warning you. Your life will be over if you don't let me go."

Ha, she's fucking warning me.

"Is that right? And how will that happen exactly? You know I got the letter from the law firm that you gave them, so how will my life be over?" She sneers at me.

"I had a plan in case this happened. It won't be long. You can kill me now but I will go knowing I got revenge on you."

I don't give a fuck what she's talking about. There are no more letters. She said the baby died. There's no proof. How did I once think she was beautiful? I must have been in a bad, desperate place back then. It's only when Poppy came into my life that the light seemed to shine again. I move away and I get a knife. I return to her and take the top of her T-shirt. Taking the knife, I slice down her front. The tee falls open to the sides. The knife was just deep enough to cut her down her front and make her bleed. It wasn't deep, just superficial. She looks down her body at the cut. It even cut one of her tits. I feel I want to slice her nipples off.

They have been in my babies' mouths. I get the scalpel from the table, I grab one of her tits and I'm just about to slice the nipple off.

"Stop Igor. Stop now."

I turn at Poppy's voice. I'm shocked not only to see her but to see she's holding the hand of a little girl who is blindfolded. She crouches down to the girl just to reassure her everything is okay. What the fuck and who is this? I turn to look at Svetlana, and I can see the look of shock on her face. I move to the doorway, step outside, shooing Poppy and the child, and shut the door. I scowl at Poppy, I'm confused.

"Come with me." She takes the little girl's hand and I follow her to the elevators, I stop in at the security room and tell them no one, not even them are to go into that room, looking straight at Sergei. We ride the elevator up to the lobby. All the while I watch Poppy who in turn watches me, she nods gently to let me know it will be okay. The doors open and before we step out Poppy takes the blindfold off the little girl and she crouches down in front of her.

"Go say goodbye to your aunt and uncle, Sabina."

I watch as she runs to a man and woman standing there. I don't know who they are but the woman looks familiar somehow. They both look old as they crouch down to cuddle her. I look to Poppy for an explanation, raising my eyebrow in question. She moves into my chest and looks up into my eyes, she's got me worried.

"I'll tell you when she's settled in bed, but meet Sabina, your daughter, Igor."

I don't know if I just heard her properly, my daughter. I only just got the birth certificate not two hours ago and found and now Poppy is telling me this is her. I look at the little girl openmouthed as Poppy puts her arms around my waist.

"Look at her, Igor, there is no mistaking she's your daughter, she's the spitting image of you. She has your blond hair and your piercing blue eyes. I heard a door slam in our apartment and went looking for you. I was in your office, Igor. I saw what was on your screen and I was infuriated. I will have no problems killing her, believe me after seeing that. I was sitting at your desk when the apartment phone went. It was this couple here asking to see you urgently, they said that Svetlana had sent them and they had been traveling all day. I was surprised when I got down here, but I knew immediately she was your daughter. There is no mistaking it. She's beautiful, Igor."

The little girl, Sabina, comes walking back to us slowly. She's scared. I watch her closely, Poppy is right. She looks just like me. My heart melts at the sight of her scared little face. I think I'm about to cry. Poppy squeezes my hand to ground me, she can see me struggle. I crouch down.

"Hey Sabina, that's a beautiful name for a beautiful little girl. I bet you're scared, aren't you? This is all strange to you, it is to me too. Shall we go upstairs and get you settled? What did your aunt and uncle tell you?"

She was shy and didn't know if she should speak, Poppy coaxes her.

"They said you were my papa."

I melt and gulp, holding back tears. I nod to her. I look at the man and woman. They both beckon for me to go to them.

"I'm just going to speak to your aunt and uncle. You stay here and I'll be back very soon."

She nods at me enthusiastically and her little eyes light up, she's fucking adorable. I can see Poppy struggle to hold it together as well. I walk over to them and shake both their hands.

"First, thank you for taking care of Sabina. Second, I had no fucking idea she existed and third, why have you only just brought her to me now and who are you?" I motion for them to sit in the seating area with me. I turn to Poppy and she nods. The woman speaks.

"I am Mila Jacoby and this is my husband Alek Jacoby. I am Svetlana's aunty, her mama Larisa's eldest sister. We live in Florida and have traveled today to bring Sabina to you under Svetlana's instructions. Can we see Svetlana, please?"

Fuck, I didn't know they had family in the States.

"I have no idea where she is. I haven't seen her for a while. I hardly see her these days." They look to each other, then back to me.

"She called last week and asked us to bring Sabina here, to ask for you, and to ask you where she was. She gave me this letter when she brought Sabina to us to look after. She told us that when the time came, she would ring us and tell us what to do with Sabina and the letter." She hands me the letter and looks over to Sabina who is sitting with Poppy talking.

I watch them for a few minutes, my heart melts again looking at my two girls. Wow, it just fucking hits me all of a sudden. My two girls, I feel a lump in my throat, I feel my eyes sting slightly. Who the fuck am I? I just can't help it, I see so much love sitting on that sofa, I have so much love for them. I try to compose myself before looking back to Mila.

"Svetlana asked us to take in Sabina. She said she was too young to look after her and that Sabina's papa, you, knew nothing about the baby. It was a lot for us to take on, we are getting on ourselves and we didn't want any more children, we were enjoying our retirement in Florida. We agreed. She said it would be short term while she got herself sorted out with you. She phoned only a few times to extend Sabina's stay. She said things were complicated, that you were with someone else and she was waiting for you to realize it was her you wanted and then you would be a happy family. As you can see, it's been nearly five years, and as much as we love Sabina—"

She stops to look at Alek, he nods and holds her hands in his.

"Alek Is not very well and I now need to concentrate on him. He has bowel cancer, it is aggressive and we don't know how long we have left together."

I see the love between these two as they smile at each other and tears run down their cheeks.

"I am really sorry to hear that, Alek. If I had known about Sabina, I would have come for her myself a long time ago. Please accept my apologies. Svetlana told me she was pregnant but that the baby died in childbirth."

They both gasp and look at each other.

"She came back and wanted us to be together but I told her I didn't love her and didn't want her. I then fell in love with my beautiful wife over there. We have two newborn boys. I have not seen Svetlana for quite a while now. She was convinced we would be together, that I would leave Poppy. I told her that was never going to happen. Svetlana has always been a little, let's just say, unhinged, delusional. I am sorry you had to take this on. Please allow me to help with any medical costs."

Mila is crying into her hands. Alek is trying to comfort her. I look at him quizzically.

"We have struggled all this time with taking in Sabina. We wanted the best for her, the best we could do. We are not well-off people. Svetlana gave us a little bit of money when she brought her, but then we have not had anything since. She told us she would send money every month, it never happened. With my diagnosis, we have been so worried about paying the medical expenses. You know what it is like here in the US. We put off me going to the doctors for so long because we did not have the money and now I fear I left it too long. You offering to help means the world to us both. We would never take money, but in this instance, we do desperately need money. We came from Russia with not much and I was able to work a little while but only as a janitor. We have just put our house on the market to sell for the money I need for my medical expenses."

I feel really bad for these two. They've looked after my daughter for the past five years and had nothing to help them.

"Will you just wait here for me. Please spend a little time with Sabina, I will be right back."

I let Poppy know what I am doing then ask her to let Sabina spend a little time with them before they leave. I'm only gone ten minutes. I arrive back in the lobby, just as I see Ryker head through the door. Fuck, it's late for him to be here. I stand where I am, not wanting him to talk in front of the others.

"Hello Ryker, what brings you here at this time?" I ask him. I haven't seen him for a while now, he doesn't come and give me physical training anymore. I see Poppy coming toward us on her own.

"I wanted to see Svetlana. Is she here?" Poppy walks to my side. She heard him ask.

"Hey Ryker, nice to see you. Did I hear you say you were looking for Svetlana?"

"Yes, I tried to phone her but there is no answer. She normally speaks to me but I haven't spoken to her for a few days now. I'm worried something happened."

Poppy looks to me then back at Ryker.

"Ryker, I'm so sorry, but Svetlana left. She finished work today, came back, and got some of her things. She rang me to tell me she was going away, maybe back to Russia but she was undecided. She couldn't be around Igor anymore. She told me it broke her heart seeing how Igor and I are with our babies. She said she couldn't take it any longer. She resigned and said she would send money for Vidana if Vidana wanted to leave. She told me not to tell Vidana she had left just yet. She didn't want her relapsing."

He hangs his head. I squeeze her hand. My wife is a fucking genius, I really met my match with her.

"Hey buddy, I'm really sorry. She was struggling. She really believed I was going to leave Poppy for her. She even came on to me the other night when she was at our apartment. I was asleep on the couch and she… well, let's just say she got herself very excited and tried to get me excited."

He stares at me in disbelief.

"You're lying, Igor. She wouldn't do that. She knew I loved her. She wouldn't do that."

He shakes his head in anger and balls up his fists. I see his eyes squint at me and a bead of sweat forms on his forehead. He's thinking about having a go at me.

"Listen, Ryker, you don't want to do this right now. Come back tomorrow. I can show you the CCTV footage. She fucking molested me while I was asleep and she tried to get me to fuck her mouth. I have it all on the computer and it's date stamped. Poppy even came in and disturbed her."

He looks shocked.

"I'm warning you now, just walk away Ryker, she's mentally unstable and very delusional."

He hangs his head, turns and walks away without saying anything.

I head over to the Jacobys and Sabina. Walking to her, watching her closely. With each step, I feel a pull in my chest, like my heart is taking in the love I feel. I have so much love for this little girl who looks just like me. How can that happen when I only met her less than an hour ago. It's like a fulfilling sense. Maybe I knew all along she wasn't dead like Svetlana claimed. Maybe I was just burying my head in the sand, not wanting to think I had a kid out there. Who the fuck knows. I thought with the boys arriving and Poppy that that would be it unless we had more babies, but seeing her I feel fulfilled. I hold out my hand, she takes it without hesitation. I bend down.

"Well, young lady, I think we will have a big shopping trip tomorrow. We have a room to make up for our little princess. What do you say?"

Her mouth opens in the biggest smile, showing me the missing front teeth, and she nods enthusiastically. I automatically scoop her up. She holds on to me, clinging to my neck. She feels so tiny in my huge arms. She smiles that goofy smile at me. I melt.

"I would love that, Papa," she says to me in Russian. I look to the Jacobys who are full of love for this little girl. I hand them an envelope. It has a check in it for a hundred thousand dollars.

"This is, for now, to help with the medical costs. I will send you money each month to help you and if you ever need anything else, please let me know. I can't thank you enough for looking after Sabina. My driver will take you to my hotel so you can rest for the night. I will also have my jet take you back to Florida tomorrow. Thank you both and I wish you well, Alek."

Poppy takes hold of my arm as I use my cane to walk, holding Sabina in my other arm as we head to our apartment. She's asleep on my shoulder by the time we get up there. The poor little thing is worn out. The boys are still asleep, Poppy had the baby monitor on her and Mavra was listening out for them also. I put Sabina down gently on the bed in the room next to ours. We both stand looking at her as she sleeps. Poppy squeezes my arm and nods with her head for us to leave. We leave the door slightly ajar and go and sit in the living area.

"Wow, what an emotional night it's turned out to be," I say as Poppy curls up beside me.

"Totally. Igor, we need to discuss Svetlana, though. She has to go once and for all."

"I know. I can't have her live, and keep reappearing, threatening me with the law to bribe me. There is no way I will live like that. Tell me, мой ангел, how do you feel about all this with Sabina? Is this okay with you, I mean, her being here?" She leans out so she can look at my face. I see the scowl and the pinched expression on her face.

"You are seriously asking me that? Do you not know me at all, Igor? I already feel love for that cute, beautiful little girl in there. Knowing she is your little girl makes me love her more. She's adorable. I wouldn't have it any other way. I agree with you though. Svetlana gave her up for selfish reasons and does not deserve to be in Sabina's life at all. I will not have her keep coming back to bribe us. She goes Igor, she goes tomorrow. I will handle Vidana, tell her that Svetlana just left, that she's done what she does best, and disappeared. I will help Vidana on whatever path she chooses. She is still young, she's barely nineteen, I want to help her. I think you should also stop paying Larisa her monthly allowance. I think she must have known about Sabina and has never helped her sister financially this whole time, even getting a monthly allowance from you. The allowance you give her can now go to the Jacobys."

I lean over and I kiss her hard.

"I love you with everything I am, мой ангел, I never expected anything less from you and I agree. We need to sort out Svetlana tomorrow, then take our little girl shopping and spoil her rotten. We will let her have the best princess room imaginable. You are my queen, she is my princess, and I have my princes. I love you all."

Nineteen

Svetlana

SERGEI CAME TO SEE ME. IT WAS A LONG TIME AFTER IGOR LEFT with my baby girl. I couldn't believe my baby was standing there. When he heard Poppy and turned around, he walked to them and I could see it was my baby. I knew it was her. I've never seen her since I gave her to my aunty Mila and uncle Alek, not even a call to hear her speak. She's never known her mama. I feel my time is up and I can't make it up to her. I planned on going back for her once Igor realized it was me he wanted as his queen. But it's taken far longer than I ever thought. It was one of the reasons I tried to get his boys to suckle me. I thought I might have some milk left from Sabina, I never got to breastfeed her. I wanted to have that feeling. The feeling of being a mama. I craved it, but then not enough to go back for her. I just wanted us all together, a proper family. Then, *she* had to get pregnant and have not one, but two boys, two heirs to Igor. My Sabina is his firstborn, she will be his heir.

I had a plan, I should have executed it earlier, now I know I've run out of time. Gaining their trust, looking after the boys, I was going to hurt them. Make it look like an accident, make it look like Poppy had been neglectful. I read on the internet that a death of a child statistically makes the parents separate as one blames the other and they can't get past it. I had my chance that night. I was going to do it that night. The setting was perfect until I saw Igor asleep on the couch. He is my talisman, I just can't help it, he's like this shiny object I just have to have. I went to get the water, making sure Poppy was out of it with the mild sedative I put in her wine. I helped her to bed that night, then after letting the boys suckle my breasts, I laid them down to sleep. I was going to put the boys on the bed next to her, then I was going to roll her body on top of them. Essentially suffocating them. Igor would come home and found them, only he was on the couch, asleep. I thought Poppy said he wouldn't be back until the next day. Then, well, I thought to myself, I can always kill them another time. I just wanted my taste of Igor more than I did that. I screwed up yet again.

Sergei has come to give me a drink. I'm in pain, half naked, hanging from my wrists. I have no feeling in my arms at all. Most of the pain I'm feeling is from seeing Igor with our little girl and wanting to be standing there by his side as he met her. I cried watching them walk away. I only got a short glimpse of her. She was blindfolded. Poppy is smart. She must have brought her down here because she knew it was probably the only thing that would make Igor leave me.

Sergei lowers me and he puts a straw to my lips. I suck up the water. I look at him. I see the sorrow on his face as he looks at me. I have trouble opening one eye and I think my nose is broken from Igor punching me. He looks down my naked torso. I can see the horror on his face.

"What did you do, Svetlana, to piss him off so much? What have you done so wrong?"

Ha, if only he knew. But I wonder if I can use him to my advantage.

"I don't know, Sergei. He hates me for some reason. I haven't done anything wrong. I don't know what he thinks I've done. Why would he do this to me? Why Sergei? I have never done anything to upset him."

He cocks his head.

"Then who was the little girl Mrs. Ustrashkins brought down here? She wouldn't bring a child down here unless it was really important."

Fuck, come on, think of something. Think. Think. I'm finding it hard to think of anything. Wait, oh.

"That was Poppy's niece. She didn't want to leave her alone, and she said she needed Igor urgently." I think he might be buying this story, after all, he was the one that came to tell Igor that Poppy had just phoned looking for him. He stands staring at me, thinking.

"I don't believe you, Lana. I don't believe a fucking word you say. I know about you and him. I know you used to live with him. Do you think I'm totally stupid? That little girl was something to do with you. Was she another sister that turned up? I saw them talking to an old couple In the lobby, I also saw Ryker come in and Igor had words with him."

Ryker was here, looking for me. Oh god, I wish he had found me, he would surely save me. Sergei obviously knows about me and Ryker, or he wouldn't have mentioned him.

"It is my baby sister, Zoya. My aunt and uncle were looking after her but they brought her here for me to take care of, she's too much for them. I'm sorry I never told you about me and Igor. I should have told you sooner. You know I have been seeing Ryker, don't you?"

He nods.

"I'm sorry if I hurt you, Sergei. It was just fun all around. After Igor, I never wanted to be serious with anyone again. I was serious about him, but he wasn't about me. He used me like he did with all his whores, you've seen them come and go over the years. You saw how Andrey and Ivan used to dispose of them. You know what he's like. I don't know why he never disposed of me. I guess I was a fool and thought he did actually love me. Sergei, I'm scared. I don't know why I'm here or what he's going to do with me. Will you help me? Please, Sergei?"

He stares at me like I'm asking for his life. He shakes his head. "I can't, Lana. He would kill me if I helped you. He will probably do something to me for bringing you this water. There are cameras everywhere, Lana. We and he never miss a thing. I'm risking my life being here right now."

I look at him sheepishly and try to shrug. My shoulders hurt so much with being hung up for so long. I look down and I cry. I want him to feel sorry for me.

"I understand, Sergei. Thank you for the water. You best leave me. I don't want you getting into trouble, I couldn't stand you being hurt for me." I look into his eyes and give him my best damsel in distress look, even with one eye half closed.

He turns and walks out of the room. He hasn't lifted me off the floor. Igor will know someone has been in here. The lights are so bright, I feel I'm going blind. I guess that's the idea in such a white room. I look around, I try to move but the shackles don't give me any slack. I can't reach the table with the knives and things on it. I can turn around but that's it.

"If I help you, Lana, what will we do? We would have to run from here. We would have to go into hiding somewhere far away from LA. Do you have a passport?"

He's back, Sergei's back. He's going to help me. I nod.

"Oh god Sergei, thank you, thank you so much. I knew I fell in love with you for a reason."

He snaps his head up to mine.

"You didn't love me. You just said it was all for fun. I loved you so fucking much, Lana. I couldn't get enough of you."

Shit.

"No Sergei, I did love you. I knew I did. I was so scared of showing my true feelings. Sergei, I was so scared. One of the last things Igor said to me when he made me leave his apartment was that if I ever loved anyone, he would kill them. That's why I always thought he loved me. Sergei, I do love you. I was scared because of what he said, so I finished it with you. I couldn't have him hurt you if he found out." I tell him in a scared voice, I shake with fear, it's all fake, remember I already have several Oscars for best liar. I think it's working. He moves over to me and takes my head gently in his hands.

"I turned the cameras off. Tell me the truth, Lana, don't lie. Do you honestly love me?"

I nod frantically at him and I cry.

"Yes, Sergei, I do. I fell for you hard. I had to leave you and start seeing Ryker, but it was always you that I imagined being with when I was with him. Only you, Sergei." I lean into him and kiss him gently on the lips. He holds my head firm and kisses me hard. I wince, my lip is split.

"Oh fuck, sorry Lana, I'm sorry I hurt you. Tell me where your passport is. I will go to your room and get what you need. Then I will get my things. I will come and get you, then we can leave through the garage on the next level. I have a car there. We need to head straight to the airport, though. We have to leave the US, is that okay? If we don't, he will find us, Lana. He will hunt us both down and kill us both." I tell him where to find my passport and I have money hidden in a box in my bathroom, a lot of money, we will need that and I will withdraw all my money from the bank so he doesn't know where we are. Sergei will have to do the same. We will have to change our names when we get to where ever we go. I can't believe he's helping me. After the way I treated him, I don't like him at all, but if lying to him gets me out of here, then I will do that.

We are out of the garage. It all went well. Sergei said no one saw him, but he turned the cameras off for his route to my room and then for us leaving. Nobody questioned him in the security office. He used to run it. We stop at an ATM and we both draw out what we can. It isn't much but it will have to do. We head to the airport. Two hours later, we are in the air. On our way first to Paris, France, then who knows from there. We got the first flight we could get, always looking over our shoulders at the airport. We were both nervous and on guard the whole time. I cleaned my face up in the car and covered my bruises with makeup. Now to sit back and relax for the time being, anyway. Landing will be a different story. We will both be on pins and needles in case Igor has someone waiting for us. I am safe for now. I lie back to try and get some sleep. Sergei is holding my hand. He keeps squeezing every now and then. I pretend I'm sleeping. I don't want to talk.

All I can picture are Igor and Sabina. I vow that one day I will return, as long as he doesn't find me in the meantime, I will return and I will be with him, *my love*. It might take a lifetime, but I will be by his side with my daughter.

I will be his rightful queen and Sabina, our princess. She will rule his empire with our help one day.

Epilogue

Igor

It's been five years since she disappeared. Five fucking years. No one has ever escaped from the basement and I mean ever, but when you have someone on the inside, I suppose it's easy enough, especially someone who can work all the cameras. I tried to find her and Sergei. I saw the first part of the encounter with them and how he walked out pretending to ignore her pleas to help her. It was all a ruse, it didn't work. I knew they were screwing. I knew right from the start. She thinks I know nothing. I also knew about Andrey and Ivan, how they all used to screw. What Sergei didn't know was I had more CCTV installed that he knew nothing about. I saw everything, like I say, never trust anyone.

I know she's plotting yet again. It's what she does. I can't believe she has done this twice to me. Disappeared, no trace of her at all. I can find anyone, anywhere, all except fucking Svetlana, it seems. If I do find either of them, they will be killed on the spot. No torture, just an end to their lives. I now still have to live my life thinking she will return and try to get me prosecuted for statutory rape. The statute of limitations is now three years according to some lawyers, but some say it's ten years depending on the situation and if there is DNA. Well, Sabina is proof enough, which means there's only less than a year to go before it ends if it's ten years. She could, however, take me to court in a civil suit for it, but I'd kill her before she did that.

It took me a long time to read the letter Svetlana left with her aunt Mila and uncle Alek. Poppy had me read it with her in the office. I had put it in my desk drawer that night I went to get the check for the Jacoby's and I didn't do anything with it. It was only when we were packing to move into our new house that I found it and Poppy picked it up off my desk. She didn't remember it either. She had me open it and we read it together.

Igor, my love.

Please don't be angry I kept Sabina away from you. You wanted me to get rid of our precious baby, and I just couldn't do that. I couldn't destroy a part of you. I had no choice but to give her to Aunt Mila and Uncle Alek. They were the only family I had in the States that you never knew about. My mama swore she would never tell you. I didn't know myself until I contacted Mama. I won't tell you how I did that, I know you would have been monitoring everything of Mama's.

Just know I did it all out of love. You are my love, Igor. It should be me by your side as your queen, not that American bitch. You deserve the best and that is me. I know you love me, Igor. I will always love you until my last breath.

If you are reading this, it is because we are either together, which I pray to God is the scenario, and I asked my aunt and uncle to bring Sabina to us or I am dead. Maybe by your hands, who knows? Maybe I am about to be killed and wanted Sabina to be with you in the hopes you don't kill me and decide we can be a family together, this is my dream.

When you receive this letter, I have no idea how old Sabina is and it could be she found this letter, which is why I have put your full name on the bottom so she can find you. She is registered on her birth certificate as Sabina Larisa Ustrashkins. It was only right she had your full name.

I know you will think I'm a terrible person for leaving my daughter, but I feel I had no choice. I wanted you more than life, Igor, even more than Sabina. I guess that makes me a horrible person, but I was only seventeen, I know I lied to you about my age right from the start and my mama went along with it and you thought I was eighteen the first time we made love, but I was young and didn't really know what to do.

I am sorry Igor, my love, my king.

Eternally yours,

Svetlana, your RIGHTFUL QUEEN.

Sabina, your papa is Igor Ustrashkins, he lives in Los Angeles in the United States. If you ever read this letter, I am sorry for leaving you and I hope you had a good life. Please find your papa. He didn't know you existed. He is a good man. I loved him all my life. You will be able to find him. Everyone knows who The Igor Ustrashkins is. I hope you will find it in your heart to forgive me one day. I did love you.

Poppy wasn't even angry with the letter, but she said it was proof that she lied about her age to me. She signed it, her signature was on the letter and it was all in her writing. It gave me some peace of mind but I still didn't trust Svetlana. She would just say I made her write it. She even dated the letter.

I love my girl Sabina so much, she's growing up just as feisty and as smart as her mama, Poppy being her mama. They have such an amazing bond. Poppy has treated her as her own since the day she came to live with us. We haven't told Sabina that Poppy isn't her real mama, we will have that talk one day. Dimitri and Nikolai are now nearly five and running us ragged, plus we now have twins, Edmon and Gala, who are at the terrible twos. Our house is pretty full with five children, three dogs, Poppy and I. We moved into our new home in the Hollywood Hills. I think if we continue like this, getting pregnant, we may end up moving to a bigger house. I thought this would be big enough but I'm having my doubts.

Business is good, we do most of it together, but there are some jobs I don't want her on, too dangerous. She has a formidable reputation, one to match mine, and together, no one messes with the Ustrashkins. She is still known as the dragon lady, she's taken it a bit far. Our office is full of all things dragon. I give my queen what she wants, always. She even has a dragon tattoo on her shoulder.

We have kept tabs on Blaine and Primrose. I have my men check in every now and then. Poppy was right, they did have children. They are as bad as us, they now have two sets of twins, all girls. I don't envy Blaine. Poppy is content to just know they are all okay.

Life is pretty good. Pretty fucking good.

Vidana

I was so fucking angry that Lana had left me. I hadn't been at the refuge that long. We were making plans, but then she up and left. Poppy told me she ran away with Igor's security man, Sergei. It didn't make sense. She said she had fallen hard for this Ryker. That bitch left me all alone again. How was I supposed to recover? I started to leave the refuge and go out and about to get my bearings. It wasn't a prison, we were allowed out. It just didn't take long for me to get drugs. I didn't have money, but I had my body. It didn't matter, really. My body had been used by countless men. I was numb to it. Poppy found out what I was doing, and she put a stop to it. I don't know why Lana had a problem with Poppy. I think she's amazing. I admire her.

I got a letter delivered to me today. I thought it was maybe from Mama. I was surprised when it was from Lana, only she used a different name. One that we used when we were little. We would play games and pretend to be different people. She was always Mary. She loved the book Mary Poppins. I was always Tink for Tinker Bell.

Tink,

I'm sorry I left you, but I had no choice. I will explain why to you one day. I hope I get to see you again. My life was in danger. I was about to be killed. I managed to escape and have now gone off the grid. Please, please do not let anyone read this unless all mail gets vetted first. I will not tell you where I am for both our safety. Please get better. I hope your recovery was not interrupted by my disappearing. If you do meet Ryker, tell him I didn't love him, even though I did.

I'm sorry for leaving, but I know you are such a strong woman. Stronger than I could ever be. I just wanted you to know I was safe and that it wasn't by choice I abandoned you.

Love you, Tink

Mary.

I'm shocked. Why was her life in danger? I bet it was Igor, he's always at the bottom of things. Maybe if I stick around I can find out. Am I strong enough to stay here? I was thinking about going back to Mama, but then she's never bothered to phone me here, and she knows where I am. Mama seems to have wiped her hands of us. Lana said Mama never called her, it was always her calling Mama. We were everything to Mama until she got all that money from Igor. It was that money that changed her. She became a different person. She didn't care Papa was dead. I found out Igor killed him for thinking he sexually abused Lana. He didn't want him to abuse the rest of us. I don't blame him for that. I blame Mama and Lana for that. They lied. Lana because she wanted Igor, selfish as ever, and Mama because she wanted money. I will never forgive them for that. Now I have to worry about Dominika, Iskra, Klara and Zoya. Is Mama neglecting them now? Maybe I need to go back home to rescue them or ask Igor to help me. Why is my family so fucked up?

I need to think carefully about what I am going to do next. I need to stay for a while at least to recover completely, that's a given. Then I need to decide if I'm going to wait for Lana to come back, but that might never happen. Or do I go back to Russia myself and rescue my sisters?

Mama and Lana are too selfish for me to worry about, but my sisters I can still try to help. I am sure if I ask Igor he will help me save them. As much as I hate him, I can use him. I can use any man after they used my body for so long. I need to do that, get strong, then get revenge on the man who wronged me. Seek out the ones who used me and exact my revenge on them. Not the ones at the bottom who were mostly killed anyway, but the man at the top. The man who had me taken just to get revenge on Igor. I saw who it was, just one time. I know he is American and not Iranian. He is the one thing that kept me sane ever since the day I saw him. But he is the one reason I was in that hell in the first place.

The End

Reviews

I really hope that you enjoyed this fictional story. Reviews are lovely! Honestly, they are! And they also help other people to make an informed decision before buying this book.

I would really appreciate it if you took a few seconds to do just that. Thank you!

Find Me and Follow Me. XX

Amazon - https://amzn.to/2H5QquX
Facebook - https://bit.ly/345Ydlr
Instagram - https://bit.ly/2SZVcwt
Goodreads - https://bit.ly/37di1oI
BookBub - https://bit.ly/3j6AmWV
www.lyndathrosby.com

Lynda XX

Books by
LYNDA THROSBY

Catfish
A dark, gritty, romantic thriller (this book contains graphic scenes) for 18+ only.

The Best Day Of My Life
A sweet, single dad of twins romance.

Chef
A semi-dark romantic thriller.

A Christmas Wish
A sweet Christmas fairy tale novella.

The Pain Series

Book 1 – *The Pain They Feel*
A dark psychological romantic thriller (this book contains graphic scenes) for 18+ only.

Book 2 – *Poppy's Revenge*
A dark psychological thriller (this book contains graphic scenes) for 18+ only.

Book 3 – *His Rightful Queen*
You just finished this book. Thank you.
A dark psychological thriller (this book contains graphic scenes) for 18+ only.

Book 4 – *You Broke me First*
Up Next, Vidana's story.
A dark psychological thriller (this book contains graphic scenes) for 18+ only.

More about Lynda

Lynda lives in Cheshire in the UK with her husband Peter and cat Bailey also with two grown-up daughters and has a two beautiful granddaughters.

She runs a successful financial business with her husband.

As a young teenager, Lynda used to read horror books with a love for everything Stephen King and James Herbert. She has always wanted to write and even wrote horror stories at age thirteen.

A little later she started reading Jackie Collins and Jilly Cooper and has always had a love of books. This then exploded with *Twilight* and *Fifty Shades of Grey*. Oh, and the introduction of e-readers.

In her spare time, she has a season ticket for Manchester City Football Club and goes to all the home games. She loves going to concerts and the theatre. She goes to the cinema at least once a week. When the weather is nice, you can see her gliding down the road on her Harley Davidson 1200T motorbike. Traveling is also high on the agenda, and her dream is to visit every state in the USA.

Acknowledgments

I wouldn't have done this without the help and support I got from my family.

First to my husband, who makes time for me to write by running our business and the continued support he gives me, encouraging me to carry on.

Thank you to ellie from My Brother's Editor - for editing and formatting my words, you have no idea what your words mean during the process.

Thank you to Rosa from My Brother's Editor for proofreading my words, such a huge, huge, help as always.

My family and friends who read the books and give me feedback.

Sybil Wilson from Pop Kitty for the amazing cover as usual.

Thank you to everyone who supports me and reads my words.

Lightning Source UK Ltd.
Milton Keynes UK
UKHW010800230721
387638UK00001B/41